MISTRESS OF POLRUDDEN

MISTRESS OF POLRUDDEN

E. V. Thompson

HEADLINE

First published in 1993 by
HEADLINE BOOK PUBLISHING PLC

10 9 8 7 6 5 4 3

British Library Cataloguing in Publication Data

Thompson, E. V.
Mistress of Polrudden
I. Title
823.914 [F]

ISBN 0–7472–0787–9

Phototypeset by Intype, London
Printed and bound in Great Britain by Mackays of Chatham PLC

HEADLINE BOOK PUBLISHING PLC
Headline House
79 Great Titchfield Street
London W1P 7FN

Dedicated to George Hardinge
Long-time editor, advisor and friend

Chapter 1

To:
Nathan Jago, Esq.
Polrudden Manor
Pentuan
Cornwall
20th March 1817

Dear Mr Jago,
I thank you for considering me for the vacant post in your
household. I am confident I will be able to perform my duties
to your full satisfaction.
    I will be arriving for an interview on Thursday, 7th April
(weather permitting).
    Your obedient servant,

Dewi Morgan (Miss)

Frowning, Nathan Jago read through the brief, neatly penned note
for the third time, but it made no more sense to him than at the
first reading. He knew no 'Dewi Morgan'. Neither, as far as he
was aware, was there a vacancy on the small domestic staff at
Polrudden. On the rare occasions when one occurred a girl would
be taken on from the village. Such matters were dealt with without
reference to him.

'Mary!' Nathan called to the servant from the top of the wide
stairway that curved down to the main hall. 'Who brought this
letter to the house?'

'One of they sailors from the ship unloading coal down on the
beach, Mr Jago. I know'd that's what he was 'cos his face was
more familiar with coal dust than with soap and water. Cheeky
with it too, he were.'

'A sailor, you say?'

Suddenly, the reason for the letter became clear. Almost a year
ago, a sea captain from one of the ships that traded into Pentuan
had toiled up the hill to pay a call at Polrudden. The purpose of
his visit was to offer condolences to Nathan for the loss of his
wife, Amy, who had died in a fire that gutted two rooms at
Polrudden. It was a tragedy that still hurt just to remember.

1

During the course of the visit the conversation between the two men was constantly interrupted by Nathan's young son, Beville. Apologising for the antics of the four year old, Nathan had commented that he would need to find his son a nursemaid or governess before he became completely unmanageable.

The sea captain had suggested one of his nieces might be suitable for such a post. Nathan remembered now that the captain's name had been 'Morgan', the same as the surname of the girl who had written the letter. The conversation had taken place so long ago it had slipped from Nathan's memory. Furthermore, as far as he was aware, he had made no positive response to the captain's suggestion at the time.

Since then, it was true, the need for someone to take care of Beville had become more pressing. Nathan's sister, Nell, had been looking after him, but pregnancy was almost an annual event with her and the latest baby was due in a matter of weeks. Nathan had intended finding someone from the village to take on the task. A Cornish girl.

With annoyance he realised that today was the sixth of April. This uninvited applicant for the post of governess to Beville was due to arrive tomorrow.

Through the window Nathan could see the clouds scudding low across the horizon beyond the foam-ridged waves. 'Weather permitting' was what the girl had written. There was an easterly near-gale blowing. With any luck her arrival would be delayed for a few days. By then he would have found a local girl to take charge of young Beville.

Dewi Morgan was not the type of young woman who would allow bad weather – or anything else – to prevent her from keeping her word.

Pale-faced from the sea-sickness which had laid her low for much of the voyage from Newport in Wales, she stood defiantly before the master of the brig *Priscilla*.

'Mr Powell,' she said in her singsong Welsh voice, 'my uncle paid you good money to get me to Pentuan today. I have an interview with Mr Nathan Jago at Polrudden Manor tomorrow. It is very important to me. Very important indeed.'

'Begging your pardon, Miss Morgan,' said the captain deferentially, 'so is the safety of my ship. It would be folly to try to beach the *Priscilla* at Pentuan in an easterly gale. If they had a decent harbour, now, it would be a different story.'

'How long do you expect the storm to last, Captain Powell?'

The movement of the ship caused the ship's master to sway in a manner she found nauseous. He shrugged his shoulders. 'Sometimes an easterly will last for a week or more. On the other hand it might blow itself out in a matter of hours.'

'What do you intend doing while the weather makes up its mind?'

'We'll stay out here and hope it improves. If it's still bad after a day or two I'll put into Falmouth. No doubt you'll be able to catch a coach from there.'

'I have no money to waste on coaches, Captain Powell, and by then the date for my interview will be long past. I am disappointed in you. *Very* disappointed indeed. I wish now I'd waited for my uncle to bring me to Pentuan. He wouldn't allow a little storm to prevent him meeting his obligations.'

In truth, Dewi's stomach threatened another rebellion at the thought of suffering the violent movements of the *Priscilla* for even an hour longer than had been anticipated.

Unwittingly, she had put forward the one argument calculated to persuade Captain Powell to complete his voyage to Pentuan. He and Dewi's uncle were both employed by the same Welsh ship-owner. Each hoped to manage the company when the ageing owner took a less active role in the business in the near future. The suggestion, however unfounded, that he lacked the skill and daring of Captain Morgan might just tip the scales in favour of his rival.

'I'll go in close enough to take a look at the beach – but I'm promising nothing more, mind.'

Tacking a mile offshore, Captain Powell studied the coast carefully with the aid of a leather-bound brass telescope. It had once been possible to berth small vessels alongside the tiny breakwater that marked the entrance to Pentuan's equally small harbour. But both harbour and breakwater had fallen into disrepair many years before and any vessel wishing to trade here needed to beach on the sand.

On either side of Pentuan's long, low-lying sandy beach the waves leaped high up the sheer brown rock face of the tall cliffs. The thunder as the water crashed back to the sea was discernible above the wind, even at this distance.

Yet a beaching was not entirely out of the question. The sea was not so angry along the length of the beach, and the tide was due to begin ebbing very soon. It *might* just be possible to run his ship ashore and secure the vessel before the next high tide returned. A glance at the barometer suggested there could be an improvement in the weather by then.

Captain Powell decided to give it a try. Ordering a further reduction in the storm-reduced sail carried by the *Priscilla* he told the helmsman to prepare to ease the vessel on to the sand. The sight of two other vessels safely secured on the beach, not far from the village, was reassuring. He ordered the helmsman to steer a course that would bring him in close to them.

Dewi was on deck when the captain took his decision to beach the *Priscilla*. So too was every member of the crew. Her delight at the prospect of keeping the appointment at Polrudden Manor was not shared by those on deck about her.

As the vessel neared the shoreline crew members began to mutter darkly that the vessel was travelling far too fast.

Very soon the noise of the waves crashing against the cliffs on either side of the beach became alarming. Captain Powell seemed belatedly to share the misgivings of his crew. Shouting above the din, he called for the last remaining sail to be lowered. Dewi knew they would be riding in on the surf, at the mercy of the running sea. Suddenly it did not seem such a good idea. The waves racing in to break on the sand appeared much larger than when she had watched them from a mile off shore.

The ships already on the beach had been to the right of the *Priscilla* when the Welsh vessel began its run in. Suddenly, Dewi realised they were falling away to the left. Ahead now was not soft sand but dark, glistening rocks, and a towering cliff had taken the place of distant hill and grey sky.

'Hard a'port, Mister!' Even as he gave the order to the helmsman, Captain Powell was gesticulating to the crew members on the deck. 'Shake the sail out . . . And be quick about it! We need to tack out of this.'

'She's not answering, Cap'n. We'll end up broadside on to the sea.'

'Damn you, man! Do as you're told . . . Get those sails out!'

Frightened and bewildered now, Dewi watched in growing alarm as the men about her scurried to obey. Captain Powell was making a desperate bid to save his ship from the rocks at the foot of the cliff.

For many terror-filled moments it seemed the power of the running sea would beat the Welsh captain. The *Priscilla* heeled over so far it seemed nothing could save her. Then slowly, reluctantly, the ship righted itself in defiance of wind and sea and was once more heading for the beach.

But the sea had not yet admitted defeat. A wave broke over the stern and a wall of water raced the length of the deck. Dewi would have been swept away had Captain Powell not snatched at her arm and held her until she managed to scramble to her feet once more.

A moment later the ship grounded, the stern rising as a wave forced the vessel higher up on the sand.

'You, girl – there's still a chance we'll be swept back off the beach! Go below and get your things. Then go ashore over the bow. There are villagers there to help you off the ship . . .'

His instructions were cut off as another wave poured along the deck and threatened to carry her with it once more.

4

When Captain Powell released her, Dewi ran for the nearest hatch, the one that led to her cabin. Behind her she heard the captain of the *Priscilla* bellow new instructions to his crew.

Here, away from the howling wind, the sound of the ship's keel grating on the sand was almost as noisy as the storm above. Dewi found her cabin ankle-deep in sea-water, poured down the hatchway from the upper deck. It was also more unsteady down here than she had anticipated, as though sea and wind were fighting each other in a ferocious bid for control of the *Priscilla*.

The bag containing her belongings was half submerged and the water added considerable weight to the contents. Struggling against the erratic movement of the vessel, Dewi reached the ladder to the deck with her burden. Here, a crewman sent after her by the captain reached out for the bag.

'No! I'll keep hold of it.' Dewi clung determinly to the bag and, after trying unsuccessfully to part her from it, the seaman pulled her and her belongings together up the ladder behind him.

Dewi was not the first to go ashore from the beached *Priscilla*. A number of crewmen were already on the beach. Helped by the villagers they heaved on thick ropes which stretched between ship and shore. Others dragged heavy timbers across the sand. These would be affixed to the ship's side to keep the vessel upright.

With the help of some fisherwomen who had gathered to watch the exciting beaching, Dewi scrambled down a rope ladder to the sand. When she was safely ashore the women helped her to where a cluster of small cottages nestled at the foot of the hillside, at one side of the beach.

She had lost one of her shoes and the other squelched soggily with every second step she took. Her long thick black hair had come undone from the neat braid in which it was normally kept and hung lank and wet about her face. Sodden clothing clung to her and its icy coldness chilled her to the bone. She was angry, both at her condition and the ignominious manner in which she had been forced to disembark from the *Priscilla*.

As the group of women passed a small building that reeked of fish, they met a man hurrying in the opposite direction.

Tall and fit-looking, he was about thirty years of age but his dress was not that of a fisherman.

When he saw Dewi he stopped. After only the slightest hesitation, he addressed her.

'You, girl. Are you from the ship that's been run on to the beach?'

'I am.' Dewi found she could hardly speak for shivering, much of it due to nerves. 'And . . . if I don't get out of these wet clothes I'll be as dead as if the damn' sh-ship had foundered on the rocks!'

She would have hurried on but the man spoke to her again.

5

'What's your name?'

Her teeth were chattering as she said testily, 'It's Dewi. Dewi Morgan – but I doubt if you're any the wiser for knowing.'

'I wouldn't say that, Dewi Morgan. I'm Nathan Jago. I believe you've come to Pentuan to see me?'

Turning away from her, he said to the women, 'Take her to Polrudden. Tell the servants to prepare a room with a fire and find some dry clothes for her.'

Chapter 2

Nathan was seated at his desk writing a letter when Dewi was shown into his study at Polrudden. It was the day after the arrival of the *Priscilla* and the weather had improved dramatically. Through the open window behind Nathan, Dewi looked out at a flat, calm sea and a watery blue sky almost devoid of cloud.

Nathan's glance shifted from the letter to Dewi – and it remained with her. This was not the cold, shaken and bedraggled woman he had seen immediately after her scrambling disembarkation from the storm-swept Welsh brig.

Convinced she had made a disastrous first impression upon her prospective employer, Dewi had taken particular care with her appearance this morning. Her long, black hair had been drawn back and plaited, the single plait folded twice and secured behind her head. The hair style emphasised both her height and slim build, as did the high-necked plain dress she wore. The dress was the only 'best' dress she possessed. Taken from her sodden bag and hung up to dry in her room, it had been carefully pressed with an iron borrowed from a sympathetic servant.

'Sit down, Miss Morgan. I trust you're none the worse for the soaking you had yesterday?'

'No, thank you, sir.'

There was a brief pause in the conversation, but before Nathan could put another question to her, Dewi said, 'I'd like to apologise for the way I spoke to you yesterday, Mr Jago. I was cold and wet, and angry with Captain Powell – angry with the whole world. But it was no excuse for being rude.'

'Had I been in your state I'd have been rude to any damned fool who kept me standing in the cold asking stupid questions. But I'm pleased to see you looking far more relaxed and comfortable today.'

Nathan felt ill-at-ease. He had already made up his mind that Beville should have a girl from the village to take care of him. By talking to this girl he was merely wasting her time, and his own. Yet she had voyaged a long way for the interview.

'Tell me something about yourself.'

'Well, I was christened Deirdre, but when my young brother was learning to talk, he called me Dewi and it stuck. Silly, really, Dewi

7

being a boy's name, but calling myself by anything else doesn't sound right now, somehow.' Dewi leaned across the desk that separated them and placed two sheets of paper in front of him. 'I've brought two references with me. One was written by a minister who has known me since I was a girl. The other is from a schoolteacher. I sometimes help with her pupils. I enjoy teaching children.'

Nathan glanced down at the two sheets of paper. One was written in a neat scholarly hand. The other was a scrawl that reminded him of his own preacher-father's untidy scrawl. But Dewi Morgan was talking . . .

'I'm almost twenty-one years old and have been an orphan since I was twelve.'

When Nathan looked up quickly she shrugged, almost apologetically, and explained, 'My father was a coal-miner. He was killed in an underground accident. A roof-fall. My mother lived for only another two weeks. I believe she died of a broken heart. She had run away from home to marry him, when she was young. They were very close.'

Nathan murmured a few meaningless words of sympathy, but Dewi shrugged. 'It all happened a long time ago now. I looked after a young brother by myself for a few months until one of my elder sisters took us in. She was a mine-widow with five young children. I took care of them, taught them to read, write and do sums, and sometimes helped out in the local school. Then my sister married again.'

Dewi shrugged again. 'A new husband doesn't want *two* women in his house. Since I left her home I've been living with an aunt – Captain Morgan's sister. They were both related to my mother. She was a Morgan too before she married. Never had to change her name, you see. But the aunt is a spinster, getting on in years and set in her ways. Although she's never said anything I know she'll be happy now I'm out of her house.'

The implication of Dewi's words was not lost upon Nathan. 'What happened to your young brother?'

It was an irrelevant question. At the same time Nathan was aware that the Welsh girl's brief account of her life hid a great deal of unhappiness. He was not an unkind man and found himself reluctant to break the news to her that she would not be taking up a post in his household.

'Daniel's at sea. On his way to China when he last wrote to me. Captain Morgan – everyone in the family always gives him his full title – says Daniel will likely be a ship's captain himself one day. I'm sure he's right. Daniel's a bright young man. Our ma would have been proud of him. I'm sure you're proud of your son too, Mr Jago. Beville, isn't that his name? I can't wait to meet him. I'm very fond of little boys.'

'Yes, Beville's his name. *Sir* Beville. But . . .'

'*Sir* Beville?' Dewi gave him a dark-eyed look of puzzlement. 'But you're not a sir, or a lord, are you?'

'No. Beville inherited his title from his grandfather – the father of my first wife. She died at Beville's birth.'

'And you've just lost a second wife?' Dewi appeared genuinely shocked. 'Life's been cruel to you Mr Jago. Cru-el.' She made the single word sound like two. 'It's terribly sad for young Beville . . . young *Sir* Beville, too. When can I meet him?'

Nathan braced himself. He could not allow this intense young girl to continue in the belief that the post of governess was hers. 'Look, Miss Morgan. I don't know what your uncle has told you, but it came as a great surprise to me when I heard you were coming here expecting an interview for a post as a governess. I *did* tell Captain Morgan I thought I'd have to employ a governess, and he mentioned he had a niece who'd be ideal for the post. However, it never went further than that. Had I been able to stop you coming all this way I would have written to you, but I only received your letter the day before yesterday.'

Dewi's expression of deep dismay made Nathan wince, but he reminded himself that this situation was not of his making.

'But . . . I . . . Captain Morgan spoke as though it had all been settled – subject to satisfactory references, of course. I . . . I've brought all my things. Left my aunt for good . . .'

'I'm sorry, Miss Morgan, I really am, but it's always been my intention to take on someone from the village. Not a stranger to these parts.'

Dewi swallowed hard and nodded her head vigorously, 'Of course. You must have someone who suits. It's that foolish uncle of mine. Got it all wrong, I'm sure. So anxious to cheer me up, I expect.'

She stood up abruptly. 'I'm sorry to have taken up your time, Mr Jago.' She made a brave attempt at a smile but did not quite succeed. 'And given you some cheek too! I'll go now, if you don't mind.'

'You don't have to leave Polrudden immediately. The *Priscilla* won't be ready to make the return voyage for a couple of days. Keep your room until then. The servants will look after you.'

'Thank you. I'll try to keep out of your way.'

Dewi fled from the study averting her eyes and Nathan felt as though he had just kicked a happy young puppy that had bounded up to greet him.

He felt even worse later that same day when he heard voices in a far corner of the garden and went to investigate.

Peering, unseen, over a hedge he saw Dewi and Beville engrossed in the study of a toad that was held in the palm of the Welsh girl's hand as she crouched beside the small boy. Dewi was telling Beville about the habits of the creature and the two were

9

so engrossed in what they were doing together they did not notice Nathan.

Walking back towards the house, he told himself that Beville would be equally happy with *anyone* who was prepared to devote her time to him.

Dewi fled from Nathan's study to the room where she was staying. With the door closed behind her against the world, she tried to busy herself. Scooping up all the clothes draped over a clothes-horse at the side of the fire, she crammed them haphazardly inside the bag she had brought with her from Wales.

No sooner was the bag full than Dewi pulled them all out again. She was not leaving for a day or two. Her clothes would be badly creased by then in the bag, especially in view of the slap-dash manner in which she had crammed them in.

When the clothes were hung over the wooden clothes-horse once more, Dewi sat down heavily on the edge of the bed. Unconsciously clasping her hands in her lap, she tried to push the hurt she felt behind her and gather her bewildered thoughts together.

Foolish old Captain Morgan! He really had led her to believe he was far friendlier with Nathan Jago than was, in fact, the case. She had arrived at Polrudden assuming the interview was to be little more than a formality. Convinced that her uncle and Nathan had reached agreement on her employment.

Glancing out of the window at the sea on which she had sailed to Pentuan, Dewi wondered how she could have been so stupidly gullible. Everyone in the family knew that Captain Morgan was prone to 'stretch the truth'.

It was not that he deliberately set out to deceive. He was a kindly man who tended to say what he thought others wanted to hear.

'There's a post as governess at Polrudden if you want it, Dewi,' he had said when he visited her at the home of his sister – her aunt. 'Mr Jago is looking for someone to take care of his poor, orphaned young son. I've told him all about you and he says you are just the girl he is looking for. You get yourself to Cornwall and the post is yours. You'll find Mr Jago is a good man to work for. No airs or graces with him.'

Dewi, who should have known better, accepted every word he had told her as the truth. She realised now that she had believed him because she *wanted* to believe. She was honest enough to admit this to herself.

The time spent living with her aunt had been a very unhappy period of her life. Strict chapel, was Aunt Phoebe. More than strict, really. 'Fanatical' was perhaps a more accurate word. Sundays were days of sheer misery. Chapel morning and evening, with the remainder of the day spent in the house with the blinds drawn, reading the bible. Any conversation would be about the message contained in the Good Book.

Dewi had been allowed no friends. If a young man so much as looked in her direction she would be subjected to a tirade on sinfulness from the barbed tongue of her spinster aunt.

Captain Morgan had provided her with a means of escape from her aunt by his offer of the post of governess at Polrudden. She could not go back to that house. *Would* not go back.

Suddenly, the view of the sea outside misted over. Lying back on the bed, Dewi spilled her tears on the pillow.

On the morning of her departure from Pentuan, Dewi received support from an unexpected source. Nathan's sister Nell, heavily pregnant, came to Polrudden to plead the Welsh girl's cause.

Seated uncomfortably on the edge of the same chair where Dewi's hopes of a post at Polrudden had been dashed, Nell looked across the desk at Nathan.

'She's intelligent, straightforward – and she and Beville get on very well. In fact, I've never seen Beville take to anyone as he has to her.'

Looking up from the mass of documents spread before him in confusion on the desk, Nathan frowned irritably. 'Nell, I'm wrestling with paperwork on a matter that affects the future of every man, woman and child in Pentuan. I've got more to do than waste time over a young woman who came here uninvited, to take up a post that doesn't exist.'

'Well, you'll need to do something, and quickly. Judging by the weight and the fidgeting of this one it won't be long in coming. I've been taking Beville most mornings, but it's becoming too much for me. I'm so far gone I can't do the farmwork as fast as it needs doing – and there are my own three to take care of.'

As though to emphasise her words, Nell linked both hands beneath her grossly distended stomach.

'I'm aware of all that, Nell. I've made arrangements for a Pentuan girl to be taken on as Beville's nursemaid next week.'

'Who is she?' Nell asked sharply. 'I can't think of any girl in the village I'd trust *my* children with.'

'I've half promised Harry Wicks I'll take on his youngest . . .'

'Sally Wicks! She hasn't got an ounce more sense than she was born with. You ask our father. He's tried hard enough to teach her to read and write, but without any success as far as I can gather.'

When Nathan remained unmoved, Nell struggled heavily to her feet. 'Still, you'll at least know where to find Sally when she's missing. She'll be in the bushes down at the Winnick with a boy. That's where she spends most of her time – as everyone in the village knows.'

11

The Winnick was the area of sand, rough grass and bushes, stretching back from the beach.

Glancing down at the profusion of papers strewn on the desk top, Nell asked. 'But Sally Wicks is your business. What's this life-or-death decision you have to take for the village?'

'It's a plan to build a proper harbour here. Now the war with France is over everyone's rushing to trade with Europe once more. Sir Christopher Hawkins bought the old harbour some years ago, now he wants to build a new one. To take large ships. He believes a number of Cornish landowners would like to see China clay and stone from our quarries going out through Pentuan. In return we'd see more goods coming in and have money spent in the village on supplies and services to the ships.'

'That would mean a big change in their way of life for the villagers. Not all of them will welcome it.'

'True,' agreed Nathan. 'but changes need to come. The fish haven't been running lately and there's little enough money to be made for those of us with fishing-boats. Another factor that needs to be taken into account is that ships are being built bigger and with deeper draughts. They won't be able to run up on a beach to load and unload. Unless we have a harbour in Pentuan, ships will go elsewhere.'

Nell's husband, Tom, was a farmer at Venn, a mile or so along the road to Saint Austell. The problems of Pentuan and its harbour were remote from her everyday life. 'You know, Nathan, I think I liked you more before you became Lord of Polrudden manor. There was time to think about *people* then. You weren't wrapped up in business the whole time.'

With this cutting and not entirely accurate observation, Nell made her ponderous way from the study. In the doorway she paused to say, 'If you want Beville, you'll find him with me – for today. I'm taking him down to the beach to say farewell to Dewi.'

When Nell had gone, Nathan grimaced at the image of himself conjured up by the sister who was almost ten years his junior. Yet, to a certain extent, Nell was right. He had been aware of this for some time. He also knew such a change in himself was inevitable.

It was more than six years since Nathan's return to the village; he had left when he was fifteen years old. The son of Pentuan's Methodist preacher, he had served in the Royal Navy before taking to the prize-ring. As Champion of All England he had made enough money to buy a fish-cellar and a number of boats.

His first marriage to the daughter of the late Sir Lewis Hearle had brought him to Polrudden. That marriage had ended in tragedy, Beville actually being taken from his mother's body minutes after she had died.

His second marriage, to Amy Hoblyn, had also been tragically brief. Now, at the age of thirty-one and twice a widower, Nathan was a wealthy man with a moral responsibility for the welfare of a great many villagers – and a young son to bring up.

Irritably, he realised his train of thought had brought him back once more to Dewi Morgan.

He had found himself thinking far more about her than he should during the morning. He told himself once more that she was not his responsibility. He had not asked her to come all the way to Pentuan from her native Wales. If anyone was to blame for her wasted journey then it was her uncle, Captain Morgan, for jumping to conclusions. It was up to him to take care of her when she returned home.

Trying to dismiss from his mind a memory of the girl as he had first seen her, wet, distressed and angry, Nathan scowled anew at the mass of paperwork in front of him.

Chapter 3

Struggling to come to grips with detailed figures of the costs involved in the proposed harbour scheme for Pentuan, Nathan was disturbed by loud voices outside the front of Polrudden. At first he took no notice of the noise, expecting it to cease quickly. When it continued, he flung down his pen, pushed back his seat and strode angrily to the open window.

A village boy, red-faced and breathless as a result of hurriedly toiling up the steep hill from Pentuan, was outside the main entrance, surrounded by an excited group of servants and stable hands.

'What the devil's going on down there? I'm trying to do some work.'

The boy opened his mouth and tried to gasp out a reply, but he was still breathless. Will Hodge, the head groom, answered for him.

'There's a rabid dog loose down in Pentuan. It's a huge animal, apparently. Probably came off the French ship that beached there yesterday. It's already bitten two children and is terrorising the whole village. Young Joe's been sent up here to find you. The villagers want you to take a gun and shoot it.'

About to retort that it could as easily be dealt with by a courageous man with a marlin spike or a hay fork, Nathan remembered that Beville had gone to Pentuan with Nell!

Calling to the boy, he said, 'Go back to Pentuan, find exactly where the dog is, then wait for me at the bottom of the hill, I'll be there with a gun as quickly as I can.'

Nathan's gun was a flintlock sporting rifle that had belonged to Sir Lewis Hearle. It hung above the fireplace in the study, together with a pouch of paper-wrapped cartridges. Biting off the end of a cartridge, Nathan primed and loaded the weapon, aware as he shook gunpowder into the priming-pan that his hand was shaking too much to complete the task as quickly as he wished. However, he succeeded in loading the weapon without spilling any of the gunpowder and ran from the house.

The village boy was waiting at the bottom of the hill from Polrudden, but Nathan did not need to be told where the dog was. The din from the beach told its own story. Whistles, shouts

14

and the banging of metal mess-kettles were coming from one of the beached vessels. From the safety of the deck the shouts of the crewmen directed Nathan to the northern end of the beach.

When an attempt had been made to build a small harbour, many years before, a small stone jetty had been constructed, extending across the beach at low tide level. The harbour had long since fallen into disrepair. So too had the jetty. Undermined and broken by years of fierce winter storms, the sea had gouged great holes in the structure.

Nell, Beville and Dewi Morgan had taken refuge in one of these holes. It was almost a small cave, large enough for them to stand upright, but shallow. Snarling at them from outside the water-made cave was the rabid dog, wild-eyed and trailing foam and slobber from its mouth.

To Nathan's alarm, he saw all that stood between the crazed and diseased animal and his son was Dewi's cloth bag, wielded determinedly by its owner.

The crew members of the nearest beached coastal vessel were making all the noise they could. Hurling chunks of their coal cargo at the dog, they were attempting to distract its attention. However, they were too far away for their efforts to be effective.

As Nathan approached, the dog launched another attack against the two women and the small boy. Once more the bag came into play, swung in desperation by Dewi.

The dog was sent sprawling on the sand, but regained its feet immediately. Attacking yet again, the animal vented its insane fury on the object that stood between it and the humans. Seizing a corner of the bag in its teeth, the crazed animal shook it this way and that, ripping the material and causing clothing to spill from a hole that quickly increased in size.

All this Nathan saw as he sprinted across the sand towards the desperately beleaguered trio.

The rabid dog did not see him until the very last moment. So fiercely was its worrying of the bag that Dewi was barely able to maintain her grip. Had the dog switched its attention to the three cowering humans now it was doubtful if Dewi would have been able to keep it at bay for longer than a few moments.

Suddenly the dog became aware of Nathan. Ceasing its attack upon the bag, it turned to meet this new and unexpected threat.

Nathan raised the gun to his shoulder when he was no more than six paces from the dog and squinted at the animal along the long barrel. Acutely aware the weapon had not been fired for a number of years, he pulled the trigger, silently praying the hurriedly prepared gun would fire.

The split second between the time the flint sparked into action and the gunpowder inside the barrel ignited seemed an eternity.

15

It took every scrap of willpower Nathan possessed to hold his aim as the dog rushed at him.

Suddenly, the gun fired. For a moment a cloud of acrid white gunpowder smoke hid the crazed dog from Nathan's view. When the smoke cleared he saw the beast lying on its side twitching violently, a musket ball lodged in its diseased brain.

Unaware of the cheers that erupted from the watching men on the deck of the nearby ship, Nathan stepped over the animal and advanced upon the two women and his son.

The noise of the shot echoing in the shallow stone cave had frightened Beville even more than had the attack by the rabid dog. As he set up a loud wail, Dewi dropped her bag to the wet sand inside the shallow cave and held out her arms. Without a moment's hesitation the small boy went to her.

When Nathan moved in closer to comfort his son he saw blood glistening on Dewi's hand.

'You've been hurt. Did the dog bite you?' The tone of Nathan's voice was an indication of the horror he felt. A bite from a rabid dog was inevitably fatal, the victim suffering a painful and distressing death.

'I don't think so. I believe it's a scratch from one of its claws.' Dewi held a trembling hand up to peer at it more closely. 'That's what it looks like, but everything was so confused . . .'

'You behaved wonderfully. If it hadn't been for you . . .'

Nathan went cold at the thought of how close he had come to losing Beville. 'You'd better come up to Polrudden. I'll have a doctor sent for to look at that hand.'

'It'll be all right, it's not much more than a scratch. If need be I'll see a doctor when we berth at Cardiff.'

Her reply took Nathan aback. In the excitement of rescuing Dewi and the others from the rabid dog he had forgotten why they were here.

Behind the Welsh girl Nell spluttered a protest, the words unintelligible, so eager was she to voice an opinion, but Nathan forestalled her.

'After what I've just seen, I'd be a fool to allow you to return to Wales, Dewi Morgan. You've saved Beville's life – and Nell's too. If you still want to take on the task of looking after young Beville and teaching him the things he needs to know, the job is yours. I'll be delighted to have you at Polrudden.'

The eventful day was by no means over when the small party left the beach bound for Polrudden. The excitement of the attack by the rabid dog proved too much for the heavily pregnant Nell. Toiling up the hill from the village, she suddenly stopped.

She clutched her stomach, her face contorted in agony for some minutes. When the pain passed it left her gasping for air. She looked at the others in dismay.

16

'Oh my God! I've started my labour. The baby's on its way.'

Nathan's immediate reaction was one of undisguised disbelief. 'But . . . you can't have it here. Not right now.'

'I don't *want* to have it here, but unless you get me somewhere else – and quickly – this is where it's going to be born!'

Staring at Nell as though expecting her to produce a baby at any moment, Nathan said he would hurry to Polrudden. There he would arrange for a horse and wagon to take her home, to Venn Farm.

'There's no time for that . . .' Nell's face contorted in pain for a second time. When she spoke again she was more breathless than before. 'This one's . . . in a hurry. Help me reach Polrudden, at least . . .'

Nell almost made it to the large house at the top of the hill. But not quite. Joseph Morgan Quicke slipped with deceptive ease between his mother's legs to a hastily produced blanket, placed on the grass at the edge of the driveway leading to Polrudden manor.

The event was watched with great interest by Beville until he was carried away during the final moments by a Polrudden servant. He went kicking and protesting angrily, unused to not having his own way.

Meanwhile, Dewi attended Nell well. Constantly reassuring the labouring mother, the Welsh girl did all that needed to be done. Behaving with great confidence, she eventually placed the new-born boy in its mother's arms.

As mother and child were being carried by stable lads and gardeners to the house on a blanket-covered sheep hurdle, a greatly relieved Nathan spoke to Dewi.

'That's twice today you've earned my heartfelt gratitude, Dewi. It's a good thing you know so much about delivering babies. Where did you learn about such things?'

'To be honest with you, it's the first time I've ever done anything like this, Mr Jago. I once saw a baby being born, but I never had any part in what went on. Mind you, your sister made it easy for me, didn't she? It would have been a very different story had things been difficult, or if it had been her first time.'

Filled with admiration for the resourcefulness of this newest member of his household, Nathan grimaced at the blood that smeared her hands, arms and dress.

'You'd better go into the house and get cleaned up. I'll find Nell's husband and tell him the good news. You'll be moving into the large spare room, next to Beville. It's got a fine view of the sea. I think you'll be happy there.'

'I'm sure I will, and thank you, Mr Jago. Tell me, though. Are things like this always happening, here in Cornwall. When I left Newport I was told I wouldn't like it here very much. Find it too quiet, they said. I must say, for a quiet place there's an awful lot going on.'

17

Nathan grinned at her. 'There's as much going on in Cornwall as anywhere else, but every day isn't like today.'

'I'm pleased to hear it,' Dewi said in the musical voice that Nathan found so fascinating. 'Now, if you don't mind I *will* go and clean myself up a bit before I take Beville to say "hello" to his new cousin.'

Chapter 4

When he took Dewi into his employment Nathan had been concerned she might not be fully accepted by the staff of his household. All his servants had been born and brought up in the village of Pentuan. It was a small and inward-looking community which excluded strangers. It even regarded men and women from neighbouring Mevagissey with suspicion.

He was relieved to learn his fears were groundless. Word of the manner in which Dewi had saved the young Sir Beville and Nell Quicke from a rabid dog, at great risk to herself, reached the house prior to her own arrival. The servants had also witnessed for themselves how efficiently she had coped with the sudden and dramatic arrival of Nell's latest baby.

They took Dewi to their hearts. Her place in the house and the tightly knit village was assured.

For two weeks Dewi took care of Nell's three children in addition to Beville, nursing the eldest boy, Tom Christian – known as Christian, to avoid confusion with his Father – through a mild bout of chicken-pox. Polrudden rang to the sounds of four youngsters as they laughed, played, squabbled and occasionally cried. Not once during this time did Nathan hear Dewi's voice raised in anger.

Her arrival could not have come at a more opportune time. In addition to the responsibilities attendant upon the birth of Nell's latest baby, Nathan was heavily involved with mounting problems resulting from the harbour proposal.

The matter was greatly complicated by the fact that, although much of Pentuan was manor land, belonging to Polrudden, the harbour itself belonged to Sir Christopher Hawkins, a political baronet. It had been sold by Beville's grandfather to pay off some of the more pressing of his debts.

Hawkins had represented various Cornish boroughs in parliament and he controlled the voters in many more. Greedy for land, he had earned a reputation for ruthless and greedy political and business dealings.

Sir Christopher Hawkins was a very wealthy man – and it was his intention to become wealthier. Among his land holdings were several of the rapidly expanding China clay quarries a few miles to the north of Polrudden. All were showing a handsome profit, but Hawkins wanted them to bring in much more.

One of the China clay industry's greatest expenses was incurred in transportation and dues at the nearby harbour of Charlestown. It was Sir Christopher Hawkins's belief that he would drastically reduce such costs if the clay was shipped through his own harbour. He hoped it would eventually be carried there from his quarries on a railway he proposed building to link the China clay area and Pentuan.

Despite his belief in the practicality of the scheme the baronet was not a man to risk too much of his own capital in such a venture. He proposed that a company, with himself as a major shareholder, should bear the brunt of the expense.

Sceptical about the venture's ultimate success, Nathan was loath to take a share in the company. Nevertheless, he was aware that unless he did so, he would lose control of the future of Pentuan village.

The first meeting between Sir Christopher Hawkins and the prospective shareholders took place on the site of the proposed harbour at Pentuan. Much of the financial backing would come from London and a lawyer, John Trubshaw, had travelled to Cornwall to represent the investors' interests. In addition to Nathan, two other Cornishmen were present. One, Sir Kenwyn Penhaligan, was a past Sheriff of Cornwall. The other was Humphrey Yates, an unsmiling banker from nearby Mevagissey, who hoped to handle the business affairs of the proposed harbour company.

A number of villagers, many children among them, unused to the sight of well-dressed 'gentlemen' in Pentuan, followed the group wherever they walked. They maintained a respectful distance, but the occasional eruption of laughter from the children seemed to annoy Sir Christopher Hawkins.

Turning to Nathan, the baronet said arrogantly, 'Jago, these people are your tenants, I believe. Will you tell them to go about their business and leave us in peace? I can't hear myself think for their noisy chatter.'

'They're interested in what's going on in the village, Sir Christopher. Having a harbour in the village large enough to take deepsea vessels will have a considerable impact on their way of life. However, if the laughter of children is annoying you, I'm quite certain their parents will keep them quiet for you.'

As Nathan walked to where the villagers stood, self-consciously falling silent at his approach, Sir Christopher spoke irritably to his fellow titled Cornishman.

'It's hardly surprising the villagers don't know how to behave in the presence of their betters. With a man like Jago in the manor they'll have forgotten the meaning of respect. He used to

20

be a prizefighter, I believe. An upstart. I can't understand what Sir Lewis Hearle was thinking of when he allowed a man like that to marry his daughter. There was some scandal, no doubt? That's the trouble with having daughters. I suppose we must be thankful the baronetcy passed Jago by and has been inherited by his son.'

Sir Kenwyn Penhaligan looked down at the ground for a moment or two, until all traces of amusement had left his face. Sir Christopher Hawkins was unmarried, but was known to have at least two illegitimate children. He had also been indicted on corruption and bribery charges in respect of his 'borough-mongering' activities. Those who knew him well considered him most fortunate to have been acquitted.

Expressionless now, Sir Kenwyn said, 'I'd say there's a very good chance of Jago picking up a title of his own right. After all, Polrudden wasn't left to him, you know. He *bought* the place. I understand the Duke of Clarence acted as his broker. I think it would be very unwise to disregard such connections.'

'Jago is acquainted with the Duke of Clarence? One of His Majesty's sons?' Sir Christopher Hawkins looked at his companion in disbelief. 'I find that very difficult to believe.'

'I'm given to believe it's rather more than a passing acquaintanceship. Nathan Jago has been a guest at the Duke's house on a number of occasions. There are rumours that the Duke has been a private visitor to Polrudden. It's said a peerage could be Jago's for the asking.'

'Good Lord!' Sir Christopher Hawkins swallowed hard. Much of his borough-mongering had been carried out in an attempt to gain sufficient power to guarantee a peerage for himself. The thought that this upstart might succeed where he had failed was too much. Nevertheless, he thought he might have been unwise to write Jago off as being of no account.

Sir Christopher was scrupulously polite to Nathan for the remainder of the tour of the proposed harbour area of Pentuan. He also accepted an invitation to take refreshments at Polrudden when the inspection was completed. Nevertheless, he found it difficult to treat either Nathan or the London businessmen as equals and at the earliest possible opportunity he made his excuses and departed.

Dewi was in the garden with Beville and Nell's children. Through the window of the room where he was entertaining the other guests, Nathan watched as Sir Christopher stopped to speak with the governess. He thought the baronet was merely passing the day with the children, and was surprised at Dewi's reaction to him. She made a short reply before turning her back upon Sir Christopher in a manner that was so abrupt as to be impolite.

Nathan frowned but just then Sir Kenwyn Penhaligan spoke to him. It was immediately apparent that the former Sheriff of

Cornwall had seen the brief exchange in the garden too.

'Surely they aren't all your children, Nathan? I thought you had only one son?'

'I do. The others belong to my sister. She's recovering from the birth of her fourth.' Nathan went on to tell Sir Kenwyn the circumstances of the birth.

'That governess of yours would seem to be a very capable young woman. Attractive too. Is she a local girl?'

'She's from Newport in Wales. A niece of one of the ship's captains who brings coal into Pentuan.'

'Um! An eligible widower like yourself in the house with an attractive young girl . . . If you're not careful you'll have tongues wagging.'

'They'll wag whatever I do – or *don't* do, come to that. Not that I mind very much for myself, but I'd like the county to give Beville an easier time.'

'Have no fear on that count, Nathan. Your son will enter society with a title, a manor, and land. This will suffice. Many of the so-called "great" families of Cornwall owe their fortunes to mining, trading – or far less lawful activities. My own ancestors were privateers – pirates. Then there are the Sir Christopher Hawkinses of this world. He almost disappeared beneath a mountain of political scandals – and personal ones too. Not only has he survived, he has actually prospered. Have you visited his new house at Trewithan?'

'No. As well as bringing up a motherless son, I've expanded my fishing fleet and I spend a great deal of time working the fish-cellars I own at Portgiskey. I've little time for socialising.'

'You should *make* time. You deserve to reap some reward for your labours. We're having a ball at my home at Golant next month. It's to celebrate my brother's return from India and to introduce his three daughters to the county. Come along and enjoy yourself. You'll find we're not all as stuffy as Sir Christopher Hawkins. By the way, this brandy is superb. I'd appreciate it if you could obtain some for me. As you might have heard, my supplier went out of business last week. I need to find a new source if I'm not to have a dry cellar.'

As Sir Kenwyn Penhaligan rode away from Polrudden, later that day, Nathan pondered the baronet's request. He must have realised the brandy he was drinking had been smuggled into Cornwall. Indeed, Sir Kenwyn's reference to his supplier 'going out of business' quite obviously referred to the French ship which had been arrested the previous week for 'moonlight trading'. Yet Sir Kenwyn was an ex-Sheriff of the County, a borough recorder and an active magistrate, dedicated to upholding the law.

It seemed he was also a man of the world – and a true Cornishman. Nathan warmed to the man. He felt Sir Kenwyn Penhaligan

22

was a man to be trusted – and one who had his duties in true perspective.

Outside, in the garden, Dewi had Beville and Nell's children with her on a blanket on the lawn, enjoying a picnic. She was aware of the approach of Sir Christopher Hawkins and would have preferred to ignore him, not from a wish to be unsociable, but because her position in the household was something of an anomaly that had not yet been settled.

Dewi was an employee of Nathan, yet she was *not* a servant. This had been made clear by Gladys Coppin, Nathan's elderly cook. When Dewi had gone to the kitchen to make herself a cup of tea on her first day at Polrudden, the indignant old woman shooed her away. 'Master Nathan employs servants to do the likes of that for 'ee,' the cook declared fiercely. 'Start doing it for yourself and they'll grow lazier than they are now.'

For a while Dewi was able to pretend she had not noticed Sir Christopher as he sat his horse nearby. Warning five-year-old Christian to take his hand out of the jam pot, she used a finger to remove a crust choking three-year-old Kate. Seconds later she was in time to substitute a piece of cake for the pebble in the mouth of the youngest child, Bessie, who was eighteen months old.

'You have your hands full, young lady.'

Dewi glanced up and as quickly returned her attention to the children. Sir Christopher's expression showed neither amusement at the antics of the children nor genuine concern for her predicament. It was an expression she had seen more than once before: the predatory look of a wealthy man-of-the-world when meeting with an attractive girl belonging to a lower social order.

Dewi was aware the horseman was speculating on his chances of bedding her. The only uncertainty she had was reserved for the method he would employ. As it was the first time he had met with her she anticipated a cautious subtle approach, but she had misjudged the political baronet.

'An attractive young girl like you could find more congenial employment than taking care of someone else's brats. I've need of a housekeeper at Trewithan. Come and see me there.'

For a moment Dewi's Welsh temper flared out of control. This man had been Nathan's guest at Polrudden. He was repaying the hospitality he had received by trying to steal her away.

Dewi bit back the retort that almost escaped her lips. The guests were to be Nathan's partners in an important business venture. She did not know how important this particular man was to her employer.

'I thank you for your offer, sir, but I'm quite well suited at present.'

The horseman shrugged. 'If you change your mind, come and see me at Trewithan. I'm Sir Christopher Hawkins. I'll find a place for you.'

'Aye, and I know just where that place will be! Hell will freeze over before I share a bed with you, Sir Christopher-bloody-Hawkins.'

Dewi spoke the words softly as Sir Christopher rode away – but not softly enough.

'Hell can't freeze over. It's a *fire*. Grandad preaches about it every Sunday . . . and there's no *blood* on that man.' Beville looked puzzled. 'And why should you share a bed with him? Hasn't he got one of his own?'

Scooping up the boy in her arms, Dewi said, 'Don't you ever take any notice of what a silly Welsh girl says when she's talking to herself, young Sir Beville. She has more foolish notions in her head than Christian has fingers in that jam pot.

'Christian Quicke, behave yourself! If the Lord had intended you to have a jampot on your hand you'd have been born with one there. Now, take it out this minute, you hear me . . . ?'

Chapter 5

'Why do you want to be gallivanting with the likes of Sir Kenwyn Penhaligan and Sir Christopher Hawkins? You've done very well these past years without getting mixed up with their sort. No good will come of this, you mark my words, Nathan.'

Preacher Josiah Jago made his gloomy prediction as he, his son and the fishermen employed by Nathan passed a new mile-long drift net through their hands and lowered it from the quay to the fishing boat, *Sir Beville*.

They were at Portgiskey, Nathan's bustling fishing-cellar, tucked beneath sloping cliffs in a small cove at the far end of Pentuan Beach.

'I reckon Nathan has ambitions to become *real* gentry himself. Before we know it he'll be coming down here wearing white gloves and wrinkling his nose when he gets downwind of the cellar. We'll need to doff our hats and call him "sir" then, I've no doubt.'

The speaker was Ahab Arthur, the oldest member of Nathan's fishing crews and skipper of his best drifter. He had held Nathan in his arms when the owner of Polrudden was no more than an hour old.

A friend of Preacher Josiah Jago for almost twice Nathan's lifetime, Ahab spoke from a privileged position. Yet, even as they laughed at his words, there were fishermen who looked askance at Nathan to see how he would take the good-natured chaffing.

'Judging by the size of your catches these days, I think you must all be coming to work in white gloves. It would be *reassuring* to get a whiff of fish downwind of the cellar.'

Nathan's response was as light-hearted as the banter of Ahab Arthur, but everyone of the fishermen was aware of the stark facts underlying the humour. The fish seemed temporarily to have abandoned the waters around Cornwall's jagged coast.

Every fishing community in the county was suffering hardship. No one knew the reason for the absence of the fish, although pilchard fishermen laid the blame squarely upon the large drift-fishing boats of the type owned and worked by Nathan. It was a deeply entrenched conviction that the fault lay with the long drift-nets hanging like giant lace curtains in the deeper waters off-shore. The seiners' complaint was that the nets prevented the fish from coming inshore to be caught by the more traditional seine-net method of fishing.

It was futile to point out that drift-fishermen too were having a lean time. The seiners retorted that even if the drift nets were not *catching* fish, they must be frightening them away.

'Will there be work for Pentuan men when you and Sir Christopher Hawkins start building this new and bigger harbour you've been talking about?'

The question came from one of the younger fishermen.

'Pentuan men will be the first to be given work. I'll make certain of that – but I also intend carrying on fishing. If the harbour's a success there'll be a ready market for fresh fish and I'll be able to ship salt-pilchards without incurring transport costs.'

'Only if the fish begin running again.'

'They will,' declared Preacher Jago confidently. 'I'm holding a special service in the chapel on Sunday. We'll be praying for a good pilchard season this year and I expect every one of you to be there. Mind you, we're not the only ones asking the Lord for pilchards, so we'll need to pray harder than Mevagissey, St Ives, Newlyn and Looe.'

Late in the evening, some weeks after Nathan's visit to the fish-cellar at Portgiskey, he was in his room, preparing for bed, when he heard the sound of cannon-fire coming from somewhere out at sea.

Throwing back the curtains he saw flashes of gunfire coming from perhaps two miles off the coast. Through the open window the sound rolled across the water to break against the high cliffs beneath Polrudden in a series of grumbling echoes.

Nathan was half undressed. Hurriedly, he put his clothes on again and pulled on outdoor boots. Leaving the room, he met Dewi outside in the passageway. She wore a dressing-gown over her nightdress and had just come from Beville's bedroom.

'There's no need to worry, Beville's fast asleep,' she said before Nathan could question her. 'But what's all the noise out at sea? I can't believe a storm would spring up so suddenly . . .'

'It's cannon-fire. A Revenue boat must have surprised a smuggler. A naval frigate has been stationed at Fowey and I hear they were keen to make an arrest. I must go down to Pentuan, to the fishing-cellar.'

'Why?' Dewi's eyes showed her concern. 'It's nothing to do with you, surely?'

'Hopefully not, but two of my boats are out fishing tonight. Revenue men get excited when they think smugglers are around. They tend to shoot at anything that's in the water.'

'All the more reason to stay ashore, I'd think.'

'I'll see you in the morning. All you need tell Beville is that

26

I've gone fishing. He's used to that.'

'Very well. Take care, Mr Jago – for Beville's sake.'

Many of Nathan's fishermen were already at Portgiskey. Among them was Saul Piper, skipper of the *Marquise*, one of the boats tied up alongside the quay.

'Get your boat ready, Saul. I'm going out to find out what's happening.'

'Is that wise, Nathan? There's a Revenue boat out there trying to sink a smuggler and probably firing at everything that's moving.'

'That's what I'm afraid of. My boats are out there, fishing in the same piece of water as a load of nervous Revenue men and a naval commanding officer who's hungry for action. If we don't do something about it my boats are likely to be lying on the bottom of St Austell Bay by the time it's light enough for anyone to see what they're firing at. Pick a crew and let's go.'

By the time the *Marquise* drifted clear of the quayside and caught the westerly wind the firing out at sea had ceased. However, every man on board the fishing boat knew to within a few hundred yards the area where the action had taken place and Saul Piper set a course accordingly.

The sky above St Austell Bay was a patchwork of high clouds, but there was sufficient light for Nathan to point out a vessel crossing the bay from west to east, ahead of them. When they were closer, he hailed the other boat.

'You there . . . what's going on?'

'Whoever you are, keep your distance. This is a smuggler's vessel with a Revenue crew on board. Stay clear or you'll be fired upon.'

'Smuggler's vessel be damned!' Nathan was now close enough to recognise the lines of the other boat. 'That's the *Sir Beville,* she's *my* boat!'

'You'll be Mr Jago then, sir? Yes, this is the *Sir Beville*. We've caught her with undutied goods on board. Ezra Partridge has ordered us to take the vessel and her crew in custody to Fowey harbour.'

'I might have guessed Ezra Partridge would have something to do with this. Where is he now?'

Ezra Partridge was the Chief Revenue officer, stationed at Fowey. Many years before, during the war between France and England, he had been taken by a French smuggler and set adrift in a French estuary. Captured and imprisoned for the duration of the war, he had always blamed Nathan for his misfortune.

'He's on board the naval frigate. They've gone off after the French smuggler. It'll be heading back towards the Brittany coast, I've no doubt.'

'Is my skipper Ahab Arthur there? I'd like a word with him.'

There was the sound of low voices, then the Revenue man called out, 'He's being brought up on deck. You can talk to him, but don't come closer than a couple of boat lengths.'

A few minutes later, Ahab Arthur called from the *Sir Beville*, 'You there, Nathan?'

'I'm here. What's all this nonsense about?'

'It's no nonsense, Mr Jago. We've confiscated a dozen kegs of brandy found on board your vessel,' the Revenue officer's voice interrupted the exchange between Nathan and Ahab.

'Is this true, Ahab?'

'They found 'em right enough – but only after we told 'em they were there! The damn fools were chasing each other in the darkness shooting off their cannon. I was afeared we were going to lose our nets to 'em, so I ordered the men to heave 'em on board. When they came in we found some kegs of brandy, linked together and caught up in the net.'

There was an outburst of derisive laughter from the Revenue men onboard the *Sir Beville*, but Ahab Arthur continued, 'No doubt the French smugglers threw everything overboard so there'd be no evidence left if they were caught. There was no sense trying to tell that to Ezra Partridge when he came on board, though. He'd put smuggled goods on board a Portgiskey boat himself if he thought he'd get away with it.'

'That's enough of such talk,' the unseen Revenue officer admonished Ahab. 'If you've nothing else to say but to insult a senior Revenue officer, you can go down below again.'

Speaking to Saul Piper in a low voice, Nathan said, 'You've sailed with Ahab recently. Is he telling the truth, or is he involved in a bit of private free-trading, using my boat?'

'Ahab? No, not him, Nathan, He'd happily do anything you told him and not question it, but he wouldn't put your boat at risk on his own account. Besides, he was saying only yesterday that with the navy at Fowey and the Revenue men patrolling at all hours of the day and night, a man would be a fool to go out night-trading until things quieten down.'

'That's what I think about all this – and Ahab's no fool. If he was smuggling he'd be cleverer than to be caught with undutied goods with navy and Revenue men about him thicker than pilchards. Unfortunately, Ezra Partridge is out to make an example of someone. It would delight him if it were my men and my boats. And the navy too will want to justify the powder and shot they've used tonight. We'll need to come up with something really good if we're to rescue Ahab and the *Sir Beville*.'

Hoping he sounded far more cheerful than he felt, Nathan called across the water, 'Don't worry, Ahab. We'll have you back home in no time. Until then don't do anything foolish.'

With the *Sir Beville* maintaining a course for Fowey, the

28

Marquise fell away and Nathan sat huddled up in the bows of the fishing boat. He said nothing for a very long time, then suddenly sat upright and turned to Saul Piper.

'Head for Mevagissey. I've had an idea. When we reach there I want you and the men to go ashore and round up every fisherman in the village. Ask them to meet me in the Crown and tell them the drinks will be on me. I've got an idea that might have Ahab free in the morning . . .'

Chapter 6

The fishermen of Pentuan, Mevagissey and the many small fishing hamlets scattered along this southern section of the Cornish coast enjoyed little sleep during the night of Ahab Arthur's arrest. Early the following morning as men on land were setting out for work, fishing-boats both large and small began converging on Fowey's natural, deep-water harbour. By the time the town's tradesmen unshuttered their shops in preparation for the day's business, more than a hundred fishing-boats were tied up at the Customs House quay – and many more were on their way in.

When the first of the Customs officers arrived for duty he took one look at the fishermen crowding the space in front of the Customs house and sent an urgent message to the town's mayor. His worship was informed that six Pentuan men were due to appear before the magistrate on smuggling charges and it seemed every fisherman on the Cornwall's south coast was in Fowey. The mayor was urged to call out the militia and clear the town.

The townspeople of Fowey, aware that something out of the ordinary was happening, took to the streets to find out for themselves. They were treated to a rare sight indeed. Fisherman after fisherman entered the Customs house, each bearing in his arms some item of undutied goods. There were kegs of wine and brandy, packages of tobacco and snuff, silks, stockings and Brittany lace . . . the amount and variety of items was seemingly endless. Many were wet, indicating recent immersion in the sea. Others were suspiciously dry. All were handed in by fishermen who claimed to have 'caught' the contraband goods whilst fishing during the night hours.

Long before such extraordinary scenes were witnessed at Fowey, at a time when the families of Nathan's fishermen would normally have been sleeping, candles burned in every Pentuan window.

Wives went back and forth between tiny cottages, discussing their hopes and fears with relatives and sympathetic neighbours.

Occasionally, wide-eyed children were despatched from the village to Portgiskey or Polrudden, seeking news that no one was able to tell them.

Yet word somehow filtered back to the anxious families that

the Revenue men had arrested the crew of one of Nathan's boats. It was not known which of the two boats out that night was involved. Someone even suggested the crew of the boat that had put to sea later with Nathan on board had suffered a similar fate.

When a weary Nathan stepped ashore soon after dawn from his boat *Marquise*, the wives and children were waiting for him. The boat had been seen heading for Portgiskey and the Pentuan villagers flocked to meet it.

Nathan was immediately surrounded by the families of his men, all demanding information.

When he managed to silence them, he said, reassuringly, 'Everything's going to be all right, believe me.'

'But what's been happening out there? We heard that one of your boats had been taken in for smuggling and the crew arrested.'

The speaker was the wife of one of the younger members of the crew of the *Sir Beville*. Guiltily, Nathan realised he did not even know her name.

'What of the gunfire? Has anyone been hurt?' This time Nathan recognised the questioner. She was Mary Mitchell, a woman whose family had suffered more than its fair share of trouble and bad luck over the years.

'The crew of the *Sir Beville* have been arrested by Revenue men, Mary, but no one's been hurt. I can assure you of that.'

A loud and agonised groan went up from the listening women.

'What will happen to them?' 'Why were they arrested?' 'Where are they now?'

The questions came thick and fast until Nathan silenced the women once more. 'Ladies, I'm going to have to leave Saul Piper to tell you what's been happening out there during the night. I need to go to Polrudden to clean up before I ride to St Austell to find a solicitor. I'll take him with me to Fowey. We need to get there before the magistrate. Please accept my word that everything is going to be all right.'

Despite the early hour, not a servant was asleep at Polrudden and few of the beds had been slept in. The first person to greet Nathan when he hurried into the hall was Dewi.

'Mr Jago! It's such a relief to see you. We've had villagers here from Pentuan every half-hour, right through the night. There have been all sorts of rumours flying around. You look absolutely exhausted. Go to the sitting-room and warm yourself by the fire. I'll have Cook make breakfast for you.'

'Tell her to make it something I can eat quickly. I haven't got much time before I need to go out again and I must shave and clean myself up! It's been a busy time.'

'But you've been up for all the night. You've had no sleep.'

'That's the least of my worries, Dewi. One of my boats has

31

been taken by the Revenue men.' Nathan gave Dewi a brief account of the night's happenings, adding, 'Unless I can persuade the Fowey magistrates that the crew are innocent, my men will spend the next few years in gaol and I'll lose a very good boat.'

Dewi could see that Nathan was both upset and tired by the night's happenings. She wasted no more time.

'You go and do whatever needs to be done. I'll arrange things with Cook. Is there anything else I can do for you?'

'Yes. Get Beville up from bed and take him down to Portgiskey. A crew will be taking *Marquise* across the bay to Fowey. I'd like you both to go with the boat. Beville's likely to see something in Fowey that he will probably never experience again in his lifetime. Every fisherman along this part of the coast, be he drifter, seiner or long-liner, will be in Fowey this morning. Every one of them united against the Revenue men. It will be a sight to see, I can assure you. I'll meet you both in the courtroom.'

Chapter 7

The small Magistrates' Court at Fowey was packed to overflowing. Outside, more fishermen than the town had ever seen together at any one time milled around the building.

The mayor had refused the Customs officer's request to call out the militia. Having visited the Customs quay for himself, he was satisfied the fishermen posed no threat to his town. Indeed, there was something of a carnival air among them. Those from the smaller fishing hamlets seldom visited a town the size of Fowey. They were taking the opportunity to explore the shops. Fishermen with money in their pockets were purchasing items they and their families rarely saw. It was good for town's business.

To Dewi, firmly holding Beville by the hand and escorted through the crowd by Saul Piper and two of Nathan's Pentuan fishermen, the atmosphere was reminiscent of market day.

At the entrance to the Magistrates' Court they were prevented from entering the building by a perspiring and harassed town constable. 'You can't go inside. It's full of fishermen. There's hardly room for the magistrate and the mayor.'

'I've been told to meet Mr Jago of Polrudden Manor here. He said to meet him inside. This is his son, Sir Beville. We've come all the way from Pentuan . . .'

Dewi's manner brooked no argument. Assailed on all sides, the flustered constable allowed them to enter the courtroom, passing responsibility for finding seats for them to an equally harassed court usher.

Accommodating Dewi and Beville meant ejecting two loudly protesting spectators. They left the room complaining bitterly that they had been the first to enter the court that morning and should have been entitled to keep their seats.

It was hot in the small and overcrowded courtroom and the air was heavy with the unpleasant odour of too many unbathed bodies. It was half an hour before Nathan arrived, accompanied by a man dressed in the manner of a solicitor. By this time Beville was complaining of the heat and the stuffiness of the room. Dewi fanned him with her hand but it was far too small to displace very much air.

Beville's excited cry of 'Dad!' was heard across the room and

33

Nathan gave his son a cheerful wave. There was no time for him to come across and speak. At that very moment a door behind the high dark wood bench opened and an usher called for everyone in the courtroom to rise. Two magistrates entered the court, accompanied by the mayor who wore the cloak, tricorn hat and chain that together constituted the trappings of his office.

Nathan gave a start of surprise when he saw the man who made his way to the high-backed seat of the senior magistrate. It was Sir Kenwyn Penhaligan. The second magistrate and the mayor waited deferentially until Sir Kenwyn was seated. Then they too sat down and others in the courtroom were allowed to do the same.

Before the proceedings began Sir Kenwyn glanced about the crowded room. If he recognised Nathan he made no acknowledgement of the fact.

This was to be a special committal hearing, with only one case on the list. It was the task of the magistrates to ascertain whether there was a case for the six defendants to answer. If, in their opinion, there was, the fishermen accused of smuggling would be committed for trial to a higher court.

'Bring in the accused.'

The usher's voice rang out above the noise of the crowded courtroom and the six Pentuan fishermen filed through a door at one side of the court. As they squashed together in the tiny wooden-sided dock there was an upsurge of sound from the spectators. It became a roar when it was taken up by those crowding the narrow streets outside.

'Silence! SILENCE! Another outburst like that and I'll have this court cleared of all spectators.' The stern-faced magistrates's clerk glared around the room. Calls for silence gained ascendancy and gradually the noise died away to a low, excited murmur.

The Pentuan fishermen were formally charged with attempting to evade the lawful duty on goods subject to taxes and conspiring with others to do so. In order that there should be no misunderstanding about the charges, the clerk of the court added, 'In other words, you are being charged with smuggling. Do you understand?'

The fishermen understood, but they protested unanimously that they were innocent of the charge.

'That is not a matter for this court to decide,' snapped the clerk. 'This hearing is merely to ascertain whether or not there are sufficient grounds for committing you to a higher court. You would then stand trial on the charges which have been laid against you. Mr Partridge, acquaint their worships with the facts of this case, if you please.'

Ezra Partridge, Senior Excise Officer for the port of Fowey and resplendent in full dress uniform, rose to his feet to address the court. There was an immediate resurgence of noise from the spectators. This time a single glance from the clerk of the court was sufficient to stifle the outburst.

'Your worships, this is a case of the utmost seriousness,' Ezra Partridge gave a sidelong glance at the men crammed in the dock. 'For very many years His Majesty's government in London has been concerned . . . *most* concerned . . . about the activities of a great many persons here in Cornwall. Fishermen in particular continually flout the laws of the land and refuse to accept that certain items entering the country must be subject to duty . . .'

'Mr Partridge, the defendants in this case are not here to answer for the unlawful acts committed by the whole populace of Cornwall. They have been brought to my court to face committal proceedings on specific charges.'

Sir Kenwyn Penhaligan peered disapprovingly over his spectacles at the Customs officer. 'Please provide the court with evidence supporting the charges.'

'Yes, your worship. I was just endeavouring to acquaint the court with the gravity of the charges. Last night's operation by my men and a frigate of the Royal Navy cost His Majesty's government a great deal of money. Men's lives were put at risk as a result of a sea battle fought between the frigate and an unidentified vessel, undoubtedly a French ship . . .'

'Enough! This court deals with facts, Mr Partridge, not rhetoric. I will not tell you again. Please detail the evidence you have to support the charges that have been brought against these men.'

'I . . . yes, of course.' Ezra Partridge shuffled the papers he held in his hands. 'The evidence is, er, quite straightforward. Whilst patrolling offshore last night, a signal fire was sighted on the cliffs between Mevagissey and Pentuan. Shortly afterwards a ship showing no lights was detected moving towards the shore. The vessel was challenged by the naval frigate but did not respond. Instead, the ship took evasive action whereupon the naval frigate opened fire and pursued the other vessel. Shortly afterwards I and my men in a Revenue pinnace boarded a vessel known as the *Sir Beville*.'

There was a sudden squeak of interest from Beville and he said loudly, 'That's me, Dewi. They're talking about me.'

Everyone in the courtroom smiled except the clerk of the court and the senior Customs official. As Dewi put a restraining finger to Beville's lips, Ezra Partridge resumed his evidence.

'. . . We were in time to witness the crew hauling in a number of kegs roped together, each filled with fine French brandy.'

At his words there was an eruption of sound, this time from the men crammed in the defendants' box. 'That's a lie!' 'Tell the truth, Ezra.' 'We were pulling in the nets, as well you know.'

'Silence! You'll speak only if and when his worship so directs.

35

Do you have anything else you wish to say, Mr Partridge?'

He shrugged. 'What more needs to be said? I've said what happened. To my mind it's as clear a case as I'm ever likely to bring before this court. They were taking undutied goods on board. I arrested them and will prove my case at the Quarter Sessions.'

'Your worships, I have been retained to represent all six of the defendants.'

The solicitor engaged by Nathan rose to his feet and addressed the bench. 'May I be permitted to ask Mr Partridge one or two questions? I feel his replies might throw a somewhat different light on this matter.'

'I protest, your worship. I have surely proved there is sufficient evidence against these men to bring them to trial. I will give my evidence in full then.'

'*I* will decide whether there is sufficient evidence to commit the defendants for trial, Mr Partridge. You may ask your questions, Mr Couch.'

'Thank you, your worship.' Solicitor Couch bowed his head in Sir Kenwyn's direction and turned his attention to the Revenue officer.

'Mister Partridge, the crew of the *Sir Beville* were hauling nets at the time they were boarded by your men, I believe?'

Ezra Partridge shrugged. 'They might have been. Then again, they might not.'

'Come now, Mr Partridge, you have spent much of your life in a fishing community. You surely know when fishermen are hauling nets . . . or shall I call upon one of your men to answer the question in your place?'

Ezra Partridge hesitated a moment longer. 'I think they were hauling nets.'

'I am not interested in your *thoughts*, Mr Partridge. Were they hauling nets, or were they not?'

'They were,' he said grudgingly.

'I'm sorry, Mr Partridge,' persisted Solicitor Couch. 'You said that very softly. I want their worships to be in no doubt at all about this.'

'They were hauling nets.' Ezra Partridge snapped the words at the solicitor.

'They were hauling nets,' repeated Solicitor Couch. 'In my experience – and yours too, I have no doubt – men engaged in smuggling activities are seldom drift-fishing at the same time. In fact, I believe you were told the kegs that are the subject of the charge had been found caught in the nets when they were hauled inboard?'

'I didn't see them come aboard in no net.'

'No, Mr Partridge. Indeed, I believe you were not even aware the kegs were on board the *Sir Beville* until one of the crew members pointed them out to you.'

'He only mentioned them because he realised I was going to search the boat and would have found them anyway.'

'That is an *assumption*, Mr Partridge, and this court – indeed any court – deals only in facts. What you are really saying is that you did *not* see the kegs taken on board and you did not believe the fisherman, even though he volunteered the information that these kegs had been taken up in the nets?'

'That's right. It's easy to say you've taken undutied goods on board by accident after you've been caught with them in your possession.'

'But his explanation was not so unlikely, surely? A ship loaded with undutied goods is being pursued by one of His Majesty's men-o'-war. The ship's master is convinced he is about to be taken. As a consequence he orders his crew to throw the whole of his illicit cargo overboard. What is more natural than that some of these goods should be caught in a net that stretches for a mile cross the path of the smuggling vessel?'

'I didn't believe it then, and I don't believe it now.'

'Really, Mr Partridge? You have told this court you do not believe this fisherman's explanation. Yet it is corroborated by many others who during the night also discovered contraband goods in their nets. They plucked goods from the sea where they had been dumped by this mysterious fleeing smuggler ship and handed them in at your office. Yet, despite this overwhelming evidence that you were being told the truth, you do not believe the fishermen on board the *Sir Beville*. I trust you can give this court an explanation?'

'I don't need to give any explanation. I found goods on board on which duty had not been paid. It's for them to provide an explanation.'

'You were *handed* goods on which duty had not been paid, Mr Partridge. Just as you have been given goods fished overnight from the sea in the same area by almost two hundred fishermen. Will you be charging them with smuggling too?'

'Of course not!'

'So positive! Yet you refuse to give this court any explanation as to why you are charging some fishermen, yet not charging others who have behaved in a similar manner? I am afraid I fail to follow the logic of your reasoning.'

Ezra Partridge stared fixedly in front of him, tight-lipped.

After a few moments of silence, Solicitor Couch spread his hands in a gesture of apparent despair. 'What more can I say, your worships? My clients, in common with some two hundred of their fellow-fishermen, recovered contraband goods from the sea. At the earliest opportunity – indeed, *before* their fellows – they

37

carried out their duty and handed their find to a Revenue officer. Much to their amazement, instead of thanking them, he *arrested* them! Yet, within a matter of hours, other fishermen do the same and receive the gratitude of Mr Partridge and the Prevention Service.

'I find it very difficult to comprehend. The fishermen of this area, including my clients, have recovered goods that will make a healthy profit when auctioned by the Excise Department. However, I would point out that all such profit and much more will be lost to the country if I am forced to call some two hundred witnesses to prove the innocence of the six men standing before you in the dock. Your worships, if these men stand trial for carrying out their duty they will be found innocent. No doubt the learned judge will echo the words I have to say now. *It is a trial that should never have been allowed to take place.*'

The murmurs of assent that swelled from the throats of the spectators went unheeded. At the bench the clerk of the court was talking animatedly to the two magistrates and the mayor. Their voices did not carry to the spectators amidst the general hubbub, but the clerk of the court appeared to be in disagreement with the others.

The dialogue went on for some minutes before Sir Kenwyn Penhaligan waved the clerk to his seat.

Straightening up, the senior magistrate looked across to the six men standing in the dock. Conversation in the courtroom faltered and then died away altogether.

Consulting the papers on the bench before him, Sir Kenwyn returned his gaze to the men in the dock. 'Ahab Arthur, Matthew Mitchell, Simon Hunkin, Malachi Hunkin, James Pretty and Samuel Dunn: you have been arraigned before me on various charges that come under the common heading of "smuggling". I find there is insufficient evidence against you to commit the case to Quarter Sessions. You are therefore discharged. You are free to go.'

Chapter 8

When the six freed fishermen stepped from the courtroom into the street, a jubilant roar rose from the huge crowd gathered outside. The sound sent startled gulls rising high in the air along the whole waterfront of Fowey and hands reached out to slap each man on the back as he passed through the throng of well-wishers.

More formal, but nonetheless genuine was the welcome given to Nathan when he left the court accompanied by Beville and Dewi.

Seizing his hand and shaking it vigorously, Ahab Arthur said, 'I don't know how you managed to get so many fishermen coming together on our behalf, Nathan, but we'm some grateful to you, I can tell you that. There's a couple of us have had scrapes with the Revenue men before. Another conviction would have meant a one-way voyage to Van Dieman's land, for sure.'

Nathan smiled wryly. 'All I did was send out word that there was contraband to be found floating in the bay. I offered to pay twice its value for every piece handed in to the Customs office. From what I've heard every single item thrown overboard from the night-trading ship has been handed in – plus most of what's been smuggled in during the last three months! It's likely to prove expensive, but it's been worth every penny I'll need to pay out. Not only has it gained your release, and that of the *Sir Beville*, but this has brought together all the fishermen of this part of the coast, whether or not they're fishing rivals. They've been given an important lesson. If we stand together instead of fighting each other, we can succeed – no matter what it is we're doing. It's something to remember for the future. I wanted Beville to witness what's happened here today.'

Nathan ruffled his son's hair affectionately before speaking to Ahab once more.

'Return to Pentuan now and take Beville and Dewi with you. Tell the men there will be no fishing tonight. The Revenue men will be smarting at their defeat in court this morning. We'll need to discuss what safeguards we can take against them before we resume fishing.'

'I thought you'd be returning with us. You need to get some

39

sleep.' Dewi's remark was accompanied by an expression that showed her concern.

'I brought a Polrudden horse with me. I'd never hear the end of it from Will Hodge if I left it in a Fowey stable. He has no more regard for the ability of Fowey men to look after horses than Mevagissey men have for their fishing capabilities.'

Will Hodge was Polrudden's head groom and his charges came a close second to his wife and nine-year-old-daughter in his affections.

'You've been up all night. You ought to stay here and sleep for a while before riding back to Pentuan.'

'I doubt if anyone at Polrudden or in Pentuan slept very much last night, Dewi. There was far too much going on.'

Reluctantly, she nodded her agreement with him. 'It's just like the mining village where I was brought up. Any disaster that happened there affected the whole community. I suppose the fact that everybody is involved brings its own comfort, somehow. It means that nobody has to suffer grief alone. It's nice to feel you belong somewhere, Mr Jago.'

As he watched the newly released *Sir Beville* put on sail and draw away from the quayside, Nathan wondered whether it was his imagination, or whether there had been a wistful note in Dewi's last remark to him? He was aware that life had not been altogether kind to her in the past. He hoped she might find happiness at Polrudden.

As the *Sir Beville* sailed between the twin forts guarding the entrance to Fowey harbour, Dewi looked back to the land-locked harbour and the steep hills fringed with houses on either side.

'I think this is probably the most wonderful harbour I have ever seen,' she said to Ahab. 'It really is a very beautiful place.'

'I doubt if there's a prettier deepwater harbour in the whole of England,' he agreed. 'Mind you, I can show you some very fine fishing villages too. I'll take you and young Beville to see some of them one day, if Nathan agrees.'

'I'd like that,' said Dewi.

Clearing the harbour, Ahab was forced to alter course, giving way to a deep-laden collier from Dewi's own country. Pointing across the bay to where a manor house stood facing the sea amidst the shrubs and trees of a large garden, Ahab said, 'There's Polrudden. It's not the largest of the manor houses you'll see hereabouts, but it's a proud house for all that – and it's a happier one these days. I hope you're settling down there?'

'I'm very happy, thank you, but why do you say it's a happier place "these days"? Hasn't it always been a happy house?'

Ahab shook his head and looked to see where Beville was. The young boy was sitting in the bows of the boat, being taught by one of the fishermen to tie a knot.

Satisfied the boy was beyond hearing, he said, 'Sir Lewis Hearle never wanted his daughter to marry Nathan. She wouldn't have either, had it not been for the accident.'

Dewi waited for Ahab to amplify his statement. When he had remained silent for a couple of minutes, she prompted, 'What accident would that be?'

'One that happened when she was riding. She was a wild one, that girl, and no mistake. I hope for everyone's sake young Beville hasn't inherited that side of her nature. She put her horse at a hedge that should never have been attempted. She came off and broke her back. Gossip had it she was carrying Beville at the time. I couldn't vouch for the truth of that but, if she was, she paid a high price for her sinfulness. She lived on, mind, until the day Beville was born. Some of the servants swear she was dead before she gave birth to the boy. They say he'll know darkness and not light because of it. Again, I couldn't swear to the truth of such rumours but I've never heard any of 'em denied.'

'That's a wicked thing of say about a poor orphaned child. *Wicked*!' Dewi's Welsh pronunciation accentuated the word.

'That's so, Dewi, and I know of no Pentuan man who would dare repeat such things in front of Nathan, but as long as you're looking after the boy, I thought you had a right to know.'

The boat bucked in the wake of another vessel that was following the collier into Fowey.

'What about Mister Jago's second wife? Wasn't she called Amy?'

Ahab's expression softened perceptibly. 'Ah, yes, Amy Hoblyn as was. Her father owned the fish-cellar at Portgiskey – 'though he landed more brandy than fish there, I reckon. He was the best known smuggler around these coasts. His daughter was a very special girl. She never had an easy life, yet she was the match of any man or woman when it came to courage. She proved it on more than one occasion. Thought the world of Nathan too. Those two should have been married when they first met up. I doubt if he would have had Polrudden now, but things might have worked out very different – for both of 'em.'

'How did Amy die?'

This was the first person to whom Dewi had spoken who was willing to talk about Nathan's two marriages. She intended making the most of it.

'Ah now, that's never been properly explained. It happened in a fire, up at the house, on the very day Nathan recovered a fortune in jewellery from one of the wrecks in the bay. There were those ready to say she'd started the fire herself. Because she didn't enjoy living at Polrudden, they said.'

'Why would they say that?'

'Amy's mother was in a lunatic asylum for a time. They said Amy had gone the same way. The more Christian of us believed it was an accident, and so did the coroner. "Accidental death", he said it was. She hadn't been well and the servants lit a fire in her room. She'd probably fallen asleep and a log tumbled out. A tragic end for a lovely young girl, it was, and no mistake.'

'Poor Mr Jago,' Dewi looked as though she was close to tears.

'Yes, if any couple were made for each other it was him and her. Mind you, you'll hear a lot of different stories because there are those who are envious of what he's got. The son of a humble Methodist preacher, destined for the life of a fisherman, yet he's found both fame and fortune. The Champion prizefighter of All England – and never defeated; friend of dukes and princes; Lord of Polrudden Manor, and owner of four of the largest fishing boats on this coast.'

Ahab shook his head in a sorrowful gesture. 'Yes, Nathan has all these things, right enough – but he's paid a terrible price for 'em. Hardly more than thirty and he's lost two wives. I was going to add that he's having to bring up an orphaned son on his own too, but you'll do a pretty good job of that, I'm sure.'

'I'll certainly do my best,' said Dewi with renewed determination. 'But I can never make up to Beville for the loss of his own mother.'

'Amy wasn't his real mother, neither, but she loved the boy as though he was her own. Anyway, the chances are he'll have another mother before too long, now Nathan's getting friendly with the likes of them who were at Pentuan the other day. Looking to build a new harbour, so they said. It doesn't matter that some of us who live in the village might not *want* a new harbour. That we might like things to stay the way they are.'

'What has that got to do with Mr Jago marrying again?'

'Well, it stands to reason that it's bound to happen sooner or later if he's going to start mixing with the gentry of the county. He's a very good catch for someone. He has lands, a manor house, money, influential friends in London – and there's a title in the family. If anything happened to Beville before he married, the title might pass to a half-brother, I suppose. Not that I know anything about such things. But it's Nathan's money as would appeal to most. Many of the so-called "great" families hardly have enough to keep their big houses in good repair because of years of bad management and squandering. No doubt Nathan would rise to the right bait too. He's lonely. I don't know of any *man* who'd get the better of Nathan Jago, but it might be a different story if a scheming woman came on the scene. Inclined to allow his heart to rule his head is Nathan.'

Dewi felt a sense of dismay as a result of Ahab's frank conversation with her. Life at Polrudden was pleasant. She took seriously the responsibility she had for Beville. Nathan took a keen interest in his son and was appreciative of what Dewi did for him. Yet he did not make her constantly conscious of the fact that she was an employee. A servant. It was an easygoing relationship and one she enjoyed.

All this would be bound to change if there were a new mistress in the house. One brought up with hard and fast ideas about the place of masters, mistresses and servants.

Dewi looked at Beville, giggling as the fishermen held up his latest tangled attempt at tying a knot. Would he be happier with a new stepmother? She doubted it.

A woman new to Polrudden and married to Nathan would have many other things on her mind, not least a determination to assure a place in Cornish society for herself and her husband. She might even resent the son of another woman, a boy who would one day inherit all that was hers only for as long as Nathan was alive.

Dewi knew her own nature. She could not stand by and say nothing if she felt anyone, even a mistress of the house, was behaving unfairly towards Beville. If that was the case, she would not keep her post as governess for very long.

She decided she did not want the master of Polrudden to marry again.

Beside her, Ahab glanced at Dewi as she pondered upon his words. He knew the seed he had sown in her mind had taken root and was well satisfied. He liked the spirited young Welsh girl. She reminded him of another young girl of whom he had been very fond.

She was a lot like Amy Hoblyn.

Chapter 9

As Nathan rode slowly up the hill from Fowey, someone called his name. Turning, he saw Sir Kenwyn Penhaligan coming up the hill behind him, mounted on a magnificent big grey.

Bringing his own horse to a halt, Nathan waited for Sir Kenwyn to catch up with him. From close at hand the big grey was even more splendid than ever and Nathan complimented the owner on his animal.

Leaning forward, the baronet patted the grey's neck, 'It's my favourite horse, Nathan. Probably the best hunter in the county. Do you hunt?'

He shook his head. 'I'm not a riding man. I can stay on a horse if it goes at no more than a canter – but only then if I'm on a good road.'

'There's no need to sound apologetic, young man. Half the riders in the county can do little better. Most lay the blame on their horses. You should try hunting some time. You'd find it most enjoyable.'

Nathan had strong reservations, but Sir Kenwyn had already put the subject behind him. As the two men rode side by side up the hill, he said, 'I'm glad I was able to stop the case against your men from going any further, Nathan. I hope you don't think it had anything to do with the fact that you and I are acquainted. My judgement was made on the overwhelming evidence that was presented on behalf of your men.'

'It doesn't matter how you reached your verdict, Sir Kenwyn. Justice was done. My men had nothing at all to do with smuggling. They were fishing, no more. I've made my own enquiries and can assure you this is so.'

'I'm very pleased to hear it. I'm not keen on this chap Ezra Partridge but, as a magistrate, I must base my findings on the evidence presented to me in court. However, I will give you a word of warning. Make quite sure your men do nothing even remotely outside the law when Partridge is around. He's a vengeful man with a long memory. He'll try his damnedest to prove he was right and I was wrong on this occasion.'

'All my boats will remain in Portgiskey Cove tonight. For the next few months they'll fish in pairs – and I do mean they'll *fish*.

If Ezra Partridge intends bringing a charge against my men he'll need to persuade the whole of his own crew to commit perjury.'

Sir Kenwyn Penhaligan sighed. 'I suppose this means I'm not likely to receive the cognac you promised me? A pity, it was excellent.'

'A keg of best cognac will be on its way to you this evening, Sir Kenwyn – and I can assure you it has nothing at all to do with the case you heard this morning.'

'I'm most grateful to you, dear boy. You'll come home with me for a drink and a bite to eat before you go on your way?'

Nathan hesitated. He had been up all night and was desperately tired, but Sir Kenwyn took his hesitation as acceptance. 'Of course you will. The last time we met I told you about my brother? Ex-administrator with the East India Company? Should have made a fortune out there, but he didn't. He's comfortably off, but no more. He's home now, with his daughters.'

'Why did he leave India?'

'Because of the girls. They lost their mother some time ago. As far as I can gather they've been running wild ever since. India's not a good country for motherless girls. He's done the sensible thing, brought them home to find husbands. I have the distinct impression that if he succeeds in getting them off his hands quickly, he'll return. He's said many times that he's got India in his blood. I think he was there too long ever to settle down in England again. We have nothing to cater for his particular talents. No uprisings to put down; no sultans to bring to heel; and he can't round up a thousand Cornishmen when there's a road or a fortress to be built!'

Sir Kenwyn looked at Nathan with a smile. 'You could give us all a lesson in handling our fellow Cornishmen, Nathan. I don't know how you did it, and I don't want to know, but bringing together a couple of hundred fishermen was something of a master-stroke.'

The horsemen fell into single file to allow a hay-laden farm cart to pass on the narrow lane. When it had gone, Sir Kenwyn asked, 'Have you thought any more about Sir Christopher Hawkins's plans for Pentuan harbour?'

'I've given them a great deal of thought. I'm no expert in such matters, but I believe the cost will be far higher than the figure quoted by Sir Christopher. I would expect it to treble, at least.'

'That's my opinion too. What will you do about it? Drop out?'

'I can't, it's too close to home. I need to retain some degree of control over what happens there.'

'Of course. I'd want as much control as possible if Sir Christopher intended such a project close to my own house. Talking of which, that's the ancestral home up ahead. And, if I'm not mistaken, here are the two youngest and wildest of the girls

45

fathered by my brother Henry. They appear to be emulating Bengal Lancers, or some such regiment from that part of the world.'

Nathan's glance went first to the manor house that could be glimpsed in the distance, through the trees. Far larger than Polrudden, it had the air of opulent solidity acquired by a big house after occupation by many generations of the same family.

He did not look at it for very long. It was impossible to ignore the horses galloping neck and neck along the narrow lane at a breakneck speed, urged on by two young riders with long blonde hair flowing out behind them. Neither girl attempted to pull up their horses until it seemed they could not avoid a collision with Sir Kenwyn and Nathan. Then, at the very last moment, they yanked the animals to a halt, so close that Nathan's mount performed a nervous jig.

'I won!'

The breathless claim was made by a girl he took to be no more than seventeen years of age and the younger of the two.

It was a claim hotly disputed by the other sister, perhaps two years her senior, who called on Sir Kenwyn to judge the dispute.

'It appeared to be a dead heat to me. What say you, Nathan?'

'I couldn't say. I was too busy trying to stop my own horse from bolting. They were certainly both level with each other when I last looked at them.'

'That argument's settled then. It was a dead heat.' Sir Kenwyn beamed benevolently at his two nieces. 'Girls, I'd like you to meet Nathan Jago. Nathan, meet my two nieces. The younger and wilder of the two is Sofia. Her only marginally more sedate companion is Lydia. Abigail, a quieter and altogether more ladylike elder sister, is no doubt at home. I hope she's engaged in activities more befitting a young lady than galloping around the lanes terrorising the populace of Cornwall.'

Sofia gave the briefest of nods in Nathan's direction before saying to Sir Kenwyn, 'May I ride your horse back to the house, Uncle Kenwyn?'

'Certainly not! You've ridden almost every horse I own into the ground. I intend keeping one good animal fit for the hunting season.'

'Then I'll race you to the house. You can't refuse, you're always telling me what a superb horse he is.'

Sir Kenwyn sighed in mock resignation and looked at Nathan. 'I regret that I really must teach this young lady a lesson. She believes quite sincerely that unless a man has wasted years in India, he can't possibly be a good rider. Start us, Nathan. Lydia will take you on to the house. Steady, wait until I've got my beast lined up.'

'Ready, steady . . . go!'

Sofia got her horse away to a faster start, but the longer strides of Sir Kenwyn's stallion soon put the baronet's horse in contention. Even so, Sofia still held a slight lead when both horses and riders were lost to view around a bend in the lane.

'Your sister is an excellent rider. You both are. You must find England very different from the life you had in India?'

'Yes. Uncle Kenwyn's a darling, but everyone else here is so dreadfully stuffy.'

Nathan smiled at the refreshing honesty of this young girl. He had further disconcerting evidence of this with her next question.

'Do you have a title or expect to inherit one?'

'A title?' Nathan was startled by the question. 'No. Why do you ask?'

'Then you must be rich. Uncle Kenwyn is only introducing us to men who are either rich or titled. They're the sort he thinks will make good husbands for us. Of course, the ideal man would have both title *and* money, but he says there aren't too many of those around.'

'I don't believe Sir Kenwyn will need to seek husbands for either of you for very long. You're both far too attractive. Once the young men of Cornwall meet you he'll need to work hard to keep them away from the house.'

Lydia bobbed her head in a mocking acknowledgement of Nathan's flattery. 'Thank you, kind sir, but I find it all extremely degrading. Every time I'm introduced to a man I feel as though I've got a rope around my neck. Being led around a show ring inviting comments on my good, or not so good, attributes.'

They were riding side by side towards the house now and Nathan said, 'I'm quite sure that isn't Sir Kenwyn's intention, young lady. He's extremely proud of you and your sisters. He wants to show you off to the county. How did you meet men in India?'

'We had an army fort quite close to the house. They were always having picnics, balls and parties. Every so often, one of the maharajahs would put on a *durbar*. They were wonderfully colourful and spectacular. People travelled for hundreds of miles to see them. They would be attended by Indian princes and princesses wearing more jewels than most people see in a lifetime. I enjoyed those.'

'There must have been a great many men there too. I'm surprised your father needed to bring you to England to find a husband.'

Lydia gave Nathan a sudden sharp look. It was too sharp. He was an astute man. She looked away again before saying. 'Oh, Father thought many of the men we were meeting were . . . unsuitable. He said we'd meet better types here in England.'

It was an evasive reply, but when Lydia next spoke it was once more in the unsophisticated manner which Nathan had no doubt would prove disconcerting for some young men – and most mothers.

'Are you married?'

'I was. I'm a widower.'

'Oh! I'm sorry, it was a rude and unthinking question.'

Lydia's question had caught Nathan offguard. She observed the sudden expression of pain which had settled briefly on his face.

'You're a very forthright young lady. It's refreshing to meet someone so uncomplicated.'

'No girl is uncomplicated, Nathan, but I say what I think. Abigail, my elder sister, says that most of the time the tongues of Sofia and I are disconnected from our brains. She's probably right. But I'd rather you didn't call me "young lady". It implies a much greater age difference between us than there is. You'll call me Lydia. And, whether you like it or not, Nathan, you've gone to the top of *my* list of eligible men. Now you can race me to the house!'

Nathan did his best to keep up with Lydia Penhaligan but, as he had explained to Sir Kenwyn, he was an indifferent horseman. When he eventually reached the house, far back in Lydia's wake, he was greeted by her uninhibited laughter.

'When I looked back to see how far behind you were, you reminded me of an Arab I saw riding a camel in Egypt. You're no horseman, Nathan.'

'That's true,' he agreed ruefully. 'I'm a fisherman and not used to riding. Does it mean I drop down your list of eligible men?'

'Oh no, Nathan. You're without doubt the most attractive man I've met since I came to England. You're still at the top of the list . . . and you might remain there for quite a while.'

48

Chapter 10

Leading the way through the huge hallway of his manor, Sir Kenwyn boasted gleefully that he had beaten Sofia in the race to the house, despite her exuberant style of horsemanship.

'Chasing after pigs and sticking lances in them – or whatever it is they do in India – can't compare with hunting foxes. There's no finer rider in the world than an Englishman. But she's damned good for a girl, I give her that.'

Sofia had gone to her room, in a sulk over losing the race, but Lydia was walking with the two men. It was impossible to tell whether she was pleased or offended by Sir Kenwyn's remarks. Her expression revealed nothing as she asked Nathan, 'Are you coming to the ball Uncle Kenwyn is giving for us next month?'

Before he could reply, Sir Kenwyn replied, 'Of course he is. Nathan is one of the very first men I invited.'

'Good!' Lydia gave him a wide smile. 'I'll see you there. I must go and find Sofia now. She'll be in a foul mood. None of us girls likes to lose at anything, no matter what it is.'

When Lydia had gone, Sir Kenwyn said, 'I'd say you've made a conquest there, Nathan. Thank the Lord she's at last showing some interest in men! I was beginning to despair of Henry ever getting any of the girls off his hands. But come and meet my brother and Abigail. When we've done that I'll send word to the kitchen that you're staying for lunch.'

'It's a very kind offer, Sir Kenwyn, but I've been up all night. I'm likely to fall asleep at the table and disgrace myself.'

'Nonsense! A fit young man like you? Stay and celebrate the victory you scored in court.'

'Another time, perhaps. I have some business I must attend to at Pentuan before the day is out.'

This was something that Sir Kenwyn was able to accept. 'A pity. Never mind, there will be another time.'

They entered a large drawing-room. At the far end, French windows stood open. Outside were extensive lawns. Nathan followed Sir Kenwyn to the edge of the first lawn. He was in time to see yet another fair-haired girl release the string of the bow she held. The arrow thudded home into the centre of a plaited straw target, a considerable distance from where she was standing.

The archer was taller than Lydia and Sofia, but there was no mistaking that she was the third Penhaligan sister.

'Well shot!'

'Well shot indeed!'

Sir Kenwyn echoed the words of a man who stood close to the blonde archer. Sun-tanned and looking remarkably like Sir Kenwyn, the other man embraced the girl.

'Henry, Abigail, I'd like you both to meet Nathan Jago. You'll remember I was telling you about him the other day, Henry? Nathan is a young man who has already achieved a great deal in his lifetime. I predict he will achieve very much more and gain enormous influence in the county.'

Henry Penhaligan's handshake was as formal and cool as the manner of the man, but Nathan hardly noticed. Abigail Penhaligan was walking towards him and he found himself holding his breath. She was a strikingly attractive girl with a beauty that appeared almost artificial. Her skin was unflawed, like wax. Her hair, blonde like that of her sisters, was worn in a most unusual style, twisted in a single plait that reached to the small of her back. But it was her eyes that he found almost mesmerising. They were of an incredible pale grey.

She was undoubtedly the most beautiful girl Nathan had ever seen. He wondered, inconsequentially, how she had managed to keep her skin so pale during a lifetime spent in India.

'I've just raced Sofia along the lane to the house and my horse beat hers,' said Sir Kenwyn. 'Didn't you race Lydia, Nathan?'

'I did, but I'm afraid I came very poor second,' he replied ruefully.

'So you've met my two wild young sisters, Mr Jago? You must excuse their manners,' Abigail smiled in Henry Penhaligan's direction. 'You see, we were allowed to run wild in India – or so everyone in England keeps telling my father.'

Abigail's voice was quiet and cultured, her manner contrasting greatly with her noisy and lively younger sisters.

'I found them charming,' Nathan protested.

'Yes, indeed, and Nathan's made quite an impression on Lydia. Quite an impression.' Sir Kenwyn's remark was accompanied by a meaningful glance at his brother.

'You must forgive my daughters, Mr Jago,' said Henry Penhaligan apologetically. 'To listen to them talk you'd think that by bringing them home to England from India, I'd deprived them of all they hold dear in life.'

Sofia, still hot and red-cheeked from the race with her uncle, came from the house in time to hear Henry Penhaligan's statement.

'You're the only one who's returned home, Father. We were all *born* in India. We've known no other home.'

50

Henry Penhaligan brushed his daughter's words aside. 'It doesn't matter where you were born. You are English. There comes a time in any English girl's life when she must put childhood pleasures behind her and take on the duties and responsibilities of a woman. For you and your sisters that time has come much later in life than for most girls. You've all been allowed your freedom for far too long. I should have packed you off to England when your poor mother died, but I couldn't bear the thought of being parted from you, perhaps for ever. That was selfish of me. Now I fear I am paying the price for my sentimentality.'

'We had a *wonderful* childhood, Father. You always gave us every single thing we wanted and we all love you for it.' Sofia linked arms with him and kissed him on the cheek. 'But I do think we could have found husbands in India quite as easily as here.'

'I don't doubt it. I want to be quite certain you select *suitable* husbands.'

Nathan wondered whether the look Henry Penhaligan cast in the direction of his eldest daughter while he was speaking contained a hidden meaning. The thought intrigued him.

On the way home to Polrudden an hour later, Nathan contemplated all the new interests that had come into his life in recent months.

First there was Sir Christopher Hawkins's scheme for developing Pentuan as a harbour for deep-sea vessels. It was a plan that had enormous implications for the village and the whole area. It would change Pentuan and affect so many people that life could never be quite the same again.

Next there was the increased vigilance of the Revenue men and the recent involvement of ships belonging to the King's Navy in their work. Smuggling had long been a part of everyday life for those who lived and worked in coastal communities. So many men were involved in night-trading that it was considered almost respectable by everyone except those employed in the Revenue service. By increasing the pressure on smugglers, the authorities would cause a great hardship in the fishing hamlets and villages around the Cornish coast, especially at a time like this, when there was a dearth of fish.

Then there were the Penhaligan girls, so different to their English contemporaries. Sofia was young and vibrantly alive. The very thought of her caused him to smile. Lydia was similar in many ways, although she was more mature than her young sister. Lydia reminded Nathan a little of Amy, his second wife. The way she had been when he first met her. The thought caused him pain.

Then there was Abigail. She was different from both her sisters. Very different. Much quieter, she possessed a breathtaking beauty.

51

He also believed there was some mystery attached to the life she had led in India. She might have fallen for someone there. A young army officer, perhaps. One thought by her father to be 'unsuitable'. It might even have been someone from a similar background to his own, thought Nathan wryly. A man who had made his own way in life without a wealthy family to ease his path to high rank.

Nathan wondered how 'suitable' the ex-East India Company official would consider him – and what difference Nathan's wealth would make to the other man's assessment?

Not until Polrudden was in sight did Nathan remember someone else who had made a considerable impact upon his life in a very short time.

Dewi Morgan, by taking on responsibility for Beville, had given Nathan the freedom to pursue a much fuller life than he had known for a very long time.

As he turned into the driveway that curved towards the house, Nathan thought that the Welsh girl, with her quiet and confident efficiency, had done more to improve the quality of his life than anything that had happened to him for many years. He must try to find a way of rewarding her.

Chapter 11

Nathan went to bed upon his arrival at Polrudden and slept until late the following morning. He was awakened by the sound of Beville's laughter coming through his open bedroom window from the lawn outside. He could also hear Dewi's voice, telling Beville to hush or he would wake his father.

For a few moments Nathan lay trying to collect his befuddled thoughts. Then he remembered the events of the previous day and smiled. It had been a good day.

Rising, he went to the window and drew back the curtains. Dewi and Beville were still on the lawn. Heads close together, they were examining something held in Dewi's hands.

'Hello there,' Nathan called from the window. As the two faces were turned up towards him he asked, 'What time is it?'

'Good morning, Mr Jago.' Dewi looked concerned. 'It's mid-morning. I hope we didn't wake you?'

'It's high time I was out of bed. I can't waste two whole days.'

'We've found a baby hedgehog. Can I keep it?' Beville's voice quivered with excitement.

'I don't see why not. Ask one of the gardeners to make a pen for it and get some straw from the stables.'

Beville was running for the stable buildings before Nathan finishing talking.

'Shall I ask Cook to prepare breakfast for you?' Dewi called out.

'Yes, please. Tell her I have the appetite of a man who hasn't eaten for eighteen hours. Oh, and, Dewi. When Beville has sorted out his hedgehog bring him along to the breakfast room. I'd like to have a talk with you both.'

Seeing her expression of sudden consternation, Nathan added, 'Don't worry, there's nothing wrong. It's just something I'd like to discuss with you, that's all.'

Before dropping off to sleep the previous afternoon, he had pondered upon the problems Henry Penghaligan had encountered with his daughters. Nathan decided it was time he gave some serious thought to Beville's future. He needed to know how much Dewi was capable of teaching him before he could make any firm plans.

* * *

53

Nathan had almost completed his breakfast when Dewi and his son put in an appearance. Beville had brought the young hedgehog with him.

'He wouldn't be parted from it,' apologised Dewi. 'It was a matter of either bringing the hedgehog along too, or suggesting we all meet up in the pen Will Hodge had made for it. Mind you, it's not much of a pet. It spends all its time rolled up in a prickly ball. I haven't seen its face yet.'

Nathan smiled indulgently. 'It doesn't matter. Here, Beville, give it some milk in this saucer. We had a hedgehog in the garden when I was a boy in the village. A saucer of milk was guaranteed to make it unroll.'

All sensible conversation ceased as the saucer of milk was placed on the floor beside the curled-up young hedgehog. Moments later the tightly rolled ball of spines relaxed. A pair of dark eyes appeared, followed by an equally dark nose, busily twitching. Then the small hedgehog was standing on four dark brown feet and turning towards the saucer of milk.

The delighted handclap of Beville sent the hedgehog into a tight, spiny ball once more, but the scent of the milk soon proved irresistible.

As the small boy crouched beside the drinking hedgehog, Dewi said to Nathan, 'Beville is very fond of animals. He has a way with them too. Will Hodge says it's time he learned to ride properly. He said he'd talk to you about getting a pony for him.'

'Good. It's Beville's learning I've asked you here to talk about. It's time he began some schooling. I wonder if it's something you can manage, or whether I need to think about a tutor?'

Trying to appear neither triumphant nor indignant, Dewi said, 'His schooling has already begun. He can read simple words. "Cat", "dog", "his" and "her". Things like that. He's also learning his alphabet. Beville, recite the A,B,C for your father.'

Without taking his eyes from the small hedgehog, Beville went through the alphabet, not faltering until he reached the letter P. He completed his task with Dewi's assistance.

'Well done, Beville! I *am* impressed.'

Nathan's loud enthusiasm caused the young hedgehog to roll up once more, but not for long. The scent of the milk was still there, the remembered taste lingering on the small creature's tongue.

'What else do you think you can teach Beville, Dewi?'

'To read properly. To write, and do simple sums. If you will buy school books I can teach him much of what is in them. I believe it will be enough for some years to come. What happens then must be up to you.'

What Dewi was saying was that she could take responsibility of educating Beville for perhaps another five or six years. Then it would be necessary either to find a tutor or to send Beville away to school. Whatever Nathan's decision then, it would mean the end of Dewi's duties at Polrudden.

'That's a way off yet, Dewi. In the meantime I'm very happy to leave Beville's education in your hands. I'll get a girl from the village to help with your other duties. I'm very pleased you and Beville get along so well. In fact, I really don't know how I managed before you came here. I must say a big thank you to your uncle when next I meet him.'

'You'll have your chance sooner than you think. A letter from him was waiting for me when I returned from Fowey yesterday. It was brought in by the captain of the ship that's down on the beach unloading coal. Uncle will be here next month, on the seventeenth. I wonder whether I might have him to tea that day – only in the kitchen, of course?'

Nathan still found her Welsh accent delightful and he mimicked her, breaking single words in two as she did. 'In the kit-chen, you say? Of course you can have him here, Dewi, but not in the kit-chen. Captain Morgan is an important man. You must eat in the dining-room. Ask him to stay for dinner. I'd entertain him myself, but I'm out that evening.'

'Thank you, but he won't be staying for dinner. Nell has invited us to the farm. I . . . we were hoping you'd be there too.'

'I'd like to be, but it's the night of Sir Kenwyn Penhaligan's ball. By all accounts it's likely to last for most of the night.'

'Of course. You can't miss that.'

Nathan thought Dewi seemed disappointed, but at that moment the hedgehog, the saucer now empty, began scuttling across the room and Beville's squeal of excitement distracted them both.

Nathan was away from Polrudden for most of the daylight hours of the next few weeks, and many of the hours of darkness too. He was having a new fishing boat built at Portmellon, a small hamlet a short distance beyond nearby Mevagissey. As the boat neared completion he spent much time at the boatyard, discussing the various innovations he wanted fitted.

There were also problems in Pentuan requiring his attention. A company had been formed for the new harbour and an engineer appointed to design and oversee the project. He had arrived with a number of assistants and thoroughly alarmed the villagers by promptly declaring that a number of houses would need to be knocked down to make way for the harbour.

When Nathan entered the village, he faced an angry delegation of residents, among them his own father.

Nathan did his best to assure them it was not, and had never been, any intention of his to knock down houses. In this he found himself in direct conflict with the engineer who insisted it would be necessary if his plans were adopted.

Eventually, Nathan rode off to discuss the matter with Sir Christopher Hawkins.

It was a two-hour ride to the baronet's house but when Nathan reached it he learned that Sir Christopher was in London on parliamentary business. He was not expected to return until the day of the ball at Sir Kenwyn Penhaligan's Golant house.

Returning to Pentuan, Nathan acted upon his own initiative. He ordered the engineer to draw up a new plan that would leave houses intact. As an alternative, he suggested the engineer should take in a section of wasteland which was owned by Polrudden manor.

The day of Sir Kenwyn's grand ball got off to an inauspicious start for Nathan. Wakened at dawn by two of his fishermen hammering on the door of Polrudden, he was told that one of his boats, the *Merry Maiden*, had almost sunk. Taking in water when fishing two miles off the coast, the crew had been forced to cut loose the nets. They succeeded in running the boat ashore on an inaccessible beach three miles along the coast, but the loss of the nets would prove expensive. Nathan needed to discover what had happened to cause the near-disaster in the first place.

With the aid of two men from the boatyard where his latest vessel was being built, he succeeded in effecting temporary repairs and sailing the *Merry Maiden* to the boatyard, but it took much of the day.

On his return, Nathan passed through Pentuan and saw Captain Morgan's ship beached on the sand. He expected to find the captain at Polrudden, but neither the captain, Dewi nor Beville was in the house.

When he asked a servant about them, she replied, 'They've all gone on up to Venn Farm for the party, sir. I believe Will Hodge, Cook and one or two from the village will be going there later.'

'Party? What party?' Dewi had said she and her uncle had been invited to Venn for the evening meal, she had mentioned nothing of a party.

'Well! I thought *you'd* have known, sir. It's Miss Dewi's birthday. Her twenty-first. Mrs Quicke's putting on a special party for her. A sort of thank you for what she did on the beach when the mad dog attacked 'em and her baby came. I would 'a thought you'd have known all about it, sir, seeing as you was supposed to be their special guest.'

As he dressed for Sir Kenwyn Penhaligan's grand ball, Nathan was angry. He was angry with Dewi for not telling him that today was her twenty-first birthday. Angry too because his sister Nell had not told him of her plans.

He was also angry with himself. Here he was dressing to attend probably the most important social event of the year, yet he cared more that he was not going to be a guest at the twenty-first birthday party of his son's governess. An employee.

He was cross that he found it necessary to remind himself of her status. Dewi never would. Although invariably polite, she spoke to him as an equal. Grudgingly, he had to admit that she spoke to others in the same manner, whether they were visiting gentlemen, house or garden servants, or villagers from Pentuan.

Nathan also felt guilty. The servant girl had said that Nell was giving Dewi a party as a thank you for what she had done on the day the mad dog attacked them. Nathan owed her as much as did Nell. He should be contributing something towards this special day.

Instead, he was going to Sir Kenwyn's ball. Momentarily, even the thought of meeting and speaking to Abigail once more failed to revive his flagging enthusiasm.

Chapter 12

Calling at Venn Farm on his way to Sir Kenwyn's house, Nathan found the party to celebrate Dewi's coming-of-age in full swing.

Beville was playing on the small lawn outside the house with Nell's children. He ran to greet Nathan when he saw him coming along the rough farm track. His reward was a ride on the horse, perched in front of his father.

Tom and Nell were inside the house. Ann Hodge, wife of Polrudden's head groom, was also there, as were many of Tom and Nell's farmer friends. Dressed in their Sunday best clothes they were cheerfully ill-at-ease.

Captain Morgan was among the company and greeted Nathan warmly. 'Found you were able to make it after all, have you? Dewi's going to be pleased.'

'I'm afraid not. I'm on my way to Sir Kenwyn Penhaligan's house. But I thought I must at least stop by and wish Dewi a happy birthday.'

'I should think so too!'

Captain Morgan's flushed face was the result of more drink than he had consumed at Venn. Nathan suspected he had been drinking with his crew at one of the Pentuan inns before climbing the steep hill to Polrudden and Venn Farm.

'Our Dewi was very disappointed when she knew you wouldn't be here to help celebrate her coming of age.'

Dropping his voice, Captain Morgan leaned forward to speak in a low, conspiratorial voice. 'Very important birthday, this is, for the girl. Comes into a bit of money, you see? From her mother's side of the family. She knew nothing about it until today. I brought a letter with me from the solicitor who dealt with the affairs of her mother and father. It's not a great fortune, mind, but enough to make her a good catch for some man.'

'I'm pleased to hear it. A degree of independence is good for any young girl making her own way in the world. Now, if you'll excuse me, Captain Morgan . . .'

Over the head of the seaman, Nathan had seen Dewi enter the room. She had not seen him. Talking to Nell, she was wearing a dress of pale blue gingham. Nathan realised she must have made it herself after Beville had been put to bed at night, probably especially for this occasion.

Nathan was halfway across the room before Dewi saw him. The manner in which her face lit up made him feel more guilty than ever. When he drew closer and she saw how elaborately he was dressed, much of the pleasure faded from her expression. He was dressed as befitted a man going to a society ball, not attending a governess's party at his sister's farmhouse.

'Dewi, why didn't you tell me it was your birthday today . . . and such an important one?'

She shrugged. 'You've had a busy time – and you're still busy. Were you able to save your boat? Everyone in the village was worried about it.'

'Yes, we saved the boat, but you don't need to concern yourself about such things. Not today, of all days. I'm not able to stay for your party, more's the pity, but I'd like you to have these.'

Reaching out, Nathan took Dewi's hand and as her fingers unclenched, dropped two small objects into her palm.

'I think I'm right in assuming that the birthstone for September is the sapphire?'

Dewi looked down at her hand and gasped in disbelief. She was holding a pair of pale blue, tear drop-shaped sapphire earrings. The cut stones were set in gold and fringed by tiny diamonds.

The rays of the late-evening sun, probing through a small lead-glass window, found the earrings and brought them vividly to life. The gasps of those standing close to her, at the sheer beauty and value of the gift, echoed her own incredulous reaction.

'I . . . I can't take these. They're far too valuable! I'd be frightened to wear them.'

'Nonsense!' Nathan was delighted with Dewi's reaction to the gift. 'I owe you far more for saving Beville and Nell from that rabid dog than could be repaid by any gift. Besides, they'll go beautifully with that new dress you're wearing.'

'Will you put them in my ears for me?' As she spoke, Dewi was removing the colourful but cheap earrings she had worn to her party.

Awkwardly, acutely aware that everyone in the room was watching his actions, Nathan carefully passed the crook-shaped clasps through Dewi's pierced ear lobes. As he did so, she asked softly, 'Did these once belong to Beville's mother?'

'No, they have a long and interesting history. They were heirlooms belonging to a noble French family. With a fabulous fortune in jewellery, they spent some time in the cabin of a sunken French ship on the sea bed in St Austell Bay. There!'

Nathan stepped back and looked with approval at the earrings now adorning Dewi's ears 'They are absolutely perfect for you.'

As she murmured her thanks, his approval was echoed by other

59

guests in the farmhouse room, but Captain Morgan went further. In a voice as loud as when he boomed orders from the deck of his ship, he said, 'Is that the best you can do, Dewi Morgan? Has Cornwall changed you so much that you can only murmur words that no one can hear? Before you left Wales you knew how to say thank you for such a handsome present. Give the man a kiss, girl! A *Welsh* kiss, not one of your namby-pamby English ones.'

Her cheeks suddenly scarlet, Dewi rose to her toes and kissed Nathan at the corner of his mouth. 'Thank you, Mr Jago. The earrings are the most wonderful present anyone has ever given to me.'

Captain Morgan shook his head despairingly. 'You're not the girl I thought you were and that's for certain, Dewi. I've seen more enthusiasm from a goldfish in a bowl. But I suppose it's going to have to do.'

A few minutes later Nathan made his apologies and left the house. Nell walked with him to his horse. On the way she said, 'Thank you for calling in tonight, Nathan. You've made Dewi's evening – and not just because of your very generous gift, either.'

'I meant every word I said in there. I owe her far more than money could ever buy.'

'You do,' agreed Nell. 'And so do I.'

She looked up at him as he gathered the reins of his horse and swung up into the saddle. 'I hope you have a good time tonight, but I'll tell you something for free. You may meet some of the most eligible young women in the county at Sir Kenwyn Penhaligan's ball, but you'll not meet one like Dewi.'

Nathan smiled. 'You always have been something of a matchmaker, our Nell. But I'll bear it in mind when I'm being introduced to all these lovely and eligible young ladies.'

As Nathan rode away from Venn farm he heard a sudden burst of laughter from behind him and a few minutes later a fiddler struck up a lively tune.

He felt a twinge of regret. At that moment he would rather be joining in the party there than riding off to meet with the cream of Cornwall's society.

Chapter 13

The ball was already underway when Nathan rode up to the impressive pillared doorway of Sir Kenwyn Penhaligan's manor house at Golant. Carriages were queueing up in the driveway, carrying those guests who lived close to the baronet's house. Others who, like Nathan, lived any distance away, were forced by Cornwall's notoriously indifferent roads to travel on horseback.

Women who had ridden side-saddle for many miles, with yards of frothy ball-gown foaming about them, hurried off to adjust their dress and repair skilfully applied make-up. All voiced relief that the evening was warm and cloudless.

Handing his horse over to a Penhaligan groom, Nathan entered through the high doorway. Standing in a line in the hall with Sir Kenwyn Penhaligan and his somewhat colourless wife were Henry Penhaligan, Abigail, Lydia and Sofia.

Henry wore a heavily braided uniform, obviously designed by the East India Company to impress the natives. Yet it was the three Penhaligan daughters who were stealing all the limelight tonight. Each wore a stunning ball-gown. Nathan thought the cost of the dresses would have paid the wages of the crew of one of his fishing boats for more than a year.

The tall, elegant Abigail, in particular, was the envy of every woman attending the ball. As Nathan passed along the line of hosts and hostesses, Abigail greeted him as correctly as she had greeted every man and woman before him, but decorum was shattered when he reached Lydia.

Before he could take her hand she gave him a hug and a kiss on the cheek. 'Nathan! I was beginning to fear you would not be coming.'

Taking his hand, she led him back to where her father stood resplendent.

'Father, Nathan is here now. May I go inside with him?'

'No, you may not!' Henry Penhaligan's severe expression was in sharp contrast to the amusement exhibited by Sir Kenwyn. 'You are joint hostess with Abigail and Sofia. You will remain here until the last guest has arrived.'

Lydia pulled a face at him and turned apologetically to Nathan, 'Bother! I'm sorry, Nathan, but I promise that my first dance will be with you – as will most of the others. Remember!'

Taking Lydia back to her place in the line, he passed on to bow the hand of Sofia. Meanwhile, Lydia was reluctantly making the disapproving acquaintance of a plump, overdressed woman and her gangling, short-sighted and pockmarked son.

'You've made quite a hit with Lydia, Mr Jago.' Sofia had her long blonde hair piled high on her head and looked as sophisticated as any other young lady attending the ball. Yet her smile was that of a young girl and it brought an immediate response from Nathan. 'I've never known her take to a man as she has to you.'

Sofia spoke softly and her next words were proof that she was more grown-up than she had seemed when challenging Nathan and Sir Kenwyn to a horse-race. 'I know you think that she and I are very young, but let her down gently, I beg you.'

In the entrance to the impressive, high-roofed ball-room, Nathan passed a self-consciously noisy group of young men who were waiting for the three Penhaligan sisters to greet the last arrival. Each was hoping to claim a dance from the sister of his choice. Nathan found he was the recipient of a great many resentful looks because of his apparent familiarity with Lydia. He found such disapproval amusing. He believed he was well down on Henry Penhaligan's list of prospective sons-in-law – if he were included at all!

Inside the ball-room, Nathan was reminded yet again that this was the Cornish social event of the year. He counted at least thirty-five of Cornwall's forty-four Members of Parliament present, although he could not see Sir Christopher Hawkins. He also recognised the Lords Mount Edgcumbe, Falmouth, Camelford and Eliot, together with a great many baronets and knights of the county. Nathan realised that those men who, like himself, did not possess a title, might actually be in a minority here tonight.

He danced twice with Lydia and once with Sofia before it was his turn to dance with Abigail. He was a competent dancer, but not a skilful one. Yet, dancing with the oldest of the three sisters, he found a new confidence and was soon convinced he was dancing as well as anyone in the ball-room.

Somewhat to his surprise, he found that conversation with Abigail was equally relaxed. They passed Lydia, dancing with a tall, uniformed cavalry officer, and the younger sister flashed them a smile aimed primarily at Nathan. It lasted only briefly. The cavalry officer made an error in his dance step, Lydia tripped and almost fell to the ground.

'I believe my sister would rather be dancing with you, Mr Jago.'

'She's a charming girl and I have enough dances booked with her already to set tongues wagging – but I'd be obliged if you'd call me "Nathan". Having you address me as "Mr Jago" makes me feel as old as your uncle.'

'Very well . . . Nathan. Would it bother you if gossip linked your name with Lydia's?'

'Not really. I pay small attention to gossip. If I did I would hardly have accepted Sir Kenwyn's invitation to come here tonight. However, it *would* upset me if Lydia read more into our friendship than is intended.'

Abigail inclined her head. 'That's much as I thought. She *is* very fond of you, but she's also something of a butterfly, so I don't think you need to fear for her too much.'

'That's the impression I've gained of Sofia too. Do I take it that *you* are of a more serious nature, Miss Penhaligan?'

'Oh, yes, far more serious, I can assure you – and since I am to call you Nathan, I would prefer you to call me Abigail.'

Abruptly, she said, 'Do you enjoy dancing, Nathan? An honest reply, if you please.'

'I enjoy dancing with you, but it's not my favourite pastime.'

'Nor mine, and it is so dreadfully crowded in here. Would you take me out to the terrace, please?'

'Of course.'

They were close to one of the tall, open French windows which led outside to a balustraded terrace extending the full length of the house. In the centre of the terrace, wide stone steps led down to extensive lawns and symmetrical flower beds.

There were lanterns on the terrace, each giving a soft yellow light. Lanterns were also dotted among the flower beds in sufficient numbers to chase away the darker shadows and hint at the colours of the blossoms on the many rose bushes. There was a bright moon. Hoisting itself clear of the horizon, it painted a kaleidoscope of light and shadow among the trees and hills bordering the winding silver ribbon of the River Fowey. The moon acted as a beacon for a trio of low-flying swans as they passed over the great house, dropping down towards the river.

'Did you ever see such beauty as this in India?' Nathan asked the question hesitantly, reluctant to lose the magic of the moment.

'Oh, yes!' Abigail's reply was immediate. 'We lived in the foothills and our house was on top of a hill. There was a river there too, but farther away. Beyond it were the mountains, stretching away forever. And the moon! Sometimes it was so large, so plump. When I was a small girl I always feared that one night it would just drop from the sky and splash in the river and be lost for ever.'

As though feeling suddenly foolish, she said, 'You have funny thoughts as a child.' Taking his arm, she suggested, 'Shall we walk in the garden?'

Nathan could have asked for nothing more, but he said, 'Our dance will be coming to an end soon. What of your next partner? I don't doubt you have every dance booked for the whole of the evening?'

'I've had enough of dancing for a while. It's really nothing more than an English-style, ever-so-civilised marriage market. When a young man comes along to claim his dance it's possible to look around the room and identify his relatives. They're the ones nudging each other and smiling unctuously as you dance by. When the dance comes to an end they crowd around their son or brother, nephew or cousin, anxious to know how we got along and what we talked about. They'll already know everything about my family, and how much money they might expect me to bring into marriage as a dowry. All that remains to be settled is whether or not I'm a fit person to rear the future bearers of their family name. I feel I should have stood in the hall handing out my pedigree to interested guests.'

Nathan smiled as he and Abigail walked down the steps to the dimly lit garden. None of the Penhaligan girls conformed to the usual behaviour expected of a girl looking for a husband. He wondered whether Henry Penhaligan was aware of his daughter's outspoken views of the ball that was to introduce the three girls to Cornish society.

'I can see how it must seem to you, although I think Sir Kenwyn would be terribly hurt if he knew you felt this way.'

'Yes, he would. Uncle Kenwyn has been very kind to us, but he knows nothing of India. Of what we've left behind us there.'

'What *have* you left behind, Abigail? Or should it be *who*?'

They were in the gardens now, passing beneath a tree, and in the shadows beyond the light from the nearest lantern. Abigail turned her face up to him, but he was unable to read her expression.

'We've left *everything* behind. All we've ever known as home. Friends; my mother's grave; things that reminded me of her. All I've ever loved.'

As they walked on together in a brief but close silence, Nathan wondered whether her failure to reply to the second part of his question was deliberate. She suddenly trembled and her grip tightened momentarily on his arm.

'Are you cold? Do you want to return to the house?'

'I was suddenly frightened of the future my father and Uncle Kenwyn see for me, here in England. Would you mind if we stayed out here for a while longer? I . . . I feel I'm able to talk to you.'

Nathan sensed a deep unhappiness inside his companion. A confused hurt. He wondered again whether there were deeper reasons why Henry Penhaligan had thrown away his own future in India and brought his family to England.

Nathan waited for Abigail to continue, but she mistook his silence for disapproval. 'I'm sorry, Nathan, I'm only thinking of myself. You've come here to enjoy a ball and I've dragged you away to the garden, boring you with my troubles. We'll go back inside . . .'

'No!' His reply was too quick. Too emphatic. He hurried to explain, 'Not only am I a very poor dancer, but my world is as far removed from the lives of the people in there as is India. It was kind of Sir Kenwyn to invite me – and I'm glad he did. It's given me an opportunity to enjoy your company and your confidence, but I don't know why he included me among his guests.'

'Uncle Kenwyn is a great admirer of yours, Nathan. When he returned from the meeting about this new harbour, he described you to my father as "a self-made man of the best possible kind".'

Nathan smiled wryly. 'Unfortunately, the county's most fashionable ball of the year isn't the place for a self-made man to shine.'

'Don't undervalue yourself, Nathan. You would stand out in any gathering. Tell me something of yourself. Uncle Kenwyn says you have a young son who has inherited a baronetcy from his grandfather. Tell me about him?'

From the formal gardens, Nathan and Abigail walked to the lake, and then back to the gardens once more. Along the way he told her much about his previous life. Of his childhood in Pentuan and the difficulties he had experienced through not seeing eye-to-eye with the rigid Methodism practised by his preacher-father.

At an age when all of those attending Sir Kenwyn's ball were still at school, Nathan had been 'night-trading', employed by Ned Hoblyn, the most notorious smuggler along the whole length of Cornwall's jagged coastline.

Nathan worked for the smuggler for some years, just managing to outpace the Revenue men until he joined the King's Navy. Here he found a niche that suited him admirably. Used to taking smuggling vessels where Revenue men feared to follow, he soon made a name for himself as one of the Royal Navy's foremost helmsmen.

There were men who considered him to be *the* finest. Among these was Admiral Lord Nelson. When the admiral was recalled from duty after a period ashore, he ordered that Nathan be transferred to the flagship, H.M.S. *Victory*.

On October the twenty-first, in the year 1805, Lord Nelson was mortally wounded on the deck of H.M.S. *Victory*, off Cape Trafalgar. In the same moment, Nathan also was struck down. His wound, although not life-threatening, left him limping for more than a year. The Royal Navy could not carry an invalid on its strength and Nathan was discharged from the service.

He did not return to Cornwall but headed instead to London. Here, when money became desperately short, he entered a fairground prize-ring to take on a well-known pugilist. He left the ring richer by more than ten pounds. Five guineas was the stake put up by the beaten man's corner, the remainder had been thrown into the ring by enthusiastic spectators. Among these was a skilful Jewish ex-prizefighter.

Too small to succeed against the heavier champions of the prize-ring, the ex-prizefighter took on the task of managing Nathan. Using all his skill and enthusiasm he guided Nathan in a prizefighting career that brought him the Championship of All England.

Nathan saved the money he won and used it to buy the fish-cellar owned and run by Amy Hoblyn, daughter of the smuggler who had once employed him. Before she became his second wife he had married Eleanor, wilful daughter of Sir Lewis Hearle of Polrudden and mother of Beville.

Paralysed as the result of a riding accident, Eleanor died at Polrudden giving birth to Beville.

Amy was also to die at Polrudden, trapped in a fire at the very moment when Nathan was recovering a fortune in jewellery from a sunken ship beneath the waters of St Austell Bay.

The jewellery revived the flagging fortunes of Polrudden and ensured the success of Nathan's fishing venture at Portgiskey, but the loss of Amy had left him a lonely man.

Nathan never expressed his loneliness to Abigail as they walked in the darkness, but it came through to her and she found herself drawn closer to him than she had ever been to any other man – except one.

Chapter 14

Nathan and Abigail arrived back at the house to find the place in an uproar. Guests had spilled from the ball-room on to the terrace and men with lanterns were hurrying in all directions, searching the shrubbery in the gardens.

As the couple moved into the lamplight, someone called, 'There she is!'

Not until then did Nathan realise that he and Abigail were inadvertently the reason for all the commotion. It had been discovered that Abigail was not in the house and a search had commenced for her.

On the terrace Nathan was confronted by a red-faced and angry Henry Penhaligan who seemed uncertain for a moment whether to address his daughter or Nathan. Eventually, as Abigail released her hold on Nathan's arm, the anger was directed at him.

'How *dare* you take my daughter off in such a manner, without so much as a "by your leave" and no thought for her reputation! Do you have no sense of responsibility, sir?'

'I'm sorry, Mr Penhaligan. I should have thought, but . . .'

'Oh, Father, don't be so stuffy. It was hot in the ball-room, desperately hot. I *asked* Nathan to take me outside. If he hadn't agreed I would either have gone outside by myself or fainted away. I'm grateful to him for escorting me – and so should you be.'

Abigail's intervention took Henry Penhaligan by surprise and for a moment he was lost for words.

'That doesn't alter the fact that he should have said something to someone . . . Or asked one of your sisters to come too, as a chaperon,' he said lamely.

'Can you imagine either Lydia or Sofia leaving the ball to walk with me because I felt faint? No, Father, I'm obliged to Nathan for acting as my escort and I'm feeling much better. Now, what's the next dance, and to whom is it promised?'

With a nod to Nathan, Abigail took her father's arm and virtually led him away, quickly passing from the terrace to the ball-room.

Gradually the excitement caused by the incident died away. When the orchestra resumed playing a few minutes later most of the guests returned to the ball-room.

Seeking out Sir Kenwyn Penhaligan, Nathan apologised for the trouble his breach of etiquette had caused.

'I should have realised everyone would be concerned for Abigail, especially her father. I must find him and apologise properly.'

'Leave it for another time,' urged Sir Kenwyn. 'My brother's sense of outrage will have subsided by then. I suspect it was never very serious. No more than an act for the sake of appearances. You've met the girls yourself before today and seen how wild they are. By all accounts they were allowed a loose rein when they lived in India. If they don't conform to the way in which young girls are expected to behave, here in England, Henry only has himself to blame. But here comes young Lydia and it looks as though she has you in her sights. We'll talk more of the girls later.'

Lydia's manner when she greeted Nathan was a mixture of injured pride and indignation.

'Nathan, do you realise you missed one of our dances by disappearing so mysteriously and outrageously with Abigail?'

'I'm sorry, Lydia.' Nathan tried not to smile at her self-centred disapproval. 'Abigail and I were talking and time just slipped away. I certainly had no intention of becoming the focus of such a fuss.'

'Fuss, you say! It fell short of a scandal by the merest whisker. Had you not returned when you did, search parties would have gone out after you. When they found you, you'd either have been obliged to marry Abigail or flee the country! Never mind, *I'll* still speak to you – but only if you have *this* dance with me.'

'Of course I will, but I don't think it's one I asked you to save . . .'

'You didn't. I just told the man to whom I promised the dance that I am too upset to dance with him.'

'He'll know that was a lie if he sees you dancing with me.'

'He knew it was a lie when I told him, but I want to know what you and Abigail were talking about that proved interesting enough to make you forget time so completely?'

Lydia repeated the demand as they danced around the floor, and Nathan replied, 'I told Abigail of Polrudden, she described life in India.'

'*What* did she tell you of India?' Lydia's question came quickly and served to increase his curiosity about the life the three girls had led there. Abigail, in particular.

'How much is there to tell? Why don't *you* tell me about life there from your point of view?'

'Would you like to take me for a walk to the lake while I tell you, and cause another scandal? No? All right then, invite me to Polrudden and I'll tell you of our life in India.'

'Is it worth hearing?'

'I thought you already knew, from Abigail. What *did* you talk about?'

'Generalities, really.'

Nathan almost added that he thought there was more than he believed Abigail wanted to tell him, but he remained silent. If there was something she wanted him to know, she would probably tell him herself, in her own time.

By the time the dance ended, all was well between Nathan and Lydia once more. He had given sufficient explanation for Lydia to accept that nothing untoward had happened between himself and her older sister.

When Lydia had been claimed by her partner for the next dance, Nathan soon realised that although Sir Kenwyn had made light of his 'indiscretion' with Abigail, the baronet's guests were less generous. At his approach men and women turned their backs in stiff disapproval. Nathan had flouted the unwritten rules of propriety. He needed to be shown that such behaviour would not be tolerated by the society in which he now moved.

After an hour of being deliberately ignored, Nathan decided to cut short his debut into Cornish society and return home to Polrudden. His name was on the dance cards of both Abigail and Lydia for one more dance, but he thought it wise to forego the one and leave his apologies for the other.

Sir Kenwyn tried to persuade him to stay, but Nathan politely thanked his host for inviting him. He pleaded the excuse that he was a working man and it was already well after midnight. The vast majority of the guests would not expect to leave the house until breakfast had been served and they had the light of day by which to see the road home.

'Yes, of course,' the baronet conceded. 'I keep forgetting about your present way of life. I'd like to speak to you about it some time, my boy. I want to put an idea to you that I'd like you to think about. Perhaps we can have a meal together, before too long?'

'I'd like that,' declared Nathan honestly. 'In the meantime, please feel free to call at Polrudden at any time. I'll be delighted to see you there.'

Nathan liked the baronet. He felt he was an honest and sincere man who returned his esteem.

Outside the front entrance to Sir Kenwyn's great house, Nathan was obliged to wait for his horse to be brought around from the stables. There was only one groom on duty at this time. No one else was expected to arrive and Nathan would be the only guest leaving before dawn.

He had been waiting for no more than a couple of minutes when a group of five young men came from the house behind him. They were noisy, in the manner of young men who have drunk more than is good for them.

Nathan's natural inclination was to ignore them, but it seemed they had no intention of going unnoticed. Indeed, it quickly became clear to him that their presence at the main entrance at the same time as himself owed nothing to coincidence.

'You leaving, Jago?'

'Good riddance, I say.'

The question came from a thick-set, black-haired young man with a face that seemed set in a permanent scowl. The comment was made, unseen, by one of his companions.

'I'm leaving,' agreed Nathan, warily watching the young men as they stopped before him. Without making it too obvious he took two short paces to one side and had one of the great, fluted entrance pillars at his back. The move made him feel less vulnerable.

'At least you've got the sense to know when you're not wanted.'

The young men were close enough now for Nathan to smell the port and brandy fumes they were breathing out in the night air.

'Should never have been invited. Don't know what Sir Kenwyn was thinking about.'

'Needs to be taught a lesson that *decent* girls can't be treated like fisherwomen.'

'I don't suppose he's ever known anything *but* fisherwomen.'

The young men were crowding him and their comments were becoming bolder, but Nathan said nothing.

'Did you think you were going to be allowed to get away with damned near ruining a decent girl's reputation, Jago?' This from the thick-set young man once more.

'I doubt if he's ever given it a thought. He may be wearing expensive clothes, but it doesn't make him a gentleman.'

Still Nathan remained silent and the thick-set leader of the small band said, 'Don't you have anything to say for yourself, Jago?'

'Not for myself – but there's something I'd like to say to *you*. Whatever you have in mind, I suggest you forget all about it. You'll have sore enough heads in the morning as a result of what you've been drinking. Don't add to your suffering.'

All five young men howled their derision in unison. When the sound died away, the thick-set young man spoke once more. 'Of *course*, we're talking to Nathan Jago, one-time prizefighter. Well, for your information, Mr Jago, *I* too was taught prizefighting. By Seamus Mallory. He was one of the best prizefighters there's ever been and he doesn't think much of your talent.'

Despite the dangers of his situation, Nathan smiled. 'Seamus Mallory never stayed in the ring with me for long enough to learn what manner of fighter I am. I fought him twice. On both occasions I knocked him out in the first round.'

The leader of the group of young men seemed momentarily

taken aback, but he recovered quickly. 'We've only *your* word for that, *Jago*, and you've proved tonight you're not a man to be trusted. Besides, you're not a young man any more.'

The thirty-one-year-old Nathan tried not to pour scorn on the younger man. He still hoped to send them on their way without any serious trouble.

'I've no quarrel with any of you. Go back inside and enjoy the ball.'

'You'd like that, wouldn't you, Jago? You'd like to think you'd got away with the way you've behaved tonight. Like to believe that no one has the guts to put you in your place.'

As the young man spoke he was slowly edging to one side of Nathan. There appeared to have been some signal passed between the group because his companions were spreading out about Nathan now. He was glad he had the pillar at his back as he tensed himself for what he knew would happen at any moment now.

Their attack was not long in coming. The thick-set young man appeared to be satisfied that he and his companions had their man safely cornered. He gave one of his companions on the far side a faint nod that might have passed unnoticed had Nathan not been looking for just such a signal.

The man who received the signal spoke for the first time, his voice as high-pitched and excited as that of a young girl. It would have made his words laughable had he not been backed up by four companions. 'We're going to teach you a lesson, Jago. Teach you that when you're in the company of gentlemen, you'd better jolly well behave like one.'

Nathan was listening but he did not allow the leader of the group to disappear from his view. Consequently he saw the punch that should have taken him on the side of the head and slipped beneath it easily. He intended returning the punch, aware that this was the man he must beat. Unfortunately, one of the others, fists flailing, had moved between them.

This man was despatched with a single punch that landed flush on his jaw. A companion was sent reeling back with a punch that had power, if not accuracy. Then Nathan was hard put fighting off the other three.

Suddenly, he heard a woman scream and caught a glimpse of Lydia in the doorway of the house. A young man accompanying her immediately advanced upon the scene of the brawl, calling upon Nathan's assailants to stop.

The newcomer came close enough to lay hands on the thick-set young man. The object of his attention immediately swung around. His punch sent Nathan's would-be rescuer staggering back towards the doorway, blood spurting from a cut on his cheekbone, beneath his left eye.

The diversion was all that Nathan needed and the ringcraft of former days came to the fore. Two punches despatched another attacker, a single punch to the stomach of the effeminate young man dropped him to his knees, gasping in pain, and the fight ended as guests flocked from the house to witness the second incident of the evening involving Nathan Jago.

At the same time, his assailants disappeared into the darkness.

There was a tight knot of guests about the young man who had attempted to come to Nathan's aid. Pushing his way through them, Nathan reached him as his bloody eye was being dabbed at by Lydia, using a silk handkerchief. At the same time she was making soothing noises, ignoring her companion's protests that he was 'all right'.

From his good eye the young man saw Nathan and gave him a sickly grin. 'I'm pleased to see you on your feet, Mr Jago, although I fear I was of little help to you.'

'On the contrary, you arrived in the nick of time. You and Lydia. Had you not appeared when you did, I'd have taken a bad beating, at the very best.'

'Nathan, you're hurt too!' Lydia's bloody handkerchief was dabbed at his face. He had a slight graze in an almost identical spot to his would-be rescuer.

'It's nothing.' He explored the graze with his fingertips. 'You'd better tend to your companion. That's a nasty cut. If you don't stop it bleeding, it will run down and spoil his clothes.'

Lydia turned back to the young man immediately and was just in time to cut off a trickle of blood that had reached his chin.

'I'm afraid I don't know your name, sir,' Nathan said to the injured man. 'I'd like to call on you some time and express my gratitude.'

'Hugh Cremyll.'

The young man extended an arm past the solicitous Lydia and shook Nathan's hand. 'You won't need to come too far from Polrudden to find me. I live at St Ewe, and I'll be delighted to see you there any Sunday morning. We have a service at ten o'clock.'

Lydia turned her head in time to catch Nathan's puzzled look. 'Hugh is Vicar of St Ewe. He was appointed only last month. He's also the *Honourable* Hugh Cremyll. His father is the Earl of Kirkliston.'

The Reverend Hugh Cremyll grinned at Nathan. 'Don't let that put you off visiting me, Mr Jago. As you can see, my blood is not blue but as red as yours – or anyone else's.'

'Yes, and it's been spilled on my behalf. I wish I knew the name of the man responsible for this.'

'I can tell you that,' said Lydia unexpectedly. 'He was one of the first to arrive for the ball and I suspect he'd been drinking ever since. He's Columb Hawkins, nephew of Sir Christopher.'

Chapter 15

It was 4 am before Nathan reached Polrudden. After stabling his horse it was a relief to reach his room and sink into the feather mattress of his bed, but he had only a brief sleep. At 7 am he was woken by Ahab Arthur.

'Morning, Nathan.' The fisherman was irritatingly cheerful for such an early hour and, taking a critical look at Nathan's face, added, 'Did you say you were attending a ball last night, or taking part in a prizefight?'

'Have you come to Polrudden at this time of day just to comment on the way I look, or was there something else?' Nathan's reply reflected the irritability of a man who has been woken from less than three hours sleep.

'What I have to tell you isn't likely to improve your temper, that's for certain. Mitchell Jane was in the village looking for you last night . . .'

Mitchell Jane was the owner of the boatyard where Nathan's new boat was being built. It was also where the *Merry Maiden* had been taken after the vessel's grounding.

'What's his problem?'

'Not his, Nathan, ours – or rather yours. The *Merry Maiden* has a couple of broken spars. Two or three more are cracked. They were probably broken before she was run onshore. It could be the reason why *Merry Maiden* began taking in water.'

'Damn! It would happen now when everything points to a good run of fish. I was told last night that the St Ives men have begun to break all records for catches. We ought to have every boat at sea if we're to show a profit this year. The *Merry Maiden*'s crew won't be happy to be ashore, either. There'll be money to be made out there this week. Did Mitchell say how long repairs are likely to take?'

'Couple of weeks, at least. It's a big job, Nathan. He won't even make a start on it until he has your say so.'

'All right, I'll go to Portmellon this morning and speak to him.'

'If the fish are on their way we'll need to have the boats and gear ready and waiting. Will we see you at Portgiskey later, or are you going to try to catch up on the sleep you lost at Sir Kenwyn Penhaligan's ball?'

Had Nathan not been so irritable from lack of sleep he would probably have ignored the part-humorous, part-sarcastic question. As it was, his temper flared. 'As the owner of the boats and the cellar, I'll do what I damned well like, Ahab! You and the others have been fishing for long enough to know what needs to be done to get the boats ready. If you can't sort it out for yourselves then I'll get men in who don't need me to supervise every little thing. Now, I've got things to do, and so have you. I suggest you get down to Portgiskey and make a start, same as I'm going to do.'

Leaving Ahab Arthur standing in the hallway of Polrudden, taken aback by this uncharacteristic display of bad temper, Nathan went off in the direction of the breakfast room. Passing a maid, he said, 'Tell Cook I'll have breakfast now – and make it a large one. I feel as though I haven't eaten for days.'

'I'm sorry, Mr Jago, sir. I don't think Cook's in the kitchen yet awhile. You wasn't expected to be back yet, and certainly not *hungry* when you got here. I'll send someone to find her right away.'

'What's the matter with everyone this morning? Is anyone doing what I'm paying them to do? Tell Miss Morgan to come and see me. I want to speak to her as soon as she's dressed Beville and given him his breakfast.'

'Miss Morgan and Sir Beville aren't here either, sir.' The girl spoke nervously, expecting another irritable explosion from Nathan. 'They stayed at Venn Farm last night. '

'Miss Morgan's party! That explains why Cook isn't working yet. Tell me, is Will Hodge in the stables or must I saddle my own horse too?'

'I'll go and find out,' said the unhappy girl, backing away from Nathan. 'I expect he's there . . .'

'Don't bother, I'll do it myself when I'm ready. Heaven help Hodge if he *isn't* there . . .'

Nathan was still feeling grumpy when he rode from the Polrudden stable, twenty minutes later. Washed and shaved, he was unfed but at least all the stable staff were at work. Will Hodge had not improved Nathan's mood by telling him what a splendid party he had missed by not remaining at Venn Farm the previous evening.

'Young Dewi sang for us,' he enthused. 'That girl has the voice of an angel. Moved your father to tears. A great asset to the village, he called her. She's promised to sing at your father's chapel one Sunday. You must go and listen to her when she does. But our little party at Venn must have been nothing compared with the "do" you went to. No doubt you had a wonderful time too, with all those fine ladies and gentlemen . . .'

Nathan met Pentuan's 'great asset' as he rode along the driveway on his way from the house. Dewi was bringing Beville home.

74

The small boy was lifted up to the horseman to exchange hugs and for a while Nathan's sour mood sweetened a little.

'I hope you didn't mind me and Beville staying at Venn Farm last night, Mr Jago? It was a wonderful party and Beville was so enjoying playing with his cousins. Nell . . . Mrs Quicke . . . suggested it would be more sensible to stay than to come home in the dark.'

Nathan nodded as he swung Beville to the ground once more. 'She was quite right.'

'How about the grand ball you went to? Did you enjoy it? I'm surprised to see you up and about at such an early hour. I was going to change Beville into some old clothes and take him out of the house for the day so you could get some sleep.'

'Ahab Arthur came to the house at seven. I need to go to the boatyard at Portmellon to sort out a problem with one of my boats.'

Dewi had moved forward to take Beville's hand and lead him clear of the hooves of Nathan's restless horse. As she looked up she saw the graze on his cheek.

'What have you done to your face? It looks as though you've had a fight with someone. Surely you didn't do that at the ball?'

'If I have to explain it any more times today I *shall* get involved in a fight. I grazed it on some bushes, riding home in the dark.'

'You ought to put something on it. You don't want it to turn septic. It could be nasty. If you have time, come back to the house now. I'll find some ointment . . .'

'It's all right, Dewi. It's not worth fussing about.' Nathan discovered that his earlier ill-temper had almost disappeared. 'I'm glad to have caught you, though. I've decided Beville should have his meals with me, in future. You'd better join us too. I want him to grow up knowing all about manners at table. We'll begin with dinner tonight. Tell Cook and the servants for me, will you?'

Watching Nathan ride away, Dewi fingered the earrings tucked safely in the purse that hung on a cord about her neck. She felt happier than she had for as far back as she could remember. Nathan had gone out of his way to drop in on her birthday party and give her a gift of a valuable pair of earrings. Now she was to share his meal table, albeit to ensure that Beville learned manners.

To think the position had almost slipped from her grasp! She was glad it had not. She liked Beville, liked Polrudden, and liked Nathan too.

'Come along, Beville. It looks as though today is going to be a lovely day. Let's find something nice to do.'

The day did not go well for Nathan. He arrived at the Portmellon boatyard to be told that the boatbuilder had found yet more damage to the ribs of *Merry Maiden*.

'It's going to need to be almost rebuilt,' he explained. 'I could skimp it and replace only what can be seen, without taking the whole boat apart. If we did that I've no doubt you could sell it without anyone being any the wiser. It *might* go on for years.'

'I wouldn't be any happier with that than you would,' reprimanded Nathan. 'It's men's lives we're discussing, not profit and loss. Do whatever's needed – but get it done as quickly as you can.'

'I can't promise to have it ready for about a fortnight, Nathan. I'll put the job ahead of everything else we have in hand, but it's not something that can be hurried.'

Nathan knew the boatbuilder would do his best, but *Merry Maiden* was not going to be ready in time to reap a harvest from the shoals of fish making their way eastwards along the coasts of Cornwall. It meant a quarter of his fishermen would be languishing on shore, earning no money for their families.

Nathan's return journey to Polrudden took him through the narrow streets of the bustling fishing village of Mevagissey. The small harbour was crowded with boats. Amidst great activity, more boats were being carried to the water and launched from the slipway of a dockside boatyard.

In answer to Nathan's question, a heavily bearded fisherman said, 'Pilchards have been seen off the Deadman.' At the same time he waved an arm airily in the general direction of the point of land hidden from view to the south west of the village. As the man spoke, Nathan recognised him as a Methodist lay preacher who occasionally preached in the Pentuan chapel of his father.

'So they've already reached us?'

'The Portloe and Gorran boats went out this morning.' The fisherman named two fishing villages to the west of Mevagissey. 'The Lord's answered our prayers, now it's up to us to grasp his bounty with both hands.'

Nathan made his way to a narrow lane off the busy harbour. He headed for a workshop where the ground floor was occupied by women mending and making fish baskets. Upstairs, in a long, narrow loft, busy-fingered women were skilfully knotting twine for nets of varying lengths and mesh sizes. Here Nathan made enquiries about replacing the net cut free from the leaking *Merrie Maiden*.

'You'll want it to be the same length as the others I've made for you, no doubt?' Gilbert Mann rubbed his hands together as though washing them. 'If you're in a hurry, as everyone else seems to be, you're in luck. I had the women make a couple of extra nets during the winter months. They're in the store, all treated and ready for use.'

'I'll send a boat from Portgiskey to take delivery of both of them,' said Nathan. 'But there's no hurry. The boat that lost my

76

last net will be laid up in the yard at Portmellon for a fortnight.'

'Makes a welcome change to find a man who's prepared to wait for something,' sniffed the owner of the premises. 'Half the fishermen around here wait until the fish are in the bay before realising they need new nets. Others come in begging me to *give* them a drift-net. "I'll pay you when the fish are running," they say – as if they're going to be rich overnight. They forget that nets are lost and boats can sink. If I was to let every fisherman have a net who promised to pay me when he got rich, I'd 'a gone out of business years ago. Like I told young Francis Hanna only this morning: "If you can't afford the tackle, you should never have bought the boat in the first place." Told him straight, I did. Well, stands to reason, don't it? A lad like that spending every penny he's ever had on a boat without tackle is sheer foolhardiness. Especially a big boat built for drifting. Costs a fortune to fit out for fishing – but you'd know all about that, Mr Jago. Not these youngsters, though, they don't think further than today . . .'

'This Francis Hanna, where can I find him?' Nathan interrupted the net-maker's commentary on youthful lack of forethought.

'Down at the harbour, I expect, where most folk are right now. Probably trying to borrow nets from someone.'

'Do you know the name of his boat?'

The net-maker shook his head. 'I wouldn't remember it if he'd told me, which he didn't. I get so many fishermen in here, telling me the names of their boats. Don't know where they find most of them.'

'It's the *Charlotte*. The boat's named after Francis's grandmother. You'll find it near the boatyard slipway. Francis will be there with it, or not very far away. The boat once belonged to his grandfather. He's spent every penny he had on buying it back.'

The speaker was a young, dark-eyed girl whose fingers were tying knots in a new net as fast as though she was knitting. But her evident skill did not impress her employer.

'Oh, listening in, were we, Pippa Hanna? I forgot you were married to Francis Hanna last month. But if you've time to listen in to other folk's conversations it means you're not concentrating on what you're doing. If I find so much as a single flaw in that net, I'll dock your pay, you mark my words. Now just you get on with what I'm paying you to do and stop minding other people's business.'

Despite her employer's warning, the girl flashed Nathan a bright smile when he thanked her before leaving the busy workshop.

He had no difficulty finding the *Charlotte* alongside the wall. Other boats about her were the scene of great activity, but on the deck of the *Charlotte* ropes were neatly coiled, sails were impeccably furled, and every strand of rigging was as taut as the strings of a well-tuned violin.

Seated in the stern of the immaculate vessel, gazing morosely at the activity all about him, was a stockily built, curly-haired young blond man of about twenty years of age.

From the quayside above the boat Nathan called down, 'Are you Francis Hanna?'

The young man looked up hopefully at the sound of his name, but the hope died swiftly. For a single moment he'd thought it might be a fisherman, wanting Francis to crew for him. Anything would be better than sitting here in his boat, in what would soon be an empty harbour. But the man looking down at him from the quayside was dressed for travelling rather than fishing.

'If you're looking for a boat to take you somewhere, I'm afraid you're out of luck. The *Charlotte*'s too large to handle on my own, and every man and boy in Mevagissey will be out today, chasing pilchards.'

'She's a nice boat,' said Nathan, looking over the *Charlotte* appreciatively. 'How did you come by her?'

Francis Hanna's resentment at Nathan's inquisitiveness lost out to his pride in the *Charlotte*.

'She was my grandfather's boat. In his day she brought in more fish than any other boat in Mevagissey. I'd go with him from as young as I can remember. When I was thirteen he died and she was sold to someone fishing out of Looe, even though he'd always said she'd come to me one day. Without her I hadn't much reason to stay in Mevagissey. I went off and learned how others fished: Scotland, Yorkshire, Ireland – Newfoundland even, for a season. I was luckier than many, I made money.

'When I came back to England I landed at Plymouth and set out to walk back here. I came through Looe – and there was the *Charlotte*, for sale. I bought her. I had my boat, but there was no money left over to buy nets or anything else I needed. It's sad to see the finest boat on the south coast stuck here in harbour when there are fish to be caught.'

Nathan looked at Francis Hanna and saw a young man who had returned to Mevagissey with a dream. The fulfilment of that dream was tantalisingly close. Yet, if help was not forthcoming, it was likely to slip from his grasp. It reminded him of his own return to Pentuan, not so many years before.

'If you're prepared to put your boat and your own skills to the test, I'll provide nets and all the other gear you'll need. We'd share all profits.'

Francis Hanna's face expressed delighted disbelief. It as quickly changed to guarded caution. 'When could you get the nets?'

'I bought two brand new nets from Gilbert Mann not many minutes ago. They've been treated and are ready for loading right now.'

Once again the younger man's excitement was tempered with doubt. 'It might take me a while to gather a crew. All those who offered to come with me are crewing for other boats now.'

He pointed to a boat that was raising sail to pass through the narrow entrance to the harbour into open water. 'There are two of them going out.'

'I've got a crew. They'll each expect a twenty-fifth of what the catch makes, and fish to feed their families for a month, but you'll have no complaints about their work. Do we have an agreement?'

Francis Hanna was so excited it seemed he might burst at any moment, but a hint of his reserve remained. 'I don't even know your name.'

'Nathan Jago.'

'*The* Nathan Jago? Of Polrudden?'

'I don't know another, and Polrudden's my home.'

All the younger man's doubts fell away and he allowed his enthusiasm to appear. Leaping to the gunwale of the *Charlotte*, he extended a hand to Nathan.

'There's my hand on it, Mr Jago. I'm proud to be in partnership with you. I promise you'll never have cause to regret it.'

79

Chapter 16

When Nathan sat down to lunch the next day with Beville and Dewi, the new routine was still strange. As a result, conversation between Nathan and Dewi was not as relaxed as he wished it to be.

Halfway through the meal Nathan glanced out of the window. From Polrudden the land sloped down to the cliffs. Beyond them was the sea. Today the water, sparkling in the sun, was sprinkled with fishing-boats, stretching almost to the far horizon.

Pointing out the scene to the others, he said, 'There's a sight we haven't seen hereabouts for many years. I hope they all bring in good catches. These have been hard times for the villagers along this coast.'

'Times *always* seem to be hard in the villages, no matter where they are,' said Dewi unexpectedly. 'Here in Cornwall the fish aren't putting in an appearance the way they used to. In Wales times are hard because coal isn't fetching the price it should, so the owners say that wages must be cut. There always seems to be some reason for money being short for those who need to work for a living.'

Nathan was intrigued by her comments about life in a Welsh coal-mining village. Apart from the brief outline when she had applied for the post of governess to Beville, she had said very little about her earlier life in Wales.

'Tell me more of your life as a girl, Dewi. From the little you've said it must have been as uncertain as life in a Cornish mining village.'

'I wouldn't know about that. I look back upon my childhood days as very happy – but that's probably because my ma and pa were still alive then. Things seemed to be happening the whole time. The men and the women worked hard but there was singing, and always something to celebrate it seemed. The women complained that the men drank far too much, but I don't think that's peculiar to Welshmen. Perhaps what I remember most of all is being part of a happy family.'

'Dewi showed me a love-spoon,' said Beville, talking through a mouthful of hot potato. 'It's made of wood. Her father made it for her mother.'

'What's a love-spoon?' asked Nathan.

'A spoon made by a young man for the girl he's courting. It's a declaration of his love and a statement that he wants to marry her. If she accepts it they're considered to be betrothed.'

'It has the names of Dewi's mother and father on it,' declared Beville.

'What a lovely custom!' Changing the subject, Nathan said, 'Will Hodge tells me you're going to sing in Pentuan chapel for my father. That will please him. He likes singing, especially when it's in praise of the Lord.'

'I like Preacher Jago. He's very like the preacher we had back home. He was Wesleyan too.'

'I like Grandad Jago, too,' said Beville, brightly. 'He says I can go to chapel and hear Dewi singing.'

'We'll all go,' declared Nathan.

'Is that because Dewi's part of the family now?'

It was a small boy's question. Innocently asked, and difficult to answer.

'That's right,' agreed Nathan. 'And a very important part of the family too. She's got to teach you to grow up to be a young gentleman.'

'If Dewi's part of the family now, why does she call you "Mr Jago"? Why doesn't she call you Nathan, like Grandad and Nell and Tom? She calls me "Beville".'

'Because they are *real* family,' explained Dewi. 'Your father was merely being polite when he agreed that I was part of the family now.'

'But he calls you "Dewi",' persisted a perplexed Beville. 'And I call you "Dewi". So does Grandad – and Nell and Tom.'

Before she could tackle Beville's latest gem of logic, Nathan said, 'Beville's quite right, Dewi. There will obviously be occasions when it's necessary to be more formal, but not here, in the house. I'd be far more comfortable if you called me "Nathan", as do most of my fishermen and the Pentuan villagers.'

'There, see!' said Beville, highly satisfied with the result of his stand. 'Now you are real family.'

'Thank you,' said Dewi jointly to father and son. 'It's lovely to be part of a real family again.'

Privately, she was less certain than her words suggested. She found Nathan an attractive man. Listening to the chatter of the servant girls, she knew they did too. However, for them such an attraction was quite uncomplicated. It was a simple master–servant relationship. Dewi was in a more ambiguous situation. As a governess she was thrown into a much closer relationship with Nathan. She now sat at his dining-table for breakfast, lunch and dinner. She shared with him a concern for the subject closest to his heart – Beville.

The relationship would move a step closer if she were to call him 'Nathan'. The fact that it would occur only in private would add to her problem. It would be a shared secret between them.

Dewi realised that Nathan was aware of nothing of this. He was merely being kind. Trying to make her feel more at home at Polrudden. But she wished . . .

Dewi deliberately dismissed such foolish thoughts. Nathan would be both hurt and bemused if he knew that his attempt at kindness had caused her to worry about such things. He would think her a very foolish girl indeed – and he would be right.

'Why don't we all take a walk to the fish-cellar at Portgiskey after lunch?' suggested Nathan. 'I'd like to see how the boats are doing. Have you ever seen a fish-cellar when everyone is working their hardest, twenty-four hours a day, Dewi?'

'I've never seen one working at all. Whenever I've been to Pentuan the talk has been of waiting for the fish to return to Cornwall. Now they've arrived it will be very exciting.'

'No, it won't.' Beville wrinkled his nose in a childish expression of displeasure. 'It's smelly!'

'Don't let your grandfather hear you say that, young man. He's been praying for the pilchards to arrive. He'd tell you that the smell that offends you so much is in reality the sweet aroma of salvation.'

'It's still smelly.' insisted Beville doggedly.

Nathan shook his head in a gesture of mock resignation. 'You'll need to make a gentleman of him, Dewi. He's not going to be a fisherman, that's certain.'

The quay and fish-cellar at Portgiskey were as busy as Nathan had forecast they would be. The *Sir Beville* and Francis Hanna's *Charlotte* were being unloaded by toiling crewmen and helpers.

As fast as wooden boxes were filled with pilchards, about a thousand silver-scaled fish in each, they were passed up the quay. From here they were dragged across the cobblestone quay to the fish-cellar.

The term 'cellar' was a misnomer. It was in reality a very large building, and above ground. In here an army of women, their tongues seemingly working as hard as their hands, were skilfully building up a great wall of fish, using coarse salt as 'cement' between each fish layer.

The salt was conveyed to the women by young children who scurried between cellar and salt store. It had been a very long time since such a rich harvest of pilchards had been gathered from the sea. Consequently the children were treating the chore as a game, their excitement fuelled by the obvious high spirits of the grown-ups about them.

A strong smell of fish already hung in the air, although this was the first day of 'bulking' – the stacking of the fish. The combination of brine and oil had not yet been squeezed from the fish by a series of processes that would take six weeks and fill the oil pits constructed beneath the cellar.

Skimmed of brine, the oil would be used in the lamps of the fishermen and sold by their wives as a cheap, if somewhat odoriferous, form of fuel.

The whole operation not yet being quite as smelly as Beville had predicted, the young boy joined in with the Pentuan children, helping to ferry wooden buckets of salt between salt store and cellar.

Beville's participation in the work of the fish-cellar had the older women beaming benevolently, and brought smiles to the faces of the younger ones. However, Beville ceased his new-found 'game' abruptly when salt entered a scratch on one of his fingers.

Wetting her handkerchief with fresh water, kept in a rain-barrel outside the fish-cellar, Dewi was wiping the salt from the cut when there was a sudden lull in the hubbub about her.

Looking up to discover the reason, she saw four horses. They were picking their way through the shallow water that ebbed and flowed between the sea and a narrow headland separating Portgiskey cove and the long beach of Pentuan.

Three of the horses were being ridden by young, blonde-haired women. The fourth rider was a man, dressed in the manner of a groom.

'Nathan!' Waving excitedly, one of the young women urged her horse ahead of the others and rode up the ramp to the quay, hooves clattering on the cobbled surface.

Scattering fishermen, women and children from her path, Lydia Penhaligan brought the horse to a halt a short distance from where a startled Nathan stood. Sliding quickly to the ground, she grasped his arm in a gesture of familiarity that raised a great many eyebrows amongst the watching fisherwomen.

'We rode to Polrudden especially to see you, but they told us at the house you were down at your fish-cellar, so . . . here we are!'

Without giving Nathan time to reply, Lydia put a hand to his cheek. 'I've been worried about your poor face, but it does seem to be healing well. It's certainly better than the faces of some of the young men you fought with. They've all called to apologise to Uncle for their behaviour – all, that is, except Columb Hawkins. When we leave here we're going to ride on to St Ewe, to visit poor Hugh. His face was far worse than yours.'

Nathan winced as he heard details of Lydia's revealing chatter repeated among the women working nearby. It would be common knowledge within a matter of hours that he had been involved in a fight at Sir Kenwyn Penhaligan's house. It would also excite a great deal of interest that a nephew of the man who had master-minded the building of a harbour at Pentuan was one of those with whom he had fought.

Over the head of Lydia, Nathan saw that Dewi had overheard Lydia's prattling. Uncomfortably, he recalled he had given her a different explanation for the graze on his face. It was evident from her expression that she too remembered.

Meanwhile, while Sofia sat her horse looking down into one of the fishing-boats, Abigail dismounted and handed the reins of hers to the groom. As she walked across the crowded quay, Nathan thought that even here, surrounded by fish, salt, nets, baskets and working villagers, she was as beautiful and as graceful as she had been at the ball.

'Hello, Nathan. I hope our visit isn't too inconvenient? You do seem to be very busy.'

'You've added to the pleasure of the most exciting day we've had for years,' he replied. 'We've netted more fish than ever before in a single day. You've arrived in time to share in the success.'

By Nathan's side, Lydia released his arm reluctantly. She had seen the way he looked at Abigail – as had most of the women working on the quay. The fact that it was the way a great many men always reacted to her made it no easier to accept.

'Do they always work as hard as this?' Lydia had loosed her hold on Nathan, but she was determined not to allow her elder sister to dominate the occasion entirely.

'It's important to bulk the fish while it's fresh,' explained Nathan. 'That's why they're working hard and fast. It will be like this, day and night, for as long as pilchards are being caught. The fishermen on the *Charlotte* were hand-lining out there too and they've caught some beautiful hake. I'll send some with the groom for your uncle's kitchen . . .'

Nathan's voice died away as he realised that Abigail was no longer listening. She was looking over to where Dewi was completing the cleaning of Beville's finger.

'Is that your son, Nathan?'

'Yes.' There was no mistaking the pride in his expression as he looked at Beville.

While they were watching, the small boy pulled his finger free of Dewi's grasp, saying, 'It's all right now. Doesn't hurt any more.'

As Abigail walked towards Beville, Nathan followed and Lydia felt she had been temporarily forgotten. She did not like it.

'Nathan, will you show me around your fish-cellar and tell me what everyone is doing?'

At that moment, Francis Hanna walked past, throwing a grin in Nathan's direction. The young boat owner was happy. He had sailed in to Portgiskey with an even larger catch than the heavily wallowing *Sir Beville*, captained by Ahab Arthur. Francis had justified Nathan's faith in him. He had also restored his own self-esteem, proving that he and the *Charlotte* were capable of out-fishing any boat in the Cornish fishing fleets.

Seeing Francis Hanna gave Nathan an idea. Calling the young man to to him, he said, 'This young lady is a niece of Sir Kenwyn Penhaligan. She was born and brought up in India and has no idea what goes on in a fish-cellar. Will you take her around and explain things?'

To Lydia he explained, 'Francis is a much travelled young man and the owner of his own fishing-boat. He and I have gone into partnership on a fishing venture.'

'I'll come too. I'd like to know what everyone is doing.' Sofia had come up behind Lydia and heard what was being said. She had remained sitting her horse looking distinctly bored while her sisters spoke to Nathan. Now, suddenly, she was the sparkling, lively girl Nathan remembered from his first meeting with her and Lydia.

'Aren't *you* able to show us around?' Lydia tried unsuccessfully to hide her disappointment that Nathan had delegated the duties of a guide to someone else.

'I'll join you soon, but Ahab, one of my captains, is preparing to go to sea again. I must have a word with him first.'

It was not a lie, Nathan told himself. Ahab Arthur had completed the off-loading of the *Sir Beville* and Nathan did need to talk to him about his next trip. He also knew the conversation would not take more than a few minutes. Ahab Arthur was an experienced fisherman and Nathan gave him a free hand. Apart from checking that all the tackle was in order, Nathan only needed to know how much fish the *Sir Beville* had brought ashore, in order to work out how much pay was due to each man.

On his return across the quay he heard the laughter of Sofia and Lydia, responding to something Francis Hanna had said. It was a happy sound and Nathan did not feel guilty when, instead of rejoining them, he made his way to where Abigail crouched before Beville. When he reached her he saw she was examining the scratched finger he had proffered to her.

'I see you two are already on familiar terms,' said Nathan. 'Has Beville introduced you to Dewi, his governess?'

Abigail nodded in Dewi's direction. 'We introduced ourselves – and discovered that all the excitement of a busy fish-cellar is as unfamiliar to Dewi as it is to me.'

As Abigail straightened, Beville said, 'I want to take some fish to Auntie Nell.'

Nathan looked questioningly at Dewi and she said, 'I promised Nell – and Beville, that I'd take him up to Venn Farm today.'

'Fine. Ask Ahab to pick out something nice for you to take there.'

To Abigail he explained, 'Nell is my sister. She and her husband have a farm on the hill beyond Polrudden. They'll welcome a change of diet.'

As Dewi gathered up Beville, Abigail discovered she still held her riding crop and walked away to hand it to the groom who stood with the horses on the edge of the busy quay.

'I'll make sure I have Beville home for dinner,' said Dewi, adding sweetly and quietly, 'be careful not to graze your face on any more bushes, Mr Jago. They can be quite dangerous.'

Chapter 17

As Abigail returned to where Nathan stood waiting, Lydia, Sofia and Francis Hanna emerged from the fish-cellar.

'Have you seen everything already?' Nathan was disappointed. He had hoped he might have a little while in Abigail's company without the presence of her two sisters, now that Dewi was taking Beville off to Venn Farm.

'No.' Lydia gave a sidelong glance at her younger sister. 'Some of us could spend the whole day being shown around without becoming bored, but we promised Uncle Kenwyn we'd ride on to St Ewe. We really ought to see how poor Hugh is.'

Nathan tried to hide his disappointment. 'Then I suppose you really must go. Please pass on my regards to the Reverend Cremyll. Tell him I intended paying him a visit long before this. Perhaps I might have the opportunity of entertaining him at Polrudden as soon as he feels able to ride over here.'

Suddenly and unexpectedly, Abigail said, 'You two girls go on to St Ewe without me. I'll stay at Polrudden. You can call for me on the way back.'

Nathan was delighted with the suggestion, but Lydia looked aghast. 'Father would throw a fit if we were to ride off and leave you behind.' She did not add 'in Nathan's company', but the inference was clear.

'I don't think Uncle Kenwyn would approve, either,' Sofia added. 'It was he who insisted we bring a groom with us.'

'Neither Father nor Uncle Kenwyn will ever know – unless someone tells them.' Abigail looked pointedly at Sofia. 'Just think of the times I've kept quiet for both of you in India. Besides, you know I don't enjoy riding as much as you two.'

Abigail was fully aware of the true reason for Lydia's objection to her remaining behind with Nathan and she now said to her, 'You don't have to be concerned for me, Lydia. I'll go back to Polrudden with Nathan and the governess. You can come there to collect me on your way back from seeing Hugh.'

Lydia gave in reluctantly to her elder sister but she looked back more than once as she, Sofia and the groom rode away from Portgiskey, taking the steep path that led in the direction of St Ewe.

Nathan was delighted that Abigail had wanted to remain with him instead of going on to St Ewe with her sisters. What was more, she had *lied* in order to be with him. Abigail had heard Dewi say she was going to Venn Farm with Beville. In fact, the two had already left. Yet Abigail had deliberately led Lydia to believe Dewi would be with her to act as a chaperon. He wondered if there was a special reason behind the deception, or whether she just wanted to be alone with him.

As Abigail and Nathan walked through Pentuan village they were in time to see Dewi and Beville pass out of sight at the top of the hill. Nathan, who was leading Abigail's horse, waved, but neither of the two were looking back.

'You must be very proud of your son,' said Abigail.

'I am,' agreed Nathan. 'But I suppose every father feels the same – whether he has sons or daughters.'

'It can't have been easy bringing him up on your own?'

Nathan shrugged. 'I've managed. It's been a lot easier since Dewi came to Polrudden.'

'She's a very attractive woman. Has she been at Polrudden very long?'

'Only a few weeks.'

Nathan had been about to tell Abigail the story of how Dewi came to be working for him, but he changed the subject abruptly. He did not want to spend his time with Abigail talking of Dewi.

'I trust the ball was a great success? No doubt you, Lydia and Sofia have been inundated with invitations from the families of all the young men who came there to meet you all?'

'There have been quite a few,' admitted Abigail. 'There was even one this morning from the parents of Columb Hawkins. However, in view of the way he behaved towards you, I think Uncle would have appreciated an apology rather more. Quite apart from that, I don't think the Hawkins family will be very welcome at Golant until Columb has written to you offering an abject apology.'

'I don't want there to be any ill-feeling between the Hawkinses and Penhaligans on my account,' said Nathan. 'I must ride to Golant and tell Sir Kenwyn so.'

'I trust that won't be your *only* reason for coming to Golant?' said Abigail. 'Lydia would be very upset were it so. Poor Lydia, she'll never forgive me for sending her off with Sofia while I remain here with you.'

'I'm very glad you did,' replied Nathan. 'It means we can talk together – and this time we're not likely to have a search party come out looking for us.'

Abigail laughed. 'Yes, that was rather unexpected.' She suddenly became serious. 'That was the reason Columb Hawkins caused trouble for you. It was all my fault. I persuaded you to leave the house and take me for walk. I'm sorry, Nathan. I do seem to have a horrible knack of causing trouble for the men in my life.'

After pondering this last remark for a few moments, Nathan pushed his thoughts aside and said, 'If it hadn't been you then Columb Hawkins – or someone just like him – would have found another excuse to pick a fight with me. It doesn't matter. It would have taken more than a few young hooligans to spoil the memory of walking and talking with you.'

An expression of contrition crossed Abigail's face and she put a hand on Nathan's arm. 'Nathan, I should have been more honest with you than I was that night – *before* you ran into trouble on my behalf – but I needed a friend. I still do. I think you might become a very dear friend – but not if you expect more of me than I can give.'

Buoyed up by the visit of the Penhaligan girls, and by having Abigail lie in order to be alone with him, Nathan's expectations suddenly foundered.

'Are you saying there's already a man in your life?'

'There was . . . no, there still *is*. I . . . I can't explain. It's very difficult for me, Nathan. Everything is far more complicated than you could possibly imagine.'

'I've never been lacking in imagination. Try me, Abigail.'

She shook her head. 'I can't. Not yet – and for a good many reasons.' She looked at him and he could see the strain she was under. 'But I really do need a friend, Nathan. Someone I can trust and who will trust me – without calling for explanations.'

The top of the steep hill had been reached now and Pentuan was hidden from view by a sharp bend and the high hedges of the lane. They walked on in silence until they reached the driveway that led to Polrudden.

Nathan was confused. His feelings for Abigail were hardly platonic. He doubted whether any hot-blooded man could look at her without his thoughts moving far beyond 'friendship'. Yet this was what she was asking of him.

It was a near-impossible situation, yet it was apparent that Abigail was desperate for someone to lean on. Someone to trust and support her in whatever trouble she was in – and Nathan had no doubt she was in some kind of trouble.

'What can I do to help?'

'Thank you, Nathan.' She gripped Nathan's arm so tightly it hurt. 'I will probably ask you to do many favours for me in the future. For now it will be enough if I could have letters sent to Polrudden, and you can find some way to deliver them to me in person.'

Nathan was taken aback. She was involving him in some illicit liaison. 'I don't like doing things like this behind Sir Kenwyn's back . . .'

'*Please*, Nathan. When the time is right I'll speak to both Uncle

Kenwyn and my father. It's not so much going behind their backs as . . . preventing me from doing something stupid. Something that might hurt everyone, including myself.'

'All right, but do you promise that you won't do anything that will make your father and Sir Kenwyn desperately unhappy? That if you ever contemplate such a thing you'll first tell me what all this is about and discuss it with me?'

Abigail hesitated for only a moment. 'I promise.'

'Then I'll trust you too and do whatever you ask of me.'

'Thank you, Nathan. Thank you so much. You don't know how truly relieved I am to have your support. You won't ever regret it, I promise you.'

Impulsively, she turned and, still clutching his arm, kissed him.

Wryly, Nathan thought he was *already* regretting the offer he had made to her. He would probably be on more familiar terms with Abigail than would any other man in Cornwall. Yet he alone would be without any hope of one day winning her for himself.

From the road far ahead of Abigail and Nathan, Dewi turned to look back. She was in time to witness Nathan and Abigail reach the gateway to Polrudden. As she watched, Abigail turned and kissed him.

'What's the matter, Dewi? Why are you looking unhappy?' Beville put the question to her as a sudden squeezing of his hand made him look up at her.

'Me? Unhappy? You're imagining things, young Beville. Come along, let's pick a bunch of wild flowers for your Auntie Nell. She likes flowers. Look, I can see some honeysuckle in the hedge over there. I'll lift you up and you can pick it for her. She'll love the scent of that.'

Held aloft, Beville turned to her and protested, 'Dewi you're not looking where you're holding me. The flowers are along further.'

'Are they? I'm sorry. I think I've got something in my eye. As soon as I find my damned handkerchief I'll get it out and help you pick some. You just stand there and see if you can see any more. I won't be a minute . . .'

Turning away, she said, 'And don't you go getting any more peculiar ideas. Unhappy, indeed!'

Chapter 18

Dinner that evening began as a somewhat subdued affair. Beville had enjoyed a busy day. As a consequence he was over-tired and irritable. Dewi had little to say and replied to questions about the day she and Beville had spent at Venn Farm in as few words as possible.

Eventually, when Beville was urged to eat some vegetables, he refused and began to cry in a low and tearless monotone.

Irritated, Nathan ordered his son to: 'Stop that.' Dewi immediately pushed back her chair and rose from the table.

'I'll take him up to bed. He's had a busy day at Venn. He and the others spent most of the time hurtling around the fields.'

'I'll call a servant and have your dinner saved and re-heated for you.'

'Don't bother, thank you. I've eaten as much as I want. I'll read Beville a story and remain upstairs with him until he's asleep. Then I'll go to my own room.'

Dewi lifted Beville from his chair and carried him from the room. She ignored his screams of outrage as he insisted he did not want to go to bed and had not finished his dinner . . .

Left seated at the dining-table, Nathan could not shake off the feeling that Dewi disapproved of him today. He wondered whether it was because he had spoken crossly to Beville. However, when he thought about it he realised she had been somewhat distant during the whole meal. He finally decided it was because he had not told her the truth about the slight injury he had received to his face at the hands of Columb Hawkins and his friends. He shrugged the matter off. It had been a very small untruth and was not serious.

Nathan did not remain alone in the dining-room for very long. He had not completed his meal when he heard voices from the direction of the hall. He frowned in annoyance. The servants knew better than to raise their voices in the house, especially after Beville had been put to bed.

The voices drew nearer to the dining-room, then he heard heavy footsteps in the passageway outside.

Before he could rise from his seat the door was flung open. Sir Christopher Hawkins stood in the doorway, red-faced and angry,

91

as though he had been drinking. With no preamble, the baronet demanded, 'What the devil do you mean by interfering with the work of my man down at Pentuan?'

Nathan was puzzled. 'To the best of my knowledge I haven't seen any of your men at Pentuan – and I doubt if I would recognise them if I had.'

'Are you saying my engineer is a liar? That you *didn't* tell him to go off and draw up a new plan for the harbour?'

Suddenly, Nathan remembered his brief discussion with the harbour engineer some days before the Penhaligan ball at Golant. 'Are you talking of his wish to knock down some of the Pentuan houses? Yes, I stopped him from doing that. It wasn't necessary.'

'Oh? So you're a harbour engineer now as well as everything else, are you? You're forgetting that having shares in the harbour company gives you a responsibility to the other shareholders. If my engineer says that's the way the harbour will go, I don't need a second – and unqualified – opinion.'

'He was wrong,' declared Nathan bluntly. 'I would remind you that I am a landlord as well as a shareholder. That gives me a responsibility to my tenants, in addition to any I have for my fellow shareholders. Quite apart from any other consideration, those houses are my property, not that of the harbour company. I never gave approval for them to be demolished – and I will not.'

'Come now, man. You must have seen the plans before you took up your shares?'

'The plans and proposals I saw mentioned nothing of knocking down any of the houses on *my* land.'

'Why do you think I invited you to take shares in the company, eh? You surely don't think it was for your business acumen?'

Doing his best to ignore Sir Christopher Hawkins's insulting words, Nathan said patiently, 'Whatever the reason, I *am* a shareholder now. In my opinion, the decision I made is in the best interest of the company, my tenants – and myself. Knocking down the houses and removing the rubble would take days. There's also a stream running beneath one of the houses which would need to be diverted. A stream, incidentally, that is the cause of serious flooding in wet weather. Something which has no doubt escaped the notice of your engineer! I suggested an alternative that means my tenants don't have to move and I'm spared the cost of re-housing them. I've already said the harbour company can take some of my wasteland to the south-west, without cost. In the circumstances, I think I've been extremely generous.'

Returning his attention to the food on his plate, Nathan said, 'Now, if you don't mind, Sir Christopher, I'll finish my meal. If you care to remain and have a drink with me afterwards, my servant will show you to the drawing-room.'

Sir Christopher Hawkins was not used to being dismissed by

anyone – certainly not by a 'common upstart', the term he had often used when referring to Nathan. He had difficulty containing his anger. 'Thank you, but you and I have nothing in common except an interest in Pentuan harbour, Jago. I *choose* my company when I am drinking.'

Turning his back, Sir Christopher strode to the door, brushing aside the wide-eyed maid who stood in his way.

Before he stepped from the room into the passageway, he turned to throw a parting shot at Nathan. 'You'll not interfere with my engineer again, Jago. My nephew Columb is to supervise the project until I offer him up for Parliament. You'll find him a very different man to deal with.'

As Nathan finished his meal alone, he mulled over what Sir Christopher had said. He wondered whether the baronet had heard of the fight between Nathan and his nephew on the night of the Penhaligan ball. He thought he had probably heard a one-sided version of the matter and for this reason had decided to put Columb Hawkins in charge of the harbour project, believing he would discomfort Nathan. Well, so he might. But he would be on Nathan's home ground. Among Nathan's own friends.

His meal over, Nathan went upstairs to say goodnight to Beville. As he approached his son's bedroom, Dewi came out. She put a finger to her lips when she saw Nathan and whispered, 'He's already fast asleep. I hope he isn't sickening for something. I'll look in on him a couple more times this evening, just in case, but I think he's probably only over-tired.'

Nathan looked in through the half-open doorway at Beville and smiled affectionately when he saw the child well tucked up, his eyes shut.

As he closed the door quietly, Dewi said to him, 'Did I hear Sir Christopher Hawkins's voice downstairs just now?'

'Yes, but he didn't stay. He came to take issue with me because I wouldn't allow the engineer at the harbour to demolish some of the fishermen's houses.'

'Would that have included the small, empty house facing directly on to the harbour?'

'It would have included the whole row. Why?'

'I met a very pleasant young girl at Venn Farm today. Her name is Pippa and she's married to Francis Hanna. I believe you've taken him on with his boat to work from Portgiskey? She's also distantly related to Nell's husband. That's why Pippa went to Venn. She wanted to see if there was a chance of getting a small house at Pentuan for her and Francis.'

They had reached the top of the stairs to the hall now, and Dewi paused. 'I suppose I took a special interest because she and her husband are living with an aunt in Mevagissey and they're not

93

happy sharing the house. It's something I know quite a lot about! She would also like to work up here in the house, helping with the cooking. I spoke to Cook and she was very taken with the idea. She said that with her rheumatics she'd like to have someone to help her – with your permission, of course. Pippa wouldn't expect much money for doing it, she just wants the opportunity to learn the duties of a cook.'

Nathan frowned. The present set-up at Polrudden was working very well. He had no wish to complicate matters.

'I'll need to meet the girl before making up my mind.'

'Of course. Actually, she says you met her only the other day. She told you where you would find Francis, when you went to the net-maker's workshop in Mevagissey.'

Nathan remembered her only as a pretty, dark-eyed girl with an attractive smile, but Dewi was talking again. 'If Pippa's husband is to continue working for you, it might be useful to have him living in Pentuan.'

'That's true.' Francis Hanna was at this very moment out on the fishing grounds once more. He would remain at sea all night. He had snatched a few hours' sleep on board the *Charlotte*, tied alongside the busy Portgiskey fish cellar quay rather than waste precious sleeping time sailing home to Mevagissey.

Having a house at Pentuan would be far more satisfactory. Francis Hanna was a good fisherman with experience of deep water work. He fitted in well with Nathan's plans for the future. Nathan would like to keep both Francis and the *Charlotte* working for him.

'I'll speak to Francis when he comes in tomorrow morning. If he would like the cottage, he can move in whenever he wishes. His wife seemed a very pleasant girl, from what I remember of her. If Cook wants her, that's all right with me. I'll leave it to her to decide whether or not the girl does enough to earn a wage. She can have her meals in the kitchen, at least.'

'I don't think you'll regret your decision, Mr Jago. Pippa's a bright girl. Quick to learn, unless I'm very much mistaken.'

'Ah! That reminds me, Dewi. Before you became Beville's governess, I'd half promised the job to a village girl, Sally Wicks. I don't think she's terribly bright, but the family could do with some extra money coming in. I'd like to take her on to help you out with Beville. Now you've taken on his schooling you need someone to cope with your other duties. You'll still be in charge, of course, and she'll do whatever you tell her.'

Dewi *did* have far more to do now she had accepted responsibility for Beville's schooling. Nevertheless, she wished Nathan had allowed her to have some say in the choice of an assistant.

'That will be fine, thank you, Mr Jago. I'll teach her all I can. Who knows? One day she might even take over from me. Not that I'm contemplating leaving, you understand. But none of us can see into the future, can we?'

With an enigmatic smile, Dewi said, 'I'll bid you good night now, Mr Jago, and go to my room. Don't worry about Beville. I'll look in on him again in a little while.'

She left Nathan looking after her uncertainly. He suddenly remembered Captain Morgan telling him Dewi had come into money on her twenty-first birthday. He wondered whether there was a hidden message for him in her words, despite her assurance that she was not contemplating leaving Polrudden.

Chapter 19

'She's not right for him, Nell. Even if she were, Abigail Penhaligan is not the sort of woman who'd make a good mother for Beville.'

Dewi was helping Nell to wash up breakfast plates in the kitchen of Venn Farm. Outside on the lawn the children played noisily on the grass, watched over by Sally Wicks. The baby's cradle was also on the grass and occasionally one of the children would pause to rock the cradle when the occupant cried in protest at their noise.

'I thought you told me the other day Abigail Penhaligan was going out of her way to be nice to Beville? She brought him some sweets as I remember – and sent some here to Venn for my lot.'

'Well, she would, wouldn't she? But there's more to mothering a boy than giving him a handful of sweets and buttering up his aunt.'

Dewi had been bottling up her resentment of Abigail Penhaligan for too long. She had to get it off her chest now. The three Penhaligan girls had visited Polrudden twice in the last ten days. On each occasion the younger girls had ridden off to St Ewe after a short while, leaving Abigail with Nathan.

'I thought Sir Kenwyn was giving a wonderful ball so that they could all find husbands? It doesn't seem to have worked very well, even though he must have spent a fortune on them.'

'You know, Dewi, if I were a stranger listening to the way you're talking, I'd say you were jealous!'

'What do you mean? Jealous indeed! Jealous because money's being spent to find them husbands?'

'That isn't what I mean as you very well know, Dewi Morgan. I think you're jealous because our Nathan is spending so much time with Abigail Penhaligan.'

'Don't be ridiculous, Nell. I'd be a very foolish girl indeed to have ideas so far above my station in life. Oh no, I have more sense than to fall in love with my employer.'

'There's nothing nonsensical in the idea, Dewi. Nathan's last wife was the daughter of a fisherman. She was ambitious, true, but she was a worker too – and Nathan thought the world of her. He may live in the Manor now, but he was born in the tiny Pentuan house where our father still lives, and so was I. If you want Nathan, then make no bones about it – and do it with my blessing.'

'Now who's getting silly ideas? All I said was that I don't want him making a mistake. Not after two such tragedies as he's already had in his life.'

'Well, I suppose he *could* do a lot worse than fall for Abigail Penhaligan. She's been brought up in India and will be more broad-minded than a lot of women he'll meet in Cornwall. She's also one of the most attractive girls he's likely to meet.'

'Beauty isn't everything,' Dewi snapped back – and regretted it immediately.

'You *are* jealous, Dewi!' Nell gave her a delighted hug, oblivious of the fact that her hands were wet from the washing-up. 'You don't know how happy that makes me.'

'You're being foolish, Nell. Even if you weren't, why should my being jealous please you?'

'Because I have more faith in you than you seem to have in yourself, Dewi. We haven't known each other for very long, but I think I understand you well enough. If you want something – *really* want it – you'll get it.'

'What I really want right now is to keep the post of governess to Beville. If I stay here listening to such nonsense for any longer I might say something to offend the sister of my employer and find myself out of work. Anyway, Beville has an hour's lesson due this morning. I'd better take him off before young Sally tires him out. She has too much energy for her own good, that one. Do you want me to take young Christian to have a lesson with Beville?'

'That would be nice.' Nell smiled fondly at Dewi. 'But don't forget what I've said. You mustn't give up trying for our Nathan. Don't give up. I certainly won't . . .'

That afternoon the three Penhaligan girls visited Polrudden yet again. As was now usual, after checking on the progress of the harbour and visiting the Portgiskey fish-cellar, the two youngest girls rode on to St Ewe, leaving Abigail at Polrudden with Nathan.

Dewi saw them walking in the garden, heads close together, talking more seriously than usual. She saw no more, choosing to take Beville for a walk to the village and a visit to Preacher Jago.

When she brought Beville back to Polrudden the two youngest Penhaligan girls had returned from St Ewe and the Reverend Hugh Cremyll was with them. It was a fine day and tea had been laid on a table placed on the lawn.

'Ah, there you are, Dewi.' Nathan waved to her as Beville ran to join the party. 'I was beginning to think you wouldn't make it back to Polrudden in time for tea. Come and join us.'

Dewi did not miss the St Ewe vicar's surprised expression at

Nathan's invitation. It served to emphasise what she had said that morning. Nell might accept her, but others belonging to the circles in which Nathan now moved were not so understanding.

'If you'll excuse me, Mr Jago, I'll take the opportunity to tidy Beville's room. I want to sort through his toys, decide what ought to be kept and what can be thrown out. It's something that's needed doing for some time now. I also promised to call in on Pippa Hanna. I'll send Sally out to stay within view. You can call on her if Beville needs anything.'

Pippa and Francis Hanna had moved into the empty house in Pentuan, bringing all their worldly goods from Mevagissey on board the *Charlotte*.

They adapted to Pentuan village life from the very first day. Neighbours called bringing tea and home-made cakes and the door to the Hannas' house was never closed against any visitor.

From Beville's room Dewi could hear the laughter of those taking tea on the lawn. Occasionally she heard the noisy shouting of Beville. He was becoming far too excited. Sally should really be making some excuse to take him away from the grown-ups but it was doubtful if she would. The young girl would hesitate to interrupt Nathan and his friends.

Dewi knew she should go down herself and take the action that was needed, but she did not feel like facing the party on the lawn.

That evening Dewi did not go down to dinner with Nathan and Beville. Pleading a headache she remained in her own room, leaving Sally to put Beville to bed.

Alone in her room, Dewi sat at the open window feeling thoroughly depressed and not a little confused. She had gained so much in the past few months, yet she was feeling thoroughly confused and unhappy.

She adored Beville, enjoyed living at Polrudden, and now had a greater degree of independence than at any time in her life. Yet this evening she felt miserable and thoroughly discontented with everything.

Even the magnificent view from her window failed to raise Dewi's spirits. Summer was almost over but it had been one of those near-perfect days so often experienced at this time of year. Close to the shore, the sea was shaded by the nearby hills to a deep seal-grey. Farther out towards the horizon, free from shadow, the dying rays of the sun tinted the water with the colour of molten steel.

To the east, tall Cornish cliffs shrank with distance until Cornwall merged with Devon and the cliffs disappeared. Westwards, the swell of Polrudden pastureland hid all except the cliff that rose above Portgiskey Cove and Nathan's fish-cellar.

As she watched, two boats appeared from the cove, bound for

the night's fishing grounds. One boat she recognised immediately as Francis Hanna's *Charlotte*. The other was soon identified as the *Sir Beville*.

Dewi had come to know most of Nathan's fishermen and she liked them all. In fact she was *surrounded* by fine people. She had also made a firm friend in Nell. Why, then, was she not happy?

Dewi thought it possible she had absorbed the mood of some of the villagers of Pentuan. The construction of the harbour was disrupting daily life in the small community. Workmen, many of them unemployed tin miners, had been brought in to carry out much of the labouring work on the harbour. They spent most of the money they earned in one or other of Pentuan's inns. Sometimes the sound of their boisterous singing could be heard at Polrudden. When they were not singing they were likely to be fighting with the Welsh seamen whose ships were beached upon Pentuan's sands.

Dewi pondered upon all these things as she tried to analyse her unhappiness and sat in the room until darkness closed its hand upon Polrudden.

Rising from her chair, she was reaching out to close the window when the sound of Nathan's voice rose to her from the driveway in front of the house. Her stomach contracted violently at the thought of Nathan standing out there in the darkness with Abigail.

Then Dewi heard another voice and realised that Nathan was talking not to Abigail but to the Reverend Cremyll. The Penhaligan girls had left long before, in time to reach the Golant home of their uncle before darkness fell.

As she quietly turned the window latch, a feeling of utter despair swept over Dewi. She had been trying to deceive herself in seeking other reasons for her unhappiness. The true reason lay within herself.

Nell had been right. She *was* jealous of Abigail. It had nothing to do with the Penhaligan girl not being the right wife for Nathan, or the perfect mother for Beville. Although both these factors concerned her deeply, they were not the principal emotion that dominated all others.

She was jealous of Abigail Penhaligan because of the close relationship she enjoyed with Nathan. A relationship about which Dewi could do nothing. Nell had expressed a belief that if Dewi wanted something enough she would get it. Dewi was honest enough with herself to know she could match neither Abigail Penhaligan's beauty, nor her standing in the society in which Nathan now moved.

All she could do was to give her love to Nathan's son and help him to come to terms with having a new stepmother when the time came.

99

Chapter 20

Two days after Dewi faced up to her jealousy, Abigail paid an unexpected late-morning visit to Polrudden. Dewi was in the room that had been set aside as a schoolroom. With her were Sally, Beville and Christian, Nell's eldest child.

Dewi was taking both boys through a page of simple printed words and she frowned irritably when a servant entered the room to announce Abigail's arrival.

'You must tell her that Mr Jago isn't at home,' she said unhelpfully.

'I have, Miss Dewi, but none of us could tell her where Mr Jago had gone and now she's asking to speak to you.'

'Sally, take over here – and ask Beville to go through the words on the first line once again. He can do much better.'

Feeling disproportionately annoyed at the interruption of the lesson, Dewi made her way along the passageway from the first-floor classroom and down the stairs.

Abigail was pacing the hall and Dewi's chin went up aggressively. She assumed Abigail Penhaligan's impatience was due to Nathan's not being at home to receive her, or because she had been kept waiting. Dewi would have something to say to *her* about visitors who arrived without any warning and disrupted the routine of the Polrudden household.

'I'm afraid Mr Jago isn't at home and he's apparently told no one what time he'll be returning.'

'Do you know where I can find him?'

'No.' Dewi's manner was unyielding.

'*Please*, Dewi. It's urgent. I need to speak to him.'

It was then that Dewi realised that Abigail's pacing was the result of agitation and had nothing to do with impatience or anything the servants had said to her.

'Is something wrong? Can I help?' Dewi's resolution wavered in the face of Abigail's obvious distress.

'Not unless you can tell me where to find Nathan. I'm not even certain he'll be able to do anything, but . . . there's no one else.'

'I don't know for certain . . . He may be at the fish-cellar, or he might have gone to Portmellon to see how the repairs on one of his boats are progressing.'

'I can find my way to the fish-cellar, but where is Portmellon? Can you give me directions?'

'Is this *really* urgent? It's not just a tantrum because you've come calling and Na . . . Mr Jago isn't here?'

It was an impertinent question, blurted out before commonsense could persuade her to hold it back. Dewi held her breath as she waited for Abigail's wrath. It never came.

'Is that what you think, Dewi? Why should you . . . ?'

Abigail's eyes widened as enlightenment came to her. 'You . . .? And you think . . . ? Oh, no!'

Abigail turned away abruptly and fled from the house. Dewi caught up with her as she struggled clumsily to untie her horse from a tree outside the main door to Polrudden. It was evident that she had been in such a hurry she had not waited for a groom to be called.

'Wait! I'll come with you. If Nathan's not at the fish-cellar I'll tell you how to get to Portmellon. I'd go there with you too, but I can't ride. You'll be quicker without me.'

For a few moments Dewi thought Abigail would ignore her belated offer and ride off. Suddenly, surprising herself, she proffered an apology to the other girl.

'I'm sorry. I shouldn't have spoken as I did. Besides, there have been many times in my own life when I've needed help. I know what it is to have someone turn away from you. I'd like to help. Truly.'

Abigail fought to retain control of herself, moved more by Dewi's kindness than she had been by her animosity.

'Thank you.'

The servant who had brought news of Abigail's arrival to the schoolroom stood uncertainly in the doorway and Dewi called to her. 'Tell Sally to carry on with the lessons as best she can. I'll be back before too long.'

Sally could barely read, but Beville would enjoy pointing out her failings.

With Abigail leading her horse, the two women walked in silence until they were almost in the village. Dewi finally broke the silence. 'I don't want to pry, but is there anything I can do to help – just in case Nathan is neither at the fish-cellar nor Portmellon?'

'No . . . yes! Would you know if there has been a letter for me delivered to Polrudden?'

The question puzzled Dewi. Why would Abigail Penhaligan have a letter sent to Polrudden?

'I couldn't be certain, but none of the servants has said anything. They usually do if anything happens out of the ordinary.'

'That's something, at least. Hopefully it will give me an extra day or two.'

Thoroughly intrigued, Dewi waited for Abigail to explain further, but the other woman remained silent. A few moments later the opportunity to ask further questions passed as a village woman hurried towards them.

Addressing Dewi, she said, 'Is Nathan Jago up at Polrudden?'

'No, we're going to find him now. Is something wrong?'

'I'll say it's wrong! Them men working on the harbour have closed off the wooden bridge over the river. Young Harriet Piper just went to cross to take bread to one of the boats on the beach and they turned her away. Told her to walk the long way round – and her a cripple too. It's disgraceful! Nathan's going to need to do something about it.'

A fast-flowing river ran along the Pentuan valley. It cut the village off from the beach and the road linking St Austell and Mevagissey. There was a permanent stone-built bridge at the far end of the village, but the wooden bridge offered the villagers a short cut to the beach and Nathan's fish-cellar at Portgiskey. It was also used by packhorses to carry off cargoes from the beached ships. If they had to use the stone bridge it would double the distance to the beach for the villagers.

'All right, leave it to me, I'm heading for the bridge now. If I can't sort it out, I'll tell Mr Jago.'

'You tell him to do something about it – and quick. Pentuan folk have been using that bridge for as long as anyone can remember. We can't have it closed. We *need* to use it.'

As they walked on, Abigail said apprehensively, 'Will this make trouble for Nathan?'

'Not if I can do anything about it.' Dewi strode purposefully towards the narrow wooden bridge.

There were men standing on either side of the disputed bridge. Both were armed with long, bulbous-ended cudgels and the man on the Pentuan side wasted no time on pleasantries.

'And where do you think you're going with that horse?'

'Over the bridge to the Portgiskey fish-cellar – not that it's any of your business.'

'It may be none of my business *where* you're going, missie – but you ain't getting there over this bridge.'

'We're on our way of Mr Jago's fish-cellar, and this is the way I always come.'

'Not no more you won't,' said the man doggedly. 'And you can tell this Mr Jago, whoever he is, that he won't be coming this way no more, neither.'

'Who's giving you your orders, and where will I find him?'

'I'm being paid by Mr Columb Hawkins and if you want him you'll no doubt find him over there, in the old Customs house.'

Doing her best to control her temper, Dewi turned to Abigail. 'I'm going to speak to this Mr Hawkins about this. Will you wait here. Or come with me?'

'Neither!' Abigail's agitation had increased at mention of Columb Hawkins's name. 'If he sees me, he'll want to know why I'm here and will probably tell my uncle. That's the last thing I want right now. I really ought to ride back to Golant. I shouldn't have come in the first place but there was no one I could turn to except Nathan. Will you give him a message for me, Dewi?'

She nodded, although the last thing she wanted was to act as a messenger between Nathan and Abigail Penhaligan.

'I am expecting a letter to arrive for me at any time. When it arrives it is most important that he finds some way to bring it to me immediately. Will you tell him that?'

'Yes, but . . . Will he know what it's all about?'

Abigail made a weak attempt at a smile. 'He knows no more than you do, Dewi, but he trusts me – as I'm trusting you to give him my message.'

Holding her horse steady, Abigail mounted the animal with the ease of a skilled horsewoman and set off at a trot, back the way she and Dewi had come.

Watching the other woman ride away, Dewi wondered what trouble she was in . . . and how far Nathan would need to go in order to help her? She would have time to ponder on Abigail's troubles later. Right now there was a problem much closer to home that needed to be resolved . . .

Columb Hawkins came to the door in response to Dewi's loud and insistent knocking. His frown of annoyance vanished when he saw her.

'Well, well, and what do we have here? My very first visitor – and such a pretty one! What can I do for you? Have you come seeking work? I'm quite certain I can find something for you. Come in.'

'What I have to say can be said right here, on the doorstep.'

'Nonsense! I can't have word getting around the village that Columb Hawkins doesn't know how to entertain pretty young ladies. Come inside and join me in a pre-lunch drink.'

'I'm here to ask why you've closed the wooden bridge across the river to the villagers? That's my only reason for coming to your house.'

'Does it inconvenience you? Well, I don't doubt we can do something about that. With goodwill on both sides we should come to some arrangement that will prove mutually satisfactory. But come in. I'm not an ogre.'

'I'll remain here, thank you,' declared Dewi firmly. 'The bridge is used by the villagers to get to the beach. It's important to them.'

Columb shrugged. 'I can't have them getting in the way of my men while the harbour's being built. They'll need to use the stone bridge.'

The more Columb Hawkins looked at Dewi, the more she aroused him. She was certainly pretty, and the simple, tight-waisted dress she wore hinted at a body that matched the face.

'Look, come inside and we'll discuss this in a more congenial atmosphere. I don't want you to feel I'm being intransigent about this matter. In fact, it's quite possible you might be able to persuade me to change my mind.'

For a moment, Dewi weakened. She would dearly like to resolve the matter of access to the bridge without involving Nathan. During the conversation with Columb Hawkins, Dewi had remembered where she had heard the name before. This was the man said by Sofia Penhaligan to have caused the graze on Nathan's cheek. There must have been an argument between them at the ball given by Sir Kenwyn Penhaligan. She did not want the matter of the bridge to cause another clash between them.

'You're not frightened of me, surely?'

'Why can't you give me a decision here and now?'

'Why? Because, my dear girl, I am not used to conducting business on a doorstep and it's certainly not the place to enjoy the company of a pretty girl. Look, come in. If it makes you feel any happier, I'll leave the front door open.'

Dewi was still not at all certain, but if she could sort out the problem of the bridge it would save trouble for everyone – especially Nathan. Two steps took her inside the small entrance hall.

'That's better.' Smiling, Columb Hawkins made as though to take her arm, but Dewi tucked it in close to her body.

'I'm in the house now, Mr Hawkins. May we talk about the bridge, please?'

'You are insistent, Miss . . . ?'

'My name doesn't matter. Do we talk about the bridge, or shall I leave again immediately?'

'Very well.' Columb Hawkins gave an exaggerated sigh. 'But at least have a drink while you're here . . . No, I'm not going to insist, but as I have one already poured, you won't mind if I drink it while we're talking?'

He opened an inner door. There were parcels, clothing and a number of bottles strewn everywhere. 'You must pardon the mess, but I moved in only yesterday. It's quite tidy upstairs, but I can't seem to get to grips with things down here. I suppose cleaning isn't in your line?'

Columb Hawkins had been studying Dewi while they were talking and found himself at a loss. She was here because of an expressed interest in the wooden bridge, but he could not make up his mind where she fitted into village life. She was too well dressed for a fisherman's woman, but her clothes were not expensive enough to place her outside the working classes.

'The bridge, Mr Hawkins.'

'Ah yes, the bridge.' Columb Hawkins entered the inner room and picked up a glass. He added to the contents from a brandy bottle and took a sip before saying, 'You want me to re-open the bridge – not just to you, but to everyone in the village?'

'That's right. To restore free use of the bridge to those who have always enjoyed that right.'

'The bridge is on private property. Having the villagers and their pack animals making free use of it will cause considerable inconvenience to the men working on the harbour.'

'I doubt that. I've found the people of Pentuan very understanding. They'll come more than halfway to meet you if you try to understand their problem.'

'Is that so? And how about you. Are you ready to come more than halfway to meet me if I'm prepared to do something about this bridge?'

'I've told you, Mr Hawkins, all I'm trying to do is prevent any trouble.'

'So you have, girl.' Columb Hawkins wrinkled his nose. 'This place can't have had any fresh air for months. Do you mind if I open a window?'

Without waiting for a reply, he opened a small transom window. A draught blew the curtains inward and behind Dewi the front door slammed shut. She turned immediately, but before she could decide whether to lift the latch or turn a heavy, wrought-iron handle, Columb Hawkins moved quickly to stand between her and her way of escape.

'I'd be obliged if you'd move out of the way and allow me to leave, Mr Hawkins.'

'But we haven't resolved the little matter of the bridge yet, Miss . . . ?'

Columb gave her an ingratiating smile. 'You really must tell me your name if we're to take this any further. I'm quite willing to make a concession to you about the use of the bridge. A *major* concession. When you return to your friends you can tell them you persuaded me to change my mind. You'll be the toast of the village. All I ask in return is that you behave no less generously than the villagers you've been telling me about. With generosity and understanding. Come now, let's be honest with each other. You're a worldly girl, I can see that. I'm not asking you for more than you'll already have given to the village lads. I can offer you a warm and profitable friendship – and real silk sheets on *my* bed.'

'The door please, Mr Hawkins?'

Dewi hoped she sounded far more assured than she felt. Her heart was beating wildly. She realised just how foolish she had been by allowing herself to be lured into such a situation.

105

'Come, girl. You entered my house of your own free will. Don't be stupid now. I've offered to give you all you have asked of me. Am I expecting too much in return?'

Columb Hawkins reached out and rested his hands lightly on Dewi's shoulders but when she tried to break free he tightened his grip and pulled her to him.

For a moment, Columb thought he had won. Dewi moved a fraction closer, but before the smile had fully formed on his face her knee came up in a vicious jerk that caught him in the groin. A fiery pain such as he had never before known exploded in his lower stomach.

As he doubled over, Dewi pushed past him to the stone-flagged floor of the hallway.

A moment later the door swung open. Turning back to the man who rocked backwards and forwards on his knees in agony, hands between his thighs, she said, 'I learned to do that when I was twelve, Mr Hawkins, against a boy who was fifteen. I've never had to do it again since, because we breed gentlemen in the valleys of Wales. You could learn a thing or two from them.'

A moment later she was outside, breathing in deep gulps of clean, fresh air. She walked away without a backward glance at the stricken man.

Chapter 21

Any hopes Dewi entertained of breaking the news of the bridge closure to Nathan in a quiet and reasonable way were quickly dashed. Preacher Josiah Jago came to Polrudden that afternoon in a furious mood.

'For sixty years I've been using that bridge. My father used it before me. When I was a small child he would carry me across the bridge on his shoulder on our way to listen to John Wesley preach the gospel. Now some whipper-snapper, who's probably never even visited the village before, says it must close! Well, he'll soon learn different. If Nathan can't persuade him to change his mind then the villagers will – even if it means cracking a few stubborn heads in the process.'

'That's hardly a Christian way of solving a problem, Preacher Jago,' chided Dewi.

'There's a time for turning the other cheek, and there's a time for smiting the ungodly,' declared the angry preacher. 'From all I've heard of Columb Hawkins, he's more at home in an unsavoury tavern than in church or chapel. I'll pray for his soul from the pulpit on Sunday, but I'll do all I can every other day to have him removed from the village.'

'Why don't you leave it to me to tell Nathan about it?' Dewi suggested, but she was already too late. As they spoke, one of the servants entered the room to announce that Nathan had returned.

Josiah Jago assailed his son with news of the closure of the bridge even before Nathan had handed over his horse to the keeping of a Polrudden groom.

As Dewi came from the house with Beville, Preacher Jago was saying, 'It's an absolute disgrace, affecting the livelihood of men and placing an additional burden on the village women.'

As Beville ran to greet his father, Josiah Jago played his trump card. 'You ask Dewi. She tried to cross the bridge today with Beville and your friend, the Penhaligan girl. They were turned back. I believe the Penhaligan girl was so upset she turned around and went home again.'

Nathan had swung Beville in the air. Now he placed him on the ground once more and scowled. 'Is this true, Dewi? Who was with you? Was it Abigail?'

'Yes, but it isn't as bad as it sounds. Abigail went home because she was short of time and we weren't certain you'd be at the fish-cellar anyway.'

'I probably wasn't. I've been to the boatyard at Portmellon and called in at St Ewe on my way back. I crossed the road bridge to Pentuan, otherwise I would have found out about this for myself. I'll go down there and sort it out right now. There's no need at all for the bridge to be closed. I'll not have my friends – or the villagers – inconvenienced at the whim of Columb Hawkins.'

'At least have something to eat before you go down there and I'll tell you about Abigail's visit.'

'Tell me when I come back.' Nathan was as angry as Dewi had feared he would be if Preacher Jago was allowed to break the news of the bridge closure to him. 'Take Beville now. I won't be long.'

'I'll come with you,' said Preacher Jago promptly.

'No, you won't. You'll remain here. This is my problem and one you can't afford to get mixed up in. It might be Sir Christopher Hawkins's doing, and he has a voice in Parliament. There are still many men there ready to seize on anything that will help discredit the Methodist movement.'

When Nathan had gone, Dewi rounded on Josiah Jago. 'I hope you're satisfied. Nathan has already had trouble with Columb Hawkins. This business of the bridge can only provoke more.'

'You heard what Nathan said, Dewi. This is *his* problem and he alone can resolve it.'

'Perhaps. But if you'd left it to me to tell him about it, I'd have made certain he had time to think about what he was going to do and not set off hot with anger. I'm going to speak with Nell. I suggest you go down to the village and round up the fishermen. There are some tough men working on the harbour. Nathan won't stand a chance alone if Columb Hawkins calls on them.'

Nathan had left Polrudden with the intention of calling on Columb Hawkins at the old Customs house and taking the matter of the bridge up with him. However, as he approached the house he saw the two men guarding the bridge turn away one of the fisherwomen from the village and he changed his mind.

The two men were standing in the centre of the bridge laughing at a shared joke as Nathan approached. When it became apparent that the bridge was his objective, one of the men sauntered to the end nearer him, fingering a long, heavy, polished wood cudgel.

By the time Nathan reached the narrow bridge the man was barring the way. He spoke first.

'And just where do you think you're going?' From the accent it was evident the man was Cornish, but he was not from the Pentuan area.

'I'm going to the fish-cellar at Portgiskey.' Nathan's reply and manner were deceptively mild.

'I don't know where this Portgiskey is, but I hope there's another way to get there, because you're not crossing this bridge.' The man gave emphasis to his words by tapping the heavy end of the cudgel against the palm of his hand.

'Oh? Who says I'm not?' As before, Nathan's words were softly spoken.

'*I* say you're not, and them's Mr Hawkins's orders.'

'I see.' Nathan half turned, as though to walk away. Suddenly swinging back he caught the other man offguard and kicked his legs from under him. The man dropped his cudgel and grabbed for the guard rail which ran on either side of the bridge.

He was not quick enough. Nathan knocked the man's arm up, at the same time using a knee to propel him off the bridge and into the fast-flowing river, ten feet below.

Even as the water closed over the unfortunate man's head and cut off his cry for help, Nathan was stepping on to the bridge to face the second man.

'Are you going to let me pass or will you join your friend in the river?'

'He can't swim! He'll drown!'

'I doubt it. He'll be in shallow water before he comes to any harm. The wetting might teach him to show good manners when he speaks to those with every right to cross the bridge without hindrance.'

As he spoke, Nathan risked a glance to where the arms of the wildly thrashing guard could be seen breaking the surface of the water far from the bridge. A few more moments and he would be swept into shallow water where the river dissipated its strength on the wide sands of the beach. He might swallow a great deal of water and be in mortal terror for his life, but he would not drown.

Returning his attention to the floundering man's companion, Nathan repeated his question. 'Are *you* going to allow me to cross, or will you join him in the river?'

The man backed slowly away from Nathan across the bridge. When his feet were on solid ground, he said, 'You're Nathan Jago, aren't you?'

'That's right, but you haven't answered my question.'

'I'm not taking *you* on, Mr Jago. As far as I'm concerned you can go wherever you like – and so can everyone else in Pentuan. Mr Hawkins can do his own dirty work.'

'Where is Columb Hawkins right now?'

'In the engineer's hut, down by the road bridge. When you see him, tell he'll need to find two new watchmen to guard his bridge. When I tell my mate who he tried to stop from crossing, he'll be going off too. If you don't mind, I'll go and help him now.'

From the bridge, Nathan could see the other watchman clawing his way from the river to the sand. Reaching safety he lay face down, the noise of his retching and gagging clearly audible on the bridge.

Columb Hawkins was coming from the engineer's hut as Nathan approached. When he saw who was bearing down upon him it looked for a moment as though he might run away, but he recovered quickly and faced Nathan defiantly.

'If you've come to cause trouble, Jago . . .'

'I'm here to *prevent* trouble. The two men you set to stop villagers from crossing the wooden bridge have quit. I suggest you don't bother to replace them. That bridge has been used by the people of Pentuan for longer than anyone can remember. You're going to need the co-operation of Pentuan people while the harbour's being built. Don't lose it before the work's even begun in earnest.'

'The bridge is on harbour land. We can't have villagers milling about when we're trying to work. It will remain closed. If the men I've put there have gone, others will take their place. I'll double their number – and double again, if I need to.'

Nathan shrugged. 'I'm not going to stand here and argue with you. I've said what I came to say, but I think you should remember my words. The success of the harbour depends to a great extent upon the goodwill of the Pentuan community – at every level. Any delay in building will cost money. It will result in the other shareholders asking questions about your suitability for the job you've been given. Besides, the man who stands to lose most, as the major shareholder, is your uncle. I don't think he'll like that. Forget the bridge and concentrate on the harbour, Hawkins. That's serious advice. I suggest you take it.'

Halfway up Pentuan hill, Nathan met Dewi hurrying down.

'Is something wrong . . . Beville?'

'No. I left him with Nell. Tom and some of the men from Polrudden will be along in a minute. I . . . we were worried about you.'

'Why?' Nathan was as much flattered as puzzled.

'When Lydia Penhaligan visited the fish-cellar with her sister that first day, she mentioned the trouble you'd had with Columb Hawkins at Sir Kenwyn's house. I was concerned there might be more between you today.'

'I'm touched by your concern, Dewi. But we'd better stop Tom and the others from going to the village.'

Nathan placed a hand on her shoulder. He removed it quickly when she appeared to flinch from his touch. 'There's more

110

involved in this than personalities. The future of the harbour is important to everyone.'

'Did you speak to Columb Hawkins?' Dewi spoke quickly to hide the foolish confusion she had felt at his touch.

'I did, and I walked across the bridge. Unfortunately, I think Hawkins is likely to increase the number of men guarding the bridge by tomorrow. If he does I have a little scheme of my own that might persuade him to forget the bridge once and for all.'

Nathan smiled at her. 'Now, why don't you tell me what Abigail had to say when she was here today?'

Chapter 22

Columb Hawkins carried out his threat. The next morning there were four loud-voiced burly men guarding the wooden bridge. Their shouted conversations from one side of the bridge to the other would have left any villagers intending to cross the bridge in no doubt of the probable outcome.

But no villagers came anywhere near the bridge. When Columb Hawkins visited his men he was assured that the Pentuan people appeared to have lost all interest in the matter.

'They'm not foolish, Mr Hawkins,' said one of the men, a giant, black-bearded man whose scarred face bore witness to many fights. 'You'm showed 'em you mean business. They won't argue with the likes of us.'

Columb Hawkins was less certain than his hired thug. When men began gathering in Pentuan that afternoon, he sent out and doubled the guard yet again. Now there were eight men prepared to dispute access to the bridge. He felt this was a sufficient number, but still made frequent visits to ensure the guards were not sneaking away to one of the local inns.

The hired men remained at their posts but they were not troubled by the Pentuan villagers. Nathan had no intention of sending the fishermen to mount a frontal attack on the bridge. That afternoon, armed with pickaxes and long-handled, triangular-bladed shovels, the villagers set about digging up the roadway on both sides of the stone river bridge, carrying their activities right through the village.

By four o'clock there was a long queue of laden wagons backing up on the roads leading into Pentuan, unable to enter the village and make their way to the harbour workings.

Nathan had expected Columb Hawkins to come to Polrudden immediately, demanding to know what was going on. However, not until the following morning did the baronet's nephew sink his pride and climb the hill to the Manor. By this time laden wagons were turning around and returning with their goods to St Austell, warning those who followed to do the same.

Unlike his uncle, Columb Hawkins did not storm into the house to confront Nathan. He came no farther than the front hall. Here he waited impatiently for half-an-hour before being shown into Nathan's study.

Columb Hawkins had contained his simmering anger so far, but when Nathan politely asked the purpose of the 'unexpected' visit, he exploded with rage.

'You know very well why I'm here, Jago. I demand an explanation from you. What the devil do you think you're playing at in Pentuan? Gangs of men are tearing up the roads, preventing anything from entering and causing me to stop all work on the harbour. When I asked what was going on I was told the men were acting upon your orders. Why?'

'There's a very simple answer. As the principal landowner hereabouts, maintaining roads in the vicinity of Pentuan is my responsibility. I am merely carrying out my public duty.'

'And how long is this "public duty" likely to continue?'

Nathan shrugged nonchalantly. 'As long as it takes. Two weeks, perhaps. It might even be four or more.'

'You're insane, Jago. Because you lost a silly little argument about a bridge you're throwing away your money, and that of your fellow shareholders in this ridiculous vendetta. Well, you can rest assured you won't get away with it. I'll take you to law.'

'Such a move will cost the shareholders more money than they're losing right now, Hawkins. Before that happens I'll demand a meeting of all shareholders and have you dismissed. Between us we can out-vote your uncle, and I'm not at all certain you're needed anyway. This "silly little argument about a bridge", as you call it, affects the livelihood of my tenants. That, to me, is of far more importance than investment in a new harbour. If you want work to resume here, you have a simple solution. One that will cost you and the company nothing at all. Allow free access to the foreshore via the wooden bridge, that's all. Now you'll pardon me if I bid you "good day" and have you shown out? I'm a very busy man.'

The following morning Preacher Jago climbed the hill to Polrudden to inform Nathan that all guards had been removed from the wooden bridge and that the villagers were once more using it without hindrance.

By late that same afternoon the road through Pentuan was passable once more and work was able to resume on the harbour.

It was a victory for commonsense, but the incident served to increase the bitterness between Nathan and the Hawkins family.

What Nathan did not know was that the decision to re-open the bridge had been made not by Columb Hawkins, but by his uncle, Sir Christopher.

After angrily upbraiding his nephew for allowing himself to be caught up in such a situation, Sir Christopher warned him, 'You should never take action without fully thinking out the consequences first. To lay yourself open to ridicule and allow a man

113

like Nathan Jago to better you is folly of the worst possible kind. I am thoroughly disappointed in you, Columb. You are not the man I thought you were.'

'If we took civil action against him, we would win. I'm convinced of it.'

Columb spoke sulkily. He had come to Trewithan to put the case before his uncle in the belief that Sir Christopher would support him and start the necessary proceedings to take Jago to court.

'Perhaps. Perhaps not. What is far more certain is that he *could* persuade the other shareholders to remove you from all responsibility for the harbour works – and I want you there. Besides, you'll be standing for Parliament very soon and it won't help your cause to be involved in a civil action. If the case went Jago's way you could forget all about a parliamentary career.'

'So what do you suggest I do? Apologise to Jago, throw open the bridge and have his fishermen laugh at me?'

'You'll do whatever is necessary to resolve this mess. It is, after all, of your own making. You'll also carefully weigh the scorn of a few villagers who count for nothing at all, against the loss of a parliamentary seat and the honours it's likely to bring to the family. There can be only one answer. Go back to Pentuan and do something about it – now!'

Chapter 23

Events at Pentuan prevented Nathan from riding to Golant to see Abigail immediately after her visit to Polrudden, but this proved fortunate. The day after the problem of the wooden bridge had been resolved, a horseman picked his way through the roadworks, bound for Polrudden. In a pouch attached to a belt about his waist he carried a letter addressed to 'Miss A. Penhaligan, Polrudden', penned in bold handwriting.

Nathan paid the money due on the letter, feeling guilty that he had not been to see Abigail sooner. He decided to go that afternoon.

It was early autumn, the day was warm and the sky cloudless. It was a perfect day for riding. It seemed others found it so too. As he entered the gates of the Penhaligan mansion he met Lydia, riding out with the Reverend Hugh Cremyll.

Hugh was delighted to meet Nathan, but Lydia appeared embarrassed that Nathan had found her in the company of the St Ewe Vicar.

After greeting him, she said, 'I'll come back to the house with you.'

'There's no need at all. I was thinking on the way here what a wonderful day it is for riding. You and Hugh go off and enjoy it. I doubt if there will be too many days like this before winter sets in. I'll still be at the house when you return. In fact, I'll wait for you and ride back as far as Polrudden with Hugh. It will be good to have company.'

Turning in the saddle as Hugh Cremyll and Lydia rode off together, Nathan thought they made a very handsome couple. Their friendship also freed him from what might have become an embarrassing situation. He smiled. Since she had met the young vicar, Lydia had not been nearly so attentive to him as before. It was a great relief!

Sir Kenwyn greeted Nathan with his usual enthusiasm, apparently delighted to see him. As they walked together through the house, the baronet said, 'You've only just missed Lydia. She and that young clergyman from St Ewe went out riding together . . . You saw them? Oh, good. You know, I thought for a while you and she might have made a splendid couple, but this young cleric

115

seems exceptionally smitten with her. He comes from a very good family. Father's an earl, I understand. Not from this part of the country, of course, but that's not a bad thing. We tend to be a little parochial in our thinking in Cornwall. Mind you, I can't see Lydia as a vicar's wife, can you? She's far too wild. Such behaviour in a man's wife might be acceptable if he were a bishop or even a dean, but with his family connections I suppose such an appointment can't be too far away . . .'

'Where are the others – Abigail, Sofia and their father?'

Sir Kenwyn smiled benevolently at Nathan. 'Probably exactly where you'd like them all to be, dear boy. My brother has taken Sofia to Bodmin. There's an estate for sale there and they've gone to have a look at it. Henry needs something to take an interest in. He must forget the past and begin building a new future for himself. I think you'll find Abigail in the orangery. She seems to spend lot of time in there, by herself. It's the warmth, I suppose. She's another one who needs to put India behind her. It would be good to think you could help her.' The baronet gave Nathan a benign smile, as though to emphasise his meaning.

As the two men left the house through the large French windows, Sir Kenwyn asked Nathan about the progress of the harbour. 'I hear there has been trouble with the villagers?'

'Nothing too serious, and it's been resolved now.' Nathan told the baronet the story of the bridge and the manner in which he had solved the problem.

Sir Kenwyn chuckled. 'It's a damned good thing we have you on the spot to sort out such matters. Young Hawkins is a hot-headed fool. I understand his uncle is going to put him up for Parliament sometime soon.'

'Heaven help the people he represents – and the country too.'

'I couldn't agree with you more, dear boy. I'm particularly concerned in case he stands for Tregony. The present Member of Parliament is very ill. I have interests there and they will *not* be best served by that young whippersnapper. Have *you* ever considered a seat in parliament?'

Nathan was startled. 'Me? An MP? No, it's never crossed my mind.'

'It should. Think about it, my boy. Think about it seriously . . . but there's Abigail. I'll leave you to go and speak to her. It's far too hot in there for me. A word of warning before you go: she's been extremely edgy these past few days. I don't know why, but then, I have never been able to understand young girls. Not even when I was a young man and such things were supposed to be important. I'll speak to you again later.'

Abigail looked up when Nathan opened the door to the orangery and her expression of delight was tinged with apprehension. Aware of her beauty as he always was when meeting her

116

again, Nathan wished the eagerness she displayed was purely for him and not for any letter he carried.

Looking over his shoulder, he saw Sir Kenwyn speaking to one of his gardeners on the lawn outside the orangery. 'Can we go somewhere a little more private, Abigail? I have a letter here for you.'

'A letter? So it's arrived!' There was more fear than joy in her expression. Blood drained from her face for a moment, and then came rushing back.

'Shall I leave you alone while you read it?'

'No! Please . . . I want you to stay with me.'

Abigail caught hold of his arm and looked wide-eyed at him. As he handed her the letter, Nathan thought yet again of what might have been had Abigail not met someone else in India.

As she read, her eyes widened even more and suddenly she gave a gasp of dismay. Turning to Nathan, she said, 'It's what I feared he would do. He . . . he's in London. I heard he was on his way. That's why I came to Polrudden to talk to you the other day. He says he wants to come and see me here – or, rather, at Polrudden, for that's where he believes me to be.'

'Would that be such a calamity? You've been expecting to hear from him for a very long time. You must have anticipated something like this. Why is there so much secrecy, Abigail? Is it because your father doesn't approve of this man?'

'Yes. I've been hoping to hear from him. Desperately hoping to receive a letter. But I never really expected him to come to England, even when I learned he was talking about it. As for approval . . . *No* one approves. Not my father . . . Not his family. No one.'

'Yet you're obviously very much in love with him and, I suspect, he with you. Perhaps you'd better tell me about him.'

Three times in the next minute it seemed Abigail was about to say something to Nathan, but she lapsed into an unhappy silence.

Gently, he said, 'There's nothing to be ashamed of in loving someone who doesn't have everyone's approval. It happened to me when I married my first wife. Her father couldn't bear to have me near him.'

'I'm not ashamed of him, Nathan. I'm *proud* of him. Proud to be loved by him. I'm only ashamed because others don't . . . *won't* see him as I do.'

Suddenly, Abigail looked up at Nathan defiantly. Deliberately, as though to see his reaction before he could hide it, she said, 'He's Indian.'

Nathan hoped he succeeded in hiding the shock he felt at her words. It was small wonder that Henry Penhaligan did not approve. Nathan knew a little of life in India. He had visited the country twice during his naval service, escorting the transports carrying soldiers whose duty it was to defend the rights of the East India Company.

Englishmen who visited the country could and did use Indian prostitutes, and most of those who took up residence in the country acquired local mistresses. These were facts of life that were accepted, even if they were not discussed.

However, an Englishman did not fall in *love* with an Indian girl. A man who did so would be ostracised by the society in which he lived, until he returned to his senses – or was sent home. As for a European *girl* falling in love with an Indian . . . it was *unthinkable*!

'Have I shocked you very much, Nathan?' Abigail had been watching him closely.

'Shocked? No. *I'm* not acceptable to many of those I meet here in Cornwall. Most of those at your ball, for instance. That's what was really behind the fight I had with Columb Hawkins and his friends. It had little to do with you. I think I told you so at the time. But your revelation has taken me aback. Who is he? How did you meet him? If he's able to travel from India to London and talks of coming to Cornwall, I gather he must come from a wealthy family?'

'He is His Highness the Yuvaraja Rao Jelal – Prince Rao. Elder son and heir of the Maharaja of Jhalapur – a State about fifteen or twenty times the size of Cornwall. My father was a senior East India Company administrator in Jhalapur. I was seated beside the Maharani at a Durbar held by the Maharaja and she invited me to teach English to the princesses in the palace. Rao had English tutors of his own and he speaks perfect English. We first met when he came to the classroom with a book he was reading and asked me a question about English law. I didn't know the answer, but I told him I would find out from my father. That, of course, meant a further meeting. After that we met frequently in the palace. When we knew each other better we would go riding round the countryside together. It was a very romantic situation, I suppose.'

Abigail gave a sudden laugh, but it caught in her throat. 'In order to escape attention, Rao would dress as a servant when we went riding. Once we met up with some of my father's friends and they insisted I go back to take tea with them. Rao was sent off to the servants' quarters. I don't know who was more appalled, me or the servants. They were sworn to secrecy by Rao under threat of their lives and he treated it as a huge joke. We were in love for two years before anyone even suspected. Then one of my father's clerks saw us riding together. He had formerly been in the employ of the Maharaja and recognised Rao. He told my father.'

'How did he take the news?' Nathan remembered Henry Pen-

118

haligan's reaction when he returned from walking Abigail to the lake on the night of the ball. That would have been as nothing compared with this revelation.

'He behaved very well . . . at first. I don't think he believed it was anything more than a single foolish escapade for either Rao or me. In fact, he behaved so well that I felt able to tell him the truth. It was a dreadful mistake. A few weeks later we were all on a boat bound for England. Father had given up his post as an administrator and we girls left behind everything we had ever known.'

'Do your sisters know about this?'

'Not everything. They are aware we left to avoid a scandal involving me. That's all.'

'And now Rao is here in England?' Nathan spoke as though thinking aloud. Abigail's life was in a mess. A far worse tangle than he could ever have imagined. 'Where is he staying?'

'At a place called Bushy Park. He wants me to write to him there. If I'd been able to write and prevent him coming to England, I would have, but he had left by the time I knew anything about it. What am I to do, Nathan?'

'He's staying at Bushy Park – home of the Duke of Clarence?'

'That's the address he's given to me. Do you know it?'

Nathan nodded. 'I've been there once or twice. The Duke was always one of most ardent of "The Fancy". A follower of prizefighting.'

Nathan did not add that when he was last at Bushy Park the Duke of Clarence, third son of George III, shared the house with his mistress, Dorothea Jordan, their ten children, and the three children of Dorothea Jordan's earlier liaisons. The house would undoubtedly be much quieter now. According to rumour she had departed and was living in France.

Suddenly, Abigail reached out and seized his hand. 'Nathan . . . is there some way you can take me to London? To see Rao before he comes here?'

Nathan was startled. 'That's completely out of the question, Abigail. You must see that, surely?'

For a moment it seemed she might argue, then she released his hand and looked away as she fought to regain control of herself. 'Yes. Yes, I *do* see. Besides, I don't think I could bear to see him again and know it was going to be for the very last time – and it would have to be. His father is very ill. Rao needs to be in Jhalapur, acting as Regent.'

Suddenly, she swung back to face him. 'Nathan . . . could you go to London to see him? Speak to him? Take a letter from me and explain how impossible it is for us to meet? Then come back and tell me everything about him. How he looks. How he feels about us.'

Nathan was about to refuse once more, but he left it too late.

'*Please*, Nathan. If you don't, I fear I'll not be able to prevent him from coming here to Cornwall. His arrival would cause a dreadful scandal for both Rao and my family. It would probably affect Uncle Kenwyn too.'

Abigail was right. Such a scandal would provide the county with gossip enough for many years to come. Yet this was really none of his business. He would be thanked by no one for becoming involved in such a mess.

'*Please*, Nathan. It means so much to me. There's no one else I can ask to do such a thing.'

Abigail looked at him with tears dulling the eyes that were like no others he had ever seen. He told himself he had to refuse to go to London for her. What could he possibly say to the man she loved?

'Nathan, I beg you.'

He had to tell her now. He could bear the torture in her eyes no longer.

'All right, I'll go.'

120

Chapter 24

'I shouldn't have allowed you to talk me into coming here with you. London is a dreadful city. A sinful place.'

Preacher Josiah Jago shook his head ruefully as he glanced over to where a jumble of houses extended to the very water's edge on both sides of the narrowing River Thames. Scattered among them could be seen the grander, ancient buildings of London. The curved dome of St Paul's. The solid forbidding bulk of the Tower of London.

The fishing boat *Charlotte* was sailing before tide and wind as it approached the Pool of London. Nathan had persuaded Francis Hanna to carry them here in his boat. It was more spacious than any owned by himself.

Turning to Dewi, the preacher added, 'When I was last here I watched a friend die on the gallows: his only crime that of preaching the true words of Our Lord to the people.'

'Why should a man be hanged for preaching?' Dewi was puzzled by Preacher Jago's statement.

'He was an American preacher and charged with sedition,' replied Nathan before his father could speak again. 'We'd just gone to war with his country and he was preaching to great crowds in the open. It was at a time when the magistrates read revolution into everything that appealed to the people. My father is right. Preacher Kemp was no more guilty of wrongdoing than he is.'

The deck of the *Charlotte* was crowded with the party from Cornwall. Nathan, Josiah Jago, Beville, Dewi and Sally Wicks were surrounded by the boat's crew. Most of the Pentuan men were catching their first glimpse of the greatest city in the world.

Informing Dewi only that he had some business to attend to in London, Nathan had said he would like Beville to pay his first visit to the capital, with Dewi to accompany him.

Excitement about the forthcoming trip had spilled over into Pentuan when Nathan decided to make the journey by fishing boat and not by coach. He pointed out, quite rightly, that a voyage by sea would be far more comfortable than land travel. The time taken would be only marginally longer, even allowing for spending the night hours in harbours along the way.

Sally Wicks had begged successfully to be allowed to accompany

Dewi and Beville. Josiah Jago had decided to join the small party at the last moment. He had taken on the self-appointed task of chaperon. It would also afford him an opportunity to visit the Methodist headquarters in City Road. Frequently in disagreement with his superiors, he hoped a visit might help to clear the air between them.

'Did they hang the American preacher at the Tower of London?' Sally Wicks was impressed by the solid building with its high walls, on the north bank of the river.

'They hanged him in public, outside Newgate gaol, with the same lack of dignity they showed to Our Lord on Calvary,' replied Josiah Jago fiercely. 'I intend spending an hour on my knees on the very spot, just as I did after his execution. Although I glory that Preacher Kemp's soul would have gone straight to heaven. He was a true servant of the Lord.'

'Preacher Uriah Kemp was a very special man,' agreed Nathan. 'But there is far more to see in London than the site of a hanging.'

He spoke largely for the benefit of Beville, who had been listening wide-eyed to the solemn words of his grandfather.

'I want to look at the shops,' said Sally Wicks, excitedly. 'I've heard you can find anything you want in the shops in London.'

'I want to see the King,' declared Beville positively.

'Well, we may not be able to arrange that,' said Nathan, swinging him off the deck up into his arms. 'But you might possibly see the Prince Regent leaving Carlton House. If you're *especially* good I might even take you to see the Duke of Clarence. He's the Regent's brother.'

'Does he wear a crown too?'

'No, but if you speak to him very nicely he might allow you to see his coronet. That's very like a crown.'

Beville was not impressed. Struggling free of Nathan's arms, he repeated. 'I want to see the King wearing his crown.'

'Then we'll need to discover whether Madame Tussaud is exhibiting her waxworks in London at the moment.'

Beville was no longer listening. With Sally Wicks in close pursuit he ran to the side of the boat to view a man-of-war, anchored in the river with gun ports open and seventy-four cannons run out of ports on three decks.

'You didn't tell me you were coming all this way to see the Duke of Clarence.' Frowning suspiciously, Preacher Josiah Jago made the comment to his son.

'I usually pay the Duke a visit when I'm in London, you know that. We've known each other since my prize-fighting days.'

'You're not thinking of entering the prize-ring again?'

Nathan smiled at his father's concern. 'You need have no fear of that. I went into the ring because I was a hungry man. I'm hungry no longer. I'm not the only one who's happy to have left

122

the ring behind, as you'll soon discover. We'll be taking rooms with John Gully, another ex-champion. He now has an inn – The Plough, on Carey Street.'

The party was given a rousing welcome by John Gully when they reached the Carey Street inn. Seemingly unable to cease shaking Nathan's hand, he kept repeating, 'You don't know how pleased I am to see you once more, Nathan. I'm shortly giving up The Plough, in favour of The Turf. There are a dozen or more friends I promised myself I'll entertain before I go – and you're top of my list.'

Suddenly the handshake came to halt, although Gully did not release Nathan's hand. 'You're not here to fight? There are some good men around at the moment. I wouldn't care for you to take any of them on . . .'

'No, John. I'm not here to fight. Those days are over for me. Like you, I lead a gentleman's life these days. I've even got a son who's inherited a baronetcy from his grandfather.'

Reaching out and drawing the child towards them, he said, 'Beville, I want you to shake hands with one of the greatest prizefighters of all time. A man who's a good friend.'

'I doubt if I was ever as good a prizefighter as your father,' declared John Gully, pleased by Nathan's compliments. Gravely shaking hands with Beville, he added, 'I'm honoured to meet you, young Sir Beville. I think we can arrange for you to have a very exciting time while you're here in London, if your father's willing.'

When he had introduced the others to the ex-pugilist, Nathan said, 'I expect to be in London for a few days, on business. Can you accommodate us all?'

'Of course! The two best rooms are taken right now, but I'll have the occupants out and the rooms ready for you within an hour. In the meantime, come to the dining-room. I'll guarantee to give you the best meal in London. You don't know how pleased I am to have you beneath my roof. Talking of "The Fancy" with one of the best, will be like old times again.'

Chapter 25

Nathan set off for Bushy Park early the following morning, riding a horse borrowed from The Plough stable. Josiah Jago had already left on foot for his personal pilgrimage to the spot where Uriah Kemp had been hanged.

The others were preparing for their first full day in the city and it was impossible to say who was most excited, Dewi, Sally or Beville. They planned a visit to the wax figures of Madame Tussaud's exhibition, currently on display in a hall close to the Tower of London. There was also to be a street fair there. Beville would be able to enjoy a great many sideshows and exhibits here that never travelled west to Cornwall.

The Duke of Clarence's home was about twelve miles from The Plough. The route took Nathan away from the busy streets of London and into the green lanes of Middlesex. However, even here the roads were far superior to those of Cornwall and he made good time.

Nathan turned his horse through the gates of the park and entered the great estate, remembering sadly that the last time he was here he had been accompanied by his second wife, Amy, shortly before they were married. On that occasion he had just taken part in a gruelling prizefight with the Irish champion and was badly battered.

As he rode along an avenue lined with magnificent horse chestnut trees, Nathan wondered about the reception he might receive from the Duke of Clarence. The Duke might not wish to be reminded of this period of his past.

Nathan also faced the problem of finding a way to speak privately to Abigail's Indian prince. Even if he were successful in this, he had to broach the extremely delicate matter of the prince's proposed visit to Cornwall to see Abigail.

To complicate matters even further, Nathan was not entirely certain just what he *should* achieve. Abigail had asked him to tell Prince Rao Jelal not to make his proposed visit to Cornwall, but Nathan was not fully convinced this was what she either expected or really wanted.

He believed Abigail secretly entertained a vain hope that Nathan might be able to perform a miracle on her behalf. Unfortunately, however he looked at the matter, he could not foresee a happy ending to the relationship.

It was all complicated still further by Nathan's own attitude to the mission he had undertaken on Abigail's behalf. If he succeeded in dissuading the Indian prince from visiting Cornwall, would Abigail be sufficiently grateful to him? Or would she always resent the fact that Nathan had been instrumental in parting her forever from the man she loved?

He had placed himself in a position where he was unlikely to win, whatever was achieved today.

Upon his arrival at the house Nathan was shown to an airy drawing-room by a dignified but friendly butler who remembered Nathan from his earlier visits to the house.

As he led the way along a lofty corridor, the butler said, 'His Royal Highness will be delighted you've called on him, Mr Jago. Unfortunately, at this moment he is meeting with the Earl Plucknett and directors of the East India Company on a matter of some considerable importance, I believe.'

'Earl Plucknett of the Whig Party?'

'That's right, Mr Jago. I understand he and his party have always taken a keen interest in the affairs of the East India Company – as, of course, does His Royal Highness.'

'I believe you also have Prince Rao Jelal staying here? Does the meeting have something to do with him?'

'Undoubtedly, sir, although the prince himself has not been invited to join His Royal Highness and the others.' Opening the door onto a large drawing-room, the butler said, 'Here you are, Mr Jago, you'll be quite comfortable in here while you wait. May I offer you some refreshment?'

'Not immediately, but I have a letter for Prince Rao – to be delivered personally.'

'You too, sir? It seems the whole world is writing to Prince Rao. Some days you'd think the drive was Epsom Downs with the number of horses galloping to and fro, all carrying messengers bearing letters for Prince Rao. He's quite turned Bushy upside down, sir, what with his huge staff and all the comings and goings. The cooks have all threatened to leave. Even the kitchen maids are close to rebellion. However, I believe the prince is in his rooms at the moment. I'll tell one of his staff you are here.'

When the Duke of Clarence's butler returned he was accompanied by an Indian dressed in expensive and colourful silks. In spite of the man's finery, Nathan was dismayed. He was short and ugly. Not at all the type of man he had expected Abigail to fall in love with.

'This is Prince Rao?'

'No, sir.' The butler's amusement stopped short of a smile. 'This is Jainu, his secretary.'

'You have a letter for His Highness Yuvaraja Rao Jelal? I will take it, please.'

The Indian servant's accent reminded Nathan vaguely of Dewi's style of talking.

'I have a letter, but it's to be delivered personally to the prince.'

'This is not a problem. I will deliver it personally.'

'I don't doubt it, but I promised the writer I would hand it to no one but Prince Rao himself.'

Jainu appeared momentarily angered. 'That is quite impossible. His Highness the Yuveraja is resting. I will take the letter.'

'I'll keep it until he's finished resting. Tell him the letter is from Polrudden, in Cornwall.'

The Indian backed from the room, bowing to Nathan, but the servility was not reflected in his eyes.

Five minutes after Jainu left the room there was the sound of voices from the corridor outside the room accompanied by the rustling of silk. A few moments later a procession swept into the room. In the lead was a tall, good-looking young man. As he passed through the morning sunshine streaming through a window, sunlight struck flames from jewels set in the prince's turban, at his throat and on fingers, wrists and belt buckle.

'You have come with a letter for me from Cornwall? From Polrudden?'

'That's right. You are Prince Rao Jelal?'

'I am. I will have the letter, please.'

As he passed the letter to the other man, Nathan realised that Prince Rao's unconscious arrogance as born of authority and was not intended as rudeness.

Nathan thought the other man would take the letter away and read it in the privacy of his own quarters, but Prince Rao was not only arrogant, he was an impatient lover. Breaking open the seal immediately, he opened the letter and read. Making no attempt to disguise his emotions, the Indian prince's expression registered delight, anguish and despair. At one stage he looked up sharply at the man who had delivered his letter.

'You are Nathan Jago of Polrudden?'

'That's right.'

Prince Rao looked at Nathan for some moments, his expression that of a man whose thoughts were elsewhere. Then he resumed reading, without uttering another word.

When he came to the end of the letter, the Indian prince frowned. Looking directly at Nathan, he asked, 'You know what is written here?'

'I am only the messenger, although I've promised Abigail I would try to explain the impossibility of having you call on her in Cornwall.'

'*Nothing* is impossible, Mr Jago. Some things are more difficult than others, that is all. Come, we will walk in the garden and talk.'

Following the other man from the room, Nathan felt he should resent the dictatorial manner of the young prince, yet he did not. Prince Rao's authority was not assumed. It was something he took as much for granted as breathing. The suggestion that it might offend would be beyond his comprehension.

When they reached the gardens they were accompanied by some ten retainers including Jainu, Rao's secretary. At a word from the young prince, the servants and Jainu dropped back. Waiting until they were at a distance which took them out of earshot, Rao asked, 'Abigail is well? Tell me of her.'

'She is very well. She misses India, but that is only to be expected. Everything in England is new to her. She will settle down.'

'What of me? She misses me too?'

'I suspect you're the reason she's finding it so difficult to settle down in England. But she will get over you too. She *must*. There is no future for you together, Prince Rao. You must realise this more than anyone else. You're both from different worlds.'

'Our two worlds meet in India, Mr Jago. Already many from both our countries have learned that love cannot be contained within frontiers.'

'Love is one of the few pleasures that can best be indulged in by ordinary people, *Prince* Rao. When you're the future ruler of a nation, a marriage is arranged to cement alliances. If love results from such marriage it is a bonus, not an expectation.'

'So you are a philosopher, Mr Jago? Then tell me, how would your philosophy view a prince who renounces his inheritance in order to marry the woman he loves?'

'You're surely not thinking of taking such action?' Nathan was incredulous. 'That would be irresponsible. Especially when there are so many other obstacles which must also be overcome. Religion . . . the objections of Abigail's father . . .'

'And also the censure of the *ordinary* people of whom you speak, Mr Jago. It would be unwise to underestimate the strength of their feelings, however hypocritical – and I choose the word deliberately, however *hypocritical* – they may be. It is, of course, perfectly all right for an Englishman to take an Indian mistress. Your people would approve. Many men would even envy him, perhaps. Similarly, should I or another prince take an English *woman* for a mistress, we would actually *gain* increased respect from our own people. But mention marriage and everyone, Indian and British, claims to be shocked! Why should this be, Mr Jago? Perhaps your philosophy can explain this to me.'

'Even if I were able to give you an explanation it would not change the situation, Prince Rao. Such intolerance – or hypocrisy, call it what you will – exists, whether it originates with subjects, religion, or family.'

'And you, Mr Jago? What are your thoughts on the matter?'

Nathan thought very carefully before replying to the prince's question.

'I would like to give you an honest answer, Prince Rao, but I don't think I can. I would marry Abigail tomorrow if she would have me – and were it not for you I believe I might have a chance.'

Much to Nathan's surprise, the prince clapped his hands together in delight. 'Mr Jago, you have told me what I most wanted to hear. What Abigail would not say to me in her letter. Had it not been for *me* she might have married you. So she *does* still love me!'

Beaming at Nathan, the Indian prince said, 'In spite of what you say, you *have* given me an honest reply, Mr Jago – and when I meet an honest man I make a friend of him. Come, we will return to the house now. The Duke of Clarence and Earl Plucknett will soon end their meeting with the directors of the East India Company. They are discussing the crisis I have caused in my country. Why they should, I don't know. My very capable younger brother is coping very well. Indeed, he has always coveted the throne of Jhalapur. The directors of the East India Company want me to change my mind, but it is made up, now I have spoken to you. It is not that I wish to evade my responsibilities, you understand? I have thought long and hard about the matter and am convinced that my brother will be a better ruler of the people of Jhalapur than I. If I were to rule without Abigail it would be because it is the will of my people I should do so. I would always resent this. Resentment of one's subjects does not lead to a benevolent reign. It is better that I abdicate. I am now more certain than ever of what I will tell them.'

Linking arms with Nathan, Prince Rao set a course for the house, and the two men returned, followed by the prince's retinue.

Chapter 26

The meeting between the Duke of Clarence, Earl Plucknett and the East India Company directors was just breaking up when Nathan and Prince Rao returned to the house.

The Duke gave Nathan a warm greeting before introducing him to Earl Plucknett and the four directors of the Company as 'an old friend'.

'I see you've already met my house guest.' The Royal Duke spoke to Nathan while Prince Rao was being held in conversation by the East India Company directors. 'The only reason he's at Bushy Park is because the Company had nowhere else to put him. He should really have stayed with Prinny, I suppose, but at this moment my brother is too busy trying to sort out the indiscretions of that foolish wife of his. The way she's behaving, it's surprising he has any time at all to devote to affairs of state. He should never have married her. We tried to tell him so at the time, but Prinny has never listened to good advice and he desperately needed the allowance that came with her. I thank God we live in England. Anywhere else and we'd all have been parted from our heads by now.'

Nathan knew the Duke was talking of his brother George, the Prince Regent. The heir apparent's estranged wife, Princess Caroline, was the subject of countrywide gossip and the cause of much embarrassment to her royal husband.

'Not that Prince Rao is very much better,' the Duke of Clarence was saying. 'His father has suffered some sort of seizure and Rao should be home carrying out the duties of a Regent. Instead, he's here threatening to throw up his heritage for the sake of some girl – and an English girl, at that. Have you heard about it?'

'I haven't heard the story of what's been happening in India, but I know Abigail Penhaligan.'

'You know her?' The Duke's surprise lasted for only a few moments. 'Yes, of course . . . She's in Cornwall at the moment, I believe?'

'What's the girl like?' The question came from Earl Plucknett, who had been listening to the conversation between Nathan and the Duke of Clarence.

Nathan took a deep breath before replying, 'She's one of the most beautiful girls I've ever met. She is also intelligent, well educated, and from a good family. She'll make an excellent wife for any man lucky enough to win her – no matter what his station in life.'

'You sound smitten with her yourself, Nathan. Do you know the girl well?' The Duke of Clarence was the questioner once more.

'Well enough to bring a letter from her to Prince Rao.'

The Duke exchanged a glance with Earl Plucknett before asking, 'Do you happen to know what was in the letter? It could be of great importance to us. Has the girl made up her mind what she intends to do? Will she marry Rao?'

'I think her main purpose in writing the letter was to persuade him not to come to Cornwall and confront her father. A scene would cause a great local scandal. One likely to prove an embarrassment to her uncle – and she's really a very responsible girl.'

'Isn't her uncle Sir Kenwyn Penhaligan? He's almost as famous a borough-monger as Sir Christopher Hawkins – but at least Sir Kenwyn supports the Whig cause.'

Earl Plucknett gave Nathan a brief, wry smile. 'From a strictly partisan point of view we don't want him to suffer any embarrassment if it can possibly be avoided – but there's rather more than a local scandal and a vote or two at stake in the matter of Prince Rao's succession to the throne of Jhalapur.'

Earl Plucknett was a prominent Whig parliamentarian. The Duke of Clarence was brother of the Regent. Both were at the heart of the country's affairs. Nathan knew little of politics and so resorted to honesty.

'I'm no more than Abigail Penhaligan's letter-bearer. Although I'm aware of the personal problems she and Prince Rao are facing, I know nothing of the politics involved.'

The Duke of Clarence put a sympathetic hand on Nathan's arm. 'I confess it leaves me at something of loss too, Nathan. However, I have always taken a great interest in the East India Company and the directors assure me the affair is likely to have wide-ranging ramifications for British influence on India.'

Turning to Earl Plucknett, he said, 'But you're the expert on this particular problem, Charles. You explain it to Nathan.'

'I'll do my best, but let me say here and now that, in common with the Duke of Clarence, I've been called in merely as a result of my long-standing interest in the company. I'm not directly involved, neither do I wish to be. Perhaps I can best be described as an impartial observer.'

Glancing over to where Prince Rao stood in animated conversation with the directors of the East India Company, Earl Plucknett explained, 'India is a somewhat uneasy federation of States. Some are the size of Great Britain, others no larger than a good-sized farm. Rao Jelal's state, Jhalapur, is one of the largest and most strategically placed. To the north are many smaller and quarrelsome states that need to have a sizeable British army on their doorsteps if they're to be kept in check. East and west of Jhalapur are two equally large states, both ruled by Rajas who have an uneasy reputation with the Company. Prince Rao's country keeps the two divided. While Jhalapur remains on friendly terms with the Company and is agreeable to the presence of the British army, it prevents a formidable alliance being formed against us.'

'But surely Jhalapur is likely to be more kindly disposed towards Britain and the Company if the Maharaja is married to an English girl?'

'Unfortunately, that is not the case. Jhalapur is a Hindu state – and one where religion is taken very seriously indeed. If Rao Jelal were to take a Christian bride, the state would rise in protest. As is usual in such circumstances, it would not be long before the Company became the target of their anger. Unfortunately, rebellious behaviour is contagious. The ideal answer, of course, would be for Prince Rao to give up all idea of marrying this girl and return to rule his country. Since he refuses point-blank, we need to think of a workable alternative. A great deal of correspondence has already passed between London and India and the matter has been discussed at the highest level. There *is* a possible solution, but it cannot be resolved immediately and will not be possible unless we can reach an agreement with the girl – and, of course, her father . . .'

Earl Plucknett broke off suddenly. 'The prince is coming in this direction. We'll speak more of the matter later.'

When Prince Rao Jelal reached the three men, he spoke to Earl Plucknett first. 'You have found a solution to our mutual problem? One that will allow me to marry Abigail?'

'We've discussed a possible compromise, Your Highness. However, much will depend upon the girl and her family – and final agreement being reached in India.'

'Abigail will marry me. Mr Jago has told me she still cares.'

The others switched their attention to Nathan. Discomfited at being the focus of their attention, he said, 'I also pointed out that Henry Penhaligan would need to be convinced it was the right thing for Abigail. I doubt if that will be easy.'

Nathan shrugged. 'But all this is none of my business, you are the ones who are discussing the matter.'

'On the contrary, Nathan. I believe you might be of great assistance to the Company.' Earl Plucknett turned to the Duke of Clarence. 'Perhaps Nathan could join us for lunch, and attend the meeting with Prince Rao this afternoon. His knowledge of the lady involved in this matter will prove useful.'

131

'Of course. There was never any question of his leaving before lunch and I agree with you about the meeting. Is it convenient to you, Nathan?'

'Thank you, yes. But I mustn't be too late returning to London. I travelled from Cornwall on one of my boats, bringing my father and son with me. My father will be all right, but I'm a little concerned about Beville. His governess is a very capable girl, but she's unfamiliar with London.'

'You should have brought him to Bushy with you. Bring him tomorrow. I've got a few animals brought in from abroad. They'll fascinate him, I've no doubt. I miss the sound of children about the place. I used to complain bitterly about them when they were here. Find I miss them now. Damned silly, eh?'

Lunch at Bushy Park did not end until almost 4 pm. By this time Nathan was almost ready to concede that a religion which forbade the use of alcohol must have an advantage over Christianity. One of the East India Company directors was so drunk he was unable to rise from his chair. Another was almost incoherent.

'I think it's time we had our meeting with Prince Rao,' said Earl Plucknett. The blue-grey cloud of tobacco smoke hanging over the dining-table threatened to envelop the men sitting about it. 'I need to be in Westminster this evening.'

'Prince Rao usually enjoys a rest in the afternoon, but he should be about now. I'll send a servant to ask him to join us in the library.'

The Duke of Clarence tugged at a bell rope beside the white marble fireplace. 'I'll also have a carriage brought to the front of the house for the two Company men. I fear they would have little to offer the discussion but vulgar noises.'

'They are probably the only remaining Company directors who have actually served in India,' explained Earl Plucknett. 'They returned so outrageously rich they were able to purchase large country estates and buy places on the board. They're known as "nabobs" at Westminster – it's a name that has caught on with the newspapers.'

While Earl Plucknett was talking, the Duke of Clarence had been briefing a servant. As the man hurried away, the Whig politician added, 'No doubt we'll find these two particular "nabobs" joining their ex-Company colleagues in Parliament when they find themselves with time on their hands.'

One of the nabobs had fallen asleep, head back, in his chair. Nodding in his direction, the Duke commented sarcastically, 'At least his snoring will keep his fellow members awake in the Commons.'

'Have *you* ever considered standing for Parliament, Nathan?' The question came from Earl Plucknett.

'Sir Kenwyn Penhaligan asked the same question recently. It's not something I've ever thought about. I'm kept pretty busy with my fishing-boats and protecting the interests of my tenants and the villagers. I'm also having problems arising from the building of a new harbour in Pentuan.'

'You are just the type of Member we need in Parliament. One eye on business, the other on the people. Parliament will be undergoing radical changes in the next few years. It will increasingly become a forum for the problems of the people, and less of a lodge where gentry meet to protect their interests. A reassessment of the representation for Cornwall, in particular, is long overdue. I think I am correct in saying your county sends more MPs to Westminster than the whole of Scotland. Some of the boroughs returning two Members have fewer than twelve votes. Meanwhile, new industrial towns with a population of many thousands have no representation at all. The whole system needs an impartial approach. That means having honest men in the House. You ought to consider the matter most seriously.'

'Don't allow Charles to launch into his favourite theme, Nathan. If he does, you certainly *won't* be back at your inn before morning . . . Ah! Here is Prince Rao. Gentlemen, shall we adjourn to the study?'

Chapter 27

Prince Rao seemed pleased that Nathan was attending the meeting. At his insistence Nathan was seated beside him. Whispering amidst the sound of chairs scraping on the polished wooden floor, Prince Rao said, 'I feel no one else in the room is really on my side. They consider me something of an oddity. You, at least, are sufficiently acquainted with Abigail to *understand* why I am willing to give up everything for her.'

For few moments the men attending the meeting talked among themselves until Earl Plucknett cleared his throat noisily and the room fell silent.

'Your Royal Highnesses. Gentlemen. We have spent all morning discussing the implications of Prince Rao's proposed abdication as Regent of Jhalapur – and, ultimately, renouncing his right to the throne of his country. We are all in agreement that this is a matter of considerable seriousness, and is of grave concern to the Company and the British government. Great Britain has committed many troops to India, to protect both the native states and the East India Company's charter. However, as we recognised this morning, the problem has been with us for some time. Consequently, we have been able to set certain wheels in motion, with a view to arriving at a satisfactory solution. One that will prove agreeable to all interested parties.'

'If it leaves me free to marry Abigail, you will not find me arguing with your decision, gentlemen.'

'It involves much more than a marriage, Your Highness – but I believe I am correct in saying that the girl's father has not yet approved of such a marriage?'

'He will,' declared Prince Rao confidently. 'But tell me, what *is* this magic solution you have found?'

'It will be magic only if it averts civil war in your own country and prevents half the continent of India erupting in violence.'

Prince Rao bowed his head in acknowledgement of Earl Plucknett's warning. 'I can assure you I have no wish to cause any suffering to my people. Explain your plan to me, please?'

Earl Plucknett cleared his throat noisily and looked about the room before fixing his glance upon Prince Rao. 'First, we have agreed you will need to abdicate in favour of your younger brother

Chait – actually, he is your half-brother, I believe? He is already acting as Regent in your absence and will continue to do so. He will become Maharaja of Jhalapur upon the death of your father.'

An expression of pain crossed the face of Prince Rao briefly, but he nodded. 'Chait will be happy, at least. He has always been more in love with the throne than I. Have you spoken to him of this?'

'He has been approached by the Company's Resident in Jhalapur. News reached us only yesterday that he is willing, subject to your agreement and your continued absence from Jhalapur.'

'You have my agreement, but what is to become of me? I am to be exiled?'

'From Jhalapur, yes, but not from India. You are aware of the death of your maternal grandfather, the Maharaja of Sikar?'

'Of course, but what is that to do with this matter? He died more than a year ago and was succeeded by my Uncle Randit.'

'Maharaja Randit proved to be a very unpopular ruler. There was an uprising and he was killed by a cousin who attempted to seize the throne. In a surprise attack upon the palace, rebels put to death all the members of the Maharaja's family who could be found. At the urgent request of your mother British troops were sent to Sikar and they deposed your cousin. A great many people were killed in the fighting. Your cousin survived, only to be taken by his own people and put to death.'

The news imparted by Earl Plucknett had dismayed Rao. 'All my mother's family? But . . . I knew them well. I spent much time in Sikar as a boy. It is a beautiful country. Who is ruling there now?'

'A British military commander is taking care of the country until a new Maharaja takes the throne. That Maharaja could be you, Your Highness. The throne is yours by right, through your mother.'

Prince Rao rose abruptly from his chair, suddenly very excited. 'Of course! The people of Sikar are a hill people. They do not take the Hindu laws as seriously as do the men of Jhalapur.'

In his excitement, Prince Rao began pacing the room. Coming to a sudden halt facing Earl Plucknett across the table, he said more soberly, 'But would they accept a *Christian* as the wife of their Maharaja?'

'They would if she did not publicly flout the country's customs – and if she had been adopted as a daughter by the slain Maharaja's mother.'

'Would my grandmother do this for me?'

'It was her idea once she was acquainted with the facts. More than anything else she wishes you, her grandson, to become the new Maharaja.'

'What of the Company? What will they expect of me if I become Maharaja of Sikar?'

'No more than would be expected if you were Maharaja of Jhalapur. They wish you to rule a peaceful country, to be a friend of the Company and accept a Resident Agent. In return you will be guaranteed the protection of the British Army.'

'Sikar has never had a Resident Agent.'

'Neither have any of the other states in that area. It would set a precedent – one I sincerely hope your neighbours will follow. You could lead a full and comfortable life there, Your Highness. Sikar is a wealthy and respected state. As Maharaja you would be entitled to a seventeen-gun salute.'

'Jhalapur is a *nineteen*-gun state.'

Earl Plucknett looked quizzically at one of the East India Company directors and received an almost imperceptible nod.

'Very well. As Maharaja of Sikar your salute will be increased to nineteen guns – in recognition of your personal importance in the area.'

'Then I agree to become Maharaja of Sikar.' Prince Rao beamed at the other men. 'It seems we are in full agreement on all matters affecting my future, gentlemen. I am truly delighted. Abigail must be informed immediately.'

'Unfortunately there are still one or two very important matters to be resolved. One is the agreement of the officials in Sikar state to your marriage. Preliminary reports indicate their willingness to accept you and Abigail, but it is vitally important to all parties, so we must await confirmation. It has already been requested, but a reply may take a month or two. Then there is the marriage itself. The girl must fully understand the situation. After all, she too will wield considerable power as your Maharani and the mother of future princes. We must also have the full approval of her father. This may prove to be a stumbling block. Indeed, I understand he brought the girl back to England when he heard of your relationship.'

'He never fully understood how we both felt. He will agree. He *must*.' Prince Rao looked less certain than he sounded and glanced anxiously at Nathan for support.

'May I make a suggestion?' Nathan directed his question to Earl Plucknett. After listening carefully to all that had been said, it was apparent that Earl Plucknett and the East India Company directors now *wanted* Prince Rao to marry Abigail and become the Maharaja of Sikar. The reason was clear. Having also negotiated a settlement on behalf of Rao's half-brother and arranged to place Rao on the throne of Sikar, it would leave the rulers of two important Indian states in their debt.

'Of course.'

'I believe Henry Penhaligan was regarded by all who knew him in India as an excellent administrator?'

The East India Company directors nodded agreement and one

said, 'The Company was most reluctant to accept his resignation. He had proved himself a quite exceptional man.'

'Then why not offer him the post of Resident Agent in Sikar? He could remain close to Abigail while at the same time pursuing the Company's interests. If a baronetcy could be included in the deal, it would put him on a par with his brother. I think that might be sufficient to tip the balance in favour of the settlement you want.'

This time it was the turn of the Duke of Clarence to nod his head. 'A baronetcy can be arranged if Penhaligan is agreeable to the plan.'

'Splendid.' Earl Plucknett seemed pleased with the way things were going. 'What will be our next move, gentlemen?'

Prince Rao was the first to reply. 'If Mr Jago will accept me as a house guest, I will pay a visit to Cornwall and try to reach an agreement with Abigail and her father.'

'That might not be such a good idea.'

Nathan was remembering the night of Sir Kenwyn's ball when he disappeared with Abigail. 'Henry Penhaligan is somewhat touchy where his daughters are concerned. He might say things he regretted if Prince Rao suddenly appeared on the scene. Once he refused to listen it might be difficult for him to swallow his pride and change his mind. It would be better if someone else came to see him first. Someone important. Perhaps a Company director?'

'I suppose I could go myself,' mused Earl Plucknett. 'Although I do have a great many commitments at the moment.'

'I haven't,' declared the Duke of Clarence unexpectedly. 'Did you say you'd come up to London by fishing-boat, Nathan? It's a long time since I was last at sea and I can't think of anything I'd enjoy more. Why don't you take *me* back to Cornwall with you? Perhaps this girl's father will consider *me* important enough? And let's not waste time. We'll go tomorrow!'

Prince Rao could hardly contain his delight. 'I thank you very much, gentlemen, for your efforts on my behalf. I assure you it will not be forgotten by me, or by my new country.'

Riding back to The Plough that evening, Nathan was at a loss to explain to himself why he had been so ready to throw Abigail into the arms of Prince Rao. He had gone to Bushy Park with some hope that the situation might be turned to his advantage, yet he had helped provide a solution that might enable Rao to marry Abigail and take her from him for ever. A satisfactory marriage between the two would be a great relief to the East India Company. It was in the interests of Britain too, but Nathan had to admit that patriotism had hardly been his prime concern.

He decided it must be because he wanted Abigail to have what she really wanted. Had it been otherwise, and he had been able to marry her, he would always have felt he was second-best. The one she turned to because the man she loved was not available. It would hardly have been a recipe for a happy and successful marriage.

Nathan also believed that Prince Rao was an honourable and sensible man who was as much in love with Abigail as she with him.

138

Chapter 28

The first full day in London got off to a good start for Dewi. Up in time to witness Nathan's early departure from The Plough, she expected tantrums from Beville because he had not been awakened to say goodbye to his father. Fortunately, he seemed hardly to miss Nathan. His chatter was filled with their plans for the day. He was going to the waxworks where he would be able to see a King with a crown . . .

Sally Wicks was coming with them and she was almost as excited as Beville. John Gully had detailed one of his cellarmen, Alf, another ex-pugilist, to accompany them. Alf would ensure they were not robbed and did not lose themselves in the teeming streets of London.

Alf was a dour, unsmiling man with a shiny, bald head that John Gully suggested would help them to find him if they became separated in a crowded street.

John Gully was up to see Dewi, Beville and Sally on their way, even though he had been awake until the morning hours, entertaining old 'friends'. The Plough was a well-known resort for ex-prizefighters, many of them down on their luck. None were ever turned away. An evening spent with an understanding and generous landlord could transform a career dogged with ignominious defeats into warm recollections of notable prizefights *almost* won.

'You'll have a wonderful time at Madame Tussaud's,' declared John Gully to Dewi as she and the others were about to set off. 'You might even see a wax model of Nathan in the exhibition. He, Tom Cribb and I were all there when I last saw the exhibition. But that was a few years ago. She might have changed things since then.'

'Well, that would be exciting indeed!' declared Dewi. 'But I do wish Alf was a bit more communicative. I haven't heard him say a word since he came in. Not so much as a good morning!'

'Neither will you,' said the landlord, casting a sympathetic glance to where Alf waited patiently by the door to the street. 'He was captured by Barbary pirates when he was a young seaman. It seems he had a bit too much to say for himself then, so they cut out his tongue. As he's never been able to write, it's set him apart from the rest of the world. Mind you, it didn't prevent him becoming a good prizefighter in his time – and he thinks the world of Nathan. Used to spar with him at one time. Nathan always made sure he was never short of a copper or two. Alf don't show his emotions very much, but he's as proud as a peacock to be going out with you and taking care of Nathan's son. You trust Alf to look after you, young lady. He'll keep you clear of any trouble.'

The small party set off from the Carey Street inn on foot. Dewi was determined not to miss a single London experience – and there was much that was new to her here. The busy main thoroughfares were bustling with all forms of traffic. There were carts of every description. The larger ones carried such loads as barrels of beer, paper for the newspapers in nearby Fleet Street, and building material for new houses. Tiny carts, most of them hand-propelled, contained goods for immediate sale, personal possessions, or tradesmen's goods. Others held meat, bread, vegetables and produce for the many shops in the area. There were carriages, coaches and an occasional prison van, its occupants shouting defiance at the world outside through tiny barred windows.

The sound of iron-clad wheels on cobblestones vied with the shouts of street vendors and the whining pleas of an army of unwashed and unkempt beggars.

They had walked perhaps half-a-mile when Beville began complaining that his legs ached. Before Dewi could pick him up, the silent Alf reached down and swung the boy on to his shoulders.

Far more sympathetic to the cellarman now she had been told his story, Dewi smiled and said to Beville, 'There, aren't you the lucky one? Now you'll be able to see more than anyone.'

Beville's reply was to reach up and set a milliner's sign swinging with such a fearsome screeching that those walking behind stepped off the pavement believing the sign was about to fall.

'Are we far from the boat?' The unexpected question came from Sally.

'I don't know,' confessed Dewi. 'Perhaps Alf will know.'

At mention of his name the dumb man turned and Dewi asked, 'Are we very far from the river at Blackfriars? That's where Nathan has his boat.'

The big, bald-headed man shook his head and pointed to the right to where the river could be glimpsed between the houses, no more than a few hundred yards away.

'Francis said on the way here that he'd like to see the waxworks,' said Sally. 'Can we go and see if he'd like to come with us?'

'I don't see why not,' agreed Dewi, albeit somewhat reluctantly. She had noticed on the voyage that Sally had spent a great deal of time talking to Francis Hanna, captain of the *Charlotte*. Sally was a notorious flirt and Dewi had not taken too much notice. Now she wondered whether there was more in the relationship than she had realised. She hoped not. She was fond of Pippa, Francis's wife.

Alf had been listening to the conversation and, when Dewi nodded to him, made for a side street that led down to the river.

Francis Hanna was on the deck of the *Charlotte*. Some of the crew were sitting about but none of them looked particularly lively.

'What's the matter with you lot?' asked Dewi, cheerfully. 'I thought that being in London, you'd be eager to be up and about. Out seeing the sights.'

'They looked too deep into London ale tankards last night,' grinned Francis. 'We discovered an inn on the river's edge with a Cornish landlord. To listen to them all talking you'd think they'd been away from Cornwall for three years instead of three days. The result was they all got maudlin drunk and they're suffering for their sins this morning. But what brings you here? I thought you'd be off seeing the sights.'

'We're on our way to Madame Tussaud's waxworks exhibition right now,' said Sally. 'You said on the voyage from Cornwall that it was something you wanted to see. We thought you might like to come with us.'

Francis hesitated for a moment. Then he said, 'Yes, I would like to see the exhibition. Just give me a couple of minutes to change into clean clothes and I'll be with you.'

Seeing Francis and his boat reminded Dewi of Nathan. She wished he had been able to come with them . . .

Ten minutes late, accompanied by Francis Hanna, they were walking alongside the river, heading for the Tower Liberties, a small, autonomous area beside the Tower of London which fell outside the jurisdiction of the City of London. Here, in a large and ancient hall, they found the waxworks exhibition of Madame Tussaud.

It was a little disappointing for Dewi. The exhibition had been on tour and much of the clothing was decidedly travel-weary and grubby. Women's dresses were particularly badly affected. Some of the waxwork figures had suffered damage too, but the likenesses were sufficiently realistic for Beville to set up a shriek of delight when he saw the image of Nathan and a crowd quickly gathered when he informed everyone within hearing that it was his daddy.

Beville's delight was complete when he found the waxwork figures of the late King Louis and Queen Marie Antoinette of France, both complete with crowns. He was less impressed with the tableau depicting the French Revolution. It included a gloomy cell and a gory guillotine scene, complete with severed heads, all liberally daubed with blood-red paint.

Beville was similarly disenchanted with a tableau entitled 'The death of Nelson', despite the information from Dewi that Nathan had known the famous admiral and been on the ship with him when he died.

Beville's hand found hers and held it tightly.

There were still a number of exhibits Dewi had not seen but she decided she would take Beville outside. Francis and Sally decided to remain behind for a while.

Even the imperturbable Alf seemed relieved to emerge into the autumn sunshine after the horrors of the waxworks, but a surprise awaited them. The street and the open spaces between the Tower of London and the surrounding houses was more crowded than it had been inside Madame Tussaud's exhibition. A busy fair was in progress. There were stalls galore and many entertainments. Jugglers showed off their skills with a whole variety of objects and a shambling, slightly mangy black bear was swaying obediently, if unrhythmically, to the music of a penny whistle. Here too were fiddlers, dancers, acrobats – and crown and anchor men. Everything from cooked pies to lace handkerchiefs was being sold from the numerous stalls.

Towering above all the many attractions was a huge pear-shaped globe of silk, suspended from which was a basket, large enough to carry two men. Anchored to the ground by a skein of ropes, the silken globe swayed in the breeze and tugged at the ropes as though impatient to be free.

When Beville pointed and demanded that Dewi lift him in order that he might see more, Alf reached down and swung him to his broad shoulders once more.

'What is it?' Beville squeaked excitedly.

'I don't know,' confessed Dewi. She was as awed as Beville by the sheer size of the object. 'I've never seen anything like it in all my life!'

'It's a balloon,' explained an elderly bystander. 'A couple of men get into the basket, release the ropes holding everything to the ground, and it soars into the air with them.'

'I want to fly in the balloon,' shouted Beville, excitedly bouncing up and down on Alf's shoulders.

'Oh no you don't, young Beville,' declared Dewi positively. 'You're as high off the ground as you're going to be today. Anyway, I can't see that thing ever getting into the air.'

The informative stranger had moved away now and Dewi added scornfully, 'It's madness even to think of such thing, if you ask me.'

For a long time it appeared that Dewi would be proven right. The balloonist and his numerous assistants had to work hard to prevent the balloon from deflating and collapsing about their ears.

There appeared to be no prospect of the balloon rising in the air with its intended passengers and after a while the spectators lost interest in the novelty and looked elsewhere for their entertainment.

Dewi and Beville were among those who drifted away. They were watching the weary antics of the dancing bear when a cheer brought them hurrying back to the roped-off area that housed the balloon.

The efforts of the balloonists had finally brought success. As the last ropes were cast off, the balloon rose slowly into the air. When the basket suspended beneath the balloon also left the ground, the huge crowd broke into applause and the two passengers waved their acknowledgement.

Beville was as excited as anyone. Shouting until he was hoarse, he returned the balloonists' waves until his arm ached. The balloon drifted into the air, seemingly as light as a wind-borne bubble from a washerwoman's tub. As it rose ever higher, the amazement of the watching crowd became disbelief. Not until the balloon was a distant speck, drifting leisurely towards the horizon, did the crowd begin to disperse, still chattering excitedly about the wonder they had just witnessed.

'What shall we do now?' Beville was still fired with excitement.

'I don't know,' replied Dewi. 'What's going on over there?' She pointed to where another large crowd was gathering.

'I can see a man talking . . . and waving his arms,' Beville's observations came as he raised himself as high as he could from Alf's shoulders, his feet supported by the hands of the big man.

'The only way to find out properly is to go over there and see for ourselves,' said Dewi.

It seemed that everyone else at the fair had the same idea and the trio were swept along with the crowd which was growing with incredible speed. It was a noisy crowd too. Dewi and the others had almost reached the speaker before Beville said disappointedly, 'There's nothing there. Only a man talking.'

By this time they were close enough for Dewi to be able to hear some of the man's passionate utterings '. . . Are we going to let Liverpool and his Tories get away with it? It's strength they understand. The power of the people . . . Are you with me?'

This last question brought a loud and prolonged roar of approval from the speaker's listeners. Dewi tugged at Alf's jacket. 'This isn't part of the fair. It's a political meeting and it's getting rowdy . . . We should leave before there's trouble.' She needed to shout in order to be heard above the din.

With Beville now silent on his shoulder, Alf nodded. He turned away and Dewi took hold of the tail of his jacket. The crush of the crowd had become alarming and it seemed to increase with every passing minute. Staying together was going to prove difficult.

A tense excitement had gripped the crowd and they began chanting in unison. This was more to Beville's liking. Secure from the crush of those all about him he took up the cry. 'Tower! Tower! Tower!'

The rabble was on the move now, away from the speaker. Heading towards the great gate of the Tower of London.

Forcing his way against the flow of the human tide, Alf fought to reach safety with Dewi and Beville. It was not easy. For every step he took forward he was forced sideways for two.

Dewi managed to stay with Alf, but she would have been swept away had the big silent man not reached back and taken her hand. Only his great strength succeeded in eventually extricating them from the vast, moving crowd.

When they finally staggered clear Dewi was aware for the first time that Beville was crying. What had begun as a great adventure for the boy had become frightening. Coming from a quiet village, unused to people in such huge numbers, he suddenly felt very small and vulnerable.

'It's all right, Beville. Don't cry.' Reaching up, she lifted him from Alf's shoulders and he clung tightly to her. 'We're safe now, Beville. Everything's all right.'

Unknown to Dewi, this had not been a spontaneous gathering. A nucleus of the crowd were members of a fanatical movement, committed to overthrowing the universally unpopular government of the Earl of Liverpool by any means possible.

They had held a meeting about a mile away at which the call had gone up for a march upon the Tower of London. They had gathered hundreds of sympathisers along the way. It seemed that the more members of the public who flocked to join them, the more they attracted.

Successful beyond all their wildest expectations and now many thousands strong, the leaders of the extremist movement felt bold enough to mount a full-scale attack on the fortress that symbolised the centuries-old authority of King and Parliament over the people.

Already paths were being cleared through the seething mass of chanting people for groups of insurrectionists, carrying stout tree-trunks between them. Appropriated from a timber yard beside the river, they were to be used in an attempt to batter down the stout doors of the Tower's gate, now firmly shut against them.

Alf took a grip on Dewi's arm and pointed. First to the battlements above the gate where armed soldiers gazed down, then over the heads of the crowd to where the fair had been sited.

Stalls, tents and barrows had been hurriedly swept aside. In their place a full squadron of blue-uniformed Royal Horse Guards were drawn up in two long lines, facing towards the mob. Behind them, nervous militiamen fingered the triggers of loaded muskets.

144

The progress of the extremists had been monitored from the time they held the first meeting. Militiamen had been mustered and the cavalry called out when their objective became clear.

'What about Sally and Francis?'

It was a foolish question. Alf could not reply. Even had he been able to speak, he could not provide Dewi with an answer. Men and women packed the space outside the exhibition like pilchards in a fish-cellar. The young Pentuan couple would need to fend for themselves and find their own way clear of the throng.

Alf's grip on Dewi's arm tightened and with Beville in her arms she followed the cellarman away from the mob.

They had gone no more than fifty paces when the hollow thud of a tree-trunk being swung against the Tower gate reached them.

Dewi turned to look back just as the soldiers on the wall above the gate took aim and fired at the crowd beneath them. She saw the white puffs of smoke, like miniature summer clouds, form above each sharpshooter. The clouds lasted for a moment only and were already wisps of vanishing gossamer by the time the flat report of the musketry reached her ears.

In the momentary hush that followed the shots a woman began screaming. Suddenly at a shouted order from the officer in charge of the cavalry, the mounted soldiers began a slow but ominous advance towards the crowd, followed by the less disciplined militiamen.

Alf snatched Beville from Dewi and they began running, ignoring Beville's protests that he was 'Not comfortable!' Behind them sections of the crowd also broke and ran. Others, missiles in hand, turned to face the cavalrymen and militia. Meanwhile, the wooden tree-trunk resumed its assault on the time-hardened wooden gate with an angry vigour.

The autumn fair at Tower Liberties had become the battle-ground for a full-scale, bloody riot.

Chapter 29

Nathan returned to find The Plough the scene of feverish activity, with men and women scurrying in every direction. At first he thought a coach must have arrived carrying a great many passengers, but he could see no vehicles in the yard.

Enlightenment came from an excited stableman who took his horse.

'I hope you wasn't caught up in all the goings-on down at the Tower today, sir?'

'No, I've come from Middlesex. What's been happening?'

'Been some terrible rioting. Worst London's seen for many a year, by all accounts. They tried to storm the Tower but the militia was ready for 'em and opened fire. The cavalry was called out too. Dozens were killed – or so I've been told. Some of the guests as is staying here got caught up in it. One of the young ladies from this very inn is still missing. Lying dead somewhere, as likely as not.'

'A young woman? Who?' Nathan was alarmed. There were probably other women staying at he inn, but Dewi had said she intended going out today. Dewi and Beville . . .

'I couldn't tell you her name, sir. But she's up here from Cornwall. You're from there too, aren't you, sir? Likely you'd know her. But don't you fret yourself, sir. Mr Gully will find out soon enough what's happened to her. He's got half of London out searching . . .'

Nathan left the stable before the other man completed his final observation. All he could think of was the possibility that Dewi was missing. Caught up in the violence of a London mob. At that moment he had no real concern for Beville. The stableman had said only that a young woman was missing. Had Beville been missing too the man would have made much of it.

Pushing through the door of the inn, Nathan cannoned into someone so hard that had he not caught her quickly she would have been bowled over.

'I'm sorry. It's entirely my fault . . . Dewi!' Nathan was so relieved when he recognised the girl he had almost knocked down that it was some moments before he realised he was still holding her.

Letting his hands drop to his sides, he said, 'Thank God you're safe! The stableman told me a young Cornish girl was missing. I thought it might be you.'

'It's Sally – and Francis too. We all went to Madame Tussaud's waxworks exhibition, near the Tower of London. Beville and I left before them. We were caught up in a mob but managed to escape. I fear Sally and Francis weren't so lucky. Mr Gully sent men to enquire at the waxworks but it had closed. The rioting has been over for hours now, but Sally and Francis still haven't returned.'

'Francis is a sensible man,' said Nathan, trying to reassure her. 'They'll be all right. I expect he was worried about his boat. They've probably gone back there.'

'That was the first place we looked. A man's been left there to let us know should they arrive.'

'How is Beville? He wasn't hurt?'

'He was upset for a short while,' Dewi said. 'He's upstairs now, playing with John Gully's children. But I *am* concerned for the other two, especially Sally. She's a kind-hearted girl, but she's not the brightest.'

'I'll go up to see Beville. Then, when I've had something to eat, I'll see what I can do to help. Where have they looked so far?'

'I'm sorry, Nathan. I'm so worried about Sally that I'm not thinking straight. You've had a long day. You must be very tired. Go and speak to Beville and I'll arrange for a meal to be prepared for you. While you're eating, John Gully can tell you where his men have looked so far.'

As John Gully related all that had been done to find Sally and Francis, Nathan realised the inn-keeper's enquiries must have encompassed every street in the vicinity of the Tower of London.

The fact that the missing couple had not been located was now a real cause for concern – especially in respect of Sally. There were back streets and alleyways not very far from the Tower where it would not be safe for any young girl – or man – to stray. The only ray of hope was that Francis was missing too. It seemed to indicate they had stayed together.

Nathan's hopeful theory was dashed before the meal had ended when a dejected and battered Francis Hanna limped into The Plough. His story added to the concern felt by everyone for Sally.

Caught up in the mob when they left the waxworks exhibition, Francis and Sally had gone along with it at first, not knowing what it was all about. By the time they learned the truth it was too late. Still on the edge of the mob, they were among the closest to the Royal Horse Guards when the cavalrymen mounted their controlled charge.

147

The Cornish couple succeeded in evading the cavalrymen, but behind the horses were Essex militiamen. Hurriedly mustered to combat the 'insurrection', they were anxious for a taste of action.

When a call went up for them to arrest the rioters, they did not attempt to dive into the crowd and seize the ringleaders, or those trying to break down the Tower gate. Instead, they grabbed those among the crowd who happened to be closest to them.

Francis knew he and Sally had done nothing to warrant arrest and when a militiaman tried to seize Sally, Francis thought it highly amusing. His mood changed when the militiaman refused to listen to his explanations about their presence in the crowd. Francis became angry.

He tried to free Sally from the man who was holding her but other militiamen came to the assistance of their colleague. In the ensuing mêlée Francis was knocked unconscious to the ground.

When he came round he was in the Fleet bridewell, along with more than a hundred others. Fortunately for him, after a couple of hours a constable came among them, taking names and addresses.

At first sceptical, the constable listened to Francis's story and then went away to speak to the magistrate who was due to try the 'rioters' at a special court.

Francis was taken before the magistrate and, after repeating his story and answering a number of questions, released. He immediately made enquiries about Sally, even visiting the women's section of the prison in an effort to locate her, but she was nowhere to be found.

As Francis left the bridewell the first of his fellow 'rioters' had already been tried and convicted and the first of many floggings had begun – but his search for Sally soon reached a dead-end.

By the time the young Cornish fisherman ended his story, Nathan had lost his appetite for food.

'Do you think Sally was arrested too?'

Francis nodded vigorously, and immediately regretted the action. The blow that had knocked him unconscious had left him with a sizeable bump on his head and a throbbing headache. 'I doubt if they would have released her, not after what happened between me and the militiaman.'

Turning to the landlord, Nathan asked, 'Have you made enquiries along the route taken by the militiamen and their prisoners from the Tower to the Fleet bridewell?'

'I've got men out right now. Don't worry, Nathan. If the girl is still in London, we'll find her before the night is out. In the meantime I'll have someone look at that head of yours, young man. You've a bump there as large as a hen's egg.'

Sally Wicks was located shortly before midnight and brought back to The Plough. She was so drunk she could hardly stand. She had been found drinking with two militiamen in a seedy, unlicensed gin-shop, just off the route taken by the militiamen with their prisoners.

One of the many women questioned by John Gully's searchers led to Sally's discovery. She had seen two militiamen, one a corporal, dropping behind the main group of prisoners in the company of a young woman. She watched them slip into a narrow alley where the gin-shop was located.

When Nathan asked Sally what had happened she immediately burst into a bout of hysterical tears and Dewi said, 'I'll take her upstairs and put her to bed. When we're alone she'll no doubt tell me.'

Dewi was right and in the privacy of the inn bedroom listened aghast to Sally's tale.

It seemed that after Francis's vain attempt to rescue her, Sally had been taken to a nearby street with others to wait an escort to the Fleet prison. Many more men and women were swiftly added to the militiamen's 'bag' during the ensuing half-hour.

She tried repeatedly but unsuccessfully to learn what had happened to Francis. One of the militiamen to whom she spoke, a corporal, kept her in conversation, asking her how she came to be mixed up in the rioting. She told him what had happened and the man appeared to be sympathetic.

When other militiamen came upon the scene and the prisoners were marched away, the corporal sidled up to Sally, telling her to fall behind by pretending she had something in her shoe.

She did as she was told and the corporal and another militiaman remained with her. When the main body of prisoners and escorts were far enough away, the corporal and his colleague hurried her into a nearby alleyway.

At this stage Sally expected to be allowed to go on her way, but the corporal told her it would not yet be safe. He explained that the officer in charge of the prisoners was likely to send someone back to look for her. Taken to an unlicensed gin-shop, she was told they would need to wait there until it was safe to emerge on to the streets once more.

Sally still believed the corporal's sole intention was to help her and as she drank he seemed to grow nicer. She was unused to drinking and it was not long before, in her own words, she was 'feeling fuzzy'. When she said she ought to return to The Plough and explain what had happened, the corporal suggested she should clean up before going out on the street again.

Barely able to stand, she was taken to an upstairs room where the corporal thought it might be better if she had 'a little rest' for a while.

When she lay on the bed the corporal lay down beside her. At

149

this stage Sally's narrative became very vague, although she seemed to recall that at one time both she and the corporal were lying naked on the bed.

Sally told Dewi that she must have fallen asleep. When she awoke the corporal was telling her to stay where she was while he went downstairs. Instead, she dressed and went down with him.

The other militiaman was still in the gin-shop and complained bitterly about the time he had been waiting. The corporal then told her she must go upstairs with his companion. Sally objected. Not from any moral standpoint, but because she said she did not like him. •

She was still arguing with the men when two of John Gully's searchers entered the gin-shop. Both men were only novice prize-fighters, but they swiftly proved too good for the militiamen.

Sally was weeping loudly now, as she ended her story, but her anguish was directed not so much at the nature of her ordeal as at the identity of the man who had been in bed with her.

'I didn't want to do it with either of them, Dewi. Honest I didn't. I wanted it to be with Francis . . . You won't tell him what happened, will you?'

'Hush now, you just lie here and get some rest. You've had a terrifying experience. Go to sleep and forget all about what's happened.'

'You won't tell him, Dewi? Promise?'

'All right, I promise – but he's a happily married man. I doubt if he cares too much who you lie down with. But try to get some sleep now.'

Dewi remained with Sally for perhaps ten minutes more. When she thought the young girl was asleep Dewi moved quietly towards the door. She had almost reached it when Sally said sleepily, 'Have you ever done it with any man, Dewi?'

'Now what sort of question is that for a young girl to ask? You just go to sleep and I hope you'll have forgotten all about such things by the time you wake up.'

'I don't want to forget. I want to remember and think about doing it . . . with Francis. I don't care whether he's married or not. My ma always says it's the only thing that rich folk can't stop us from enjoying. Haven't you even *thought* about it, Dewi? Thought about doing it with someone like Nathan Jago? You tell me you haven't and I'll call you a liar. I've watched you looking at him sometimes and I knew very well what you were thinking about.'

Outside the room, Dewi leaned back against the door trying to compose herself before she went downstairs to face Nathan and the others.

First Nell Quicke and now Sally! Were her feelings for Nathan

150

so obvious to everyone? They could not be, surely? She wasn't even certain of them herself. Sally Wicks was talking drunken nonsense.

Dewi reassured herself with the thought that the young girl would remember nothing of their conversation by the morning. Besides, she would have more important matters to think about.

Mentally bracing herself, Dewi set off to give Nathan and the others a diluted version of Sally's ordeal at the hands of the two militiamen.

Chapter 30

The news that the Duke of Clarence was coming to The Plough before embarking on the *Charlotte* to take passage to Cornwall, caused great excitement among the inn's employees.

Late to bed after the excitement of the previous day, John Gully was up before dawn, personally supervising the cleaning of every room likely to receive a visit from the Royal Duke.

The *Charlotte* too was cleaned from stem to stern – and then cleaned once again. The accommodation on the vessel was virtually non-existent. Despite this, room was somehow found to enable the Duke of Clarence to take his ease in comparative, albeit cramped, privacy. Here, below decks in what would normally have been a fish-hold, he would be sheltered from the rigours of the weather and the work of the upper deck.

In the event, the occupants of The Plough and the crew of the *Charlotte* waited in vain for the third son of King George III. He had announced his intention of being at the inn by midday. Not until four o'clock was a message received from the Duke. He regretted that it was now impossible for him to make the voyage that day. He would be at the inn ready to make the voyage to Cornwall at midday the following day.

There were no excuses made in the note and no apology for causing a major disruption in the routine of The Plough and upsetting the plans of Nathan and his crew.

When Dewi commented on the Duke's apparent lack of consideration, Nathan shrugged. 'Royal Princes shouldn't be judged by the standards set for ordinary men. The Duke is no different from his brothers in that respect. But he's basically a very generous man. I've had occasion to be grateful to him in the past. He'll have his own reasons for not coming today. Reasons that are important to him. I look forward to welcoming him onboard the *Charlotte* tomorrow.'

John Gully was standing with them. In spite of the inconvenience that had been caused to him, he suddenly chuckled. 'I seem to remember that your Amy used him as a runner to lay a bet when you fought Abraham Dellow.'

'That's right.' Nathan's answering smile contained a mixture of pride and sadness. 'She risked all the money she had in the world to buy Polrudden for Beville. To ensure he grew up with his rightful inheritance.'

'Amy must have been a very special person.' Dewi spoke quietly, looking at Nathan's face. But it was John Gully who replied.

'She was a girl in a million. There wasn't a man who frequented The Plough who wouldn't have given his life for her.'

John Gully had also been watching Nathan and he steered the conversation away from talk of Amy. 'Mind you, the Duke had a special lady in those days too.'

'Dorothea Jordan? Yes, he seemed very happy with her and their children. It came as a great surprise when I heard they'd separated.'

'It must have been a shock to Dorothea Jordan too. Ten children she had by the Duke, and others before she met him. She must have thought it was family enough to keep 'em together. Mind you, I don't think it was her fault they parted. Rumour around London has it that the Duke ran up so many debts the King threatened to cut off his allowance altogether. Told the Duke to find himself a rich heiress. It was practically a royal command, by all accounts.'

'Poor woman!' murmured Dewi. 'After having ten children by the man, she might have expected at least *some* loyalty from him, no matter who he might be.'

'Ah, well, we're not supposed to judge Royal Princes as other men when it comes to their women, it seems. The Prince Regent flaunts his mistresses everywhere, yet he wouldn't even acknowledge his wife if he passed her by in the park. The other Princes are no better. They're the scandal of London. Why, the other night at the theatre . . .'

John Gully proceeded to tell a story about the Prince Regent and his foremost mistress attending a performance at which his wife, the Princess Caroline, was also present. As she listened to the story, Dewi wondered what Nathan and the Royal Princes could possibly have in common.

'Did any famous actors ever come to Wales, Dewi?' The question was posed by John Gully.

'I don't know. Come to think of it, I can't even remember there being a theatre in Newport, 'though I suppose there might have been. I never really thought about it.'

'Never been to a theatre? Bless my soul, it's one of the great pleasures of life, girl. You ought to take her, Nathan, especially now you have an extra night in London. Edmund Keane's playing Romeo at the Drury Lane Theatre and London's raving over him. If you want to go I can offer you the use of Lord Queensberry's box. It's mine whenever I care to use it – which isn't very often these days.'

When Nathan hesitated, Dewi said quickly, 'It's a very kind offer, Mr Gully, but I couldn't leave Beville with Sally. Not after last night. She's hardly capable of looking after herself, let alone a lively small boy.'

'That's no problem,' said the landlord promptly. 'He's as happy as a sand-boy playing with my boys. The missus said so herself not an hour ago. Besides, we've so many of our own that putting one more to bed will be no chore. He can share a room with whichever of them he chooses. It'll make the evening something of an adventure for him.'

'I couldn't . . . really.'

Dewi found herself in near-panic at the thought of going out to the theatre with Nathan. She told herself it was to save him any embarrassment, but it was far more than that. She would dearly love Nathan to take her to the theatre . . . to take her *anywhere*, but it would need to be his own idea. Not something that had been forced upon him by a well-meaning friend.

'Even if I wanted to go, I have nothing to wear. But it's a kind thought. Thank you.'

Dewi spoke in what her nieces had always referred to as her 'no-nonsense voice'. It should have meant the end of the matter, but Nathan decreed it should be otherwise.

Remembering the home-made dress she had worn on her twenty-first birthday party, he said, 'I think it's a wonderful idea. As for a dress . . . every woman should buy a new dress when she comes to London for the first time. There's little opportunity to buy one in Cornwall. John, could your wife spare a while this afternoon to take Dewi out to look for one?'

When she opened her mouth to speak, Nathan anticipated her protest about the cost of such a purchase. 'It can be a late birthday present to you . . . from Beville.'

'You've already been more than generous for my birthday, but . . .' Dewi hesitated, not certain whether this was Nathan's own idea, or whether he had been pushed into taking her. 'If you really *would* enjoy going to the theatre, I should love to come with you. It would be a thrill to write and tell my sister in Wales about it.'

'Then it's settled, and I'll have no argument about a new dress. You'll buy one this afternoon and we'll go to Drury Lane this evening.'

154

Chapter 31

Nathan came down from his room that evening to find John Gully and most of the inn's female staff in the parlour. All were busying themselves with tasks that should have taken a quarter of their number and a tenth of the time to complete.

He waited fifteen minutes for the appearance of Dewi. He was becoming impatient, fearing they would be late for the theatre, when she came downstairs – and made an immediate impact upon everyone in the room.

As a gasp of admiration arose, Nathan turned towards the door and his mouth fell open in delighted disbelief.

Dewi's long black hair had been styled in a classic Greek chignon with a blue velvet bow holding it in place behind her neck. Her dress was of pale misty blue silk, drawn in tightly at the waist and with a contrasting bodice decorated with darker blue velvet bows, matching the one in her hair. Beneath the hem of her dress it was just possible to see pale satin evening shoes also decorated with a bow to match those in her hair and on her dress. In her ears she wore the earrings that had been a birthday present to her from Nathan.

The silence that followed his initial surprise temporarily unnerved Dewi. 'You don't like the dress? There's something wrong?'

Nathan gathered his wits together quickly, yet he found himself strangely tongue-tied. 'There's nothing wrong. Nothing at all.'

'It's not too showy, is it? I mean . . . you don't think I look as though I'm trying to be someone I'm not?'

'Dewi, you look absolutely lovely, and if Nathan doesn't say something very quickly I'll whisk you off to the theatre myself. Tell the girl how she looks, Nathan.'

'She looks very lovely indeed – and it's a beautiful dress too.'

'You're not just saying that because you don't want to embarrass me?'

'Dewi, you can stay here fishing for compliments all evening if that's what you want to do, but the reply will still be the same. I am proud to be taking you out this evening. Very proud indeed, I promise you.'

John Gully's wife had entered the room behind Dewi and now

155

she gave her an affectionate kiss on the cheek and a quick hug. 'There you are. It's exactly what I told you Nathan would say – even though it took him a while. You're a beautiful girl, wearing a beautiful dress. Now off you go before I start feeling jealous because of the way my husband's looking at you!'

The Drury Lane Theatre was only a few streets away from The Plough, but Nathan had a carriage waiting and Dewi felt like royalty as she was handed in by a liveried carriage driver.

Dewi's thin veneer of sophistication cracked a little when they neared Drury Lane. There were lots of narrow streets and alleyways around here, occupied by some of the poorer residents of England's capital city. The carriage attracted a small crowd of begging urchins who hurled obscenities after them when the coach failed to slacken speed.

The area outside the theatre was being kept clear for carriages, but there was a fair-sized crowd of onlookers who uttered audible expressions of admiration as Dewi stepped from the carriage with the grace of a princess.

Many people were entering the theatre. Most were making their way to the 'pit', on the floor of the theatre, immediately before the stage. These were members of the public who would pay least to watch the play, yet even for them it was a special night out. They were as interested in the other theatregoers as they would be in the Shakespearean play they had all come to watch.

John Gully had sent word ahead that Nathan and Dewi would be taking the Marquess of Queensberry's box and the theatre manager was in the foyer personally to escort them to their places.

In the box were two comfortable armchairs from which they would watch the play in comfort. There was also a bottle of champagne in an ice-bucket and two exquisite tall glasses on a nearby table.

Dewi found the sheer luxury of her surroundings breathtaking. As she sat beside Nathan, looking about her, she realised with a start of surprise that others in the theatre were equally interested in her.

Heads were turned towards her from the well of the theatre and to Dewi's intense embarrassment two army officers in a box on the other side of the stage rose to their feet and gave her a deep bow.

Acknowledging their gesture with a brief nod of her head, Dewi turned to Nathan apprehensively. 'They must have mistaken me for someone else. Who do you think they believe me to be?'

Nathan smiled indulgently. 'It *could* be because you're occupying the box of the Marquess of Queensberry, but I doubt if that's the reason. They are bowing to you because you're the most beautiful girl in the theatre. They are publicly acknowledging the

156

fact – and I'll raise my glass to that too.'

Handing her a glass of champagne in which small bubbles raced each other to the surface of the golden-tinged liquid, Nathan raised his own glass before taking a sip from it. 'Here's to you, Dewi.'

She followed his example. As the champagne coursed down her throat, she looked surprised, blinking rapidly.

'Is something wrong?'

'No.' Dewi smiled at him almost shyly. 'It's just . . . I've never drunk champagne before. It's very nice. Very nice indeed.'

'It certainly is, but take it easy. I don't want you returning to The Plough in the same state as Sally Wicks.'

'It can't make you drunk, surely? It's far too nice for that.'

This time Nathan laughed out loud. 'Dewi, you're priceless. I'm glad you found your way to Polrudden.'

The glass paused on its way to her lips once more. 'Are you, Nathan? Are you really?'

'Yes. Re-ally.' He broke the word in two, imitating her Welsh accent.

'Why?' Dewi asked the question softly, watching his face as she waited for his reply.

'For one thing, Beville couldn't have found a finer governess. He's a lucky boy.'

'You said, "for one thing". Is there another reason?'

'Yes.' Nathan was floundering for a reply. 'It's meant that tonight I'm escorting a young lady who is the belle of the Drury Lane Theatre, and who has made me the envy of every man in the house.'

Dewi looked at Nathan silently for long moments, but before she could speak again, the theatre orchestra struck up.

The music was very loud but it died away suddenly and the manager of the theatre parted the curtains and stepped to the front of the stage. As a surprised murmur broke out among the crowd, the manager held up a hand, calling for silence.

'My lords, ladies and gentlemen, before we begin the play tonight I have a sad announcement to make. I have learned today that one of our best loved actresses, a lady who has trodden the boards of this very stage, has died suddenly in France. May we please have a few moments' silence to show our great respect for the late Mrs Dorothea Jordan?'

'Good God! She was the Duke of Clarence's mistress!'

Nathan thought he knew now why the Duke had postponed his trip to Cornwall. After all the years he'd lived with her, he would be greatly upset.

Dewi would have questioned Nathan, but at that moment the orchestra struck up once again, playing dramatic music now. The curtains were drawn back and the play began.

The players at the Drury Lane Theatre were among the finest in the country, but when Edmund Keane strode on to the stage in the role of Romeo, he immediately dominated the scene.

Dewi hardly noticed when Nathan poured her a second glass of champagne. As the story of the play unfolded she was held spellbound. Caught up in the magic of the evening, the rich prose of William Shakespeare's lines, and the genius of Edmund Keane, she felt as though she were part of some wonderful dream.

Once or twice during the performance Nathan found he was looking at Dewi and not at the actors. She was so entirely absorbed in what was happening that he was able to study her without her being aware of his interest.

She really was an extremely attractive girl. He wondered why he had never noticed before. He decided that she deliberately played down her appearance. It was probably a habit that had come about while she was living with her spinster aunt in Wales. Sympathetically, he thought that life could not have been easy for her there.

Guiltily, Nathan realised that in the time Dewi had been at Polrudden he had never before noticed her in this way. He wondered why? No doubt it had something to do with the arrival of Abigail on the scene so soon after Dewi had come to work at Polrudden.

On stage, Juliet was faced with the devastating discovery that she had fallen in love with the son of a family that had been feuding with hers for many years. In the moment of awareness the stage curtains closed and after a momentary hush the theatre erupted in applause, Dewi joining in.

'Enjoying the play?' Nathan lifted the champagne bottle from the ice bucket but saw that Dewi had not touched a drop from her glass during the first act. He filled his own instead.

'It's *wonderful*. Just as though it's all really happening out there and not actors playing a part.'

'That's what good theatre is all about, Dewi – and you won't see anything better than this.'

For the remainder of the brief interval Nathan and Dewi spoke of the play and the Welsh girl was more animated than he had ever seen her. Her delight made it a very gratifying evening for him.

Dewi's involvement with what was happening on stage was so absolute that, in the final act, Nathan had to give her his handkerchief to mop up the tears that flowed freely when hero and heroine met their dramatic deaths.

When the final curtain fell, the applause for the cast was deafening. Edmund Keane came to the front of the stage on numerous occasions to acknowledge the continuing ovation and he reserved his deepest and final bow for Dewi, thus setting the seal on her joy at a wonderful evening's entertainment.

Outside the theatre, as they stood on the pavement together, Dewi was still bubbling over with the sheer joy of the performances she had just witnessed. She hardly noticed the young boy who bumped against her with a murmur of apology. At the same time the handles of her purse were cut so skilfully that she was not even aware it had been taken from her arm.

But Nathan saw what happened. Before the young thief could pass the bag to another boy of a similar age who was hovering nearby, Nathan pounced upon him.

'No, you don't, young man.' Nathan took back the handbag with one hand, at the same time maintaining a tight grip on the boy's arm that it would have needed the strength of a grown man to break.

'Let me go!' He emphasised his demand with a kick from heavy, steel-tipped boots that would have skinned Nathan's shin had he not held the struggling boy at arm's length.

'I think this calls for a visit to the magistrate for you, young man. A whipping might teach you to have a little respect for other people's property.'

The struggling ceased and suddenly the boy showed genuine fear. 'Don't put me up before the beak, mister. It'll be the convict 'ulks for me this time, for sure.'

The boy suddenly began to shiver. Whether he was really frightened or it was merely a good act Nathan could not tell. 'Me brother died on the 'ulk at Woolwich only last month. It'll break me sister's 'eart if I'm sent there too.'

'You should have thought about all that before you took up thieving.'

'Please, guv'nor. *Please*! I won't do any more thieving. Honest, I won't.'

'I doubt if you know the meaning of the word. What's your name?'

'Charlie. Charlie Philpotts . . . Oh Gawd!' Letting out a sudden wail of misery, the boy sagged in his grasp. 'Here's a runner. I'm done for now, and no mistake.'

The crowd from the theatre was thinning now, and making his way towards them was the large man whom Charlie Philpotts had identified as a Bow Street runner, one of the select band of men employed by the Bow Street magistrates to take thieves.

Still held fast in Nathan's grasp, the young thief began to tremble and now Nathan was convinced this was no act. Leaning closer to the boy, he said, 'You're not likely to get another chance like this. Make the most of it. If you're serious about giving up thieving, go and speak to John Gully, landlord of The Plough in Carey Street. I'll see there's work for you. Now go, before I change my mind.'

159

Nathan released his grip and Charlie Philpotts sprinted off along the road as though the devil was after him. As Nathan gave her purse back to Dewi, the Bow Street runner reached them.

'I saw you had hold of young Charlie Philpotts, sir. Has he been up to his old tricks again? Stealing ladies' purses?'

'Are you talking about that young boy? No. The lady dropped her handbag and he and I went for it together. I thought it might be better for everyone if I reached it first.'

'You were very wise in your thinking, sir, but not so wise in allowing the young scoundrel to go free. The handles of that purse have been cut – and with a razor, likely as not. He's a wrong 'un, that lad. He's been in trouble with the law before now, and will be again. I've had my eyes on him for a very long time.'

'Oh, well, we have the purse now and, as I said, as far as I'm concerned, it was dropped. I'll be laying no charges. But, here, please take this for your trouble and concern.'

Nathan took a guinea from a pocket and passed it to the Bow Street runner.

As Dewi and Nathan walked away from the theatre, she said, 'The runner was right, you know. The handles of my purse have been cut.'

'I was aware of that, but you had only to look at the boy to realise how poor he is. There were more holes than cloth in his coat and his trousers were so threadbare they'd likely have split when he ran away.'

They walked together in silence for a few moments before Dewi said, 'Do you think he will ask for work from John Gully?'

'I doubt it, but he's been offered a chance. I'll sleep happier than if I'd sent a boy of his years to a prison hulk for at least seven years. You saw the hulks when we came upriver past Woolwich. The smell of them is enough to make an honest man's skin creep. Life on board is the closest thing to hell anyone will find on this earth. I wouldn't send a boy there if he'd robbed me of half my possessions. Besides, I worked with a smuggler for many years when I was little more than Charlie Philpotts' age. I dread to think what might have happened to me had I been taken and handed over to the magistrates. Fortunately I wasn't and joined the navy instead. That led to my having all the things I enjoy today. I hope one day Charlie Philpotts may have similar luck.'

Dewi looked at Nathan with a new respect. This was a side of his nature she had not witnessed before. She decided she liked it.

'There's a carriage for hire over there.' He was about to step off the curb and cross the road to the waiting vehicle when Dewi stopped him.

'Can we walk instead? It's not very far.'

'Of course, if that's what you want to do. Are you certain you'll not be cold?'

She nodded and took his arm. In fact, despite the chill of the night she was warm. It was a warmth that had its source deep inside her. This had been a wonderful day. A day for her to savour for the whole of her life. She wanted the evening with Nathan to last for as long as possible.

Chapter 32

The Duke of Clarence arrived at The Plough at twelve noon the following day. Nathan was the first to greet him and was able to say in privacy, 'I was very sorry to hear the news last night of Dorothea Jordan's death. She was very kind to me, and to Amy, my wife.'

'Yes. Yes, indeed. She was a fine woman. A damned fine woman. I heard the news only yesterday morning myself. Didn't feel like travelling afterwards. I hoped you might understand. No more of it now, Nathan. I don't want to make a damned fool of myself, eh?'

The Duke of Clarence turned away from Nathan and was soon involved in a noisy conversation with John Gully. The two men had met before and when the talk turned to the subject of prize-fighting, Nathan thought they might be delayed for a further twenty-four hours.

However, the Duke and his luggage were eventually conveyed to Blackfriars Wharf where the *Charlotte* was in full readiness for them. Josiah Jago was not returning to Cornwall on board the vessel. Never a good sailor, he had pleaded Church business and remained behind. He would travel at a later date on the regular London to Penzance coach.

It was immediately apparent that the Duke had been expecting to sail on a somewhat larger vessel, but he was quick to recognise the potential sailing qualities of the Cornish lugger. After under-taking a brief tour of inspection he expressed his satisfaction. 'She's a damned fine boat, Nathan. I shall enjoy sailing in her. By the way, I hope you don't mind but I've arranged for one of the Navy's new-fangled steam tugs to take us down-river as far as Sheerness? It will be waiting for us off the Tower. I thought it might be able to make up some of the time I've lost you. Also gives me an opportunity to see how effective these steam-tugs really are.'

The paddle-driven steamer put up an impressive performance. With the *Charlotte* in tow, the vessel wheezed and splashed its way towards the sea on a windless day and against a turning tide. Around them only multi-oared vessels were making any progress at all and the tug-towed *Charlotte* soon left them all behind. By four o'clock they were off Sheerness, but the Duke ordered the disgruntled steam-tug captain to take them on to Margate.

The *Charlotte* spent that evening tied up alongside Margate pier while the Duke, Nathan, Beville and the women went ashore to a local inn, causing a stir among the local residents.

The weather on the return voyage to Pentuan was livelier than it had been on the outward voyage but the Duke of Clarence seemed to enjoy every moment. Standing straddle-legged on the upper deck of the *Charlotte*, he struck a pose that Nathan thought was vaguely reminiscent of the Duke's late friend and hero, Admiral Lord Nelson.

The sea brought back memories of that famous man for the Duke too and he was constantly urging Nathan to tell of his own experiences of the time when he sailed as Nelson's coxswain.

They were stories that enthralled the others on board *Charlotte*. Nathan's standing with the crew – and with Dewi – had never been higher.

In many ways it was a difficult voyage for her. Her duties as governess to Beville were not onerous on board the boat and she had little to do. Each of the fishermen assumed an unspoken responsibility for the young boy's safety and he was constantly supervised.

She spent a great deal of time talking to the Duke of Clarence. He was unfailingly charming to her, but she felt in awe of the Royal Duke.

The only person on board to take no part in caring for Beville, or anything else, was Sally Wicks. The young nursemaid was not a good sailor and events of recent days had done nothing to improve matters. It was generally felt that Sally's known weakness for men had contributed greatly to what had occurred between her and the militiamen. For this reason the attitude of the crew to her was far cooler than it might otherwise have been.

She spent most of her time sitting alone at the stern of the fishing boat, wrapped in a blanket. A lone, dejected figure, she willed the hours away until they would finally arrive at Pentuan.

It was mid-afternoon on the third day of the voyage when the *Charlotte* sailed past the entrance to Fowey harbour and entered St Austell Bay.

The weather had deteriorated still further during this last day. A strong easterly wind, combined with a high tide, meant that sailing into Portgiskey Cove, where Nathan's fish-cellar was situated, was too dangerous to attempt.

For the same reason, beaching the *Charlotte* on the sand would be equally hazardous. She had not been built for beaching. As well as the risk of structural damage to the boat, it could result in the Duke of Clarence suffering a ducking, at the very least.

'Do you think you can take the *Charlotte* into the old channel?' Nathan spoke to Francis Hanna who was at the the helm of his own boat. 'It will be more sheltered there and we can moor alongside the steps at the old Customs house. It should prevent any accidents – providing you think you can avoid the rocks at the entrance.'

'Don't you concern yourself about me, Nathan. I haven't enjoyed myself so much in years. I ought to spend far more time at sea.'

His face glistening with spray and his wet hair plastered down against his head, the Duke of Clarence wore an old oilskin and was indistinguishable from any of the fishermen.

'The channel is the safest place to land in weather like this,' replied Nathan. 'It leads to the new harbour that's being constructed. It's the course the large ships will need to take and it's also closer to Polrudden.'

'Can I do something to help?' The Duke was determined to savour every last minute of his sea-going experience.

'You can do the same as me – stay out of Francis's way while he brings his boat in.' Nathan led the Duke to where Dewi, Beville and Sally huddled at the stern of the fishing boat.

As the *Charlotte* rode the waves, heading inshore towards the narrow channel, Nathan glanced towards Francis Hanna. He was ready to offer his expertise to the younger man, but it was not needed. Francis was fond of declaring he could handle his own boat better than any other man. This was an opportunity to prove before a royal witness that it was no idle boast.

Edging alarmingly close to the rocks to the north of the harbour entrance, the *Charlotte* suddenly surged forward, propelled irresistibly by wind and tide. The fishing-boat continued to gather speed until the twin motivating forces suddenly dropped away without warning. Those on board relaxed as the *Charlotte* slowed and gently bumped against the pier wall.

As one of the fishermen scrambled up the uneven wall, a rope was thrown ashore. Seconds later the *Charlotte* was safely moored beside the old Customs house. They were as close to the village as they could go. Immediately ahead were stout lock gates, keeping the sea at bay from the work going on inside the harbour basin.

Nathan sent a young fisherman hurrying to Polrudden to arrange for horses and a light carriage to carry the Duke and his luggage to the Manor. As the considerable amount of luggage was being carried ashore the Duke wandered off, still wearing the fisherman's oilcloth coat as protection against a persistent drizzle.

He wandered happily among the harbour workings until he stopped to look in a deep hole where men were at work building a side wall of the harbour. Nathan was keeping the Duke in view, at the same time supervising the unloading of the luggage. Suddenly he saw Columb Hawkins striding towards the Duke, with Sir Christopher in his wake.

There was aggression in every line of Columb's appearance and Nathan hurried to intercept him and avoid trouble for the inquisitive Duke.

He was too late. Columb Hawkins reached the Duke first.

'What the hell do you think you're doing here? Isn't it bad enough having villagers using the harbour workings as a main thoroughfare? I'll not have fishermen wandering around as well. Clear off, before I throw you off the harbour land myself.'

The Duke was startled. He had never been spoken to in such an outrageous manner before. He looked to Nathan for an explanation, but Sir Christopher Hawkins spoke first, 'Is this one of your men, Jago? I might have known! I'm damned if I know why you became a shareholder of the harbour company. You seem to be set on delaying work by every means at your disposal . . .'

Stepping between the belligerent Columb and the Duke, Nathan said, 'Your Royal Highness, may I introduce Sir Christopher Hawkins and his nephew, Columb?'

Startled by Nathan's deferential manner in addressing the Duke, Sir Christopher Hawkins snapped, 'What nonsense are you up to now, Jago?'

'His Royal Highness, Prince William, Duke of Clarence, has just arrived from London. He was merely taking a passing interest in the harbour. As his Royal Highness's host, please accept my apologies for the trespass upon your land.'

Turning away from the two men, Nathan addressed the Duke. 'Shall we return to the boat and await transport, Your Royal Highness?' Nathan made exaggerated use of the Duke's titles and the Duke of Clarence followed his lead.

'Of course, Nathan. Please accept my apology for any embarrassment caused to you by my inquisitiveness.'

The moment the Duke began talking it was evident he was no fisherman and now Sir Christopher Hawkins observed that underneath the oilcloth coat the Duke was wearing fashionable white trousers with straps disappearing beneath the insteps of elegant and expensive boots. He remembered too the stories of Nathan's friendship with the Duke.

'Your Royal Highness . . . please accept my abject apologies.' Struggling for words, the baronet continued: 'The rudeness of myself and my nephew is unforgivable.'

'Yes.'

The single word of agreement from the Duke was more scathing than any reprimand.

Columb Hawkins looked at his uncle as though he had suddenly gone mad. He refused to believe Nathan's story that this rather insignificant and damp man was the third son of the reigning monarch of England.

Behaving as though the two Hawkinses no longer existed, the Duke of Clarence said, 'Perhaps we should return to the boat, Nathan. I would like to thank your young captain and the crew for a most enjoyable voyage. I will remember it with a great deal of pleasure.'

Taking Nathan's arm, the Duke of Clarence turned his back on Sir Christopher and his nephew without a word to either of them.

When Nathan and his royal companion had passed beyond hearing, Sir Christopher gave vent to the anger he felt.

'Damn the man! I'll not forgive Jago for this humiliation. He'll pay one day, I swear it.'

'You don't think that really *was* the Duke of Clarence?'

'You wouldn't know a duke if he rammed his coronet down your throat, you damned young fool! It's *your* quick temper that's the cause of this humiliation. I'm damned if I know why I put you in charge of the harbour construction in the first place. You've been nothing but trouble from the very beginning. I've a good mind to send you packing and bring in someone I can trust . . .'

Chapter 33

At Venn Farm, Dewi sat in the kitchen telling Nell of the adventures experienced by the party from Pentuan whilst in London. Outside it was a miserable grey day with a steady drizzle. The children, supervised none too graciously by Sally, were in one of the farm barns. They were watching Tom Quicke and a carpenter making repairs to a wagon that had seen better days.

'Fancy our Nathan bringing the Duke of Clarence back to Polrudden!'

It was the third time Nell had said the same thing. Glancing up at her visitor, she smiled. 'But tell me about your visit to the theatre with our Nathan. Did you have a nice time?'

Kneading a small mountain of dough, Nell looked across the kitchen at Dewi. She was baking bread for the farm, with some to spare for the older people in the parish.

'It was a *wonderful* evening. I can't ever remember having a better one. I had a new dress especially for the occasion. Nathan bought it for me and said it was a present from Beville. I must show it to you when you next come to Polrudden. It's really beautiful, Nell. At the theatre we sat in a box that belonged to the Marquess of Queensberry! Can you imagine it? Me, Dewi Morgan, sitting in a box that belonged to a famous peer. While I was there two army officers actually stood up and bowed to me across the theatre, in front of everyone. Then on the way out Nathan caught a young boy who tried to steal my purse. He cut the handle, without me knowing a thing about it. Clever, he was.'

'Did our Nathan hand him over to the magistrate?'

'No. He said the boy would have been sent to one of the hulks we saw on the way up the Thames. They were horrible, Nell. It doesn't bear thinking about. Nathan said he didn't want that on his conscience. I admired him very much for that. He's very kind and caring, really.'

'You're as soft as he is,' retorted Nell, but it was not said unkindly. 'That young boy is probably busy robbing other people at this very moment. Where's Nathan now?'

Dewi lost much of her sparkle as she replied, 'He's taken the Duke to Golant with him, to see Abigail Penhaligan. Couldn't wait to go and see her. He was up at the crack of dawn and the

167

pair of them left while I was still giving Beville his breakfast.'

'Never mind, it was you he took to the theatre, not Abigail. Did he enjoy it too?'

'I thought so at the time. Walking back to the inn I took his arm and for a while I felt very close to him, Nell. I thought he felt it too.' Dewi shrugged. 'I was fooling myself. I should have known better. Nathan's an important man. A friend of Royal Princes. He owns a manor house, lands, and a fishing fleet. He'll marry Abigail – that's if *she's* got any sense.'

'What would you do if he did?' Nell put the question almost casually as she pounded away at the dough on the table in front of her.

Dewi looked unhappy. 'I think I'd have to leave Polrudden, Nell. It doesn't make sense, I know, but I couldn't remain in the house if Nathan got married. Come to that, I doubt if a new wife will want me around. She'll have her own ideas about bringing up children. Have children of her own too, no doubt.'

Nell glanced up sympathetically. Wiping her hands on the apron she wore, she said, 'I need to leave this dough to rise for a while. Let's have a cup of something while you tell me all about the Duke of Clarence. I hope Tom and I will have an opportunity of meeting him while he's here.'

'It will raise Nathan's standing with Abigail's father like nothing else could. Nathan and the Duke have sailed to Fowey on board the *Sir Beville*. I doubt if we'll see anything of either of them for the rest of the day.'

Immediately upon his return to Polrudden, Nathan had sent a letter with one of his grooms to Sir Kenwyn Penhaligan. The letter explained that the Duke of Clarence was on a private visit to Polrudden and had expressed a wish to visit Sir Kenwyn's house at Golant to speak with Henry Penhaligan. Nathan hinted that it was in connection with East India Company business, with whose affairs the Duke was closely associated.

As the *Sir Beville* sailed through the spectacular Fowey harbour heading upriver to Golant, a number of spectators lined the river-bank. By the time the Golant tidal shoreline came into view it was evident that, private visit or not, Sir Kenwyn had no intention of allowing the occasion to pass without due recognition. Local militiamen were drawn up on the quayside in immaculate order and the small group of officials gathered here included Cornwall's High Sheriff, the militia commander, magistrates, town mayor from nearby Fowey, and a number of Members of Parliament and other local dignitaries. Behind them stood an impressive carriage. Borrowed for the occasion from a great house forty miles away, it had been driven through the night to convey the Royal Duke a few hundred yards from the river's edge up the hill to Sir Kenwyn's house.

'Not quite what I was expecting,' commented the Duke of Clarence drily. 'Nevertheless it is preferable to my reception from Sir Christopher Hawkins.' Minutes later he was stepping ashore to planking laid across the mud of the creek with all the dignity and graciousness expected from a son of the ruling monarch.

Nathan followed the Duke along the line of dignitaries, gravely shaking the hands of men who had been foremost among those who turned their backs upon him at Sir Kenwyn's recent ball.

The brief official welcome at an end, the Duke of Clarence, Sir Kenwyn and Nathan entered the carriage and set off for the Penhaligan Manor.

'I hope you did not mind the official welcome, Your Royal Highness,' said Sir Kenwyn, apologetically. 'But a visit to Cornwall by a member of the Royal Family provides a rare opportunity for the county publicly to state its loyalty. I felt it was something to be encouraged.'

'Of course,' agreed the Duke amiably. 'But that's an end to it, I trust?'

'Er, well . . . almost.' Sir Kenwyn squirmed a little. 'I have arranged for a few prominent members of our little community to join us for lunch.'

'I'm afraid they'll need to wait until I have completed my business with your brother. I must return to London tomorrow and I have promised the directors of the East India Company I will have a reply for them.'

Sir Kenwyn was beside himself with curiosity. Why should the Duke of Clarence have travelled all the way to Cornwall to speak to his brother on behalf of the Company? It had to be a matter of great importance, yet he could not imagine what it might be.

'Of course. My guests will be delighted to await your convenience, Your Royal Highness.'

Any hopes Sir Kenwyn entertained of eliciting an explanation from Nathan when they reached his home were dashed immediately by Abigail. The three Penhaligan girls, accompanied by the Reverend Hugh Cremyll, were introduced to the Duke who took an immediate interest in the eldest of the three sisters.

'Ah! So *you're* the young lady I've been hearing so much about lately. Now I've seen you I can understand why. You're a very attractive girl, my dear. Most attractive.' His gallantry coming to the fore, he added, 'But you're all so attractive I don't know how any young man could put any one of you before the others.'

Turning to Henry Penhaligan, he said, 'Your wife must have been a rare beauty, sir.'

The introductions over, Sir Kenwyn offered the Duke refreshments, but they were declined. He was eager to begin his talk with Henry Penhaligan.

While Sir Kenwyn was showing his brother and the Duke to the room set aside for them, Abigail led Nathan away, ignoring

Lydia's protests that she wanted to hear about London and learn what Nathan had done while he was there.

Abigail took Nathan to the orangery where they had spoken on his last visit to Golant. Once here she turned to him eagerly. 'Nathan, what is happening? Why has the Duke come here with you? Why does he wish to speak to Father – and what of Rao? You gave him my letter? How is he? Did you have an opportunity to speak with him?'

'Find us a place to sit and I'll tell you everything that happened at Bushy Park. It's all very exciting. I only hope it is what you really want. First of all, your prince is well and is as eager to have news of you as you are to hear of him . . .'

Nathan told Abigail all that had occurred at Bushy Park. Long before he finished speaking she was on her feet pacing up and down the orangery before him.

When his narrative ended she came to a stop in front of him and held out her hands to him. When he grasped them, she said, 'All this is really happening? The Company is actually in *favour* of Prince Rao marrying me?'

'That's why the Duke of Clarence has come to Cornwall – and it's proof of how important the whole issue is to everyone. The outcome is very much up to your father now. The Company is hoping the Duke will be able to persuade him to accept their offer – but most important of all, how do you feel about it?'

Abigail suddenly dropped to a seat opposite Nathan. Keeping his hands clutched tightly in hers, she spoke in a voice that was choked with emotion. 'How do you *think* I feel, Nathan? I love Rao. I have since the very first time we met. But I never for a moment believed anything would come of it. How could it? He is . . . was, heir to the throne of a rich and powerful state. I wasn't even certain that he really loved me in the same way – until now. To give up his right to the throne of Jhalapur for me! How much more proof could I need? I feel the whole world has suddenly come to life again. So much of it is due to you, Nathan. You know, if I didn't have Rao, I might easily have fallen in love with you.'

He tried to pass off her statement as a joke. 'Here I've been, working hard to smooth the path for you and Rao, and now you tell me that if I hadn't worked so hard I might have stood a chance with you. What sort of a thank you is that?'

'A heartfelt thank you. You are a very dear friend. One who cares enough for me to want to help. Without you I would have gone out of my mind with worry by now. I am grateful, Nathan. Truly I am.'

Abigail grasped his hands more tightly. 'But I'm not the girl for you, Nathan. My heart is in India. It always will be. Rao is aware of this. So too is my father, but he refuses to face the fact.'

Releasing his hands, she suddenly stood up. 'I fear that even the Duke of Clarence will find it difficult to convince my father that I should be allowed to marry Rao. It is too great a leap for an Englishman's mind to make.'

'The Duke has a great prize to offer your father in return for his consent. Sikar is a very important state in the Company's scheme of things. His appointment as Resident there would be recognition of his undoubted ability. Add to this having a Maharaja for a son-in-law – plus an immediate baronetcy. It's a very tempting offer for any man.'

'It's the son-in-law part that will prove difficult for him to accept. There is a great deal of prejudice among officials of the Company in their dealings with Indians.'

'I don't doubt it. I admit to qualms about the situation myself, if only because of the religious differences. But wealth and position will ultimately overcome the prejudice of others. I feel certain your father will be more concerned with the implications of such a marriage for *you*. What if Rao takes other wives? He's fully entitled to do so under Hindu law. Indeed, it will be expected of him. Then there are the duties expected of you. What if he dies before you? To contemplate *suttee* is out of the question. Nevertheless I understand it's part of Hindu tradition.'

Nathan was talking of the barbarous Hindu practice in which, when a great man died, his wife was expected to throw herself upon his funeral pyre and accompany him on his journey in the world beyond life.

'Rao and I have discussed both these customs. He will not take other wives. I have his solemn promise. He says he does not want other wives. Quite apart from his personal feelings it only leads to intrigues and constant resentment. As for *suttee*, he is as opposed to its practice as I am. It was his intention to have the practice banned when he became Maharaja of Jhalapur. He will no doubt do the same in Sikar.'

'If you're confident he'll keep his word and you both love each other, I can only offer my blessing and hope your future will be very happy.'

'I wish the same for you, Nathan. You'll find the one for you – and I don't think you'll need to look very far for her.'

'Oh! Do you have someone in mind?'

Nathan thought she was referring to Lydia. He was taken aback by her next words.

'Yes, Beville's governess. It will no doubt set tongues wagging, but you once told me they would wag no matter what you did. You're advising me to flout convention. I suggest you do the same.'

'You're echoing the words of my sister, Nell. She thinks there's no one quite like Dewi.'

171

'Then take notice of what we say. We both care about you.'

'Thank you, but for today I think we should concentrate on your problems and hope the Duke of Clarence can win your father over.'

'He *must*. It would be unbelievably cruel for matters to have progressed this far only to have my own father dash all my hopes for the future.'

'Don't worry. The Duke is a very persuasive man and there's a great deal at stake for everyone. He'll convince your father. I'd wager Polrudden on the outcome.'

Chapter 34

By mid-afternoon it seemed Henry Penhaligan might be proving resistant to the persuasive powers of even such a personage as the Royal Duke. Both men were still closeted in Sir Kenwyn's study.

The guests who had been invited to lunch with the Duke of Clarence were milling around in the drawing-room of the large house. Doing their best not to appear anxious for their promised lunch, they consoled grumbling stomachs with prodigious quantities of wines and spirits ferried from the cellar of their host.

With Nathan's help, Abigail managed to keep a degree of control over her own nerves. Then, at three o'clock, a servant hurried to the drawing-room to summon her to the study.

The blood drained from her face and for a few moments Nathan feared she might faint.

'Why do you think they want to speak to me?'

'There's only one way you're going to find the answer to that,' replied Nathan, gently. 'Would you like me to come with you?'

Colour began to return to Abigail's cheeks. Taking a deep breath, she shook her head. 'I'll be all right now . . . but pray for me a little, Nathan. No, not a little. Pray very hard!'

Abigail had not left Nathan's side since his arrival at the house. For much of the time they had avoided the company of others. Now, at Abigail's sudden and unexpected departure, Nathan was immediately accosted by Lydia, Sofia and Sir Kenwyn, with Hugh Cremyll in close attendance.

'What *is* going on, Nathan?' 'Why all this mystery?' 'Please tell us, you must know.'

'You'll all know, in good time.' Nathan felt he could not give them an explanation until a decision had been made by Abigail's father.

'It must be something of great importance for the Duke of Clarence to travel all the way from London to speak to Henry. Surely you can tell us *something*?'

'I can only say that the Duke is on a private visit to Polrudden, but has agreed to speak to your brother on behalf of the East India Company directors.'

'Are they going to offer Daddy another appointment with the Company?' The question came from Lydia. 'Will it be in England, or do they want him to return to India?'

'I would say it is highly probable they want him to return to the Company.'

'But where?' Lydia persisted.

'I've said all I can for the moment. Anything more must come from your father.'

'Is all this mystery really necessary, Nathan? Surely the Duke and Henry could at least take a break for some lunch? My guests will be fainting from hunger if they have to wait for very much longer.'

Sir Kenwyn could see the social occasion he had so hurriedly organised becoming a drunken débâcle. His cellar was depleting at an alarming rate.

'Your brother and the Duke are discussing a very delicate and important matter. As soon as it's been resolved I'm certain you'll be the first to learn all about it, Sir Kenwyn. I regret that I'm unable to tell you more.'

'Well, I hope they come out for lunch soon. Another half-an-hour and everything will be totally ruined.'

Still grumbling, Sir Kenwyn went off to offer more excuses to his hungry guests, leaving Nathan to parry the more insistent questioning of Lydia and Sofia.

The meeting between the Duke of Clarence and Henry Penhaligan broke up fifteen minutes later. One look at Abigail's face was enough to tell Nathan that the East India Company, represented by the Duke, had won the day.

Nathan had a moment of sadness for what might have been. He had lost Abigail, yet her happiness was so much in evidence that he knew he had been right to help her achieve her aim. He could not, and would not, say anything to spoil this moment for her.

The arrival of the Duke of Clarence was the signal for Sir Kenwyn's guests to commence their social jockeying. Abigail took the opportunity to take Nathan by the hand and lead him away from the others, ignoring their protests at being kept in the dark. Leaving the house, they returned to the orangery.

The moment they were lost from view amidst the greenery, Abigail flung her arms about Nathan and gave him a kiss that would have outraged the most broad-minded of Sir Kenwyn's guests.

When she released him, Nathan said shakily, 'I assume by your exuberance that your father has agreed to your marrying your Indian prince?'

'Yes!' Abigail took his hand, but she found it difficult to remain still. 'And Father will be returning to India, taking the girls with him. He will represent the Company as their Resident in Sikar. He's to be given a baronetcy right away – the Duke of Clarence

174

said that is your idea. Father is thrilled about it.'

A more sober note came into her voice. 'But we mustn't tell anyone what is happening until word is received from India that the Company's solution is acceptable to everyone. Even worse, I'm forbidden to see Rao until such confirmation is received.'

She let out a sudden wail that startled him. 'Oh, Nathan! How am I going to keep it a secret for all that time and not see Rao when he's so close and I love him so? I shall burst trying to keep everything to myself!'

'You've been nursing an impossible dream for a long time, Abigail. Now a miracle has happened and the dream is almost yours. You'll only need to keep your secret for a month or two at the most. Enjoy that time. It's going to be the last opportunity you'll ever have to lead your own life. Once the secret is out you'll need to fight off all the people who want to know more about you. You and Rao. Then you'll be off to India and a life spent in a palace, surrounded by servants and guards. I have no doubt at all that you'll be very happy with Rao, but your life is never going to be the same again.'

'I've thought of all that, Nathan. Very many times. But it's what I want more than anything else in the whole world. It's what I've wanted from the very first time Rao and I met.'

'You've flouted all the rules of convention, but I don't think the outcome is in any doubt now, Abigail. You've won. You've got what you set your heart on. I admire you greatly for that. I hope you'll always be very happy. You deserve to be.'

Nathan gave a strange, rather lost gesture that was half admiration, half resignation. 'I envy Rao. Not for his riches, or the power he'll wield in this new state of his, but because he's got you – and because I know in my heart he deserves you. There can't be many men in the world prepared to give up all that Rao has for the woman he loves.'

Chapter 35

The Duke of Clarence left Cornwall by carriage the day after his meeting with Henry Penhaligan. His visit had been highly successful. He had persuaded Abigail's father to accept the East India Company's offer. By so doing, it was to be hoped he had resolved the crisis involving the Indian states of Jhalapur and Sikar.

With the Duke's departure invitations began to flow in to Polrudden. Nathan was invited to parties, luncheons and functions of every variety. He refused them all.

It was not that he was particularly anti-social. He still regarded himself as a working man and had a great deal to occupy his time.

One of his first, more unpalatable tasks was to discipline two of his young employees. One was a stable lad named Walter Tripp. The other was Sally Wicks.

Will Hodge, the Polrudden head groom, had caught the young couple making love in the hayloft above the stables. He took them both to Nathan who was in his study trying to bring the Polrudden ledger up to date.

'I wouldn't normally have troubled you at all,' Will Hodge apologised. 'I'd have kicked the boy's backside and had a word in the ear of the girl's father. But it's the second time I've caught young Sally – and not with the same boy, either.'

'I see.' Nathan did his best to look stern as he eyed the young couple standing before him, but he could not help thinking how absurdly young they both were to be standing before him accused of such conduct. The boy especially seemed ready to burst into tears at any moment and it was to him Nathan spoke first. 'Is there anything you'd like to say to me, Walter?'

'I'm sorry, Mr Jago, truly I am. I've never done nothing like this before and I won't do it again, I promise. It was just . . . I . . . I'm sorry. I really am.'

'And you, Sally? What do you have to say for yourself?'

'Nothing.'

Nathan waited, but it seemed that Sally Wicks meant exactly what she said. She had nothing to say to him.

'Do you both realize the consequences of what you were doing? The ruin of both your lives and the disgrace to your families if Sally were to become pregnant? You would either have to marry, or face the possibility of one or other of you going to prison. Magistrate Tremayne is notorious for his severity in dealing with bastardy cases that come before him.'

'It won't happen again, Mr Jago, I swear. Please . . . give me another chance.'

The contemptuous glance Sally threw at Walter Tripp was not missed by Nathan. He realised too that much of the young man's distress stemmed from his concern that he might be dismissed from Polrudden.

Walter supported a widowed mother who suffered from the wasting disease. Nathan also suspected that the brief encounter in the hayloft had been Sally's idea. It heightened the suspicion he had entertained since London that Sally's account of the incident involving the two militiamen had not been entirely truthful.

Nathan looked questioningly at Will Hodge and the groom said, 'I don't have any complaints about Walter's work. Until now he's been a good, well-behaved lad. Like I said, if it hadn't been the second time I'd caught Sally in the hayloft with my lads I'd have dealt with it in my own way. As it was, I couldn't bring her to you and not him.'

'That's true. All right, Walter. I confess that I'm very disappointed in you, but I'm prepared to give you another chance. Just make sure you don't get into any more trouble of any kind. Do you understand?'

When Walter Tripp had left the study, stuttering his gratitude, Nathan turned his attention to Sally. 'What am I going to do with you? When I took you on at Polrudden I expected you to settle in and become a trusted and valued employee. To share the responsibility with Dewi of taking care of Beville and becoming a useful member of my household.'

Sally's chin rose defiantly and suddenly she snapped, 'Why all this fuss because I went up in the hayloft with a stable boy? It would have been different if I'd done it in a house with a gentleman, like Dewi does, wouldn't it?'

Sally's unexpected outburst rocked Nathan and he demanded, 'What's that supposed to mean?'

'Don't you know? They do down at Pentuan. Anyway, you don't need to tell me to leave. I'm going anyway. I'm fed up being told what to do all the time by *her*, when she's no better than me.'

With this parting shot, Sally turned and stalked from the room before either man could make a move to stop her.

Frowning at the head groom, Nathan asked, 'What was all that about, Will? Was it just a spiteful outburst or are there some malicious rumours running around the village?'

'I don't know. Not that I'd believe Sally Wicks. She'd say anything about anybody right now. She was defiant enough to you, but she's really very upset at being caught and having to leave Polrudden. When her father hears of this she'll take a thrashing that will put a stop to her goings-on for a week or two. But rumours are like weeds. Once they get to spreading they choke the life out of the truth. I'll find out if there are any going about and put a stop to them.'

Despite the absurdity of Sally Wicks's accusation, Nathan found it impossible to settle down to work at the ledger when Will Hodge had left the study. Each time he tried he found his thoughts sliding away. Having to dismiss an employee was a rare event at Polrudden and, as a nursemaid to Beville, Sally Wicks had been closer than most.

Yet it was not her going that kept invading his thoughts, but the allegations she had made against Dewi. Nathan tried hard to dismiss them, as Will Hodge had suggested, but they continued to trouble him.

Eventually, he gave up any thought of work. Dewi was at Venn Farm with Beville. He would go there and speak to her – not about Sally's wild accusations, of course, but to tell her that her assistant had been dismissed.

Dewi was taking lessons in one of the farm rooms. When Nell led Nathan there she was teaching not only Beville but Christian, Nell and Tom's oldest child, together with five children from neighbouring farms.

'I hope you don't mind,' said Dewi as Nathan looked about the room in surprise. 'It seemed just as easy to teach seven as only two. Beville won't suffer by it. In fact he enjoys proving how much better he is than the others. He has lessons every day. I take classes here only three times a week.'

Looking at Dewi, Nathan realised there was much that went on with this girl that he knew nothing about. 'I think it's an excellent idea. Children who live on farms tend to miss out on any schooling that's arranged at the chapel in the village. But I've come to Venn to talk about some bother that Sally's been involved with.'

'What has she been up to?' Dewi spoke sharply. 'I left her with instructions to tidy up the nursery and to sort any clothes that are too small for Beville. If she's let me down again she'll be in trouble when I get back to Polrudden.'

'Sally won't be there,' said Nathan, bluntly. 'Can we go outside and talk about it?'

'You go off with Nathan,' said Nell. 'I've got milk and saffron cake in the kitchen. That will keep the children quiet for a while. If young Sally Wicks has left Polrudden for good she'll be no loss. I told Nathan when you first came here what I thought of *her*.'

'Has Sally gone for good?'

Dewi asked the question as Nathan ducked out of the low

farmhouse door into yard. It was early October now and with a thin but discernible mist rolling in off the sea it was decidedly chilly.

'Yes.' As they walked up and down outside the house Nathan told Dewi what had happened.

'I should have seen this coming,' she said. 'I *did* see it coming. Sally's always been far too interested in boys, but I thought I could sort her out without bothering you. I was wrong. I'm sorry.'

As Dewi spoke, Nathan thought again of Sally's wild and vague accusation against her. He refused to believe there was any truth in her words . . . and yet, Dewi was an attractive girl. The awareness had remained with him since the evening when he had taken her to the theatre in London. It was not beyond the realm of possibility that someone should fall for her. Yet who could it be?

Dewi shivered and Nathan was immediately solicitous. 'I'm sorry. You're not dressed to be outside in this weather. I wasn't thinking.'

'It's all right,' Dewi smiled at him. 'It's nice to get a little bit of fresh air after being in a room with seven young children. But what will you do now? Will you get someone in to take Sally's place, or not bother?'

'I think you need someone to help you, but it might not be such a simple matter to find a good, trustworthy girl. What do you think?'

'As it happens there's someone who I think will be ideal to take Sally's place. Francis Hanna's wife Pippa was talking to me the other day. She said she'd like to work with children and asked how she should set about finding such work. She's a bright girl and very pleasant. I doubt if you'll do any better. You can ask Nell about her if you like, they've known each other for a long time. Cook likes Pippa too – and she isn't the easiest person in the world to please!'

'All right, speak to her when you return to Polrudden. She can begin work right away, if she's agreeable.'

'You won't regret it, Nathan. She can read and write and is quick at figures. She'll be able to help me with Beville's schooling.'

Nathan had the sudden uncomfortable realisation that such a girl might be perfectly capable of standing in for Dewi if she wanted to be elsewhere at any time . . . He dismissed the thought again immediately. If it had not been for Sally Wicks's angry outburst he would never have had such an idea in the first place.

Despite his resolve to put Sally's resentful accusation out of his mind, it returned to Nathan when Dewi had taken her charges back to the impromptu classroom. He was in the kitchen with Nell. His sister was clearing away after the children and was reminding Nathan that she had told him of Sally Wicks's character many months before.

179

'From what I hear she behaved completely in character while you were all in London. She's a trull that one, make no mistake about it. You're well rid of her.'

'Probably, but before she left Polrudden she accused Dewi of behaving just as badly – but with a "gentleman"!'

Nell was as shocked as Nathan had been. 'I said she's a trull. She's a *lying* trull at that.'

Nell looked sharply at her brother. 'You don't believe a word of it?'

He shrugged. 'I don't rate Sally's honesty any higher than her morals, but she says they're talking about Dewi in the village. I was wondering whether you've heard anything?'

'I haven't – and if I do I'll put a stop to such talk right away. You get something like that repeated often enough and folk who ought to know better begin to believe it. Now, *you* might have nothing better to do than stand around repeating gossip. *I've* to to clear this kitchen up and get dinner ready before I go out to milk the cows and feed the calves . . .'

Nell had rejected the rumours about Dewi out of hand. Nevertheless, she was unusually thoughtful as she busied herself cleaning the farmhouse kitchen. She had not completed the task by the time Dewi ended her lessons. She gave a groan of frustration as children erupted from their room and made for the garden via the kitchen.

'I'll make a cup of tea then give you a hand before returning to Polrudden, Nell.'

'That sounds a wonderful idea, Dewi. The kettle's already boiled. By the time it's made I'll be almost finished here.'

Dewi made the tea, poured it into two cups then sank into one of the kitchen chairs, saying, 'Some days children are harder work than others. This is one of the hard days.'

'You still happy at Polrudden?' Nell threw the question over her shoulder as she stowed a brush into a cupboard in a corner of the kitchen.

'Happier than ever now Sally's gone. That girl worried me. It was nothing I could really put my finger on, you understand, but I could never relax when she and Beville were out of my sight. I don't know what it was. I just had a *feeling* about the girl, that's all.'

'Funny how you get that way about people, isn't it?' Nell took a seat across the table from Dewi and pulled a cup of tea towards her. 'Get feelings about them, I mean. I had the feeling as soon as I saw *you* that you were right for Beville – and for our Nathan, come to that.'

'Now, Nell, you're not going to start that talk again, I hope?' Dewi eyed the other woman warily across the thick rim of the cup she held to her lips.

'I've never put an end to it,' confessed Nell, cheerfully. 'That's why I've told our Nathan that the rumour he's heard about you is a load of nonsense.'

'A rumour about *me*?' Dewi lowered the cup so swiftly she spilled some of its contents in her lap. Placing the cup on the table she took the wet cloth that Nell passed to her and began rubbing the stained spot vigorously. 'The chance of doing anything to justify rumour would be a fine thing! What am I supposed to have been up to?'

'Been in some gentleman's house with him, it seems. When Nathan was telling young Sally off about the way she'd behaved she complained that nothing was said to you when you did the same thing with a "gentleman" in his house. Said the rumour was all over Pentuan, so it must have originated down there.'

'Well, of all the nerve! I can't think how such a rumour could have got started. The only times I go down to the village are when I take Beville. Anyway, there's no one down there that Sally would refer to as a gentleman . . .'

Dewi gave a sudden start and broke off what she was saying.

'What is it, Dewi? Have you thought of something?'

'Indeed I have. I went to Columb Hawkins's house when he first arrived and had the bridge closed. I suppose he could loosely be called "a gentleman", although that isn't what I called him.'

Dewi related the reason for her visit to Columb Hawkins's house and told Nell of the outcome.

'He got exactly what he deserved,' said Nell, outraged. 'It's a good job our Nathan never got to hear of it. He'd have given Hawkins a thrashing he would never have forgotten.'

'That's exactly what I was trying to prevent,' said Dewi. 'There's been bad blood between the two of them since the night of Sir Kenwyn Penhaligan's ball. I thought that if Nathan went to see him about stopping the villagers crossing the bridge there might be more serious trouble between them.'

'And our Nathan knew nothing about it?' Nell smiled at Dewi. 'It's no use you trying to tell me you're not soft on him, Dewi Morgan. Why else would you risk your reputation in such a way? But what we've got to do now is find out who saw you and started the rumour going the rounds. It shouldn't be hard to put a stop to it before it grows too much in the passing-on.'

'I shouldn't bother about it. I just went upstairs to fetch your Christian's coat before he went out. From the bedroom window I could see some riders going along the lane. It was too far away to be absolutely certain, but I think it was those Penhaligan girls. With that Abigail about the house, Nathan is not going to bother himself with rumours about me.'

'I don't know about that, Dewi, but you've given me an idea. Miss Abigail Penhaligan can't spend twenty-four hours of every day at Polrudden and it will do our Nathan good to have something else to think about when she's not there. We might just allow these rumours to spread their wings and fly around a little before we shoot them down once and for all.'

Chapter 36

After Nathan's return from the voyage to London, the visits to Polrudden of Abigail and her sisters had assumed a regular pattern once more. Soon after their arrival Lydia and Sofia would ride on to St Ewe to visit Hugh Cremyll, leaving Abigail behind. At some time in the afternoon the two younger sisters would return to Polrudden, accompanied by Hugh, and they would all have tea together.

It was quite apparent to everyone who observed them together that the relationship between Lydia and the Vicar of St Ewe had blossomed into something more than a casual friendship. Yet Lydia seemed embarrassed by any show of affection between them when they were in Nathan's presence. It was as though she felt she was being disloyal to him. It seemed not to matter that others assumed a romantic interest between Nathan and the oldest Penhaligan sister.

On this occasion, when Dewi had seen the sisters passing Venn Farm on their way to Polrudden, they were accompanied by Sir Kenwyn.

It was a cold, blustery day. Not the weather for riding seven or eight miles to pay a social call. Nathan was not at all surprised when Sir Kenwyn declared he had business to discuss. The baronet suggested the girls should *all* ride on to the Vicarage at St Ewe.

Abigail did as her uncle wished, albeit sulkily. Before riding away she demanded that their business be concluded by mid-afternoon as *she* had something of importance she wished to discuss with Nathan.

Waving farewell to the three girls and their accompanying groom, Sir Kenwyn stamped his feet unnecessarily enthusiastically upon the mat inside the small outer hall of Polrudden. He bemoaned his fate in having to share his own house with three such young and lively women.

'I always thought my wife and I were unlucky not to have children, you know,' he confided to Nathan. 'Thought it would have been splendid to be able to pass my baronetcy on to my own son. Now I'm not so certain. What if they'd all been daughters, eh? Life's not your own with so many young women about the house. They're constantly demanding attention, or sulking because you haven't read their thoughts and given them something they've never asked for – or even hinted they wanted.'

As he and Nathan passed through the inner hall, Sir Kenwyn stopped to shrug off his heavy riding coat. 'They're all being so damned mysterious too. I know Henry has been offered some high office in India but, in my opinion, there's far more behind it than anyone is saying. Even an old fool like me can see *that*. But will they tell me what it's all about? No, not a single word. So today I'm getting my own back on all of 'em. They know I'm here to speak to you on a matter of importance, but I refuse to tell 'em a word of what it's about. Let 'em sweat on it, I say – although I'm given to understand that "sweat" is not a word you use when you're talking about young girls. That's another thing! I haven't been able to enjoy a good cuss at anyone since they came to Golant. I haven't been so damned screwed-down since I was a boy at school!'

'What is this deep secret you've come to discuss with me?' Nathan smiled at the thought of Sir Kenwyn having to watch his manners and language in the privacy of his own home. It was hardly in keeping with his reputation as an autocratic magistrate and land owner.

'Ah, yes! Well, it's something I've mentioned to you before, my boy. This time it's come from Earl Plucknett. He's an influential member of the Whig Party in London. As you probably know he's a friend of the Duke of Clarence. He mentions that you met when you were in London, at Bushy Park. It seems they are all in agreement. Earl Plucknett has suggested I invite you to stand for Parliament. The candidate at Tregony has died after a long illness. Earl Plucknett feels you would stand a very good chance of taking the seat in the election being called there. I agree, and have recently bought enough property in the area to influence the outcome of any election.'

Nathan was taken by surprise by Sir Kenwyn's suggestion. He had never taken the earlier remarks of the baronet and Earl Plucknett with any seriousness. Consequently, he had given the matter no thought whatsoever. He told Sir Kenwyn so.

'Think about it during the course of the next few days. I mentioned it to you before because I sincerely believe you are the type of man we need in Parliament. Someone who understands the people. Times are changing rapidly in England, but the present government refuses to change with it. They still cling to the past. To a way of life that no longer exists. If they are not very careful the country will go the way of France. It is something we all fear, of course, but the Whigs and Tories have differing ideas on how to avert such a calamity. I, and an increasing number of other responsible people, believe the Whigs are more in touch with the present mood of the country.'

'I couldn't possibly argue with you, Sir Kenwyn. I have already confessed to Earl Plucknett that I have no knowledge whatsoever of politics.'

'Couldn't be better, my boy! You'll enter the Commons with no preconceived loyalties other than a sense of duty towards your constituency. *Those* are the politics of the future. While we're on the subject of loyalties . . . don't you think it's time you told me something about this mystery surrounding Henry and his appointment with the East India Company?'

'You must ask your brother about that, Sir Kenwyn. I'm sure he'll tell you everything when he feels the time is right.'

'I hope so. Mind you, I don't think he's said anything to those girls of his – unless Abigail knows something. Lydia and Sofia certainly don't and it will no doubt affect their future far more than it does mine. Damned peculiar way of going on, if you ask me.'

'Never mind, Sir Kenwyn. Come inside and have a drink while you tell me more of what's involved in becoming a Member of Parliament.'

The three Penhaligan girls did not return to Polrudden that morning. After lunching with him, Nathan accompanied Sir Kenwyn to the harbour at Pentuan to check on progress.

There seemed to be a great deal of activity around the site but very little noticeable progress. Sir Kenwyn was less than enthusiastic about what he saw. He would have liked to discuss the work with Columb Hawkins, but Sir Christopher's nephew was elsewhere.

Walking away from the harbour office, Sir Kenwyn said gloomily, 'I can't see the harbour being completed in a twelve-month and we'll be lucky to see a return on it in much less than three years. What do you think, Nathan?'

'Much the same as you. It will be three years before there's any suggestion of a profit – and the cost will be at least three times as much as was originally estimated.'

Sir Kenwyn whistled. 'That won't please the London shareholders. They'll expect a very good return for such money.'

'According to my fishermen the harbour is never going to make anyone rich. The river brings tons of silt down from the clay and tin workings on the moor above St Austell. They say the planned jetty is too short to prevent the silt drifting across and blocking the channel to the harbour. But, of course, my men are fishermen, not harbour engineers.'

'No doubt their opinion is far more honest because of it. Do you think Hawkins is aware of this?'

'He wouldn't pass the time of day with my men, but he's not a fool. He'll have taken advice on all aspects of the project.

Frankly, I don't see what he hopes to gain from having a harbour built here.'

'A great deal more than any of his fellow shareholders. With his own harbour he could drastically cut the cost of shipping his clay. If others saw Pentuan harbour working well they might shift their business here too and the harbour dues would add to his profit.'

When the two men reached Polrudden Sir Kenwyn stopped and looked out towards the sea. 'There's another thing. If the channel keeps silting up, the other shareholders would probably decide to cut their losses and sell their shares for whatever they will fetch. A man like Sir Christopher would buy them up, extend the jetty far enough to eliminate the silt problem – and what does he have? I'll tell you – he owns a profitable, working harbour, most of the cost of which has been paid for with the money of others.'

'Would Sir Christopher do that?'

'If he can get away with it – and I'm afraid I can see no way to stop him. We could suggest extending the jetty now, but that would mean calling in even more money. I doubt if anyone will be prepared to commit such an amount of capital. I for one am prepared to cut my losses right now and get out, much as I would like to see the harbour scheme succeed. I think we should call an extraordinary meeting of the shareholders, send for Columb Hawkins, and try to establish the facts.'

'All right, but don't do anything with your shares before you've spoken to me. If you decide to sell I'll buy them at a fair price. Whatever the outcome of this project it will affect me and the people of Pentuan. I want to retain some say in what happens, at least.'

The arrival of the three Penhaligan girls with Hugh Cremyll brought their discussion to an end. There were squeals of delight and excitement when Sir Kenwyn disclosed he was putting Nathan up for election to Parliament and he was subjected to warm and exuberant congratulations.

They insisted he bring up champagne from the Polrudden cellar and the celebrations went on well into the evening.

186

Chapter 37

Nathan's announcement that he would be standing for Parliament received a mixed reception from his own family. It was the morning after Sir Kenwyn's visit and Josiah Jago was breakfasting at Venn Farm when Nathan arrived to break his news.

Nell was so excited she hugged her brother to her, oblivious of the fork and carving knife she held in her hands.

'Your hair smells of cooking fat,' he complained as he struggled free.

'And so would yours if you had to cook for a hungry family like mine. I suppose you want some breakfast too, or is it beneath the dignity of a future Member of Parliament to eat breakfast with his poor relations in a farmhouse kitchen?'

'It's my second breakfast of the day, but I'll need to build up my strength if I'm to fight an election. Sir Kenwyn believes I'll probably be standing in opposition to Columb Hawkins.'

'I'm glad *somebody* is,' said Nell. 'You'll beat him too. He's not the sort of man we want representing anyone in Parliament.'

'It will make a pleasant change to have someone in Parliament who knows something about the problems of the small farmer,' declared Tom Quicke as he speared a piece of ham thick enough to have soled a farmer's boot. 'It's getting so a man doesn't know when he tills a crop whether it's going to be worth his while reaping it.'

Preacher Josiah Jago provided a dissenting note in the general approval for Nathan's prospective parliamentary career.

'Are you quite certain you're doing the right thing, Nathan? You'll be mixing with *gentlemen* up there in Parliament. Men with unlimited resources. Many of them haven't seen the inside of a church since the day they were baptised. You've had a God-fearing upbringing, even though I don't see much of you inside a chapel these days. But you were born in a poor cottage in Pentuan. It's not good for a man to get too far above his station in life.'

'You said much the same sort of things when I took on Polrudden.' Nathan spoke across the table as he carved himself a slice of ham on the same proportions as that now almost consumed by his brother-in-law. 'That hasn't worked out too badly.'

'All the more reason not to tempt fate yet again,' his father retorted.

'There's another factor to consider.' Nathan sat back to allow Nell to pass two fried eggs over his shoulder to the plate on the table before him. 'If I'm elected to Parliament I'll have an opportunity to do something about all those ideas you're always putting forward. You know, allowing Methodists to control their own Church. Gaining recognition from the government for your Church and the way you want to worship.'

It was an aspect of Nathan's election to Parliament that Josiah Jago had not considered. He lapsed into thoughtful silence as he chewed on his breakfast. Perhaps there might after all be considerable advantages to be gained by having his son in the House of Commons.

'What does Dewi think about all this?' Nell asked as she served up her own breakfast and sat down at the table with the others.

'I haven't said anything to her about it yet,' said Nathan. 'I wanted to tell you first. Anyway, it won't make any difference to Dewi. She'll carry on looking after Beville as she does now.'

'It will make a great deal of difference. If you're going to spend much of your time in London, she'll need to make decisions about Beville without you. It will mean a great deal more responsibility for her.'

'I don't intend spending any more time away from Cornwall than I have to,' declared Nathan. 'I have a fishing business to run and that's still important to me. As for Dewi, well, she's a good sensible girl. I can rely on any decision she makes. Besides, she has Pippa to help her now.'

'What happens if you hear any more rumours about her?' asked Nell, mischievously. 'Won't you spend your time up in London wondering what she's up to, instead of sorting out affairs of the country?'

'What are you talking about, Nell?' Preacher Jago spoke through a mouthful of food. 'What rumours are these?'

When Nell told him of the rumours linking Dewi with 'a gentleman', Josiah Jago so puffed himself up with indignation it looked for a while as though he might burst.

'You should know better than to believe such things,' he said angrily. 'You know what Pentuan is like for gossip.'

'I wouldn't be too sure,' said Nell, innocently. 'Dewi's a very attractive girl, you know. It would hardly be surprising if some gentleman found her attractive. Good luck to her, I say.'

'No.' Josiah Jago shook his head vigorously and the children watched in fascination as a dribble of fat slid down his chin unnoticed. 'I don't believe it. Dewi is a good, God-fearing girl. Had you been in chapel on Sunday you'd have heard her, Nathan. She sings like an angel.'

'I had intended to be there.' Nathan was embarrassed. He had promised to go to hear Dewi singing, but had forgotten. 'I was busy.'

'You're always busy these days. I can't remember when I last saw you in the chapel. If you have time to listen to rumours you could surely find time to spend an hour praising God for all he's given to you. Talking of rumours, it's a good thing you got rid of that Wicks girl . . . Sally. I've heard that she's been coming from Columb Hawkins's house in the dead of night. The rumour-mongers have probably confused her with Dewi. I intend speaking to her about it.'

'And who was it saying no notice should be taken of Pentuan rumours?' retorted Nell. 'You'd be best forgetting all about it. For what it's worth, I've heard she's taken up with one of the sailors from a Welsh coal-boat beached on Pentuan sands. It's serious, so I've been told. Are you going to take that up with her too?'

'Let's forget all about rumours,' said Nathan hastily. He had stood between Nell and their father during many arguments. Both were far too outspoken and stubborn. 'None of you has yet answered my question. Shall, or shall I not, put myself up for a seat in Parliament?'

'It doesn't really matter what we have to say about it,' declared Nell. 'You'll please yourself anyway – and that's exactly the way it should be. It's a very big decision. One that will change your life-style and change things for Beville – and Dewi too.'

Dewi heard the news of Nathan's intention to stand for parliament from Nell, later that same morning. She had come to the farm to take her usual lessons for Beville, Christian Quicke and children from neighbouring farms.

Shrugging her shoulders, she said, 'I doubt if things will change very much for me. I'll just get on with my work and mind my own business, same as now.'

'Nathan will have more need of you than ever before. He'll be spending time in London and will want to know there's someone reliable at Polrudden to take care of Beville.'

'I'm left to take care of Beville on my own most of the time as things are now. Nathan always seems to be with Abigail when he's not working. If she's not at Polrudden with him, he's at Golant with her. Perhaps they *should* get married. At least there'll be one of them at home all the time to run the house. Anyway it doesn't worry me any more.'

'You don't mean that, Dewi. You care for both Nathan and Beville far too much.'

'What difference does that make to anyone? There's nothing either you or I can do now, Nell. Any objection Henry Penhaligan might have to his daughter marrying Nathan will fly out of the window when he becomes a Member of Parliament. She'll no doubt want to make her own arrangements for Beville then.'

'What bothers you more, Dewi? Having someone else looking after Beville, or knowing that Nathan will be married to Abigail?'

'I've told you before, what Nathan does is his own business. I'm thinking of Beville. He was lucky with one stepmother. Abigail Penhaligan doesn't impress me as someone who will put her own interests second to those of a child. She's not right – for either of them.'

'Perhaps our Nathan already knows that. He's no fool, Dewi.'

'Don't they say that the cleverest of men are fools when they fall in love? He's besotted with her. Far too much to think straight about anything.'

Suddenly, Dewi had the look of a thoroughly dejected woman. 'I don't know, Nell. I sometimes think I should never have come to Polrudden. I've grown too fond of everything about the place, and too fond of the people I've come to know. You and Beville especially. It's going to be heartbreaking to have to leave now.'

She managed a bleak smile. 'Talking of Beville, I'd better make a start with the schooling. I don't want his new stepmother saying that he needs an education and packing him off to school right away. He's still too young for that.'

Nell felt deeply sympathetic towards Dewi, but all she could say was, 'Don't give up. There's a great deal can happen between now and a wedding. Please don't give up . . . for everyone's sake.'

Nathan brought up the matter of his proposed new future that evening. He and Dewi were finishing off the meal without Beville. The young boy had felt tired and been taken to his bedroom by Pippa Hanna.

'Yes, I've heard about it. Nell told me when I was at Venn today.'

Sensing a slight chill in her reply, Nathan said, 'I should have spoken to you about it earlier. You're the one who'll be left at Polrudden to take care of Beville on the occasions when I'm in London. I know you have Pippa to help you now, but will you be happy to be left in charge of things?'

'I'm sure I'll be able to cope very well, thank you. That's if you want me to?'

'Of course I do, Dewi.' Something about the way she phrased her reply caused him to add, 'You can't have any doubt about that, surely?'

'I don't know. As a Member of Parliament you'll be a very important man. You might decide you need to make changes in your life. Send Beville to some grand school, perhaps. There would be no need for you to employ a governess then.'

'I have no plans to send Beville away to school for many years yet. To be perfectly honest, I'll be very unhappy when he needs to leave Cornwall and take his place in the world.'

'I'm very pleased to hear it, but there *are* going to be changes in your life and none of us can see into the future now, can we?'

Dewi's Welshness was always more pronounced when she was under any pressure. Although unaware of the reason for it, Nathan found it an endearing trait.

'Well, for as far as I can see into the future, I want you to remain at Polrudden. To give Beville something in his life that doesn't change. But I suppose I shouldn't place such responsibility upon you. After all, you might want to leave Polrudden one day.'

'Oh? And why should I want to do that?'

'You might get married, Dewi. Go off and have a family of your own.'

She had it on her tongue to retort that as governess to Beville she rarely met anyone outside the family circle. Then she remembered the rumour Nathan had repeated to Nell. Dewi had a strong feeling that this lay behind the present conversation.

'Perhaps. As I just said, none of us can look into the future, can we?'

Chapter 38

Tregony, where the by-election was to take place, was a borough some eight miles from Polrudden. Of all its residents, less than two hundred were entitled to cast a vote to elect the man who would represent them in the House of Commons.

Sir Christopher Hawkins believed he owned sufficient property in the borough to ensure the candidate he put up would be elected. It was a lucrative business for the baronet. The late Member for Tregony had paid him six thousand pounds for the privilege of taking his seat in the House of Commons. There had been many others before him who had done the same. It was known that Sir Christopher Hawkins was 'borough-monger' for at least six of the constituencies which sent members to the Parliament in London from Cornwall.

Although Sir Christopher was confident he could ensure his nephew's election, news that Nathan intended standing against Columb came as a shock. It was not that he thought Nathan stood the slightest chance of winning. But, as he told his nephew, such opposition would set a dangerous precedent.

After contemplating the matter for some time, Sir Christopher decided he needed to discuss the matter with Nathan Jago.

He found Nathan in the garden at Polrudden, supervising the cutting up of two large elm trees, brought down in the winter storm of the previous night. It was still squally and the wind coming off the sea had dropped only marginally below gale force. Trying to hold a conversation in such conditions was impossible and the subject of his visit was not something to be shouted on the wind in the presence of the Polrudden gardeners.

Once inside the house, when Sir Christopher had divested himself of his wet riding clothes, Nathan led him to the study. Here, standing in front of a crackling fire with a pot-bellied glass of brandy in his hand, the baronet did his best to assume an air of joviality.

'I expect you're wondering why I've come visiting on such a foul day, eh, Jago?'

'No doubt it has something to do with the election at Tregony?'

If Sir Christopher was startled by Nathan's forthrightness it showed in only the briefest of blinks.

'You're a man after my own heart, Jago. You get straight to the point. No shilly-shallying. I like that. You're quite right, of course, and I'll be as straightforward as yourself. I would like you to stand down.'

'I don't doubt it! Unfortunately, you've had a long ride on a filthy day for nothing, Sir Christopher. I'm not only going to stand for election at Tregony, I intend winning.'

Sir Christopher's fiery nature almost got the better of him, but he held himself carefully in check.

'Look, Jago . . .'

The baronet seemed oblivious of the faint tightening of Nathan's lips at being addressed only by his surname, as though he was one of Sir Christopher's servants.

'. . . I know what's behind all this nonsense. I think it's high time this foolish vendetta between yourself and young Columb was brought to an end. I don't know what it's about, and I don't want to know. All I'm concerned with is the time and money it's wasting – both yours and mine. I'm being perfectly frank with you when I say you haven't a hope in hell of being elected. Tregony is *my* borough. It always has been. Ask any of the householders there. Most are my tenants and they know better than to vote against me.'

'Then you have nothing to fear from my intervention, Sir Christopher. No doubt the voters will enjoy being wined and dined by both of us.'

Once again Sir Christopher needed to keep a tight grip on his temper as Nathan sipped on his own drink.

'Be reasonable, Jago. I've already told you that I'm aware you and Columb don't see eye-to-eye. I'm offering you an opportunity to settle your differences. Meet Columb socially. I'm sure you and he will get along famously.'

'We've already met socially, Sir Christopher, at Sir Kenwyn Penhaligan's ball. Columb brought a number of his young friends along with him. I regret I can't refer to them by name because he failed to introduce either them or himself when they set upon me. Ask him about it.

'However, my standing for election has nothing to do with liking or disliking your nephew. I've been asked to stand at Tregony because it's felt I'll represent the voters in a fair and impartial manner. That's what I intend to do.'

'You'll soon discover the House of Commons is no place for innocents, Jago. It's about power and the rights of those who are most fitted for the task of governing. Men with families who have educated and trained them for high office. Something you can know nothing at all about.'

Aware that his journey to Polrudden had been unsuccessful, Sir Christopher dropped his pretence of affability. 'You're a fool,

Jago. An even bigger fool than I thought you were. I came here prepared to offer you the hand of friendship. I might even have been able to use my influence to gain a parliamentary seat for you elsewhere, in the future. However, you've chosen to ignore my overture. So be it. You'll find that your loss will be considerably more than mine.'

There was nothing more to be said and Nathan sent for a servant to conduct Sir Christopher to the hall. The angry baronet was donning his outdoor clothes when Dewi came down the staircase leading Beville by the hand.

The anger momentarily left Sir Christopher and he gave her a long and calculating look. When Dewi reached the bottom stair, he said, 'Have you given my offer any consideration, young lady?'

'I have.'

'Well, what is it to be? Will you come to work for me at Trewithan?'

'No thank you, Sir Christopher. I'm quite well suited here.' Dewi's reply was deliberately polite.

'You might be well suited now, but my advice to you is to get out while you can. There's more than one way of skinning a cat – and Nathan Jago will be well and truly skinned, I can promise you that.'

The last button on his coat done up, Sir Christopher headed for the door. As the waiting servant swung it open, he stopped and turned to address Dewi once more. 'The offer is still open. I urgently need a housekeeper. Take the post and I'll pay you twice as much as you're getting here. Think about it, girl, before it's too late.'

The baronet had not quite reached the door when Beville said in a very loud voice, 'That's the man who wanted you to share your bed with him, Dewi. Has he got one of his own yet?'

Sir Christopher Hawkins's next call was upon his nephew, at the old Customs house alongside Pentuan's partly constructed harbour. His foul mood was not improved when his bellowing brought a tousle-headed Columb from upstairs, fumbling with the fastenings on his trousers as he hurried to greet his uncle.

'What are you doing in bed at this time? It's mid-afternoon?'

'You've seen the weather for yourself. The men can't work in this. I had a couple of glasses of wine with my lunch and thought I'd catch up on my sleep. Seemed a sensible thing to do.'

'Sensible? Lazy is the word I'd use! Now you're up you can find something for me to drink. We have things to talk about. I've just been up to see Jago, to try to persuade him not to stand for Tregony. The man refuses to see sense. No doubt he's got the backing of Sir Kenwyn Penhaligan. I've heard that Jago and the daughters of Sir Kenwyn's brother are as thick as flies around a blackberry bush. We both know Jago doesn't stand a hope of being elected, but I'm taking no chances. Sir Kenwyn has bought a deal of property in and around Tregony during this past year or two. You're living here in Pentuan – do a bit of digging. Find out what scandals the man has been involved in. There must be something. Dig as deep as you like, but make sure you find *something*, you understand?'

'I understand, Uncle.'

'Good. Now fetch me that drink and I'll be on my way. This is no weather to be travelling after dark. The state of the roads in Cornwall is a disgrace.'

When his uncle had left the old Customs house, Columb Hawkins breathed a great sigh of relief. He had been close to panic when Sir Christopher had asked him why he was in bed in the middle of the afternoon. For a while he had feared his uncle might go upstairs and check for himself.

'It's all right, he's gone now. It's safe to come downstairs.'

'I don't want to come downstairs. You come back up here.'

Now the fear of discovery had passed, Columb's confidence was returning. He smiled as Sally added, 'Are you coming back to bed, or shall I come down there? I might even go outside and dance in the rain, just as I am . . .'

'You'll do no such thing, young lady. You'd catch your death of cold – and I have plans for you.'

'You're all talk, Columb Hawkins. Any hot-blooded man would have been back here in bed with me the moment the door closed behind his uncle. Perhaps I should have invited him up here instead? I've heard he's one of the randiest men in Cornwall.'

'You be careful what you say about him, young lady. Randy my uncle may be, but he's not a man to take a slight lightly.'

As Columb climbed the stairs he winced at the thought of what his uncle would have said had he known that there was a young village girl lying in his bed upstairs while he told his nephew to dig up any scandal concerning Nathan Jago.

Had he come upstairs and discovered Sally Wicks it would have been the end of Columb's prospect of becoming a Member of Parliament. Sally was bright, lively and sexually avaricious. She was also embarrassingly brazen. She would have flouted the relationship in front of Sir Christopher. Columb decided he would need to cool off the affair in the weeks that lay ahead. Until after the election, at least.

He did not know that even as he climbed the stairs heading for the bedroom, Sally was tentatively exploring her stomach with her fingertips. She wondered whether a baby could possibly begin to show after only a few weeks of pregnancy.

Chapter 39

Three weeks after Sir Christopher's visit to Nathan he proved that the threats he had made then were not idle ones.

Humphrey Yates, the tall, serious banker from Mevagissey, toiled up the hill to Polrudden in a small gig, arriving in the first light flurry of the winter's snow.

A servant brought the news of the banker's arrival. Nathan was in the nursery, listening to Beville reading a simple story comprised of mainly three- and four-letter words written out for him by Dewi.

'I put Mr Yates in the downstairs library, sir,' said the servant. 'He looked shrammed with the cold. He's shivering so much he could hardly state his business.' Lowering her voice meaningfully, she added, 'If you asks me, I'd say he's a sick man. He should never be out in weather like we've got today.'

Nathan hurried downstairs to check on the state of his visitor and found the servant had been exaggerating somewhat, but not by very much. Humphrey Yates's complexion was as grey as the sky outside. Although he was still shivering, Nathan suspected that his state was the result of nerves and not caused by the inclement weather he had encountered on the way to Polrudden.

The banker's first words confirmed Nathan's suspicion. 'Mr Jago . . .' Yates stuttered the words. 'I fear I'm the bearer of bad news. Dreadfully bad. I . . . I really don't know how to tell you.'

'Just sit down, Mr Yates. Let me fetch you a drink and you warm yourself by the fire before you try to explain.'

'No, sir. I have never touched alcohol in my life and will not now, though sorely tempted. When I impart my news I doubt very much whether you will wish to waste your hospitality upon me.'

'Allow me to be the judge of that, Mr Yates. What *is* this dire news you bring?'

'I can hardly bring myself to talk of it, sir. My whole world . . . my whole reason for being, all gone. And with it the hopes and fortunes of all those who have trusted me. Forgive me, Mr Jago, I beg you. Please forgive me.'

'What are you trying to tell me, Mr Yates?' With a sinking feeling, he prompted, 'Is it the bank? Has something gone wrong?'

'Wrong? Worse than that, Mr Jago. The Bank of Mevagissey has failed. My bank . . . I'm a ruined man. A disgraced man – and I fear I have dragged you and many, many more down with me. Men and women too, widows many of them. Hundreds of people whose only mistake has been to trust me with their money.'

'How can this be? Such a state of affairs can't have happened overnight. Why haven't you said anything before? Given your investors at least a hint of what might happen to their money?'

'How *could* I?' the stricken banker wailed. 'Have you ever heard of a bank warning people not to invest their money with it because there was a possibility they might lose it? Besides, I never for one moment believed it would ever come to this.

'Times are hard for everyone, Mr Jago. We've just fought a hard war with France. Penniless ex-soldiers roam the countryside like plagues of locusts. Farmers struggling to earn a living are having their crops stolen as fast as they ripen. The government doesn't seem to know what to do about anything . . .'

Humphrey Yates saw Nathan's expression of impatience and brought his tirade to a halt. 'Even so, I would have been all right, Mr Jago, I know I would. It was Sir Christopher Hawkins. If he hadn't withdrawn all his money, my bank would have survived, I know it would. Every penny, he took – and then told me he was calling upon the bank to honour its obligation as a major share-holder in the Pentuan Harbour Company.'

'What obligation?'

Nathan was trying to think of all the implications of the failure of the Bank of Mevagissey. He hoped there might be some way of saving the bank, but if Sir Christopher Hawkins was behind its closure, the baronet would not have struck until he had closed all possible loopholes.

He believed he knew the reason for Sir Christopher's unex-pected move. It would not have been difficult for him to discover that Nathan banked with Humphrey Yates. If he lost all his money and was declared a bankrupt he could not stand for Parliament. It was a Draconian measure, but typical of the ruthlessness of the man.

'Sir Christopher is calling for the shareholders to treble their investment in the company. The cost of the harbour is apparently far higher than was first estimated.'

'Is he within his rights to do this?'

Nathan knew what the answer would be before the banker spoke, but he was buying time. Time to think of some possible solution.

'Yes, Mr Jago. It was in the agreement we all signed. If anyone fails to meet their obligations then their shares will be offered for sale to the other shareholders. That's what I will have to do. But who will want to buy them?'

197

'Mr Yates, I suggest you put aside your aversion to strong drink for tonight. I don't think I've ever seen a man who needed a drink more!'

News of the failure of the Bank of Mevagissey and rumours of Nathan's impending bankruptcy spread to every household within five miles of Pentuan with the inevitability of dawn.

Tom Quicke deserted his farm chores to rush to Polrudden, arriving as Nathan, Dewi and Beville were eating breakfast.

Entering the house through the kitchen, he arrived in the break-fast room unannounced and wearing his working clothes. The muck of the farmyard still clung to his boots, and he was pursued by an anxious maid.

'Is it true, Nathan? Has the Mevagissey bank really gone broke? Wilf Hunkin just came up to tell me the news. He said his brother came up from Mevagissey to tell him about it before dawn this morning.'

'It's true I'm afraid, Tom. You bank there. Do you stand to lose much?'

'Not me, Nathan. We've had a couple of bad years and I had no more than a couple of guineas put away there. Luckily I still have the money from my autumn sale of bullocks up at Venn. I hadn't got around to taking it down to the bank – but how about you, it's your bank too? You must have lost a small fortune.'

'I've lost a lot, Tom. Humphrey Yates came here to tell me about it late last night.'

'How did it happen? I've heard of other banks failing, but Humphrey Yates is such a careful man. He's the last one I'd expect to go under.'

'I don't think he would have if it hadn't been for Hawkins.'

'Sir Christopher? How is he mixed up in this?'

Nathan told his brother-in-law what the banker had said to him the previous evening.

'I might have guessed he'd be behind it somewhere. He's no friend to any of us around here. It was a sad day when he got control of the old harbour and foisted his grand schemes on us.'

Tom Quicke scratched his head and looked quizzically at Nathan. 'What are we going to do about it?'

'*You're* going to go back to Venn and say a little prayer of thanks as you work that you did not have time to put your autumn sales money in the bank.'

'It's not me I'm worried about. What are *you* going to do? Will you have to sell up anything? It's not a good time, not for land. Nor, as far as I can gather, for selling boats or fish-cellars.'

'I'm doing nothing right now, Tom. I'll just sit tight at Polrudden and let the world come to me. Unless I'm very much mistaken about Sir Christopher Hawkins's motives in all this, it won't be long in coming.'

When Tom Quicke had gone, there was silence around the table until Beville asked permission to leave. When it was granted he ran from the room unaware of the drama going on about him. Dewi looked across the table to where Nathan sat sipping his coffee, his thoughts seemingly far away. She thought he appeared very tired. It was hardly surprising. If all his money had been in the Bank of Mevagissey he would have suffered a devastating blow.

'How serious is your loss, Nathan?'

He attempted a weak smile but it ended as more of a grimace. 'You needn't worry, Dewi. If some things *do* have to go, I promise you'll be the very last. It's serious, but I've faced worse things in my life.'

She hesitated before saying, 'I inherited some money on my twenty-first birthday, Nathan. It's not a lot . . . at least, I don't suppose it is to you . . . but if it will help in any way you're welcome to it.'

Seeing the astonished expression on his face she said, 'I mean . . . you might not want to accept it as an outright gift from me, but you're welcome to accept it as a loan, and I won't expect you to repay it until everything is all right again.'

Dewi was alarmed to see tears suddenly spring into Nathan's eyes. He bowed his head for so long that she felt obliged to speak again.

'I'm sorry, Nathan. I didn't mean to shame you in any way. I only thought . . .'

'Shame me, Dewi? You haven't done that. Humbled me a little perhaps . . . and more. I'm deeply touched. I was remembering the last woman who was willing to risk her inheritance for me. It was Amy, my second wife. You're a lot like her, Dewi. A lot like her.'

Rising from the table, he left the room without saying another word, leaving Dewi still seated at the breakfast table, her mind in a turmoil.

Chapter 40

The day after Humphrey Yates's visit to Nathan, the banker's housekeeper discovered her employer hanging from a beam in his stable. He must have committed suicide immediately upon his return from Polrudden. Incongruously, before killing himself he had carefully wiped the snow from his gig and stabled and fed his horse.

With the banker's death went the last hope that something might still be saved from the collapse. The Mevagissey fishermen were hit particularly hard by the bank's failure. It had been a good fishing season and many of them had deposited all their money with Humphrey Yates. Thinking it safe, they had looked forward to spending the winter months cosily planning for the new season. Some had already ordered new boats, new nets and items of furniture for their homes. All these would now need to be cancelled. The repercussions of the bank's failure would spread throughout the whole community.

Pentuan was less affected on a personal level. Only two fishermen had money in the failed bank. However, the rumoured bankruptcy of Nathan cast an air of gloom and uncertainty over all those who lived here. Anything that affected Polrudden would have an effect upon them too.

There were many visitors to Polrudden during this anxious time. One of the first was Sir Kenwyn Penhaligan.

He expressed his deepest sympathy for the losses Nathan had suffered, but could offer little else. Times were bad for everyone, he explained, and with Sir Christopher Hawkins calling upon the harbour shareholders to treble their investments . . .

The two men were together in Nathan's study for a very long time. When the Golant baronet left he was deep in thought. Yet, as one of the servants said in the kitchen during their tea-time, 'It didn't seem as though Mr Jago's plight was worrying him as much as it might. But then, 'tisn't him as is going to the wall.'

Much more concern was expressed by Abigail. She arrived at Polrudden on her own, riding her horse as though she had been urging it to a full gallop all the way from Golant. Her hair was flowing loose behind her and, with her face flushed, Nathan thought she had never looked more beautiful.

Passing her horse to a Polrudden stable lad who came running when he heard the hoofbeats on the gravel of the drive, she went into the house through the open front doorway without waiting for a servant.

Nathan had seen Abigail's arrival from his study and was coming down the stairs when she ran in to the front hall.

The clatter brought Dewi from the nursery. She looked over the banisters from the first-floor gallery in time to see Abigail run up the first three stairs to intercept Nathan and clutch his arm.

'Nathan . . . I've only just heard about the collapse of the Mevagissey bank. Everyone is saying you've lost everything. That you're to be declared bankrupt. Is it true?'

'You mustn't believe all you hear, Abigail. Look about you. I still have Polrudden, the lands, my fishing-boats . . .'

'Oh, Nathan! You poor, brave dear.'

When Abigail kissed him, Dewi turned away and hurried to her room. She did not want to see or hear any more. Since she had offered her inheritance to Nathan there had been a warmth in his manner towards her that had lifted her spirits to a new high. Seeing Abigail with him sent them back down again.

Dewi told herself it served her right. She had temporarily forgotten all the principles she had quoted to Nell. No girl in her position should ever become too fond of her employer.

Had Dewi remained listening, she might have learned something that would have startled her and also proved that Abigail's present concern was not entirely for Nathan.

Clutching his arm, the eldest Penhaligan girl walked back down the stairs and across the hall. As they headed towards the sitting-room, she said, 'I've had a letter from Rao. He's received news from India – good news. So good that he wants to come to Cornwall. Says there's no reason for us not to see each other now, and we have lots to discuss.'

'Does your father agree?'

'I haven't told him. I wanted to come here first. You see . . .' Abigail looked up at Nathan pleadingly. 'I thought you might let him stay here, with you. It would make things so much easier for everyone. I don't like to ask you, with all the problems you have right now, but . . . will you. For me?'

Looking down into Abigail's flushed face with its pleading expression, Nathan had a sudden, uncomfortable feeling that she had probably given very little serious thought to his problems. He could not help comparing her reaction with that of Dewi.

He told himself such a comparison was not fair. This was the most momentous event that would happen in Abigail's life. The threshold to a way of life that would not come to most young women in their most exotic dreams.

'Of course he can come here – but not for a week or two. I

201

have some business matters to put straight first.'

Abigail's squeal of delight and hug of gratitude was witnessed by one of the maids. Repeated with embellishments in the servants' hall, it had become a passionate and intimate embrace by the time Cook passed on gossip of the incident to Dewi that night.

It served to fuel the unhappiness created by the scene she had witnessed for herself earlier in the day.

Forty-eight hours after the collapse of the Mevagissey bank, Nathan rode away from Polrudden, saying only that he expected to be away for at least seven days. In fact, he was absent from Cornwall for ten. He returned just in time to attend a meeting of the Pentuan harbour shareholders, called by Sir Christopher Hawkins for the second week in December.

The meeting was held in Sir Christopher's great house of Trewithan, a few miles from Pentuan, and Nathan arrived there in the company of Sir Kenwyn Penhaligan. Two bitterly complaining shareholders who had travelled from London were also present. Their complaints were directed as much against the cheerless atmosphere of Trewithan as with being prised from their homes. They did not appreciate travelling to the depths of rural Cornwall on the whim of the company's chairman and senior shareholder.

Impervious to the complaints of his guests from London, Sir Christopher was in an unusually affable mood. After ensuring everyone in the room had a drink, even Nathan, the baronet regretted the absence of the other London investors. He then called upon his nephew to read a report on the progress made to date on the harbour project at Pentuan.

Somewhat nervously, Columb read from a prepared document. It made gloomy reading. The harbour construction was progressing more slowly than had been anticipated; the costs far exceeded the original estimates; expenditure had already exceeded the original investment – and would rise still higher. Much higher.

His duty done, Columb resumed his seat to the accompaniment of noisy protests from the two London investors.

Calling for order, Sir Christopher said, 'There you have it, gentlemen. I regret the report could not strike a more cheerful note as we enter the festive season, but I felt it could not be put off any longer.'

'It's a damnable report!' retorted one of the London men. 'Much more to the point – what are you going to do about it?'

'There is only one thing I can do,' replied Sir Christopher, carefully avoiding looking at Nathan. 'I must ask each shareholder to treble his investment. At the same time I must warn you that I am likely to call for increased capital yet again in the foreseeable future.'

There was a great deal of noise from the London investors and

Sir Christopher needed to bang angrily upon the desk in front of him before they quietened enough for him to be heard.

'May we have some order, please, gentlemen? I regret the necessity for calling in more funds, but I would point out that I am obliged to take such action in the interests of the company. Your obligation to provide additional funds is equally clear. It is set out in the terms of agreement signed by each and every one of you when you first invested money in the company. It is a *legal* obligation, sirs. One that would be upheld by any court in the land. The only escape would be by having oneself declared bankrupt. In such an event the shares would be offered to the highest bidder – within the existing shareholders, of course.'

Sir Christopher looked directly at Nathan for the first time as he made this final declaration.

One of the London men snorted derisively, 'I can't see anyone, within the company or without, offering more than a few pence per share.'

'Nevertheless, gentlemen, I regret I must ask each of the shareholders, those present and absent, to advance a further three thousand pounds each, to meet their obligations. In view of the urgency of the matter, I suggest a stipulation that the money be paid to the company within, shall we say, one calendar month?'

'You can *say* whatever you wish,' declared one of the London men defiantly. 'You'll need to send the bailiffs in before the Pentuan Harbour Company gets another penny of *my* money.'

'I note your comments with regret, Mr Marsh, but they will be duly entered in the minutes of the meeting.'

'There is another way of dealing with this.' Nathan spoke for the first time.

'Oh!' Sir Christopher gave him a sardonic look. 'Pray enlighten us, *Mr* Jago. I trust your suggestion will not suffer a similar fate to the Mevagissey bank.'

'I think it's a suggestion that will meet with the approval of the majority of the shareholders. I move that we dismiss the manager of the Pentuan Harbour project and appoint another man to take over the work. He will assume the task of re-assessing how much money needs to be spent in order to complete the project.'

Sir Christopher showed his anger momentarily. His expression was swiftly replaced by one of contempt. 'I thought you might have something sensible to put forward, Jago. I don't think we need to record such comments in the minutes of this meeting.'

'On the contrary, Sir Christopher, I demand we not only put my suggestion in the minutes, but take a vote on it.'

'I agree,' interjected Sir Kenwyn. 'I second the motion.'

His face exhibiting cold fury, Sir Christopher said, 'In view of Jago's totally unreasonable vendetta against my nephew I can understand him wishing to place his displeasure on record. I find your conduct reprehensible, Sir Kenwyn. You should understand that in view of my one-third shareholding it is impossible for you to out-vote me. There are five shareholders absent from this meeting. I therefore move . . .'

'Wrong, Sir Christopher,' Nathan interrupted the baronet. 'I returned from London only today. While I was there I bought out the shares of three of the London investors. I now hold *almost* a third of the shares. With Sir Kenwyn's backing for my proposal, I believe you are out-voted – although, of course, it depends entirely upon the votes of the other two shareholders.'

Turning to the two London men, Nathan asked, 'Gentlemen, do you vote with Sir Christopher to pay a further three thousand pounds, or will you support my motion and freeze further payments until a professional assessor can be brought in?'

'You're bluffing, Jago. Your bank has failed. You can't possibly buy up shares in the company.'

'The Bank of Mevagissey failed, yes, and I lost money – far more than I wished. Fortunately most of my capital is banked elsewhere. Having money in the Bank of Mevagissey was a matter of convenience, nothing more.'

Drawing a sheaf of papers from his pocket, he said, 'Would you like to see the letters of transfer from the other shareholders in respect of their holdings?'

'You've been clever, Jago, I grant you that – but you still haven't won.' Appealing to the two London investors, Sir Christopher said, 'Gentlemen, you have heard how Mr Jago has been to London in a bid to take over the Pentuan Harbour Company. The opportunity to tell him what you think of his underhand methods is in your hands. Is your trust with him or with me?'

The first London investor licked his lips nervously and looked from the baronet to his companion. The other man looked to Nathan uncertainly.

'The decision is in your hands,' he said quietly. 'Do you wish to pay another three thousand pounds, or would you prefer to have an independent assessment?'

'I'm with you,' said the second Londoner promptly. After only a few moments' hesitation, his companion said, 'Yes, me too.'

'Then it seems the motion is carried,' declared Nathan. 'Columb Hawkins, the Pentuan Harbour Company will accept your resignation here and now. Failing which you will receive your dismissal notice in the morning.'

'You can have my resignation – and welcome. You and the company deserve each other.'

'Don't be so hasty, Columb. I'm still the chairman of the company.'

'Not for long, Sir Christopher. Gentlemen, I propose a vote of no confidence in our present chairman.'

'I second that.' The reply came from the London investor who had been uncertain of voting for the dismissal of Columb Hawkins. 'Now we've got this far we might as well wipe the slate clean. I also propose that Nathan Jago is elected as chairman of the Pentuan Harbour Company.'

'I second that.'

Both Sir Kenwyn Penhaligan and the other Londoner responded in unison.

'Does anyone wish to register their vote against the motion?' Nathan asked the question, but Sir Christopher Hawkins was already gathering up his papers, disdaining to make a reply.

'Then it would appear the company has a new chairman,' said Nathan cheerfully. 'Now, since there would appear to be no other business, I suggest we thank Sir Christopher for his hospitality and adjourn to Polrudden. I believe a small celebration is in order.'

Chapter 41

Word that Nathan had not been bankrupted by the collapse of the Mevagissey bank and had managed to turn the tables on Sir Christopher Hawkins travelled as fast as had the earlier bad news. So great was the rejoicing in Pentuan that the villagers asked Preacher Josiah Jago to hold a special service of thanksgiving in the small Pentuan chapel.

The service was held in the darkness of a winter evening. Voices raised in joyful song from the packed chapel could clearly be heard by Columb Hawkins as he packed his belongings in the old Customs house, at the edge of Pentuan's partly completed harbour.

The arrival of Sally Wicks, slipping quietly into the house through the unlocked door, did nothing to improve his mood.

'What do you want? If you've come to gloat, then forget it. I'm pleased to be leaving Pentuan and the harbour project. I can't remember when I enjoyed anything less.'

'I wouldn't gloat over anything that upset you, Columb. You know that.'

'Then if you're here to ask me to take you to bed, you can forget that too. I'm too busy packing. No doubt your family is among those celebrating my being ousted by Nathan Jago?'

'You're not the most popular man in Pentuan,' admitted Sally, 'but the villagers are celebrating Mr Jago still being at Polrudden rather than anything that's happened to you.'

She seemed ill-at-ease. She had come to the old Customs house to speak seriously to Columb, but had been put off by his boorish greeting.

He stamped about the house gathering his personal possessions and stuffing them into a number of trunks gathered on the floor of the living-room. Although he needed to push past her more than once, he ignored Sally and she found his indifference hurtful.

At last she asked timorously, 'What's going to happen to us, Columb? Now you're going away from Pentuan, I mean?'

'What do you expect?' he replied callously. 'It's over. We had a bit of fun and enjoyed it, but we both knew it couldn't last.'

'It was more than a "bit of fun" for me, Columb. I love you. I've told you so often enough.'

'More fool you. I enjoyed what we did and so did you, but it wasn't the first time for either of us, and I doubt it will be the last.'

There was a long silence before Sally said tearfully, 'I . . . I'm expecting a baby, Columb.'

Momentarily startled, he gathered his wits together and shrugged. 'What's that to do with me?'

'Everything. You're the father.'

He gave a short laugh, not pausing in his packing. 'You'll be hard put to prove that, Sally Wicks, even to yourself.'

The tears in Sally's eyes overflowed and her bottom lip trembled as she said, 'You're not being very nice to me, Columb.'

'What do you expect? Here I am packing all my things because I've been ousted from my house and work by some Pentuan . . . *fisherman*, and you come here to tell me you're pregnant, wanting to lay the blame on me. It's hardly surprising I'm not being very "nice". Look, I just told you, what happened between the two of us is over. It's as though it never was – and as far as the rest of the world is concerned, nothing *has* happened between us. No one knew you were coming here and it would just be your word against mine.'

'I can prove I did come here, Columb.'

Suddenly ceasing his packing, he swung round to face her. 'How?'

'I could tell people about what was said between you and your uncle. Remember the time he came here, when I was upstairs in bed and he didn't know? He told you to find some scandal involving Nathan Jago. I could tell people about that and I bet they'd believe me.'

'It would prove nothing.' Despite his assertion, Columb sounded far less assured.

'I don't *want* to tell, Columb. I just want you to be nice to me. Especially now I've got your baby inside my belly.'

He put down the pile of carelessly folded clothing he was holding. 'Look, Sally, I *will* be nice to you. I'll even give you some money so you'll not need to want for anything. But acknowledging that this baby you're having is mine is impossible. You know it is, and so do I. If it ever comes before a magistrate my uncle will have a lawyer in court to deny everything, on my behalf. There's no doubt we would win, no matter what you told the court. I'm not the only one you've been with, we both know that. There are the village boys – you've told me about them, yourself. Then there are the stable boys at Polrudden . . . Yes, I listen to gossip too. When it comes to rumours . . . I've heard talk on the harbour of what went on when you were in London with Jago.'

'That wasn't my fault,' she protested. 'Them soldiers took me off and got me drunk.'

'I'm not interested in who was to blame, only in what happened – and any court would feel the same. Then, of course, there's the sailor from the Welsh coal-boat . . .'

'He's not just a sailor,' Sally said sulkily. 'He's going to be a second mate.'

'Whatever he is, or is going to be, he's your best bet, Sally. Tell him you're pregnant and that he's got to marry you. You'll make him a good wife, and he'll be a good husband for you. A mate, eh? You'll really be someone as a mate's wife, Sally.'

The idea appealed to her, but she said, 'Wouldn't you care if I became someone else's wife?'

'Of course I'd care,' Columb lied. 'But I'm thinking of you. My uncle is very ambitious. If he thinks you're out to make trouble for me he might very well have you thrown in prison. He can do it too. He's a magistrate and so are many of his friends.'

'I don't know,' said Sally querulously. 'Owen – that's the sailor – might not want to marry me.'

'Of course he will – especially when he hears you've got fifty pounds put away. That's what I'll give you as a present when I hear you're to be married.'

The idea of being married to the future mate of a ship, plus having fifty pounds, more money than she had ever possessed in her life, appealed to Sally. Nevertheless, she did not want to seem too eager.

'All right, I'll think about it – but only if you and me go upstairs now . . .'

Abigail and her two sisters arrived at Polrudden early on the morning after Nathan's meeting with Sir Christopher Hawkins. They had come to congratulate Nathan on his coup against the baronet. All were delighted with the outcome and reported that Sir Kenwyn was positively gleeful.

'But why were you so secretive about everything that was going on?' Abigail put the question when the others had ridden off, on their way to St Ewe to visit High Cremyll. 'You could have trusted me, surely?'

'I could,' admitted Nathan. 'But I only formed my plans as I went along and I didn't return from London until late yesterday. That reminds me. I found time to visit Prince Rao while I was in London. I have a letter in my study for you.'

'*You went to see him!* Nathan, how could you visit him without first letting me know? I would have given you a letter for him.'

'Don't worry, you'll be able to deliver it in person. Rao's letter will give you the details. He's coming to Cornwall next week. I've invited him to spend Christmas at Polrudden.'

For a moment all the colour drained from Abigail's face before it returned in a rush that turned her cheeks scarlet. 'You've arranged all this and kept it to yourself! Nathan, how could you? I've been here a whole hour and you haven't even dropped so much as a hint!'

Chapter 42

Abigail was still at Polrudden that afternoon when Nathan was called to the fish-cellar at Portgiskey. One of his boats, attempting to enter the small bay in a squall, had been forced by tide and wind against the rocks. The incident has caused some damage. It would need to go to the maker's yard for repairs. It was a problem that required Nathan's personal attention.

Lydia and Sofia had not returned from St Ewe when Nathan left. As there was a cold drizzle outside, Abigail remained at Polrudden and found her way to the nursery. Dewi was teaching Beville to paint, using water-colours. Opening the door quietly, Abigail stood watching them for some minutes before Dewi looked up.

'I'm sorry. Am I disturbing you?' Abigail apologised. 'Nathan's been called away to the fish-cellar, there's been a minor accident involving one of his fishing-boats. I brought a present with me this morning for Beville. I thought this might be a good opportunity to give it to him. If you're busy I can leave it with Nathan.'

'We're only painting, it isn't important. Beville, Miss Penhaligan has a present for you. Put your brush in the water and wipe your hands on this cloth before you take it, please.'

Beville obeyed her hurriedly, eager to discover what Abigail had brought for him. Eventually, with clean hands and a smile of anticipation, he stood before her.

Crouching down until she was on a level with him, Abigail produced a carved wooden animal from behind her back. 'Here you are, Beville, I've brought this for you. It was carved for me by the man who was my bodyguard in India. He looked after me for fourteen years and died saving me from a mad buffalo. He was a very brave man. A very *special* man, as is your father.'

Placing the carving in his hands, she asked, 'Do you know what animal it is?'

Holding the carving carefully in his two hands, Beville shook his head.

'It's an elephant. There are lots of them in India. They are used for riding, for hunting, and for doing heavy work, like moving trees that have been cut down, and helping to make roads. They are huge animals too. Some of them stand almost as tall as the ceiling, in this room.'

Beville looked up to the high ceiling above him and frowned. 'One of Uncle Tom's horses is *nearly* as high as the ceiling.'

'Is it now? Your Uncle Tom must be as proud of his tall horse as Indians are of their elephants. You must show him your elephant and tell him how large a real one is. I don't expect he knows anything about elephants.'

'Uncle Tom's a farmer. He knows *everything* about animals.' Beville spoke indignantly.

'I'm sure your Uncle Tom is a very clever farmer, Beville. In fact, you're a lucky boy. You have a special uncle and a very special father.'

'I don't have a mummy though,' said Beville, very seriously.

'No, Beville, you don't have a mummy.' Abigail reached out hesitantly, as though to take hold of the small boy. She was not bold enough and her hands dropped to her sides. 'I grew up without a mummy too. I know how you feel.'

'I'll leave you two alone for a while,' said Dewi abruptly. 'It will be a good opportunity for you to get to know each other better.'

Her words seemed to startle Abigail. 'That's not necessary, Dewi. Beville is a lovely little boy, one of the nicest I've ever met, but I'm not very good with children. Perhaps I'll be better when I have children of my own, but I don't want to interfere. Beville is your charge.'

'Not for long.' Dewi did not know why she spoke now and could sense the chasm opening up beneath her feet as she spoke, but the words had to come out. 'I'm leaving Polrudden.'

'But . . . why? I thought you were so happy here. We all thought so.'

Abigail's apparently sincere dismay puzzled Dewi. She had thought the other woman would be pleased to know she intended leaving. It would leave her free to bring Beville up in the way she thought best. As his stepmother that right would be hers alone.

'I've been offered another post. As a housekeeper.'

Dewi was aware that Beville was staring at her with an expression of confusion and disbelief that cut deep into her. She tried to will herself not to look at him.

'Does Nathan know about this?'

Dewi shook her head. 'I've only just made up my mind.'

'He'll be devastated, Dewi. He relies upon you so much. He's told me so many times.'

'Dewi! I don't *want* you to go!' The anguished words escaped from Beville.

'You'll be all right.' Dewi tried hard to make the words come out normally, although they threatened to choke her. 'Daddy loves

211

you very much. He and Miss Abigail will take very good care of you. I know they will . . .'

Her voice broke and she could not trust herself to say any more. Thrusting Beville towards Abigail, she turned and fled from the room.

Once safely inside her own room she turned the key in the lock and flung herself face downward on the bed. Here, alone, she allowed the tears to come. She had made her decision now and announced it to Abigail. Once the other woman had time to think about it she would not try to prevent Dewi from leaving. The thought made her weep even more.

It must have been twenty minutes later when there came a soft knock on the door of her room.

'Dewi, it's me, Abigail. I'd like to talk to you. It's very important – to both of us. Please let me in.'

She made no reply.

'Dewi . . . I must talk to you. It concerns all of us. Things are not as you believe.'

Abigail broke off and a few moments later Dewi heard the voice of one of the servants speaking to her.

Shortly afterwards, Abigail knocked once more. When she spoke again her voice was quieter. 'Dewi, I need to speak to you but it's impossible through a locked door and I haven't very long. My sisters have arrived and are waiting downstairs for me. Please . . . I want everything to be right for Nathan and Beville.'

Had Abigail not brought Nathan and Beville's names into the conversation, Dewi would probably have opened the door. She was half rising from the bed. As it was, she froze and minutes later heard Abigail walking away from the door.

Much later, Dewi rose from the bed and washed her face in cold water from a jug on the wash-stand in a corner of her room. She saw herself in the mirror and put her fingers to the puffy redness about her eyes.

But her appearance was not important. Beville's agonised outburst kept coming back to shame her. She should never have said what she did to Abigail in front of him. She should have thought about the hurt and confusion it would cause to him. Her outburst was unforgivable.

Turning her back on the mirror and its unflattering honesty, Dewi unlocked the bedroom door and went off in search of Beville.

She found the small boy in his bedroom, next to the playroom. He too had been crying and even now dry sobs racked his body as he lay on his bed. Pippa Hanna was seated beside him.

Pippa was pale and obviously concerned about her charge. Her relief when Dewi entered the room was short-lived when she saw her reddened eyes.

'Has something happened, Dewi? Miss Penhaligan called for me to come to Beville's room and I found him on the floor, crying his eyes out . . .'

Pippa had taken the afternoon off to catch up on some sewing she needed to do.

When Beville saw Dewi he began crying again and held out his arms to her.

'It's all right, Pippa. You go off now and I'll look after Beville. You and I will talk in the morning.'

'Are you quite sure, Dewi. It looks as though you're upset too. I don't mind staying with Beville . . .'

'There's no need. We'll both be all right, I promise. Off you go now.'

As Pippa edged uncertainly towards the door, Dewi sat on the edge of the bed and Beville put both his arms tightly about her, crying, 'I don't . . . want you to go, Dewi. I . . . want you to stay . . . at Polrudden, with me.'

He had been sobbing for so long he had lost control of his breathing and his sentences came out disjointed.

'Hush now, Beville. There's nothing for you to worry yourself about. I'm not going to go off and leave you unless I know you're happy and being looked after here.'

'I . . . don't want you to go . . . at all.'

He spoke with his mouth against her shoulder and as she leaned over him she felt his tears wet against her cheek. His skin felt very hot too, so upset had he become.

Rocking him gently in her arms, Dewi felt a great surge of love for this little boy.

Chapter 43

Dewi was still holding Beville in her arms, his sobs almost over, when Nell entered the room unexpectedly, her hair dishevelled from the wind and rain outside the house.

'You're here! I wondered what I was going to find when I arrived. The Penhaligan girls called in at the farm on the way home. Abigail said something had happened and that you were very upset. She said I was to tell you that everything will be all right and you're not to do anything silly before she's had time to speak to you.'

'Dewi's going to leave Polrudden. She's going away.' Another sob escaped from Beville and he clung more tightly to her.

'Hush now.' She kissed the top of his tousled head. 'I've told you, there's nothing at all for you to worry about. Everything's going to be all right.'

Nell had taken in the situation almost immediately. Beville had obviously been extremely upset and Dewi's puffy eyes added to the untold tale. Abigail Penhaligan had not exaggerated the drama. Nell was bursting with curiosity, but realised that Dewi could not speak in front of Beville, and the young boy was far too upset to be left alone right now.

'I'd have been here sooner,' said Nell, 'but Christian has the measles. No doubt the others will be out in spots before the week's out. I don't know where Christian caught it. He hasn't been off the farm for a week.'

'There's an epidemic in Mevagissey,' said Dewi. 'It must have come from there, somehow. I'm sorry you've been dragged away from the farm like this, Nell. It's not necessary, really. You can go back now.'

It was a relief to turn her thoughts to the measles of Nell's children and put the drama of the afternoon to the back of her mind for a while. She felt as though there was a vast cavern of aching emptiness inside her. The thought of leaving Polrudden made her feel physically sick. She wished she could undo all that had occurred during this afternoon, but told herself it had needed to be said, sooner or later. Putting it off would only have meant more unhappiness for everyone in the long run.

'I'll go to the kitchen and fetch a pot of tea. Then, if you're certain you're going to be all right I'll get back to Venn. I left Tom in charge of the children, but there are things he needs to do around the farm before nightfall.'

'Go on home,' said Dewi. 'I'm very grateful to you for caring enough to come here, but Beville and I will be fine now.'

Hugging the small boy to her, she said, 'It was just silly old Dewi having a peculiar few minutes, that's all.'

'I've been waiting for just such a "peculiar few minutes" from you for some time now, Dewi, but there's only one person who could have prevented it. Unfortunately, that brother of mine seems to spend his time wearing blinkers. He doesn't realise what's going on under his own nose most of the time. We'll talk about it later, you and I. I'll go and see about that tea.'

Tea had been brought to the room and Beville was almost asleep in Dewi's arms when there were sounds from downstairs and a man's voice in the hallway.

'That's Nathan now,' said Nell. Giving Dewi a shrewd look, she asked, 'Do you want to see him right now, or would you rather leave it until later?'

'Later, Nell.' Dewi felt panic rising in her. 'I'd like time to put myself and my thoughts together first.'

'Right, I'll go and tell him.'

Nell put her tea down and stood up with the intention of going downstairs and heading Nathan off, but she was too late. Before she could even start across the room heavy footsteps were heard hurrying along the passageway outside, the door was thrown open and Nathan stood in the doorway.

Bemused by the scene before him, he said, 'What's been going on? Are you all right, Dewi?'

'Dad!' Beville had been almost asleep. Now he started up, bleary-eyed. 'Dad, don't let Dewi go away. Tell her she's to stay with us, at Polrudden.'

Nathan looked totally bewildered. 'Does someone mind telling me exactly what's going on? I have a note from Abigail apologising for upsetting you, Dewi. The note was brought to me by one of the grooms who'd been ordered to search until he found me. What's been happening?'

'Dewi said she was leaving us. She's going away,' Beville repeated.

When Nathan looked to Dewi for an explanation, she glanced down at the small boy before shaking her head at Nathan. She was not prepared to talk in front of Beville.

Taking in the situation quickly, Nell said, 'Give Beville to me for a few minutes, Dewi. You and Nathan go downstairs and sort things out.'

Dewi would have preferred to tidy herself before facing Nathan to explain the situation, but Nell was already taking Beville from her arms, ignoring the boy's protests.

Nathan was no tidier than Dewi. After making temporary repairs to his boat, he had sailed the vessel to the boatyard at Portmellon. The weather was far from ideal for a sinking fishing-boat and he had received a thorough soaking. Reaching Portmellon, cold and wet and the boat dangerously low in the water, he had found Abigail's hastily scribbled note awaiting him when he stepped ashore. He had hurried back to Polrudden on the groom's horse, leaving that unfortunate man to plod back to Polrudden in the rain.

In the light of the drawing-room, when Nathan turned to face her, Dewi realised his condition for the first time. Forgetting her own worries for a moment, she said, 'You're soaking, Nathan. You ought to go and change before you think of anything else.'

'It will wait. What's all this about? Why did Beville tell me not to let you go away? You're not considering leaving Polrudden, surely?'

Avoiding his eyes, Dewi nodded. 'I've decided to go. I'll stay until I'm quite certain Beville will be all right without me, then I'll leave. I think it will be better for everyone, really.'

'But . . . why, Dewi? Why? I believed you were happy here. I thought you enjoyed being at Polrudden as much as Beville and I enjoy having you here. Why are you leaving – and why so suddenly? I don't understand . . .'

Dewi had expected this moment to be hard, and it was. Even harder than she had imagined.

Discarding the many explanations she had rehearsed in her mind many, many times, she said lamely, 'I've been offered another post.'

Nathan waited for more details to be added to the bald statement. When they did not come, he said, 'Is that the only reason? I don't know what this new post is, but whatever salary you're being offered, I'll pay more. Beville *needs* you, Dewi. We *both* need you.'

Dewi agonised over what to say next. She finally settled upon the truth.

'No, that isn't the only reason, Nathan. I know you'll probably be married soon. Your new wife will want to bring Beville up her way. Any woman would. I'll no doubt have different ideas to her. I've never been very good at holding my tongue and arguments about Beville wouldn't be good for him. Nor would it be the right way for you to begin a marriage. I'd rather leave now, of my own accord, than be dismissed later on.'

'What makes you think I'm about to be married, Dewi?' Nathan ran a hand through his hair and it came away wet. 'Who am I supposed to be marrying?'

216

She looked at him disdainfully. 'What sort of question is that? I have eyes in my head, same as the servants. It would take a crowbar to prise you and Miss Abigail apart sometimes. I'm not saying that's wrong. It's the way people should be who are to be married, but you shouldn't be surprised when folk notice such things.'

'Supposing you were right and I were to be married? Would you stay if you were given an assurance that you would be allowed to bring up Beville in the way you thought best? Without interference?'

It was a totally unexpected question and Dewi could not find an answer.

'No wife could accept having another woman in the house who had more authority over her husband's child than she did herself. It wouldn't be human.'

'You haven't answered my question, Dewi. If you did have that assurance, would you stay?'

Again she hesitated before replying, 'No, because it just wouldn't work.'

'Very well, I'll put another question to you. Are you just using this as an excuse to leave Polrudden, Dewi? Have Beville or I – or anyone else here done something to upset you so much that you feel you just can't stay with us any longer?'

Dewi thought of how happy she had been at Polrudden. Of how much she loved Beville . . . and, yes, this man standing before her too. Suddenly the tears welled up again. She turned to flee from the room, but Nathan was too quick for her. Catching her by the arm he swung her around to face him.

'I don't pretend to understand why you're putting yourself – and us – through all this, Dewi, but I don't think you want to leave Polrudden any more than Beville and I want you to go. You can tell me what it's all about some other time. Right now it's my turn for talking. I'm *not* marrying Abigail Penhaligan, or anyone else.'

Dewi looked up at him in total disbelief. He was lying. He had to be.

'But . . . I've seen you. So have the servants.'

'You've seen Abigail showing me the affection she would have given to a brother, if she had one.'

Propelling her to a chair, he said, 'Sit down, Dewi. I'll get you a drink – get us *both* a drink, and then I'll tell you a true story. It's about Abigail and it must remain a secret for another week or so. After that the whole world will know. When you've heard it you'll understand everything about the relationship between Abigail and me.'

Nathan poured very large brandies for Dewi and himself and then told her the story of Abigail and Prince Rao and of the part

217

he had played in helping to bring them together.

When the story came to an end he poured another brandy for himself and would have given Dewi another had she not shaken her head. She was thoroughly bewildered.

'Is this why you went to London? When we came with you?'

They were the first words she had uttered since he had informed her he was not marrying Abigail.

'That's right. I saw Abigail's prince again when I went to London recently. Prince Rao is coming to stay at Polrudden next week. If everything goes according to plan their forthcoming marriage will probably be announced then – although it might be decided to keep it quiet for political reasons. That's a decision for the Company to make.'

'It's a wonderfully romantic story.' Dewi's Welsh accent was as ever very apparent in times of stress.

Swilling the brandy about in her glass, she gazed down at it for a long time before glancing up and saying to Nathan, 'I've behaved very stupidly, haven't I?'

'In order to answer that I'd need to know what your motives were in deciding to leave Polrudden, Dewi. Your *real* motives.'

Gazing down into her glass once more, she deliberately ignored the question. 'You must have thought me foolish too when I offered you money after it was rumoured you'd been seriously affected by the collapse of the Mevagissey bank.'

'Oh no, Dewi. I thought of many things then, but never that you were foolish. Generous, caring, warm-hearted – they were some of the words I thought of, but never foolish. You offered me help when most others sat back to see what was going to happen to me. I was deeply touched by that. More than you could ever know. That's why I find it so difficult to understand why you want to leave Polrudden now.'

When Dewi made no reply, Nathan said, 'Do you still want to leave Polrudden? Now I've explained everything?'

When she still did not reply, he said, 'Dewi, don't leave Polrudden. Beville and I both want you to stay here with us. Say you will. Please?'

It took Dewi many moments of staring into her brandy glass before she dared answer Nathan's plea. When the reply came she hoped it showed none of the emotion she felt.

'Yes, I'll stay at Polrudden. I'll stay for as long as I'm really wanted.'

When she looked up at him Nathan glimpsed the old Dewi once more as she said, 'You'd better go and change out of those clothes before you catch your death of cold. I'm going up to Beville's room now to tell him what a foolish governess he has. Then Nell can go home and I'll see that Beville has an early night in bed. Poor little chap, he's had a hard day.'

Chapter 44

Abigail rode to Polrudden early the next morning, accompanied only by a groom. At the house she was told by a maid that Nathan had left even earlier. If Abigail wished to speak with him she would find him at the Portmellon boatyard, discussing the fate of his damaged fishing-boat.

Abigail's reply was that she had not come to see Nathan, but to speak to Dewi. The thought of her unhappiness had given Abigail a sleepless night. Having spent innumerable hours agonising over what *she* had always believed to be an impossible love, Abigail thought she understood something of Dewi's predicament. She felt the other girl would be in need of a sympathetic ear this morning – if she was still at Polrudden.

Much to Abigail's relief, she was informed that Dewi was in the playroom, discussing with a carpenter the changes that would need to be made in order to keep up with the growing needs of the young boy who would one day inherit Polrudden.

While she waited, Abigail was shown into the tiny sitting-room that had been allocated to Dewi some time before. It was a place where she could escape the attentions of Beville and carry out her sewing, mending and letter writing.

It was a very private little corner room with two windows. The larger of the two looked out upon a walled orchard. Now leafless, the gnarled and distorted apple tress had supplied fruit to generations of Polrudden residents. Abigail thought the aged trees must have witnessed a great many of Polrudden's changes of fortune and circumstance.

The second, smaller window gave an oblique view towards the cliffs that dropped sheer to the sea from the high ground between Pentuan and Mevagissey.

The furniture in the room was well worn, but everything was neat and the room had an air of warm cosiness about it. A splash of colour was provided by two bright green chair backs, each embroidered with the red dragon emblem of Wales. Abigail thought Dewi had managed to make the room reflect her own character.

Abigail was examining a large, hand-carved wooden spoon when the door opened quietly and Dewi said softly, 'That's a love-

219

spoon. A young man in the valleys of Wales will carve one for his sweetheart and present it to her if he wants to court her seriously. That one was carved for my mother by my father.'

'What a delightful custom – and practical too! It must eliminate much of the agonising over whether a man is seriously interested or only being flirtatious. Has Nathan seen it?'

'Yes, he saw it soon after I came here.'

Abigail smiled at Dewi, a trifle apprehensively. 'I'm glad you're still at Polrudden, Dewi. You were so upset yesterday I feared you might do something drastic and leave before I could get here to speak to you. I called in at the farm to see Nathan's sister, Nell. I also wrote a note and sent it with a groom to Nathan. I didn't know what else to do.'

'You were very kind. Far kinder that I deserved after my stupid outburst. You also showed far more sense than I did. I'm very sorry, Miss Penhaligan – both for my silly behaviour and for the trouble it has caused you.'

'I would rather you called me Abigail, Dewi – and you behaved with remarkable restraint in the circumstances. When my life changed and I believed I was going to lose everything I loved, I threw a tantrum that's probably still spoken of with awe among the servants who worked for us in India.'

'Was that when they learned about you and your Indian prince?'

Abigail was taken by surprise by Dewi's question, but it showed only by the rapid blinking of her eyes.

'Nathan told you?'

'Yes, but he said it had to remain a secret until the prince came to Polrudden and an announcement was made. Nathan told me because . . . I thought you and he were going to marry. That I wouldn't be wanted at Polrudden any longer.'

'I knew that was at the heart of your upset yesterday. Does working here matter so much to you, Dewi?'

'I like Polrudden. I like it very much indeed.'

Abigail gave her a long and very shrewd look. 'Is it Polrudden, Dewi, or is it Beville . . . and Nathan?'

'Beville is a wonderful little boy. I love him very much.'

'And his father . . . do you love him too?' Abigail put the question very quietly, believing she already knew the answer.

Dewi shrugged and looked away from Abigail's forthright gaze. 'He's a special man, but he's the lord of the manor of Polrudden. I'm only Dewi Morgan, daughter of a Welsh coal miner, and governess to his son. I'm not a fool, I'm quite happy to stay here – as Beville's governess – for as long as Nathan wants me to.'

Unexpectedly, Abigail stepped forward and grasped both Dewi's hands in her own. 'Dewi, I knew there was something more to what happened between us yesterday than the affection of a governess for her charge. You're in love with Nathan!'

220

She opened her mouth to deny the charge, but Abigail did not allow her to speak. 'It's all right, Dewi. Quite all right. You're keeping my secret, I'll say nothing to anyone else of yours – but don't sell yourself short. You're a lovely girl, warm and intelligent. It's the man who chooses you who'll be the lucky one, not the other way around – and it doesn't matter whether he's a lord, a miner, or a prince. If you love Nathan – go after him. If he has any sense he won't run very fast. I'm fond of him too, Dewi. He's been very kind to me without asking for anything in return. I'll do whatever I can to help you. I believe that's the greatest favour I can do him in return for his kindness to me.'

The arrival in Cornwall of His Royal Highness Prince Rao Jelal, future ruler of the State of Sikar, caused as much interest throughout the county as though he had been heir to the throne of Britain.

The East India Company had supplied the prince with one of its newest merchantmen to convey his party to Cornwall. Details of his plans had been sent ahead of the party. When the ship sailed into Falmouth harbour Prince Rao received a nineteen-gun salute from one of the two forts guarding the entrance to the major sea port.

An excited crowd assembled to witness the historic arrival and they were not disappointed. Prince Rao was dressed in the bejewelled finery expected of an Indian ruler. With him he had brought an escort of richly dressed *Rajput* horsemen. Each man was taller than six foot in height and carried an unsheathed sword that glinted ominously in an obliging spell of winter sunshine.

The Indian prince travelled with a huge retinue of servants. The mountain of baggage they brought with them had the watchers gasping as it was carried from the ship and piled ever higher on the jetty.

Horses and carriages had also been brought to Falmouth by the East Indiaman vessel. As the vehicles were off-loaded, the excitement of the spectators grew. Eventually the royal party itself disembarked from the ship and entered the coaches. Accompanied by its colourful escort it set off through the narrow streets of Falmouth, bound for Polrudden.

The distance from Falmouth was some twenty-four miles and the procession would be talked about by those who lived along its route for years to come. It would have taken a brave man to demand money from the fierce *Rajput* escort and the notoriously grasping turnpike operators lifted their barriers and waved the party hastily through. As the cavalcade passed through Truro, Tresillian, Probus and Grampound, the streets were lined with cheering crowds.

Once off the main roads farmers with slow-moving farm vehicles made the party's progress somewhat less triumphant. Nevertheless,

221

the sight of a band of richly dressed horsemen bearing down on him with drawn swords was enough to galvanise the slowest-moving farmer or carter into action. Inside his coach, Prince Rao frowned in annoyance at each delay, but his impatience was that of an eager lover and not the arrogance of royalty.

The presence of Prince Rao Jelal at Polrudden created more interest among local people than anything that had occurred in the county for a great many years. Communications in the duchy were far from satisfactory, but news of the prince's presence reached every lonely village and hamlet with incredible speed.

Each day sightseers gathered outside the gates of the house in the hope of catching a glimpse of the Indian ruler. The more daring of the small boys sneaked inside the gardens and hid among the bushes for the same reason and the gardeners were kept busy chasing them out.

The women of Pentuan chose a more direct method. They arrived at the house with messages and gifts for relatives among the Polrudden servants, some of whom they had not spoken to for many years. These women were usually rewarded by a glimpse of the prince's servants at work in the Polrudden kitchen, preparing food for their master and his staff.

The initial introduction of Indian servants to the Cornish kitchen came close to causing a rebellion among the Polrudden kitchen staff. Prince Rao's own cooks spoke very little English. When they had difficulty making themselves understood they simply appropriated whatever cooking utensils they needed. This upset Gladys Coppin, the elderly Polrudden cook. It took all Dewi's diplomatic skills to arrange a satisfactory division of cooking facilities amidst a babble of raised voices and brandished kitchen knives.

Despite the uneasy armistice sinister tales seeped from the Polrudden kitchen. Most were of the strange ingredients and unusual methods of cooking employed in preparing food for the Indian prince and his party.

When Nathan decided to hold a reception to honour the prince's presence in his house it was explained that Prince Rao's cooks would be cooking traditional Indian delicacies for the occasion. The conservative-minded cook sniffed in professional derision. She could not see why the Indian could not eat: 'Good, wholesome Cornish food, same as other folk. If it was good enough for the son of an English king, it ought to be good enough for an Indian prince.'

It was to be a small, family-and-friends reception, a reunion between Prince Rao and the Penhaligan family. A few additional guests would be present, the two East India Company directors who had accompanied the prince from London among them.

Beville had been given permission to attend, but on the day of Prince Rao's arrival he was taken ill with a bout of measles, caught from Nell's children, who were now recuperating.

Dewi was invited and Tom Quicke and Nell were coming from Venn. From Golant, Sir Kenwyn and his wife would accompany Henry Penhaligan and his three daughters. The final member of the party would be the Reverend Hugh Cremyll from nearby St Ewe. Nathan's father had also been invited, but he rarely attended social functions at Polrudden and pleaded that his church duties would not allow him to attend.

On the day of the reception the weather was crisp and cold. Hugh Cremyll was the first to arrive and was introduced to Prince Rao by Nathan as 'a very close friend of Lydia, Abigail's sister'.

The prince put the correct interpretation upon Nathan's pointed introduction and the embarrassed clergyman received an effusive greeting.

Prince Rao was so excited at the prospect of his reunion with Abigail that he was unable to stand still. In sharp contrast, Hugh Cremyll remained much quieter, but he too had some momentous news to impart to Nathan.

'It's news I had intended breaking to Lydia first,' he said, almost shyly. 'But I can't keep it entirely to myself any longer. I have been offered a post as the Dean of Gloucester. It's really rather exciting.'

'It's *wonderful* news!' exclaimed Nathan. 'I'm delighted, Hugh – and Lydia is going to be so proud of you.'

'I hope so.' Hugh Cremyll coloured up alarmingly, 'You see . . . I intend asking her if she will marry me.'

'She'll be a fool if she refuses you,' said the delighted Nathan. 'But there can be little fear of that. If ever two people were made for each other, it's you and Lydia. I've known it since the night the two of you met, when she mopped up the blood you spilled in my defence.'

'I think I have known it too,' said Hugh shyly. 'Although I feared at first that you and I were destined to be rivals.'

'I'm very pleased we became friends instead,' said Nathan warmly. 'Come and have a drink, Hugh – a stiff one to bolster your courage.'

When the two Penhaligan families arrived, Prince Rao was nowhere to be seen. For a few moments there was an expression of panic upon Abigail's face, but Nathan came to her rescue swiftly, apologising for the prince's absence.

'Prince Rao needed to go to his rooms for a few minutes,' he explained. 'He'll be down shortly. While we wait, would you come upstairs and visit a very spotty Beville, Abigail? He is very disappointed not to be meeting you tonight – you *have* had measles?'

'Yes, but . . . can it wait until after I see Prince Rao?' Abigail was more agitated than Nathan had ever seen her.

'Beville will probably be asleep by then. Please, it won't take a few minutes. If the others will excuse us. Dewi, would you take everyone through to the drawing-room? Hugh is in there. I think he might have something special to tell everyone.'

The Penhaligans, Lydia in particular, were happy enough to go and greet Hugh and Nathan took Abigail upstairs. When they came to the door of Beville's room Abigail would have gone inside. Grasping her arm, Nathan said, 'We'll go and visit him in a few minutes.' Without any further explanation he hurried her on to his study.

'Nathan, where are you taking me? I thought you said Beville . . .'

'It's all right.' Opening the study door, Nathan said quickly, 'Rao is in here. Don't be longer than ten minutes or I suspect your father will come looking for you.'

Before she could regain her composure, Nathan had thrust her inside the room and closed the door behind her.

Nathan waited outside his study door for fifteen minutes before he knocked. He could keep the party downstairs waiting no longer.

Abigail and Prince Rao came out of the study enveloped in happiness and Nathan breathed a sigh of relief. He had begun to wonder whether one or other of them might change their mind once they met again.

Abigail echoed his relief as they made their way to Beville's room to pay the small boy a brief visit while Rao went to meet the other guests.

'I am so happy, Nathan. I had been concerned that I might be more in love with the magic of India than with Rao. Now I know my fears were groundless. When I saw him again my legs turned to jelly. Oh, Nathan, I *do* love him – and I know he loves me too. Everything is going to be all right!'

They did not remain in Beville's room for more than a couple of minutes. Pippa was sitting with him and he was almost asleep. After he had given Abigail a sleepy greeting, they tip-toed from the room and made their way downstairs.

Preacher Josiah Jago had arrived in spite of his earlier doubts about attending. He was talking to Dewi, while the Penhaligan family crowded about Prince Rao. The young girls were eager for news of India and the friends they had left behind among the political agency staff in Jhalapur.

All conversation ceased when Nathan and Abigail entered the room. Even the most hardened cynic would have recognised the powerful emotion in the look that passed between Abigail and Prince Rao. For many seconds there might have been no one else in the room.

Looking from one to the other, Sir Kenwyn Penhaligan began to have an inkling of why there had been so much secrecy surrounding the affairs of his brother in recent weeks. Taking out a handkerchief he mopped his brow and murmured, 'Good God! Good God!'

Prince Rao crossed the room to greet Abigail formally. Taking her hand, he carried it to his lips, at the same time bowing low.

It was a moving moment that touched everyone in the room, but Dewi was standing facing the door when Jainu, Prince Rao's secretary, entered the room. He did not share the pleasure of the others.

He displayed such disapproval that Dewi was taken aback. She wondered what powerful reason there could be why the secretary did not share the joy of his master at the reunion with the English girl he loved.

Chapter 45

Contrary to Nathan's secret fears, the evening party at Polrudden was a great success. Part-way through the evening Henry Penhaligan and Prince Rao asked if they might have the use of Nathan's study for a few minutes of private discussion. The few minutes extended to half-an-hour, but it was evident from the demeanour of both men upon their return that their talk had proved entirely satisfactory.

Not long after this, Prince Rao asked Nathan if the servants of the house, together with his own Indian servants, could be summoned to the room. He had an announcement to make and he wished them all to be present to hear it.

It was an unusual request but Nathan sent a message to the servants' hall. While this was being done, Prince Rao had an earnest conversation with his secretary. In another corner of the room, the red-faced but beaming Hugh Cremyll was talking equally earnestly with Henry Penhaligan. Across the room Lydia watched the two men anxiously.

Nathan smiled benevolently about him. He had no doubt why Prince Rao wished all the servants to come to the drawing-room. Nathan also believed he could hazard an accurate guess as to the subject of Hugh Cremyll's discussion with Lydia's father.

It was about ten minutes before the Polrudden servants assembled in the room, huddling together in a self-conscious group. Nearby were the retainers of Prince Rao. Much more colourful in their Indian dress, they were also considerably noisier.

The sounds ceased immediately Prince Rao advanced to the centre of the room to make his announcement.

Displaying no nervousness whatsoever, the prince smiled about him before speaking.

'My very good friend, Nathan Jago. Ladies and gentlemen. Faithful servants. It is customary in my country that on certain occasions a proclamation is made that should be heard by every man, woman and child in the land. This is one such occasion. As I am not in my country I have asked for you to gather here because each of you, in his or her way, has helped make this a momentous day for me.'

Prince Rao beamed around the room. 'You see, I am shortly

to be returning to India, to the State of Sikar, to become their Maharaja. Henry Penhaligan – *Sir* Henry Penhaligan, for he has been granted a baronetcy – will also serve in Sikar on behalf of the East India Company, as my Resident Agent. I look forward to receiving his wise guidance and assistance.'

Prince Rao nodded in the direction of Henry Penhaligan before continuing, 'Also at my side will be my Maharani. The Maharani Abigail.'

It took a moment for his words to sink home. Then there was a gasp from most of those in the room, followed by squeals of astonished delight from Sofia.

As Lydia and Sofia hugged their sister, Dewi's attention was once more caught by the expression on the face of Jainu, Prince Rao's secretary. It showed none of the delight registered by the other servants.

Sir Kenwyn Penhaligan appeared to be perspiring freely, but when his handkerchief disappeared from view he gave his niece a kiss and a hug of congratulation.

'There is one thing more . . .' When Prince Rao had everyone's attention, he continued, 'Abigail and I will, of course, have a Hindu wedding ceremony befitting a Maharaja and Maharani when we return to India. However, I have spoken to Hugh Cremyll and he has agreed to marry us in a Christian ceremony, here in his small church, according to the customs of England. It will be performed as soon as it can be arranged. I am assured the necessary formalities will take no longer than three weeks. I regret the haste but, as the two directors of the East India Company who are guests tonight will tell you, I am needed in Sikar. They are experiencing troubled times.

'Finally, I wish to thank you, Nathan Jago, for your efforts on my behalf, and for the caring friendship you have shown to Abigail. I will be forever in your debt.'

The excitement was still running high in the room when Henry Penhaligan called for silence.

'This has been a very, very eventful evening for all of us,' he said. 'Now I am delighted to announce one more surprise. This evening I have agreed to give not one daughter away in marriage – but *two*! Hugh Cremyll, soon to become Dean of Gloucester, has asked Lydia to marry him. She has accepted and I am most happy to give my consent and my blessing to them both.'

Now it was the turn of Lydia to be showered with good wishes from all those present in the room. Nathan was one of the last to offer his congratulations and she offered her cheek somewhat apprehensively for his kiss.

Seemingly relieved by the warmth of his embrace, Lydia said, 'You're not angry with me, Nathan?'

Her question took him by surprise. 'Why on earth should I be angry? I'm delighted for you. And for Hugh too. You make a wonderful couple.'

'That makes me very happy, Nathan. Relieved too. After all, I did tell you you were my favourite man – and so you are, after Hugh. But I thought you were interested in Abigail, not me. Now I realise you were only being a good friend to her.'

'Lydia, any hopes I entertained of remaining your favourite man went out of the window the first time I saw you with Hugh. It was quite apparent to me – and, no doubt, to everyone else – that you are made for each other. I've already told Hugh so.'

'You're a dear, Nathan – no, you're not!' Lydia suddenly pouted, something she had always done most appealingly. 'You knew about Abigail and Rao yet you kept it all to yourself. You could have told *me* at least.'

'My sentiments exactly,' Sir Kenwyn said ruefully. He had heard Lydia's words. As she was led away by her father to receive the congratulations of the East India Company directors, Sir Kenwyn added, 'I'm not sure I will ever forgive you for this, Nathan. Fancy knowing what was going on and not saying a word!'

'I daren't,' Nathan protested. 'It was an extremely sensitive matter. Had anything leaked out it might have upset the plans of the East India Company and the Duke of Clarence – not to mention the governments of Britain and Sikar. Sometimes I wondered how I'd managed to entangle myself in the whole business.'

'I quite see your point, dear boy. It also explains why the powers-that-be would like you to have a seat in Parliament. You know when to keep your mouth shut, and when it's time to act. Too few men do, these days. Mind you, who would have thought that one of Henry's daughters would marry an . . . Indian?'

Sir Kenwyn mouthed the word silently.

'He's an extremely wealthy man,' declared Nathan, 'and I believe his family – on both his mother's and father's side – have ruled their countries for about a thousand years longer than our own royal family.'

'No doubt you're right, dear boy, but I find the idea of having a prince – an *Indian* prince – in the family a little hard to get used to.'

At that moment Henry Penhaligan came across the room to join his brother and Nathan. His face flushed with the excitement of the events of the evening and the amount of brandy he had consumed, he exclaimed, 'What a day this has been! I can't remember another quite like it in all my life. I came to England to find husbands for three girls and now I'm returning to India with two of them, plus the husband of one of them.'

Looking at his brother with a shrewdness that belied the amount he had drunk, he added, 'I'm proud of Abigail and Lydia,

Kenwyn. Damned proud. Proud of their husbands too. Abigail, in particular, has chosen a brave course. I'm glad I'll be around to give her my help, if ever it's needed.'

Beaming at Nathan with more warmth than he had ever displayed before, he added, 'Mind you, my boy, I still have one very attractive daughter on my hands . . .'

It was almost three o'clock in the morning before the celebrations came to an end. When he had handed Lady Penhaligan into the coach taking her and the others back to Golant, Nathan looked up at Polrudden. It seemed every window was lit, as though the house itself was celebrating the events of the evening.

He was about to enter the door when Will Hodge, who had brought the Golant coach horses from his stables, suddenly darted into the bushes nearby. The sound of a brief struggle reached Nathan.

A moment later the groom entered the pool of light cast from the open doorway of the house, half dragging a still-struggling boy.

'Let me go, I ain't done nuffin'.'

The accent was cockney and the voice sounded vaguely familiar.

'I saw him skulking in the bushes earlier,' explained Will Hodge. 'He's not from these parts and he's up to no good, if you ask me. Probably hoping to steal something while no one was looking. He might have done it already.'

'I 'aven't pinched anything. Wasn't going to, neither.'

Looking up at Nathan, he added, 'That's the truth, Mr Jago. I swear it.'

The face was dirty and the boy looked half-frozen, but at that moment Nathan remembered where he had seen him before.

It was young Charlie Philpotts. The boy who had tried to steal Dewi's bag when she and Nathan were leaving the Drury Lane Theatre in London!

Chapter 46

Charlie Philpotts sat in the Polrudden kitchen, warming himself at the huge range. Between bouts of prolonged shivering, the boy wolfed down every piece of food that was handed to him.

'Lord bless us!' grumbled Gladys Coppin. 'There ain't more than a half-penn'orth of him, but I swear he'll eat us all out of house and home before he's through. There's been more food disappear down his gullet than I cooked for all the guests we've entertained at Polrudden tonight. Where's the boy putting it all? If he was a Pentuan boy I'd say it was going down to fill his boots, but them as he's wearing don't look as though they'll keep his feet inside of 'em for very much longer, let alone a barrow-load of food.'

Charlie Philpotts's boots were scuffed, dirty and very badly worn. The sole on one of them had parted company with the upper and was secured with a loop of stout rope that must have made walking both difficult and uncomfortable.

'I've 'ad enough now.' Charlie's actions belied the muffled words as he crammed an oversized piece of pastry into his mouth. A moment later he gave out a gargantuan and noisy belch that sprayed crumbs across the kitchen as far as the fire itself.

'The boy's learned no more manners than he's seen soap on his face,' grumbled the aged cook. 'And what was he doing skulking in the bushes out in the garden at such a time of night, that's what I'd like to know? He was up to no good, that's certain.'

'What *were* you doing?' Nathan asked. 'If you were looking for me, why didn't you come to the house and ask – and how did you know where to find me?'

All the party guests had either gone home or retired for the night. The servants too had been sent to bed to snatch a few hours' sleep before tackling the chores of a new day.

Nathan and Dewi were in the kitchen with Charlie. The cook had insisted on remaining with them. She declared that if *she* went to bed the uninvited guest would most likely eat the food she had put by for that day's meals.

One quick gulp emptied Charlie's mouth of the food that remained there. Wiping his mouth on the sleeve of his ragged jacket, he said, 'I got a right fright that night you collared me outside the theatre, Mr Jago. I thought you was going to turn me over to that runner for sure. When you didn't, I thought you was probably a soft touch and hoped this geezer you told me to go and see at The Plough might be a soft touch too. So I went along to Carey Street to see him.'

Charlie gave a derisive snort that proved he had not swallowed all the pastry in his mouth. 'Cor! Some soft touch 'e turned out to be. You an' all. Champion prizefighters, the pair o' you. He told me all about you. How you'd started off. What you'd done. Where you'd been in your life. He told me 'ow I was likely to end up, if I didn't stop what I was doing and make something of meself.'

Charlie shrugged. 'It made a lot of sense. I knew it was no good me staying around London trying to do something new. I wouldn't last long with all me mates if I told 'em I was going straight. They'd think me a right sissy. The only way was to get out. So 'ere I am!'

'How did you get here?'

'I walked.'

'You walked? From London to Cornwall? How long did it take you?'

'I dunno. Three weeks. Four maybe. Might even have been more. Days and weeks 'ave never meant very much to me. I gets up when it's light and I doss down when I'm tired. Anyway, I'm 'ere now, ain't I?'

'What did you have in mind to do once you arrived here? What *can* you do, Charlie?'

'Me? I can't do nuffin'. Never learned 'ow. But I'll try, Mr Jago. Anyfing you want me to do, I'll give it a go.'

'We'll need to think about that in the morning. We must also find something for you to wear that doesn't look as though it would fall apart if ever it were washed. Right now I think we'd better find somewhere for you to sleep.'

'I ain't going to sleep inside no house – not even this one. I was brought up in a workhouse, until me ma died, then I ran away. I swore right there and then I'd never sleep in no house again.'

'Where have you been living, in London?'

'In an old warehouse, down by the river. Me and some of me mates. Me young sister, Liz, would 'ave been with us too, if she could 'ave got away from Ma Kettle.'

Nathan and Dewi exchanged glances and Charlie attempted to clarify his statement. 'The poor-house master sold Liz off to skivvy for a woman who runs a boarding 'ouse. She's locked in the cellar every night. "To keep 'er out o' 'arm's way," the old woman says. Liz would 'ave been better off wiv us.'

Charlie Philpotts was a real urchin of the London streets.

231

Nathan felt that settling down to anything, anywhere, was not going to be easy for him.

'I think the best place for you tonight will be the loft above the stables. There's plenty of hay to keep the chill off you, at least.'

Gladys had been listening to the conversation. In a strangely gruff voice, she said, 'Here, I'll find a little bit of food for you to take with you. With an appetite like yours you're likely to wake up hungry in the night.'

When Nathan returned from the stables, Gladys had already gone to bed, but Dewi was still in the kitchen. She had made a pot of tea and now she poured a cup for him.

Setting it on the table when he dropped into a chair, she asked, 'Do you think Charlie was telling the truth about the sort of life he led in London and his reasons for coming to Cornwall?'

'I believe him when he talks of his harsh life in London. I saw something of the East End when I was prizefighting. There are a lot of youngsters like him. Boys *and* girls. As for his reasons for coming to Cornwall . . . I'm not so sure. I believe he's probably running away from something, but I'm not going to question him about that just yet. If he'd stayed in London his way of life would have led him first to the hulks, and eventually to the gallows. At least he's got *some* chance of a better life in Cornwall.'

'Poor Charlie. What will you do with him?'

'I don't know yet. I'll need to think about it.'

Nathan finished his cup of tea in silence, then stood up wearily. 'It's been a very long day – and night, Dewi. Time you went to bed and snatched a couple of hours' sleep, at least.'

He smiled warmly at her. 'Thank you for acting as my hostess at the reception tonight – and that's what you were, you know. Hostess of Polrudden. It's a role you carried out very well. We must have another reception some time.'

'I'd like that. Perhaps next time Beville will be well enough to stay downstairs for a while and I can feel I have a right to be there.'

'You did a splendid job tonight. Everyone at Polrudden has a very high regard for you.'

'Thank you.'

For a few moments they both stood in the kitchen, saying nothing. It was almost as though neither wanted to be the first to leave.

Looking at her, Nathan felt a stirring in him that he had not known for a long time. Dewi was an attractive woman and she and he lived beneath the same roof. In his house. In Polrudden.

He remembered the allegation made about her by Sally. That Dewi had been seeing a man. If it were true, would she welcome an advance from *him*? Become his mistress, even?

Dewi raised her glance to his face and he felt she was able to read his thoughts. He was suddenly ashamed of them.

'Time you were in bed, Dewi.'

'Yes. Good night, Nathan.'

'Good night. Before I go to bed I want to check I locked the door when I came in from the stable. I'll see you at breakfast. Don't worry if you're late waking up. Pippa can deal with Beville.'

In her bedroom, Dewi heard Nathan go along the passageway on his way to his own room. She held her breath as her imagination had him pausing outside the door . . . but then she heard him walking on.

She had seen the look on his face when they were both in the kitchen. For a moment she had thought he was going to reach out for her. She almost stepped forward to meet him. Had she done so she would have made an utter fool of herself.

Pulling the bedclothes up about her, Dewi resolved not to allow such foolish notions to enter her head again. She was a governess to Nathan's child. A good governess. Tonight she had played the part of a hostess at a Polrudden reception and Nathan was grateful to her for performing the task. That was all there was to it.

Snuggling into the bed, Dewi thought it must have been the emotional aftermath of an evening at which two marriages had been announced that had given her such foolish notions.

She had a good position at Polrudden. She was very happy here. It was all very well for Nell to suggest she should set her cap at Nathan. Such romantic ideas could lead to her dismissal from Polrudden. All the same, she could not be dismissed for her dreams. Dewi went to sleep wondering what would have happened had she *not* been mistaken about Nathan's intentions when they were both alone in the kitchen . . .

Chapter 47

Finding a niche for Charlie Philpotts at Polrudden proved more difficult than Nathan had anticipated. Self-conscious in new clothes bought from one of the chandler's shops in Pentuan, the London urchin began his first day at Polrudden working in the stables.

It soon became apparent that, despite Charlie's early boast to one of the Polrudden stable-lads that he was 'afraid of nuffin'', the cockney lad was in fact terrified of horses.

Switched to work with the gardeners, Charlie was no more successful. He knew nothing at all of plants and had no interest in learning anything about them. Furthermore, Charlie's blasphemous cockney language proved deeply offensive to the ears of the head gardener who was a staunch Methodist with deeply held beliefs and an abhorrence of drink and bad language.

Fishing proved to be a disaster of equal proportions. The fishing-boat carrying Charlie had hardly left the quay at Portgiskey before the London boy was in trouble for wanting to fight one of the fisherman whom he believed to be laughing at him.

Ahab Arthur was skipper of the small boat and he refused to allow the boy's anger to be used as an excuse for idleness. Charlie was given the task of baiting hooks used on the long-lines, cast over the side to catch deepwater fish while the drift nets were out.

Two hours later Charlie was landed at Mevagissey to receive the attentions of the village doctor. One of the large, barbed hooks had torn through his right hand, causing a severe wound. For the remainder of that first week, he was allowed to perform light odd-jobs in and around the kitchen, under the benevolent supervision of Gladys Coppin who believed the young boy needed a great deal of 'feeding-up'.

But Charlie soon ceased to be the main topic of conversation at Polrudden. A few days after the reception at which Prince Rao announced his future intentions, the future ruler of Sikar was taken violently ill.

When the doctor from Mevagissey was summoned to the house he suggested the prince had eaten something that had disagreed with him.

'It's hardly surprising,' explained the doctor confidently. 'People from Eastern countries are not used to our foods. Fortunately, the severest symptoms rarely last for longer than a day or two. You should see an improvement by then.'

After two days Prince Rao was worse than ever and Dewi had doubts about the accuracy of the physician's diagnosis. No one else on the Prince's staff had fallen ill and all the food was prepared in the Polrudden kitchen.

The doctor was called in once more and when Dewi voiced her observations, the doctor admitted there were certain 'puzzling' elements to the case.

'He has all the classic symptoms of poisoning,' mused the doctor. 'Yet, as you quite rightly say, no one else seems to have been affected in the same way. Of course, he does hail from a foreign country and they have many maladies in such places. Diseases of which we in England know nothing. Some might take months to show themselves. If it *is* something he has contracted in India, then I doubt if we have a doctor in the country able to identify Prince Rao's illness. All I can do is make up some physic when I return to Mevagissey and have it sent to you. We must hope it will have some success.'

The surgeon left, leaving Dewi far from confident that his 'physic' would have any effect.

Contrary to Dewi's expectations, Prince Rao's condition *did* show some improvement over the next couple of days. However, just when she believed he might be on the mend, he was struck down once more. This time the symptoms were even more severe than before.

Abigail had become a daily visitor during the illness of her fiancé. When she left the sick-room after his latest bout of sickness she was close to tears.

'I feel so *helpless*,' she confessed to Dewi. 'I would like to stay with him for every hour of the day, but feel he'll rest more if I leave him. It's not as though I am doing anything by remaining in the room.'

In the passageway, not far from the room, they met Jainu. Prince Rao's secretary was heading toward's Prince Rao's room bearing a tray on which was some food, prepared by the Indian servants in the Polrudden kitchen.

'You're wasting your time, Jainu,' said Abigail. 'The prince is in no condition to eat.'

'His Highness must eat,' declared Jainu, positively. 'He is very sick. Food is necessary to keep up his strength. I will personally feed him.'

'Something about that man gives me the shivers,' confessed Dewi. 'Has he been with Rao for very long?'

'For much of his life,' replied Abigail. 'He was appointed by Rao's father, the old Maharaja.'

235

She shook her head despairingly. 'If the Maharaja weren't so ill himself he would probably say that Rao's illness was a punishment from the gods, brought about because he's flouting Hindu law by marrying me. The Maharaja was always scrupulously polite to my father and to the rest of us when we were in Jhalapur, but it was well known that he really had no time for Europeans and our ways. There wouldn't have been an English Resident in Jhalapur had the Maharaja not been defeated in battle by the British army, years before we went there, and if he'd had his way Rao would never have been allowed English tutors. He would never have forgiven Rao for marrying me and would be happy to know that Rao's brother will rule Jhalapur in his place.'

'Jainu is aware of all this?'

'Of course. He probably holds the same views as the old Maharaja. But why do you ask? You don't think he would deliberately do anything to prevent Rao from getting better?'

'No,' lied Dewi, anxious not to add to Abigail's worries. 'I've taken a totally unreasonable dislike to the man. I do that sometimes, it's a bad fault of mine. Now, I'll go and get you something to eat from the kitchen before you return to Golant. And you mustn't worry, I'll keep my eye on Rao. He'll be well long before the wedding . . .'

In spite of her reassurances to Abigail, Dewi believed Jainu knew more about the illness of his master than anyone else. When Rao adamantly refused food for two days he improved noticeably. When he began eating once more his illness returned with renewed ferocity.

Dewi made enquiries in the kitchen and confirmed that Jainu alone took food to the prince's room. When she asked why, she was informed by Rao's servants that the secretary had a responsibility to the prince's father for the well-being of his son. Furthermore, Jainu had told the others it was not right for a servant to see a royal prince in such poor health.

When one of the East India Company directors, alarmed at the increasing seriousness of the prince's condition, suggested he should send for the Company doctor on board the Company merchantman lying in Falmouth harbour, Dewi agreed. But she intended carrying out a plan of her own before the doctor reached the house.

Dewi believed Jainu was poisoning the prince. She could not convince herself the secretary intended killing his master, only that he intended keeping the prince in such a weak condition that he would be prevented from marrying Abigail.

She hid herself away in various rooms along the route taken by Jainu when carrying food to Rao, peering at him through partly open doors, but saw nothing remotely suspicious. If he was adding anything to the food it must be taking place inside the sick-room. She found an opportunity to search the room but again drew a blank. Undeterred, she told herself the secretary would hardly leave an incriminating substance in the room where it might be found. He would be carrying it upon his person – and Dewi thought she knew a way to prove once and for all whether her suspicions were well founded. She would call upon the services of Charlie Philpotts.

Charlie was still spending much of his time in the Polrudden kitchen. Gladys complained constantly that wherever she turned around she found the cockney boy 'under her feet'. Yet she had become fond of the young orphan and Dewi suspected she encouraged Charlie's presence.

Dewi sent for the London boy, but her heart sank when he entered the play-room and she saw the heavy bandage on his right hand.

'They said in the kitchen you wanted to see me, miss?' For some reason, Charlie showed a deference to Dewi that was sadly lacking in his dealings with the other members of the household.

'That's right, Charlie. There was something I wanted you to do for me. Something that no one else could possibly do, but I'd forgotten about your injured hand. I fear it will make what I have in mind impossible . . .'

'Don't you believe it, miss. I often used to go out thieving with me right 'and bandaged up like this. Most gents would ignore me because they thought I couldn't do nothing with an injured hand. The fing is . . . I'm left-'anded, see? While they were eyeing me bandaged 'and, the other one would be in their pocket, lifting their purse. But you won't want to 'ear about that.'

'That's just where you're wrong, Charlie. In fact, it's a bit of pick-pocketing I have in mind for you. Do you think you could go through the pockets of Jainu, Prince Rao's secretary, without him knowing?'

'Wiv the loose clothes 'e wears?' Charlie said scornfully. 'I could strip the 'airs off 'is chest without him knowing anyfing about it, if that's what you wanted.'

Despite the seriousness of what she was about to do, Dewi could not hide a smile. 'No, I'm not interested in the hairs on his chest, Charlie, but I'm going to share a secret with you. This must remain strictly between the two of us if we're not both to get into serious trouble, do you understand?'

'Cross-me-'eart, miss, I won't say a word to no one.'

'Good. Now, I believe Jainu is adding something to Prince Rao's food to make him ill. I don't know what it is, and I don't know where he keeps it, but it's my belief that it's added in the prince's room when Jainu takes him a meal. Do you think you

237

can somehow go through his pockets and see if there's anything there?'

'Course I can! Blimey, when them lot are preparing food for the prince in the kitchen there's so much pushing and shoving and chatter going on you could pinch everything they owned wiv'out being caught. Don't you worry, miss. If he's up to any mischief I'll bring the proof to you – and 'appy to do it. You'd fink 'e was the prince the way 'e lords it over the other servants. Gladys'll be glad to be rid of 'im.'

Dewi told Nathan nothing of her suspicions, nor of her efforts to have them proven. She was glad she had kept her own counsel when, that evening, Charlie reported to her that he had 'inspected' the Indian secretary's pockets in the kitchen without finding anything.

She began to doubt her suspicions still more when the East India Company doctor arrived from Falmouth after dark that night. After a thorough examination of the prince, he suggested that the Mevagissey doctor had probably been correct. Prince Rao showed all the symptoms of a man who was suffering from a very severe attack of food poisoning.

Dewi lay awake for much of the night worrying. If her theory was wrong, as it would seem to be, what could be causing Prince Rao's illness, and what could be done to bring him back to health? It was quite apparent from what the East India Company doctor had said, and from her own observations, that if something was not done to reverse the prince's decline very quickly, he would die.

Dewi was still worrying the next morning as she dressed when there came a sudden, soft knocking at her door.

Still buttoning up her dress, she called, 'Who is it?'

'It's me, Charlie. It's urgent, miss.'

Hurriedly fastening her buttons, Dewi opened the door and Charlie slipped into the room. In his hand he held a small wooden box inlaid with elaborate patterns formed from slivers of ivory. 'I've got this for you, miss. I fink it's wot you're after.'

Charlie placed the box in her hand. Opening it carefully, she discovered it to be half full of a greyish powder.

'Where did you get this?'

'From Jainu. He came to the kitchen early, same as 'e always does, to take an early morning cup of tea to the prince. This was in his pocket.'

'He wasn't aware that you took it?'

'Don't be daft, miss. I could nick a crust from a baby's mouth and it'd still be sucking 'appily for another 'alf-hour.'

'Thank you, Charlie. If this is what I think it is, Prince Rao owes you his life. Away you go now – but keep clear of the kitchen until everything's sorted out. Jainu may realise it's you who has taken the box from him. If he would kill his prince, he's not going to think twice about harming you.'

Chapter 48

Nathan was on his way to breakfast when Dewi waylaid him to tell of what she had done, with Charlie's help.

Far from being pleased with her, Nathan was aghast.

'Why didn't you discuss it with me before doing something like this, Dewi? Jainu was appointed to be Prince Rao's protector by the Maharaja himself. He's been his guardian angel since Rao was a small boy. What would persuade him to harm Rao now? I think you've made a grave error of judgement, Dewi.'

'I don't think so.'

But suddenly Dewi felt far from sure. It had not occurred to her that Nathan might question her actions. If he failed to support her she would be in serious trouble.

'I know Jainu has been with Prince Rao for a very long time, but he was appointed because the Maharaja feared the influence a Company-backed education would have upon him. I believe Jainu's real task is to ensure that Rao maintains the Hindu customs of his people. Rao has already said his father didn't believe in progress. His younger brother was favoured because he's a more orthodox Hindu.'

'I can't believe a father would sanction the death of his son, whatever the reason. What's more, I don't approve of Charlie's part in this. You really should have spoken to me before taking such action, Dewi.'

Nathan gnawed on his lip as he thought about Dewi's theory and what she had done in her attempt to prove her suspicions. 'We'll take this powder to the East India Company doctor and see what he makes of it. If he says it's harmless then we'll think of some way to return it to Jainu without causing too much embarrassment to anyone.'

The East India Company doctor was in his room speaking with one of the Company directors when they took the powder to him. He listened in silence as Nathan told him how the powder had been obtained and of the theory that had prompted such action. Nathan said nothing of Dewi's part in the matter.

Doctor Ian McKay was a cautious and conservative man, not given to jumping to wild conclusions. Opening the box as Nathan was speaking, he examined the contents and frowned. Taking out a small, folding magnifying glass, he examined the powder in greater detail. After sniffing the powder a number of times, he wet the tip of a finger. Gently touching the powder, he carried a minute quantity to his tongue.

Immediately reaching for a glass of water, he proceeded to rinse out his mouth, spitting out the contents into a bowl on the washstand.

'You say Jainu was carrying this when he was taking food to Prince Rao?'

'That's right. Do you know what it is?' Dewi asked the question anxiously, eager to vindicate the actions she had taken.

'I will need to make some tests before I can be absolutely certain, but it reminds me very much of a potion I came across in India a few years ago. It was made up from the seeds of a plant closely resembling digitalis.'

'But is it poisonous?' This time the question came from Nathan.

'The potion was used by an Indian servant to kill his English master. The Englishman was believed to be responsible for the pregnancy of the servant's young daughter. It was a tragic story . . .'

Catching the horrified glance that passed between Dewi and Nathan, the doctor added hastily, 'As I say, I will need to make further tests. However, the symptoms of the prince fit many of the known attributes of digitalis poisoning. Slow pulse rate, irregular heart-beat . . . I feel it would be better were the prince's secretary kept well away from his master for the time being.'

'I'll have Jainu removed to the Company ship, at Falmouth,' said the East India Company director grimly. 'If this *does* turn out to be a case of poisoning, then he'll be sent for trial in India.'

'In the meantime I'll ensure someone is with the prince day and night,' said Nathan. 'Some of the other servants may also be involved.'

'I doubt it very much,' said the director of the East India Company. 'If Doctor McKay proves this substance to be a poison from India, it would seem Jainu was fully prepared to murder Prince Rao when he left that country, should he deem it necessary. He would not have needed to involve anyone else. However, it's a wise precaution – but I suggest we confront Jainu immediately.'

While Dewi hurried away to arrange for someone to remain with the prince, Nathan and the East India Company director set off in search of Jainu – but the murderous secretary was nowhere to be found.

There was evidence in his room of a hasty departure and enquiries among the servants revealed that soon after taking breakfast to the prince's room, Jainu had returned to the kitchen, highly agitated. He was seeking a small, wooden box, claiming it contained something of great importance.

When the box could not be found, the secretary must have realised it had been stolen from him. There could be only one explanation for such a theft. Suspicion had fallen upon him for the condition of the prince. He had fled hurriedly.

Nathan sent out men to scour the countryside, but the Indian secretary had made good his escape.

That evening Doctor McKay was able to report to a greatly relieved Abigail that Prince Rao's heartbeat and pulse rate had improved. It was the doctor's opinion that Jainu had been detected just in time. The East India Company doctor was now convinced that the powder was poison. Had it been administered to Prince Rao for another twenty-four hours, his heart would have failed and he would have died.

Quite late that evening there was a knock on Dewi's door. It was unusual for her to have visitors at this time of the day and she was preparing for bed.

'Who is it?'

Even as she spoke Dewi was gathering up her nightdress and other clothing to tidy the room should she need to open the door, although she believed it was probably a servant, seeking her advice about Beville.

'It's Abigail. I'd like to speak to you.'

She and her uncle had arrived during the afternoon to visit Rao. The weather had deteriorated to such an extent, snow mixed in with a persistent rain, that a groom had been sent to inform Lady Penhaligan that the two would remain at Polrudden overnight.

Dewi re-doubled her efforts, at the same time calling out, 'Just a minute.'

Putting the final touches to her whirlwind bout of tidying, she glanced in the mirror, smoothed back her hair, and opened the door.

'I'm sorry I was so long,' she apologised. 'I wasn't expecting company. Won't you come in?'

Stepping into the room, Abigail said, 'I was in two minds about calling on you at such a late hour, but I've just come from Rao. I wanted to thank you. He is so much better this evening. I will sleep happily knowing that he's going to recover now.'

She shuddered. 'If it hadn't been for you, I dread to think what would have happened.'

'We're all very relieved that it's over,' said Dewi, placing a sympathetic hand on her arm. 'It's been a horrible time for you.'

'Yes.' Abigail sat in the chair pulled forward for her by Dewi. 'I had hoped to see you at dinner, but Nathan said you needed to be with Beville.'

'That's right. He's had a bad day. I wanted to tell him a bedtime story and see him settled down for the night.'

242

Dinner had been attended by Nathan's house guests, Doctor McKay, the two East India Company directors and Abigail and her uncle. Dewi would not have been comfortable in their company. Pippa Hanna had a heavy cold and had been sent home by Dewi earlier in the day. She was able to use this as an excuse to have her dinner with Beville, who was still recovering from measles.

'He's a very lucky boy to have someone like you to care for him – and to live here, in Polrudden. I think this is a wonderful house. It seems my whole future has been decided here. First by Nathan's efforts, and now by your astuteness. Doctor McKay said at dinner that another one or two doses of the poison would probably have been enough to kill Rao. Can you imagine such a thing, Dewi? Not only would I have lost Rao and the future we've planned together, but . . . I would always have believed his death to be the result of coming to England to see me. How could his father have sent such a man to spy on Rao, Dewi? His own son!'

Abigail's emotions overcame her and she began weeping.

Dropping to her knees beside the anguished woman, Dewi took her in her arms. 'You can put it all behind you now. Look forward to the future you and Rao are going to enjoy together. Besides, you don't know for certain that Rao's father was behind this. Jainu probably misinterpreted his instructions. Rao's father would probably be as upset as you if he'd known what Jainu would do.'

Abigail shook her head tearfully, 'No, Dewi. I haven't told Rao, and I never will, but I've learned that the servants were always aware of Jainu's real role among them. He comes from a family that has supplied assassins to generations of Maharajas. Among Rao's servants he was known as "The Executioner".'

'They knew? Yet nobody said anything about it to Rao?'

'No one dared. On board the ship on the way to England one of Rao's attendants had a bitter quarrel with Jainu. He died in agony and the ship's doctor said it was the result of eating bad food, bought at their last port of call. The other servants knew better, but no one dared risk upsetting Jainu.'

'It's unbelievable! I'm so glad he's gone. He made my skin creep!'

'Rao shares my gratitude. He's a very rich man and he said you are to be rewarded with anything you ask.'

Dewi smiled. 'My reward is knowing you and Rao are to be married. There are some things money can't buy, Abigail, and there's very little I really need. I have money put by, enough to provide me with a small income should I need it in the future. For now . . . well, I'm very happy here at Polrudden.'

Abigail also smiled, for the first time since entering Dewi's room. 'You will be even happier if things work out the way both you and I hope they will. You're a very special woman – and

Nathan is a very special man. You're both made for each other. I can see it, and so can Nathan's sister, Nell. One day he will open his eyes and see it for himself.'

Chapter 49

By Christmas Day, Prince Rao was a wan but cheerful version of his old self. He was familiar with the story of Christmas and his first journey outside Polrudden was to the church at St Ewe with Nathan, Dewi and Beville. They were joined here by Sir Henry Penhaligan and his three daughters. Sir Kenwyn was unable to come with them as he traditionally read the Christmas lesson in his own local church.

After the service Hugh Cremyll accompanied the party to Polrudden where they exchanged presents before lunch. It was difficult to know what to give to a prince who had so many possessions, but Nathan's gift of a specially made saddle was received with delight by Rao.

The present given to Nathan in return was truly breathtaking. The prince gave him an ornate box of carved and well-polished wood. The box itself would have delighted the owner of Polrudden, but when he opened it he gasped in disbelief. It was half filled with beautifully cut gems, each the size of a man's thumbnail.

Before Nathan could recover from his astonishment, Prince Rao said, 'That is more than a present for Christmas, my friend. It is an expression of my gratitude for giving Abigail hope when a future together seemed impossible for the two of us. It also expresses my appreciation for your part in making the impossible a reality.'

Nathan was about to protest that such a present was too generous, but Rao had already beckoned a servant forward to hand him a box similar in design to the one handed to Nathan, but longer in shape.

Turning to Dewi, Prince Rao presented her with the box.

'This is for you. It is a token gift only, for who can put a value on life? When I return to India and am formally accepted as Maharaja of Sikar I will have a letter sent to you. It will inform you that whatever you ask from my country shall be yours – and Sikar is a rich country. Until then, this necklace will remind you of my promise. It will also be a beautiful match for the earrings you are wearing.'

Dewi was wearing the sapphire earrings given to her by Nathan. When she opened the box her reaction was no less incredulous than his had been. It contained a gold and sapphire necklace of breathtaking beauty. She could not even hazard a guess at its value, but she realised she would never be a poor woman again.

After everyone had eaten Christmas lunch it was the turn of the Polrudden servants to receive presents. Assembled in the hall each received a token but expensive gift from Prince Rao. Among those present was Charlie Philpotts. Having been at Polrudden for only a couple of weeks he did not expect to receive anything, but was singled out by the prince for a special gift.

The servants gasped when Charlie was handed a gold watch encrusted with jewels. Unable to contain his delight, he said, 'Gawd! This must be worth a fortune!'

'Should I value my life at less?' Prince Rao gave Charlie an amused smile. 'I have been told how you obtained proof that Jainu was trying to poison me. Had you been brought before me in Sikar I would have been obliged to order that your hand be cut off. Instead, I am rewarding you. It is a novel experience. One I will remember with much pleasure – and immense gratitude. For you, Sikar will always provide a refuge, should there come a time when it is needed.'

On New Year's Day 1818, Sir Kenwyn Penhaligan held a dinner at Tregony to introduce Nathan to the borough's voters. Many were tenants of Sir Christopher Hawkins and, in order to ensure their attendance, the Golant baronet let it be known that Nathan would be accompanied by Prince Rao.

The dinner was held in a huge canvas pavilion, erected just outside the town, and every man to whom an invitation had been given was there.

Prince Rao was attended by his own cooks and servants and his every gesture followed closely by the fascinated guests. Nathan gave an election speech, setting out what he hoped to achieve as the Member of Parliament for Tregony, but his words did not matter. He had given the voters of the borough an opportunity to dine with Prince Rao, future Maharaja of the far-off Indian state of Sikar. It was something the guests would boast of for many years to come. A milestone in their rural lives. Because of it, Nathan had already gained the votes of many of them.

But Columb Hawkins was also standing for the seat and he had no intention of allowing Nathan to steal votes in such a fashion. When the dinner was well underway a commotion was heard outside the pavilion.

At first Nathan thought the noise was no more than a few drunken men making their way home from the local inn. However, it was soon evident this was a more organised disturbance.

The noise soon became a chant promoting Columb Hawkins as Member of Parliament for Tregony. But the men outside the pavilion did not intend restricting their expressions of opposition to chanted slogans.

Two men had been left at the door by Sir Kenwyn Penhaligan to check the credentials of guests attending the dinner. The disturbance outside moved closer and first one and then the other doorman was thrown backwards through the doorway. They were closely followed into the pavilion by the leaders of the dissenters.

Nathan recognised one of them immediately. He was the man he had thrown into the St Austell river when Columb Hawkins had closed the bridge to the residents of Pentuan.

He rose to his feet, intending to take him on once more, despite the heavy clubs wielded by the man's companions who were crowding through the door behind him.

Nathan's intervention was not needed. Prince Rao had guessed what was going on and had sent a servant hurrying to a canvas door at the rear of the pavilion. While the troublemakers were still looking around the pavilion, deciding where to begin their mischief, the canvas flap to the annexe was thrown back and silk-clad *Rajputs* poured into the pavilion. When they saw the intruders they let out shrieks that terrified even those who were there by invitation.

Drawing their curved swords as they came, they ran around the tables, heading for the startled men in the doorway. Long before the Indian warriors reached them, the intruders were falling over each other in their haste to flee into the night.

Nathan began to apologise to his guests for the intrusion, but one of the men seated close to him at the table said, 'There's no need for you to apologise to us, Mr Jago, nor to concern yourself with what's happened. The story of how Hawkins's bully-boys were routed by an army of sword-bearing Indians will win you more votes than a bookful of words ever could. Them as couldn't come here tonight are going to regret it for the rest of their lives. Those warriors with their swords are the most fearsome sight I've ever seen in my life – and I was with Wellington at Waterloo! If I could give you two votes, I would, Mr Jago. I wouldn't have missed such a sight for worlds!'

The cold, wet weather that had held Cornwall in its grip for almost three weeks relented a day before the wedding of Prince Rao and Abigail Penhaligan.

It was an occasion that attracted representatives of the oldest and most dignified families in the land. The pews of the small, ancient church of St Ewe were filled to overflowing with well-dressed men and women. Around the altar and in the window spaces exotic flowers grown in the greenhouses of Cornwall spilled from huge vases and added myriad colours to the whitewashed interior.

Prince Rao arrived at the church in a closed carriage escorted by only four *Rajput* guards. The remainder of his fierce, mounted soldiers had been despatched to Golant to escort the bride to her wedding.

It was not only a colourful gesture, but a practical one. Jainu was still at large and the honour of his ancestors dictated that he should succeed in the mission entrusted to him by the ailing Maharaja of Jhalapur. He had failed in his bid to kill Prince Rao. His mission might still be accomplished were he to murder Abigail instead of her intended husband.

As a 'thank you' to Dewi for her part in thwarting Jainu's plan, Abigail had invited her to serve as one of her bridesmaids, together with Lydia and Sofia. Dewi had accepted because it would enable her to stay close to Beville, who was serving Abigail as a page.

The wedding was all that a bride could have wished. It was doubtful whether Abigail even heard a small group of dissenters who objected to the marriage of a Hindu prince in a Christian church. They were jostled to the back of the huge crowd by determined onlookers. The Cornish villagers were angry that anyone should attempt to spoil the day for 'the lovely young maid' who was marrying her prince.

After the ceremony was over the bride and bridegroom were cheered from the church by the crowds and the guests returned to Polrudden. Here they enjoyed a reception such as the house had not seen for very many years.

Before the festivities began, Rao and Abigail, together with all the Indian servants, went to a specially prepared room. Here a Brahmin holy man performed a much shortened version of the traditional five-day-long Hindu marriage ceremony. The full ceremony would take place upon the couple's arrival in Sikar. However, this was sufficient to ensure the young couple were man and wife according to the laws of both their countries.

As the newly wed couple emerged from the room where the Hindu ceremony had taken place they were showered with rice grains by Rao's servants.

Nell and Dewi were standing outside the room and Dewi said, 'Abigail was telling me about this part of the ceremony. Rice is a symbol of fertility. It's a wish that they might have lots of children during their married lives together.'

Nell made a strangled sound in her throat. 'If that's what they really want then they should forget the rice and come to spend a few weeks at Venn Farm!'

Dewi looked at Nell in disbelief. 'You're not saying you're pregnant *again*?'

'Not yet, but I expect I shall be before the year's out.'

Chapter 50

Three days after their marriage, Prince Rao and Abigail took passage in an East India company vessel from Falmouth, bound for India and their new life in Sikar. Sir Henry and Sofia Penhaligan sailed with them.

Nathan, Dewi and Beville went to Falmouth to see the party off as did Lydia and Hugh Cremyll. It was a tearful parting for the sisters. Lydia, in particular, looked very forlorn standing on the quayside as the ship carrying her family set off to sail halfway around the world.

Those on the quayside remained waving until the ship was lost in the mist that reduced visibility to no more than a mile. Then Hugh Cremyll led his tearful bride-to-be to a waiting carriage, leaving Nathan and the others to follow.

Whilst at Falmouth they learned that Jainu was also on his way to Sikar. He had been arrested by the master of another East India Company vessel when he tried to buy a passage to India. Travelling in irons on the other ship, he would go on trial in India for attempting to murder Prince Rao. His fate was a foregone conclusion, his death more certain than that of the prince he had attempted to kill.

Nathan was unusually silent on the journey from Falmouth and Dewi said to him, 'Are you going to miss Abigail?'

Startled from his thoughts by the question, Nathan said, 'Yes, I suppose I am . . . But I'm going to miss the whole family. Rao too. No doubt the servants at Polrudden will be breathing great sighs of relief now his staff have left, but the house will seem very empty without them.'

'Yes, it will.' Dewi had become very close to Abigail during the last couple of weeks. She would miss her too. 'But you'll probably have another nephew or niece this year. That's something for you to look forward to.'

Nathan groaned. 'Poor Pa finds it difficult to remember all their names now. If she has any more she'll need to stitch numbers on them.'

'Preacher Jago called at Polrudden earlier this morning. He said there's been no work on the harbour at Pentuan for two days.'

'That's right. There has been so much rain work has stopped

249

until the weather improves. The men have been paid up. They'll no doubt remain in Pentuan until the money's all been spent, then they'll make their way home and wait for the weather to break.'

'Does that mean the harbour will take longer to complete than you thought?'

Nathan gave a mirthless laugh. 'There have been so many problems it's no longer possible to predict a realistic completion date. There are times when I wish I'd allowed Sir Christopher Hawkins to buy up all the shares. All the headaches I have now would be his.'

Nathan had never been convinced the harbour was either needed or practicable. His involvement in the first place was solely to curb Sir Christopher Hawkins's more grandiose plans and so prevent the destruction of Pentuan as a community. The problems associated with the building work were taking far more time than he had to spare right now, especially with the by-election at Tregony looming on the horizon.

Nathan was not the only man with troubles originating in Pentuan. The weeks of bad weather that had caused the temporary cessation of work on the harbour, had also kept the fishing fleet from venturing to sea. As a result, the attention of the villagers turned inwards upon their own community.

It did not take them long to find a subject for gossip.

In an attempt to keep her pregnancy a secret for as long as possible, Sally Wicks had gone to great lengths to conceal her condition. She let out the seams of her dresses and tried to wear clothes that hung loosely. More recently, she never left the house without a length of linen bound tightly about her midriff. Yet all her efforts were to no avail.

Walking along the village street she was aware of the nudges and whispers accompanying glances in her direction, whenever she passed by a group of women. Even more hurtful to her, the young men who had once been happy enough to linger on the Winnick with her for an hour or two now studiously avoided her. Each seemed anxious that his name should not be linked with hers.

Eventually, she could take the scornful looks, the innuendoes and the ostracism, no longer. It was Columb Hawkins's fault she was in this condition. His baby she was carrying. He must do something about it.

Columb Hawkins was living in Trewithan, his uncle's large house some nine miles from Pentuan. Sally set out during a lull in the rain but still had an hour's walk ahead of her when it began raining once more.

By the time she reached Trewithan she resembled a drowned rat and was shaking with cold and apprehension. Approaching the great house, she knew a moment of uncertainty. It was much larger than she had imagined. Larger than Polrudden.

Her hesitation lasted for only a few minutes. She had come here to talk to Columb Hawkins. She would not be overawed by a large and imposing house. Neither would she go to the servants' entrance. She had been good enough for Columb Hawkins when he took her to bed. He would see her at the front door.

The maid who answered the door to her took one disapproving look at her and mistook her for a gypsy girl. 'Whatever it is you'm selling, you can take it to the back door.'

Even as she spoke the maid was closing the door and before Sally could state her purpose it was shut in her face.

For a few moments she stared at the wooden door in dismay. Then anger took over. Reaching out, she tugged at the bell-pull again and again.

The door was opened by the same maid, but this time a large frowning man dressed in the livery of a butler stood behind her.

'I told you it would be her again,' said the maid. 'These gypsies never take no for an answer.'

'What do you mean by ringing the bell in such a manner?' The butler's voice was as large as his body, but Sally told herself firmly that he too was a servant, same as the maid.

'I'm no gypsy and I'm not selling anything. I've come here to speak to Mr Hawkins. Mr Columb Hawkins.'

The butler hesitated. The girl looked and spoke like a village girl and her clothing was totally inadequate for the weather. Had she come asking for Sir Christopher, he would have sent her packing. But she was demanding to speak to Columb – and the baronet's nephew had some peculiar friends. He could also be extremely angry when crossed.

'If you care to come inside – to the *outer* hall, if you please – I'll see whether Master Columb will speak to you, Miss . . . ?'

'Miss Wicks. Sally Wicks from Pentuan – and he'd *better* see me, if he knows what's good for him.'

Columb Hawkins was fully aware of the consequences of refusing Sally, but it did not prevent him from being very angry when he came to the outer hall.

'How *dare* you come to my uncle's house and demand to see me? Look at the state of you! I'm surprised they even opened the door to you.'

'I've walked all the way from Pentuan. I had to see you, there's no one else I can turn to. You don't know what it's like in Pentuan for a girl in my condition. Everyone looking at me, saying things behind my back . . .'

Sally's lower lip trembled as self-pity gripped her.

'For God's sake, don't start blubbering here, girl.' Columb had seen his uncle's butler standing in the shadows in the hall. 'You'd better come inside – but keep your mouth shut until we get

251

somewhere where we won't be overheard.'

As Columb and his sodden companion passed into the main hall, the butler stepped forward. 'Is there something I might get for you or for the young lady, Master Columb?'

'No . . . I mean, yes. The young lady has come a long way to bring me a message. I'm taking her to the library, there's a fire in there.'

'Yes, sir. Would you like me to have a maid bring a towel? Or something dry for the young lady to put on? A maid's uniform, perhaps?'

'I'll attend to the young lady. You may go now.'

'Thank you, sir.' The butler inclined his head in Columb's direction, gave Sally an expressionless glance, then went off along the passageway.

'He doesn't believe you. He thinks I'm just a trull. I don't like him.'

'I don't give a damn what you do or don't like! Or what my uncle's butler believes. We'll get to the library and you can tell me why you're here. Once you've done that you can get on home again. I'll not give the servants anything to talk about in this house.'

When they reached the library and Columb closed the door behind them, Sally's lower lip began trembling once more. 'Why are you so angry with me? You never used to be. Not when you were in the old Customs house in Pentuan. You were nice to me then – and look where that got me.' She patted her stomach meaningfully. 'This is why I'm here, and well you know it. Well, it's *your* bastard, what are you going to do about it?'

'You know the answer to that. We discussed it months ago. Get your sailor lover to marry you and I'll give you a wedding present of fifty pounds. In view of the fact that any one of twenty or thirty young men could be the father of the baby you're carrying, I think that's a very generous offer.'

'No, it's not. You're its father. I know it and so do you. As for marrying the sailor . . . I can't. He's already got a wife in Swansea.'

'Damn the man! He ought to be whipped! Well, isn't there someone else you could blame! How about the village boys? Isn't there one of them who would marry you? My offer stands, no matter who you wed.'

'There'll be no wedding, I'm too far gone for that now. I'll just have to have the baby and manage the best I can – but I'll need more than fifty pounds to help me along. I'll need at least . . .' Sally cast a quick glance at Columb's expression and reduced her demand by a hundred pounds. 'At least a *hundred* and fifty pounds.'

He almost exploded with indignation. 'You must be mad, girl! I've made you a very fair offer in the circumstances. I've a good mind to have you thrown out of the house.'

'If you did, I'd sit on the doorstep until Sir Christopher came home and then I'd tell him all about us.'

'Don't you threaten me, young lady, or you'll be answering to the magistrate in addition to all your other problems.'

'I'll be answering to him anyway when the baby comes along, so it won't make any difference to me. When I name you as the father no doubt he'll want to speak to you too. Before then I'll probably go up to Polrudden, tell Mr Jago what's happened and ask his advice.'

Sally was blackmailing him. Columb Hawkins knew it, but there was very little he could do. Relations between his uncle and himself were already strained. He could not afford to upset Sir Christopher any more. There was also the matter of the forth-coming by-election which promised to be a very close-run contest. Far closer than he or Sir Christopher would have liked. If Sally went to Polrudden and told Nathan Jago about the child, Columb's prospects of being elected to Parliament would fly out of the window. The electors *should* be loyal to Sir Christopher, but they were staunch Methodists to a man. A scandal such as this would cause them to hand their votes to Jago, whatever the consequences for themselves.

'Look, Sally, let's not be hasty about this. You've come here tonight and taken me by surprise. I am a very busy man at the moment, what with the forthcoming election and helping my uncle to run his estates. I can't give you the money you want tonight. I don't have that sort of money with me. But if that's the amount you need to take care of things, then I'll get it for you as soon as I can. But . . . are you quite certain this sailor isn't in a position to marry you? He might only have pretended to be married in order to evade his responsibilities. When did you speak to him?'

'Yesterday. His ship's on the beach at Pentuan until the day after tomorrow – and there's no doubt about him being married. I asked one of the crew.'

'Very well, I'll have the money tomorrow night – but you're not to come here again. I'll meet you on the beach at Pentuan, as soon as it's dark. Make it the end farther away from the village. Is that all right?'

'I knew you wouldn't fail me, Columb. It will be the last time I trouble you for money, I promise you.'

Even as she made the statement, Sally knew it was a lie. She intended that Columb Hawkins should provide her with a regular income. She would make sure of that.

Columb Hawkins's thoughts were echoing those of Sally. He was aware that if he paid her the sum she was demanding then he would be milked of money for the remainder of his life.

To have such a threat hanging over his political life was not something he intended to allow.

Chapter 51

The heavy rains of the past weeks gave way to a relentless drizzle, shrouded in a grey mist that seemed to penetrate even the warmest clothing.

Standing on the cliff edge in one of his fields, Nathan shivered and thrust his hands deeper into the pockets of his greatcoat. He was inspecting the spot where one of the farm-hands had reported a collapse of the cliff, brought about by the water draining down from the sloping field.

Looking at the scene, Nathan thought it was as though some giant creature had taken a bite from the cliff edge. Below him, surf surged over the newly won territory and thundered against the exposed and still crumbling cliff-face.

'We'd better get a fence put around this,' he said to the man who had reported the fall. 'Have it done today. There's more cliff to go yet. We don't want to lose any cattle over the edge.'

Nathan was still inspecting the extent of the fall when Will Hodge, the Polrudden head groom, rode out of the mist.

'Hello, Will. What are you doing out on a day like this? Not exercising the horse, surely?'

'I've come looking for you, to see if you can spare some of the men. They're getting a search party together in the village to go looking for young Sally Wicks. She went out last night and never came home.'

'That's not unusual, surely? Since she left Polrudden she's spent more than one night on the ships, from what I've heard.'

'She's never valued virtue very highly, it's true, but her mother says she's been behaving herself much better these past few months. It could mean she's becoming steadier, or it could mean that village gossip is right, for once.'

'Oh? What does gossip have to say about her?'

'She's pregnant. Either way, she's missing and her mother's very worried about her.'

'All right, send all the men we can spare down to the village – but I want the carpenter and his men to have a fence around this piece of cliff before nightfall. The edge is crumbling badly.'

'I'll tell him when I get back to the house. Do you know that young Charlie Philpotts is working with him now?'

'No.' Nathan had not seen the young cockney boy for some days.

'It seems he's quite clever with his hands. He's taken to carpentry like a duck to water.'

'I'm glad we've found something he enjoys. He's better off here than he was in London.' Nathan turned back to the cliff as the surf broke against it with a loud roar and a six-foot slice of land slid in to the sea.

'You'd better tell the men to put the fence right across the bottom of this field. Fence off a strip of about twenty paces. While you're at the house have a horse saddled for me. I need to show my face at Tregony. Sir Christopher Hawkins has been carrying out some serious canvassing there on behalf of his nephew. I think we're ahead on promised votes, but I must make sure we stay there.'

In Tregony, Nathan learned that Sir Christopher Hawkins's 'canvassing' had taken a more direct line than was usual when votes were being solicited. Those voters who were tenants of Sir Christopher were threatened with immediate and arbitrary eviction if they failed to support the nephew of their landlord.

The tenants of properties not owned by Sir Christopher were told that if they failed to support Columb, he would 'move heaven and earth' to purchase their properties and have them out before the next election came around.

Nathan was able to allay the fears of those whose homes were not owned by the baronet. To others, threatened with immediate eviction, he made a promise that either he or Sir Kenwyn Penhaligan would re-house them in similar properties to those they now occupied. It was a promise he had been authorised to make by Sir Kenwyn. Whether it was sufficient to secure their votes was uncertain.

Nathan was on his way home to Polrudden when, rounding a sharp bend in the narrow lane, he saw a horse standing at the side of the lane. Crouching beside the animal was a young woman, dressed in a dark green, waterproof riding habit. She appeared to be trying to lift one of the animal's hooves.

Reining in his mount, Nathan called, 'Is your horse giving trouble? Perhaps I might be of some assistance to you?'

The woman looked up at him when he rode alongside her. Aged about twenty-eight, she had dark eyes, black hair and a face that was somewhat pinched, but not unattractive.

'I would be obliged for your help, sir. I was on my way home when the horse began limping rather badly. I suspect it's picked up a stone, but it's a stubborn brute and won't lift its hoof for me.'

Swinging down from his own horse, Nathan tied it to a field gate only a few paces away.

The woman held the bridle of her horse as Nathan walked towards the animal.

'Whoa, there, fellow!'

Nathan spoke softly as the horse threw up its head, nervously. 'Steady, now! Which leg seemed to be lame?'

'The front left, I believe.'

Her accent was that of an educated woman and from a cursory glance, Nathan had observed that her clothes were both stylish and expensive.

The horse stood still and allowed him to run his hand down its front left leg. When his hand reached the fetlock, the horse shifted its weight to the other legs and lifted the hoof obligingly for him.

'It's quite apparent it's a man's horse!'

The woman spoke with some exasperation as Nathan inspected the underside of the hoof. There was a small amount of mud here, apparently picked up from the grass verge on which the animal was standing, but no stone.

'I'll have a look at the others, just in case there's something there.'

The other hooves were as clear of stones as the first and when Nathan walked the horse along the lane there was no trace of a limp.

'I feel such a fool!'

The woman took the reins from the horse's neck and, stepping into Nathan's cupped hands, mounted the horse. Settling herself in the side-saddle, she adjusted the long skirts of her riding habit about her high riding boots.

'I am very sorry to have delayed you, sir. May I be so bold as to ask your name?'

'It has been a most pleasant diversion, ma'am – and my name is Jago. Nathan Jago.'

'You're standing for election here in Tregony! I am indeed honoured.'

In spite of her apparent surprise, Nathan had a feeling he had seen her somewhere before today.

'You are from these parts?'

'Forgive me, I haven't introduced myself. I am Felicia Brandon. Lady Felicia Brandon. I lived in Cornwall as a child, but have spent the last few years abroad. Latterly in Italy, with the Princess Caroline.'

Now it was Nathan's turn to be genuinely startled. Princess Caroline of Brunswick was the estranged wife of the Prince Regent. Since separating from her royal husband she had lived on the Mediterranean coast, much of the time in Italy. Her conduct there had been such that she had been the subject of numerous scandals.

'I see you are familiar with the stories concerning the Princess, Mr Jago?' She smiled at his embarrassment.

'I've heard the gossip, Lady Brandon. I don't doubt it's been exaggerated out of all recognition,' he replied hastily.

'Regrettably not.'

Felicia Brandon readjusted her skirts unnecessarily. 'If anything the rumours fall far short of the truth. One has to feel great sympathy with the Prince Regent for being wed to such a woman.'

She smiled at Nathan. 'You are acquainted with the Prince, I believe?'

Her question took him by surprise. He wondered how this woman knew so much about him. 'I have met the Prince, but I'm more closely acquainted with his brother, the Duke of Clarence.'

'I have heard as much.'

As though reading his thoughts, Felicia Brandon added, 'You must know you are the talk of the county, Mr Jago? From fishermen and prizefighter to friend of royalty and host of Indian princes – not to mention having a considerable landholding.'

Once again Nathan had the uneasy feeling he had met this woman before, but he could not recall the occasion, and she was speaking to him once more.

'Won't you ride a little way with me? I promise not to take you too far out of your way. I am renting Golden for a while. Do you know it? It's a delightful manor house between Tregony and Grampound. It belongs to the family of my late husband.'

'You're a widow? I'm sorry.'

But Nathan was not sorry at all. Mounting his horse he pulled it alongside Felicia. 'I'll be delighted to ride to Golden with you.'

As they set off he glanced at his companion. She smiled at him and he returned the smile. He found he was looking at her in a new light now he knew she did not have a husband.

Chapter 52

It was dark before Nathan returned to Pentuan. He had ridden as far as Golden with Lady Felicia Brandon but had declined her offer to stay and have tea. The weather was threatening another storm and he wanted to be home before it broke.

As he entered the village sheet lightning was trembling on the horizon out at sea and the rumble of thunder rolled across the waters. Yet, above these natural sounds, he could hear a hulla-baloo coming from the direction of the cliffs on the Polrudden side of Pentuan. Flaming torches could be seen dancing like fire-flies along the cliff edge path. He wondered what could be causing such a commotion. It did not take him long to find the answer.

In the darkness of the village street he almost bowled over Charlie Philpotts. He recognised the boy by his swearing as he leaped out of the path of Nathan's horse.

'Charlie! What are you doing here – and what's going on over by the cliffs?'

'Mr Jago! They've been looking for you. All Hell's broken loose here in the village. They was searching for some girl – the one as used to work for you, up at Polrudden.'

'Sally Wicks. Have they found her?'

'They found her all right. Down by the edge of the beach, close to your fish-cellar. She was as dead as a doornail. She'd been strangled with a piece of rope. It was still tied around her neck.'

Nathan was aghast. Sally was a totally amoral girl, but she was lively and affectionate. It was hard to think of her as being dead. Murdered.

'Who would have done such a thing? Does anyone have any idea?'

'Oh, everyone in the village knows who did it – or they think they do. Last night this Sally was heard having an argument with a sailor from one of those Welsh ships on the beach. Seems he's got her into trouble and she wanted him to marry her. Only snag is, he's got a wife already.'

'Where's this sailor now?'

'He's run off along the cliff path, up towards Polrudden way. It seems he'd prefer to 'ave a rope put 'round 'is neck by a Jack Ketch than by a Johnnie Cornishman.'

'They wouldn't lynch him. He'd be put on trial.'

'Don't you believe it, Mr Jago. The mood the men are in they'll string him up to the nearest tree. They've even got the rope with them.'

'I'd better get after them and stop them before they do something they'll regret for the rest of their lives.'

'That's what your father said not three or four minutes ago. He's gone after 'em to try to stop what's going on.'

'I'll ride to Polrudden and try to head them off from there.'

As Nathan was about to urge his horse on, a thought made him pause. 'What are you doing in the village alone, Charlie? Why didn't you go off with the others?'

'Me? I've seen enough hue an' cries in London, Mr Jago. I've seen men – and boys – 'ung by the neck until they died, my own brother among 'em, and 'im no more'n fifteen. This sailor may 'ave killed someone and 'e probably deserves to die because of it, but I don't want to 'elp catch 'im. Neither do I want to see what 'appens when 'e is taken.'

With this revealing disclosure of his life and views, Charlie disappeared into the darkness. After only a moment's hesitation, Nathan heeled his horse into motion and set off up the steep hill towards Polrudden.

On his way up the hill, he had time to think out his strategy. Instead of turning in at the Polrudden drive he carried on along the lane and turned into a field that led to the cliff edge.

The field was steep here and he was forced to allow the horse to pick its way down the slope, but the flickering lightning out at sea allowed horse and rider glimpses of the route they were taking.

Nathan could see the torches of the villagers too. They seemed to have assembled in a semicircle at the spot where there had been the cliff fall, earlier in the day.

The crowd was still noisy but sounded angry now rather than revelling in the excitement of the chase as when it was passing through Pentuan.

As he drew nearer, Nathan could see that the Pentuan men were forming a semicircle about a figure which crouched at the cliff edge. He was on the wrong side of the fence erected to keep Polrudden cattle away from the ground which had fallen during the night.

In his hand the man wielded what appeared to be a pick-axe handle. Facing him, the villagers carried a variety of staves and cudgels, yet none ventured too close to the sailor.

All this Nathan could see in the uncertain light from flaming torches that cast weird, ruddy shadows across men's face, augmented occasionally by flickering lightning.

Inconsequentially, Nathan was reminded of a scene from the

stage play of *Romeo and Juliet* which he had attended with Dewi in London. The scene where the citizens of the watch turned out to pursue Romeo after the death of Tybalt . . .

Suddenly, another figure entered the scene. Nathan's father had laboured up the cliff path from the village as fast as he was able. Now, unsteady from his exertions, he put himself between the threatening villagers and their quarry.

'Wait . . . I pray you,' he appealed breathlessly to the villagers. 'Wait . . . lest you bring everlasting damnation upon your souls.'

''Tis his soul that's damned already, Preacher Jago,' growled one of the village men. 'He killed poor young Sally Wicks. Strangled her with a piece of rope and left her lying down on the Winnick. Now it's his turn to know how it feels to die with hemp about his neck.'

'His guilt is for a court to find,' pleaded Preacher Jago. 'His fate decided by a judge, within the law. Let no man here stand before The Lord on judgement day with the death of a fellow man staining his soul.'

'My father's right.' Sliding from his horse and leaving it to stand free, Nathan pushed his way through the villagers to where Preacher Jago faced them. Indicating the man cowering on the cliff edge, he said, 'Kill him and you'll climb the gallows' steps to pay for it.'

Nathan's manner became suddenly contemptuous. 'There isn't one of you here who'd give Sally Wicks so much as the time of day while she was alive. Why this sudden urge to hang for her now she's dead?'

There was an uncomfortable silence that lasted many seconds before one of the villagers said, 'She was one of us. We look after our own, you know that well enough, Nathan.'

'Yes, I know it – and I agree with it. But the best way you can look after your own families as well as avenging the death of Sally Wicks is to take this man and hand him over to the magistrate.'

There was another long silence, broken eventually by a villager saying, 'That's all very well, but he doesn't look as though he's ready to be taken before cracking a few heads.'

'He'll give himself up once he knows he's not going to be hurt.' Eager to follow up the advantage won by Nathan, Preacher Jago turned to the man crouching at bay behind him.

'You've heard what's been said. Give yourself up. My son and I will see you are taken before a court and given a fair trial.'

'I didn't kill Sally, I swear I didn't. I don't even think I was the father of the child she was expecting. I told her so last night. The last time I saw her.'

The seaman spoke with the same sing-song accent as Dewi.

'If that's the truth, you have nothing to fear. You can prove your innocence before a court. Come, give me that handle.'

As the seaman hesitated, Preacher Jago took a pace towards him.

Still the man seemed uncertain and the elderly preacher advanced closer.

'Come, you have nothing to fear from anyone now.'

The Welsh seaman stood up and held out the pick-axe handle to the preacher.

Suddenly, without any warning and with hardly a sound, seaman, preacher and the ground upon which they were both standing, disappeared before the horrified eyes of Nathan and the villagers.

Nathan's immediate instinct was to step forward but as a prolonged flicker of sheet-lightning lit the sky over the sea he looked down and leaped back immediately. Beneath him he could see black, cold rocks fringed with white foam, more than a hundred feet below. There was no more than a hand's breadth of ground between him and the fate that had befallen his father and the Welsh seaman.

The Pentuan men who only a few minutes before had been intent upon avenging Sally Wicks's death were now running for their life up the slope of the field.

Nathan went with them – but he was chasing his horse. When he caught the animal he leaped to the saddle and set off for the village, riding through the darkness at a reckless pace.

He was as close to blind panic as he had ever been in his life. He was not thinking straight. He had seen his father disappear as though snatched by an unseen hand. It had all happened so quickly he could not accept that the cliff had collapsed and taken his father with it. He was rushing to the village now, to take out a boat and find him. He refused to believe the fall had taken him to his death. Yet he had seen the rocks, far beneath him . . .

Nathan galloped the horse across the sands to his fish-cellar in Portgiskey Cove. On the way he passed the ships on the beach. The seaman accused of killing Sally belonged here yet there was not a light showing on any of the vessels. It was as though the men on board had cut themselves off from the happenings about them. Not wanting to know. Fearful, perhaps, that if the villagers were thwarted in their chase they would turn upon the companions of their intended victim.

Nathan's intention had been to take out a dinghy from the cove, but Francis Hanna was here with two of Nathan's fishermen. Taking advantage of the lull in fishing activities they had been fitting new rigging to the *Charlotte*. Tucked away in the tiny cove, they had been unaware of the drama taking place so close at hand.

Nathan's sudden arrival startled the crew who were enjoying a drink of ale at the end of a long but successful day's work.

Francis was a man of action and when Nathan jumped onboard and ordered him to put to sea he did not waste time demanding an explanation. Not until the fishing-boat was clearing the entrance to the small cove did Nathan explain that his father had gone over the cliff below Polrudden. He was going to look for him – or his body.

It was a hazardous quest, but Francis Hanna did not hesitate. Ordering the crewmen to light every lamp they carried on board, he shook out the mainsail and set a course for the Polrudden cliffs.

Chapter 53

Nathan and the crew of the *Charlotte* searched for the bodies of Josiah Jago and the Welsh seaman throughout the night. It was dangerous work but above them the cliffs were manned by shocked servants and villagers. Carrying lanterns on long poles or wielding firebrands, they provided a guide for the searchers who sailed perilously close to the rocks below them.

The storm that had threatened earlier in the night slowly grumbled its way eastwards along the English Channel leaving behind an angry swell that swirled over the rocks and spent itself against the tall cliffs.

As soon as a grey dawn replaced the black of night a whole flotilla of boats put out from the fishing communities along the whole length of the coast. Those without boats combed the foreshore, helping in the sad search.

Preacher Josiah Jago had been a well-known and much loved figure in Methodist chapels for miles around. To a great many people, he epitomised Methodism and had done so for the whole of their lives. The tragedy of his death would touch households far beyond Polrudden and Pentuan.

All day the boats remained at sea. Then, an hour before dusk, a body was seen washing in and out with the tide, about half-a-mile from the scene of the cliff collapse.

A small boat manned by two fishermen from nearby Polkerris braved rocks and an ugly swell to retrieve the body. Once in the boat they swiftly identified it as the missing preacher.

The body was transferred to the *Charlotte* and a sad convoy of boats returned to Nathan's fish-cellar at Portgiskey. There would be no further search. The boats had gone out seeking Preacher Jago. They would waste no time trying to find the seaman who had been the indirect cause of the tragedy. His body would never be found and no one outside Wales mourned his passing.

Men from Polrudden led by Will Hodge were waiting at Portgiskey with a sheep hurdle. In silence, Preacher Jago was conveyed to the Pentuan chapel he had built himself.

When the sad procession reached Pentuan they found the street lined with weeping women and sombre, bare-headed men. Josiah Jago had been their preacher for much of his life. He had shared their joys and their tragedies and played his part in births, marriages and deaths. They had lost a friend, a very good friend, and all shared Nathan's grief.

Inside the chapel, Josiah Jago was laid out by two old women who then left Nathan alone in the darkening chapel to pray for his father.

He remained in the chapel long after it became dark. He was not a deeply religious man, but he prayed tonight as his father would have wished.

He did not hear the door of the chapel open but suddenly became aware of someone kneeling beside him. It was Dewi.

She remained in silence for a while and Nathan knew that she too was praying. Then she said quietly, 'He was a truly great man in his way, Nathan. He'll be sadly missed.'

'Yes.' He hardly recognised his own voice, choked with emotion, as the words came out.

'It's been a hard time, a tragic time for you, but I think you should come home to Polrudden now.'

'Does Beville know?'

'Yes. He is very, very upset. He's cried himself to sleep but I've left Pippa with him, in case he wakes.'

'Poor little chap. He'll miss his grandpa.'

'We'll all miss him, but I think you should come home now, Nathan.'

Dewi expected to have a hard time persuading him. He was obviously stricken with grief. To her surprise, he said, 'Yes. Yes, you're right. I must go home. There's a lot to be done.' He spoke like a man who was thoroughly exhausted.

'There's nothing to be done that won't wait until tomorrow,' she replied. 'Come on now.'

Nathan climbed heavily to his feet. It seemed that every muscle in his body ached but it was hardly surprising. The past thirty-six hours had been gruelling ones, the sheer physical exertion sustained only by grief.

When he stood up he felt dizzy with exhaustion but Dewi was beside him and when he staggered she supported him.

It was a long trudge up the hill to Polrudden that night and Nathan and Dewi spoke very little along the way.

When they arrived at the great house it seemed at first as though it was in darkness but Dewi quickly realised that, in common with the houses of Pentuan, every window had a blind drawn out of respect for Josiah Jago. They would remain drawn until after his funeral.

In the light of the hall a tearful maid took Nathan's coat and Dewi observed that his unshaven face was more haggard than she had ever seen it.

'Come into the library. There's a nice fire going there. I'll have

Cook send up something from the kitchen for you.'

'I'm not hungry.' Nathan wearily waved aside the suggestion of food.

'Maybe not, but you'll have *something*. I'll tell her to send you up some soup, at least. You may not fancy it, but your body must be crying out for sustenance. I'm surprised you're still on your feet. Sit down here and I'll pour a drink for you. A very large brandy, is it?'

Without waiting for his reply, Dewi went to the brandy decanter and filled a tumbler two-thirds full. 'Here you are, you've earned it after all that's happened these past twenty-four hours.'

Nathan took the drink without protest and was halfway through a second by the time a bowl of soup and chunks of home-made bread arrived.

The drink had made him light-headed and as he ate he had trouble focusing his eyes upon Dewi.

He paused with the spoon halfway to his mouth and said fiercely, 'He was a good man, my father. A damned good man!'

'He was indeed. We've had to put a maid at the door all day, just to tell callers there was no news of him. He'll be sadly missed.'

'I didn't always see eye-to-eye with him, you know.'

Once again the spoon paused and Dewi said nothing, hoping it would complete its course to Nathan's mouth. He had eaten hardly anything yet. Instead, it was lowered to the soup dish once more.

'We didn't always see eye-to-eye . . . Have I already told you that?' Nathan frowned as he tried very hard to focus *both* eyes on her.

'I think you have, but it doesn't matter. You can tell me as many times as you wish.'

'Didn't see eye-to-eye . . . but I admired him. He was his own man. No matter what he did for anyone, he was always his own man. Not many men can say that, can they?'

'No, Nathan. Not many men.'

He nodded and this time the spoon traversed the full distance between soup dish and mouth.

'Does our Nell know? Has anybody told her?'

'I went to Venn and told her myself, last night. Tom's been to the house a couple of times today and he was one of the men searching along the foreshore. A servant went to tell her when he'd been found, but I'll go there myself a little later tonight.'

'You're a good girl, Dewi. One of the best. Don't know how I managed without you. Couldn't do without you now. Couldn't . . .'

Nathan stood up abruptly and Dewi just managed to catch the plate before it tilted and deposited its contents on the carpet.

'I'm going to bed, now . . . I feel so damned tired, Dewi. Why do I feel so damned tired?'

265

'Because you've been up and about for two days and a night. Because you're under a great strain – and because you've just lost your father . . .'

Dewi caught Nathan as he was about to sidestep away from the door. Putting his arm about her neck, she supported him to the door.

One of the maids was in the passageway and with her assistance Dewi managed to get Nathan as far as his bedroom. Inside, she and the maid removed his coat and shoes and got him to the bed.

'It's all right, you can leave him now. I'll settle him down for the night.'

The maid looked horrified. 'Wouldn't you rather I got one of the men up here, Miss Morgan?'

'I'm not going to undress him, if that's what you think. He won't know what he's wearing in bed tonight, and he certainly won't care. What he needs is a really good sleep, then he'll be able to face whatever tomorrow brings.'

When the maid had gone, Dewi built up the fire then pulled the sheets on Nathan's bed up to his chin and tucked him in.

Looking down at him, she thought that he and Beville were really very alike. Both had similar bone formation. Both had ears that stuck out rather more than they should.

Dewi remembered what Nathan had said to her before they came upstairs: 'Couldn't do without you, Dewi.' She wondered how much of that had been meant, and how much was merely the brandy talking?

It didn't matter too much. He had said it and that in itself gave her a warm glow.

Suddenly, and so impulsively that she startled herself, Dewi leaned over Nathan and kissed him, full on the lips. Straightening up, she remembered that the last time she had kissed him was on the evening of her birthday party, at Venn Farm. Her Uncle Morgan had not approved of that kiss. Too 'namby-pamby', he had said. He could not have said the same about this one.

She leaned over Nathan to kiss him once more but as her breath fanned him his eyelids flickered and he opened his eyes. For a moment Dewi held her breath, horrified that he might not have been as drunk as she had believed. That he realised what she had done.

Slowly, Nathan closed his eyes once more and with a feeling of embarrassed relief, Dewi tiptoed to the door and let herself out of his room.

Chapter 54

Walking to Venn Farm, Dewi hoped Nell would not be in bed. It was still early, despite the winter darkness, but the past two days would have been a great strain for her.

She was relieved to see a light on in the farm kitchen and entered to find Tom seated by the fire and Nell working at the kitchen table, with flour-covered hands and forearms.

Looking at the domestic scene, Dewi hesitated before asking, 'You know . . . ? You've heard about your father?'

Nell nodded without pausing in what she was doing, but Dewi had known her long enough to realise she was keeping a tight rein on her grief. 'Will Hodge came from Polrudden to tell us, but we realised last night that he'd never be found alive. He's at the chapel?'

Dewi nodded.

'Is our Nathan still with him?'

'No, I went down there and brought him back to Polrudden. I thought he would collapse before he reached home, he was so tired.'

'Poor Nathan. He'll be taking it particularly hard because he and Pa didn't always get along as well as they have in recent years. He'll be thinking of all the wasted time and blaming himself.'

Nell looked up from the mountains of dough that were heaped upon the table. 'I spent most of my grief last night. I was thankful I had Tom here to see me through it. Our Nathan has no one.'

'That's why I brought him home and made sure he went to bed with some food inside him, but I couldn't comfort him in the way he needs.'

'I'm sure you did very well, Dewi. I'm so glad you're there at Polrudden.'

Tom stood up from his seat at the fireside and carefully knocked his clay pipe out in the fire. 'If you'll excuse me, I've a pig and a cow both looking as though they're due to give birth some time tonight. Let me know when you're ready to go back to Polrudden, Dewi. I'll have a lantern ready for you. This rain has left so many potholes in that lane you're likely to break a leg in the dark.'

When he had gone, Dewi said, 'I don't really need a lantern. I came here all right.'

'Tom's a real old fusser – but he's the kindest man I know. I'm lucky to have him, and that's for certain.'

Nell brushed back a strand of hair, forgetting her hands were covered with floor. She left a streak of white across her forehead, 'I'm baking for the funeral. Our pa had so many friends I'll likely need to bake for two days and two nights to make enough.'

'I hadn't thought about that. I'll speak to Cook at Polrudden. She can get the girls working on something there.'

'Thanks.' Without pausing in her work, Nell looked across the room to where Dewi sat. 'You'll keep an eye on our Nathan? Make certain he gets enough to eat – and doesn't blame himself for what's happened?'

'Why should he do that? No one could have known the cliff was going to collapse when it did.'

'Perhaps not. From what I hear it was both Nathan and Pa who stopped the villagers from forcing that sailor over the cliff edge. If they hadn't, Pa wouldn't have gone over with him.'

'No – but most of the Pentuan men *would*. Think what a disaster *that* would have been! Anyway, there was nothing else either Preacher Jago or Nathan could have done. They couldn't allow the Pentuan men to take the law into their own hands – however guilty the sailor might have been.'

'That's perfectly true, Dewi. Besides, although the sailor and Sally had been heard quarrelling on the night she died, he was by no means the only man who might have wanted her dead before she could name the father of the baby she was carrying.'

'What do you mean?'

'I was talking to Winnie Doyle the other day – she's the woman who started the rumour about you and Columb Hawkins. She's a gossip and a mischief-maker, but she doesn't miss anything that goes on in the village. She told me that Sally Wicks might have set her sights higher than a seaman to father her child. Seems she'd been in the habit of calling on our Mr Columb Hawkins after dark when he was down at the old Customs house. She also overheard part of the quarrel young Sally was having with the sailor. Sally said she'd come to him with a dowry of a hundred and fifty pounds if he'd marry her.'

'Sally has never had such an amount of money in all her life!'

'Exactly. But there's a certain man we've already mentioned who *has*. No doubt he'd be happy to give such a sum for her to marry someone else – especially if that someone thought *he* was the father of her child. The only trouble was, the sailor was already married. Now, I ask you, Dewi. Who would have most to lose if he was to be named as the father of Sally's baby, the married sailor – or Columb Hawkins?'

'Are you saying that Columb Hawkins is the killer of Sally and not the sailor?'

268

'I'm saying nothing, Dewi, and never will say anything outside of what I've said to you, here in this kitchen. I'm repeating gossip, and that's a dangerous thing. What I *will* say is that Pa and Nathan were right to stop the villagers from taking the law into their own hands over the sailor. It's an almighty tragedy that they weren't *both* saved so that everything could have come out in a courtroom. But there we are. It isn't only the Good Lord who looks after his own. The Devil does the same.'

Nathan leaned very heavily upon Dewi's organising ability during the few days before the funeral. The rain of recent weeks had cleared and the men who had been working on the harbour began to drift back. There was work for them, but the engineer-in-charge was missing. Consequently, Nathan found he had to assess the work to be done and detail the men to carry it out.

The fine weather also meant that fishing-boats were going out, with a consequent resumption of work at Portgiskey.

As if these two activities were not enough at this time, the Nichols shipyard at nearby Fowey was reported to have a hundred-ton schooner for sale at a bargain price. Nathan had wanted to fish the Newfoundland banks for some time. This vessel had been built for the Newfoundland trade by a shipowner who wanted to add the ship to the two he already had trading there. Unfortunately, both his other vessels had been lost in the Bay of Biscay, en route from the Mediterranean. This had so discouraged the shipowner that he decided to give up his business. He no longer wanted the ship he had ordered and was prepared to lose the money he had already advanced on her.

It was too good an opportunity to be lost. Nathan went to Fowey to inspect the boat, named the *Heron*, and negotiate the purchase of her.

Dewi was left to make many of the arrangements for the funeral of Preacher Jago and for feeding the mourners at Polrudden afterwards.

She did not mind taking on such a task. It meant that Nathan could concentrate on other matters. Each night they would spend a couple of hours together, discussing what she had done and what remained to be completed.

On more than one occasion, Nathan repeated that he did not know how he would have coped without her. Dewi was pleased to know her efforts were appreciated. Her only regret was that it had taken the tragic death of Preacher Jago to bring them so much closer.

The funeral attracted one of the largest crowds seen anywhere in Cornwall for very many years. Not only were most of the county's Methodist preachers in attendance, but so too were the majority of their congregations. Local magistrates attended *en masse*, to endorse the actions that had led to the preacher's death.

But the vast majority of mourners were men and women who had known Preacher Jago – and they came from every walk of life. Sir Kenwyn Penhaligan was there. So too were dozens of vagrants from Polgooth Downs. The Pentuan preacher had regularly taken the word of God and more material items to them. They would miss him sorely.

Hugh Cremyll and Lydia were not at the funeral. Hugh had gone to Gloucester to take up his new appointment only days before Josiah Jago's tragic accident. Lydia had accompanied him. Until their marriage she would live in nearby Cheltenham, with a relative.

At the graveside, Dewi stood beside Beville when the coffin was lowered in the ground. As the grief of the mourners became more voluble she spoke over the boy's head to the ashen-faced Nathan.

'Are you all right?'

Looking across at her, he could trust himself to do no more than nod.

'I'm going to Polrudden now. I'll take Beville with me. He's upset enough already.'

Once again Nathan could only nod and Dewi took the quietly weeping small boy up the hill, the huge crowd making a respectful path for them to pass through.

Dewi had hoped the grief and eulogies in praise of the dead preacher might have been left at the graveside, but there were many Methodist preachers among the mourners who came to the house. Some had wished to make a speech at the funeral but had been restrained by the officiating preacher. Thwarted there, they made their speeches at Polrudden. They could be found in rooms, on the staircase overlooking the hall, and even out on the drive, preaching to the crowds who had followed the mourners up the hill to Polrudden.

'This isn't what our pa would have wanted.' Nell made the comment to Dewi as Beville was taken upstairs to the nursery where Nell's children were being cared for by Pippa Hanna. 'He always said that funerals should be quiet, dignified ceremonies. The peaceful passing on of a man or woman into the hands of their creator. He once told me that.'

When Dewi made no reply, Nell looked at her quickly. 'Are you all right?'

'Yes . . .' Suddenly, Dewi shook her head. 'No, that's a lie. I'm *not* all right.'

Nell stopped on the stairs. 'What is it? Has something happened to upset you?'

270

'Yes. I keep telling myself I'm silly to be upset over an expression, but I've seen it before. I *know* what it means.'

'I'm sorry, Dewi. You'll need to explain yourself. You're talking in riddles. Does it have something to do with our Nathan?'

Dewi nodded, 'One of the servants brought him a hand-written note, shortly before we came upstairs. I overheard the servant say it had been brought to the back door by a messenger. Nathan read it and then someone spoke to him as he was slipping the note into his pocket. He missed his pocket and it dropped on the floor as he moved away. I went to pick up the note for him. I didn't intend to read it, but I just couldn't help myself. It was lying open when I picked it up . . .'

'Well, don't just stop there, what did it say? What was in it to upset you?'

'All it said was, "I am deeply distressed to hear of your tragic loss. Please accept my sincerest sympathy and call in to see me when you are next passing Golden." It was signed by a Felicia Brandon.'

Nell looked perplexed. 'I don't know her, but it sounds like a perfectly polite note of sympathy to me.'

'I know . . . and you're probably right. I'm just being silly, but it was Nathan's expression, Nell. It was a look I saw him give to Abigail when she first came to Polrudden. For a moment I thought it was from her. Then I realised it couldn't possibly be.'

Dewi shrugged but was unable to shake off the unhappiness she felt at that moment. 'I know it should really be none of my business, Nell, but I think Nathan has fallen for another woman.'

Chapter 55

For three days after the funeral, Nathan was kept at Pentuan dealing with business matters. They included the harbour, fishing from Portgiskey – and his proposed venture into Newfoundland waters. He had bought the Fowey schooner *Heron* and now he took on Nicholas Dunne from Mevagissey as Master.

A very experienced seaman, Dunne had sailed the triangular route Cornwall–Newfoundland–Italy–Cornwall, carrying on the trade Nathan intended entering.

It was an ambitious venture. Francis Hanna would take his boat, the *Charlotte*, to the cod-rich fishing-grounds off Newfoundland and spend the summer months fishing there. His catches would be taken to the timber-clad shores of Newfoundland to be smoked and cured by men shipped there for the purpose by Nathan.

The *Heron* would take a cargo of the fish to sell in the insatiable Italian market and either return to Newfoundland with a cargo of salt or sail back to Cornwall with wine and any other trade goods found by Nathan's agent in Italy.

It was a trade pattern established by Cornish fishing-boats and ship-owners for more than two hundred years. As a boy Nathan had listened to retired Cornish seamen outside the fish-cellars of Pentuan and Mevagissey. They would spin yarns of fishing around Newfoundland and of the fortunes to be made in the trade between there and the Mediterranean. He had dreamed of one day taking part, as a seaman. Now he would make the dream come true for other adventurers.

With most of his problems solved close to home, Nathan turned once more to his other great venture: the election at Tregony.

He was increasingly excited at the thought of becoming a Member of Parliament, but he needed to work if he were to secure his place there. Word had reached him that Sir Christopher Hawkins had been very busy in the constituency and was putting up a powerful argument in favour of his nephew. Few men felt strongly enough about Nathan to risk dispossession by voting for him.

Sir Kenwyn had sent Nathan a list of Hawkins's tenants to visit. For the next few days he called on then, offering reassurance that should they be dispossessed for not voting for the Hawkins camp,

272

Sir Kenwyn would offer them the tenancy of one of his own properties. There would also be a substantial sum to 're-settle' them in their new home.

Somehow it always happened that the last potential voter visited by Nathan each day lived no more than a mile from Golden Manor, where Felicia Brandon was staying. Being so close, it would have been churlish not to call at the house and thank her for her letter of condolence.

Each day it came as an increasing disappointment to learn that Felicia was out riding or 'visiting'. On the fourth occasion, Nathan received the same reply accompanied by a knowing look from the maid who answered the door to him.

As he was returning the way he had come, he heard the sound of a horse being ridden fast along the lane behind him. As it drew closer a voice called his name. He turned to see Felicia riding at a reckless pace towards him.

Tugging her horse to a halt beside him, she said breathlessly, 'I'm so glad I was able to catch up with you. I went out riding and when I returned to Golden a few minutes ago they told me you'd called yet again. I leaped straight back on my horse and chased after you. I would have been most unhappy had I not caught up with you.'

Reaching across the space between the two horses, she rested her hand on his arm and squeezed gently. 'I was so terribly sorry to hear of the tragic death of your father. He was a well-loved man, I believe. It must be a grievous loss to you?'

'Yes. I've been calling to thank you for your message. It was greatly appreciated.'

'We all have tragedies in our lives. I've always found that sincere sympathy is one of the greatest comforts we can receive.'

Felicia gave his arm another squeeze before releasing it. 'You will return to Golden and have some tea – or something stronger?'

'I will. Thank you.'

Riding together to Golden, they chatted about many things: Cornwall; Princess Caroline; the weather – and Nathan's election prospects.

'I think I stand a very good chance of winning,' he declared. 'There are still one or two voters who could go either way, but I should win by a reasonable margin.'

'Really?' Felicia sounded surprised. 'I thought the borough had been comfortably secured by Sir Christopher Hawkins?'

'I hope he thinks so too. It might make him complacent. A great many voters are disenchanted with the men selected by Sir Christopher to represent them – and with the party supported by them in Parliament. There's a general feeling that's it's time for a change.'

'How very interesting.' For a moment Felicia seemed deep in

thought. Then she brightened. 'Here we are at Golden. Tie your horse and I'll have a groom bring it a drink.'

'I can't stay too long. I have a great many things to tend to.'

'And I am low on your list?' Felicia laughed at his protest and took his arm as they entered the house. 'I'll try not to delay you for too long.'

Nathan thought he would be happy to forego a great many of his tasks for the company of this woman but as they passed through the door his first comment was about the Manor of Golden.

'What a charming old house. How long have you lived here?'

'Not long. As I think I told you, it's owned by family. It also has a fascinating history. Have you heard of the Catholic martyr, Cuthbert Mayne?'

'Wasn't he a Catholic priest who was hung, drawn and quartered at Launceston?'

'That's right. He was taken here in this very house. As a result the then owner, Francis Tregian, spent most of his life in prison, much of it in the Tower of London. Before you go I'll show you the secret room where Mayne was hidden . . .'

Nathan found Felicia excellent company. Bright and vivacious, she was also generous with her attention. She asked a great many questions of him, although she was less forthcoming when Nathan tried to probe into her background.

Her very reticence added to her fascination. Nevertheless, after enjoying her company for more than an hour, Nathan said, 'I fear it's time I left. My boats will be sailing for the fishing grounds tonight. I would like to speak to the men before they go.'

'Must you leave so soon, Nathan?' She sighed. 'I have so enjoyed your company. But you cannot leave until I have showed you the priest-hole where Cuthbert Mayne used to hide. Wait while I light a candle.'

Felicia lit a taper from the fire and applied it to the wick of a candle standing in a holder on the side-board.

Shielding the candle flame with one hand, she led Nathan from the small room where they had taken tea, to a larger room closer to the passage-like entrance hall.

Making her way to the huge fireplace, Felicia ducked beneath the mantelpiece and her voice, echoing within the chimney, called for him to follow. By the time he too had ducked inside the fireplace, Felicia was mounting a series of stones, projecting like steps from the wall.

No more than eight feet up the wide chimney was a low doorway, set back into the wall. Pushing it open, Felicia crawled inside the opening.

Nathan followed her and found himself in a small chamber containing a wooden chair and table and a narrow trestle bed which was, rather surprisingly, made up ready for use.

'How would you like to spend days and nights shut up here, Nathan?'

'I wouldn't like it at all – but Cuthbert Mayne was taken and executed more than two hundred years ago. Surely the furniture hasn't been here for all that time?'

Felicia laughed. 'The table and chair may well have been here since Mayne. They are very old. But the young son of the family who last lived here used this as a den. The bed is his.'

She laughed again and this time the sudden exhalation of breath extinguished the candle flame abruptly. Felicia gave a small gasp of surprise. Whether she moved forward towards him or whether Nathan reached out fearing she might stumble he never knew. What was certain was that a moment later she was in his arms. He smelled her hair and the faint aroma of her perfume – and then he felt the same breath that had extinguished the candle against his lips and he kissed her.

Her mouth moved beneath his and her arms went about him, drawing his body to her, straining to him.

He pulled his mouth away, to draw breath, but she pulled him to her again, and now her body moved against his. 'Please, Nathan . . . it's been so long . . .'

There was not the faintest of lights in the small chamber. Somehow, in the darkness, Felicia shed her dress and Nathan was holding a nearly naked woman.

Then he too was removing his clothes, helped very efficiently by Felicia. Moments later they were lying on the bed together. Here, in the room where a martyr had spent his last moments of earthly freedom, they made love in a frenzied fashion that left them both gasping. Afterwards in the darkness, when they had stopped panting, they lay together for long moments until her mouth found his once more and they made love for a second time.

'We must go now or the maids will have a search party sent out to find me.'

Felicia's words reached Nathan as he lay in a blissfully drowsy state somewhere between sleep and wakefulness. She stirred beneath him and he moved to allow her to rise from the narrow bed.

He sat up but was unable to see a thing. It seemed Felicia was having similar difficulties because she hissed, 'I can't see a damned thing in here. I'm going to open the door.'

There was a slight creaking sound and a dim light revealed the various objects in the room. Naked, Felicia rose from the floor holding her dress. As he watched she pulled it over her head and was naked no longer. Reaching out, Nathan located shirt and trousers and five minutes later was following Felicia down the utilitarian stone steps to the fireplace below.

Much to Nathan's surprise he ducked into the room to find lamps lit and the curtains drawn.

It seemed that Felicia too was concerned at the passing of time.

'You must go now, I have company arriving tonight. It would be embarrassing, to say the least, if they found us both here in this condition.'

'Yes.' Nathan was taken aback by her matter-of-fact manner. She had just participated in an orgy of abandoned love-making that was more reminiscent of a street-girl than of a lady of breeding. Now she suggested he should leave with no more emotion than if he had been a tradesman who had tarried too long. 'When will I see you again?'

'I don't know. It might be difficult. I'll send a messenger to Polrudden. Please, you *must* leave now. I will see you to the door.'

As Felicia escorted him along the passageway they passed a servant girl who avoided looking at him, casting her glance to the flagstone floor instead. Nathan felt that something was wrong. The girl halted at the rear of the passageway, as though waiting for something.

At the door, Nathan expected Felicia perhaps to step outside into the darkness where the servant girl could not see them and kiss him goodbye, with at least a brief repetition of the passion she had shown not many minutes before.

Instead, she left the door open and in a loud and formal voice said, 'I bid you good evening, Mr Jago.'

This was too much! 'Felicia, surely . . .'

'You will leave now, if you please.'

It was as though Felicia was saying it not to him but for others to hear. The servant, perhaps, in order to protect her reputation.

Nathan almost accepted his own excuse for her, but it jarred. Surely she would have given him some sign? A secret message between them. Even a squeeze of his arm . . .

When he was still within sight of the lights of the house, Nathan pulled his horse to a halt. Felicia had said she was expecting visitors. That would explain her wanting him out of the house so quickly – but it did not explain her baffling change of attitude towards him.

He wondered who her visitors could be? On an impulse, he dismounted from his horse. Spying on a lady was an ungentlemanly thing to do, but Felicia had hardly behaved in a ladylike manner. Allowing . . . no, *begging* him to make love to her and then suddenly acting as though he were a stranger. There was something here that was not right and it both hurt and alarmed him. He was deeply smitten with Felicia. He hoped he might find a logical reason for her confusing change of attitude. He *wanted* things to be right between them.

276

Nathan took his horse into a field before tying it to the gate. He had no way of knowing from which direction Felicia's visitors would be coming. He did not want them to see his saddled horse tied beside the road.

Nathan walked back to the house and found a spot back from the short driveway. Hidden by the overhanging branches of a tree he had a very good view of the front door of Golden.

He had been waiting for about twenty minutes and was beginning to feel the cold in his feet when he heard the sound of a coach creaking and rumbling along the lane, coming from the opposite direction to that in which he had left his horse.

At the entrance to the driveway of Golden the coach turned in. Rings of light from the flickering lanterns fell on two horses side by side in the traces.

The coachman pulled the horses in a tight turn in front of the door. An assistant coachman leaped to the ground and unfolded the steps before opening the coach door.

At that moment the door of the house was thrown open and light shone past the slim figure of Felicia. The first figure to leave the carriage was an elderly man who descended the steps stiffly. He had hardly taken a step towards the door before Felicia flung herself at him, crying, 'Harold, my *dear* husband. I was beginning to fear you would never arrive.'

Before Nathan had time to recover from the shock of Felicia's words, the light from the door fell upon the faces of the two men descending from the coach behind the man she had called husband. His blood froze as he realised his intuition had not played him false.

Something was wrong. Very, very wrong.

The two men descending from the coach were Sir Christopher Hawkins and his nephew, Columb.

In that instant Nathan knew why he had sometimes felt uncomfortable when he looked at Felicia. It was because of the strong family resemblance she bore to Columb Hawkins. He believed she was most probably young Hawkins's sister!

Chapter 56

Nathan's initial confusion over Felicia's behaviour quickly passed. On the ride home to Polrudden he began to assess the meaning of everything he had learned tonight. Coupled with Felicia's peculiar behaviour after they had emerged from the chimney priest-hole, the implications were ominous. But why had she behaved as she had? Why had she lied about being a widow – and why had she been so eager to have an affair with him?

Nathan was angry with himself for having been so infatuated with her that he had not bothered to learn anything of her background. It was something he needed to do now, and quickly. He wondered how much time he had before she showed her hand.

Instead of returning immediately to Polrudden, Nathan went first to Venn Farm. He needed to talk things over with someone. Dewi had a clearer and more objective mind than any other person he knew, but this was not something he could talk about with her. In a moment of truth, he admitted to himself he was too ashamed to speak to her about the brief affair with Felicia.

He felt as though he had been disloyal by having had such a relationship.

He might have thought more deeply about this revelation had he not been so worried. He wanted to talk the matter over with Nell. It would not be the first time he had confided in her when he was in trouble.

Nell listened in perplexed silence to Nathan's expurgated version of his brief liaison with Felicia. When it ended, he shrugged his shoulders. 'There you have it, Nell. She's up to something, I'm sure of that. I only wish I knew what it was.'

'You're a damn' fool, Nathan!' There had been a number of gaps in his story, but Nell felt she could fill them in with a fair degree of accuracy. 'You risk injuring your brains every time you jump on a horse! But perhaps that's a qualification for Parliament. It certainly doesn't seem to have done Sir Christopher Hawkins any harm.'

She rose from her seat and poured Nathan a second cup of tea. 'It must have something to do with living the life of a "gentleman" or "lady". I'm sure I don't have time even to think of such things

– and neither does Tom, I'm pleased to say.'

Tom Quicke was in one of the barns with the Polrudden carpenter, assisted by Charlie Philpotts. They were repairing a wagon that had overturned on Pentuan hill that day.

'I accept the sisterly censure. I deserve all of it – and more – but how can I find out something of Lady Felicia Brandon?'

'How can *we* find out? you mean. Have you said anything to Dewi about this woman?'

'What's it to do with her?'

The reply came back so quickly and with such a defensive tone to his voice that Nell raised an eyebrow, but she ignored the question.

'You said this woman had travelled with Princess Caroline in Naples. When the Duke of Clarence was here he was talking of the Princess and her behaviour there. Apparently it was so outrageous that the Prince Regent is seriously thinking of divorcing her. If so much is known it means someone has been reporting to the Court in London all that's been going on out there. Why not write to the Duke and ask him if anyone knows of your precious Felicia?'

'I can't bother the Duke with such a trivial and personal matter.'

'Tell him the lady is probably related to the man who was so rude to him in Pentuan. If she's out to cause trouble for you, he'll probably be delighted to help.'

'No.' Nathan shook his head. 'Anyway, I have a nasty feeling that things will start happening very quickly. I'll have to try to find an answer right here in Cornwall.'

'That's up to you. It's your future that's in the balance. I'll see if anyone around here knows anything about this Felicia. Now, I think I can hear the baby crying. I'll let you know if I learn anything, Nathan. In the meantime, for goodness' sake keep away from these so-called "ladies". If you have to go somewhere where you know you're going to meet up with them, take Dewi with you. She'll look after you.'

Riding home, Nathan wondered why Dewi should have been on both his and Nell's mind that evening.

'. . . And that's the story of it so far, Dewi. What do you make of it all?'

It was the afternoon after Nathan's visit to his sister. Dewi had come to Venn Farm for her usual teaching session with the children from nearby farms. They were now playing in the hayloft, attached to the stable. Nell and Dewi were in the farmhouse kitchen preparing a tea for the boys. Nell had just told her about Nathan's visit and the web of deceit woven by the writer of the message of sympathy she had found.

'Is Nathan upset because he's fond of this Lady Felicia or

279

because she might damage his chances of being elected to Parliament?'

'I certainly don't think he's too romantically involved with her, Dewi. He was flattered because she's a so-called "lady of breeding" and gave him the come on, that's all. It's happened once or twice before. Nathan finds it hard to believe that well-bred women have the same emotions and bodies as the rest of us. If you'd come to Polrudden as Lady Dewi he'd have been at your feet long before this.'

'I'm not at all sure I'd want him to fall for me just because I had a title, or so-called good breeding. Mind you, that's probably the only way he'd ever notice me. But that's not the main problem right now. We've got to stop Lady Felicia Brandon from making any trouble for him. We won't be able to do that until we know a great deal more about her.

'Nathan should have written to the Duke of Clarence. He would be pleased to help. He told me the story of Amy, Nathan's second wife, getting him to place all the money left to her by mother on the result of one of Nathan's prizefights. He is very fond of Nathan.'

'I know, but he was adamant about not bothering the Duke.'

'Well, he's said nothing to me and I think we need to move very quickly. Do you know anyone reliable who might be prepared to ride to London to take a letter from me to the Duke?'

'You have the very man at Polrudden,' said Nell. 'Will Hodge's young brother is staying with him at the moment. In the summer months he rides as a jockey at many of the race meetings throughout the country. I believe he might have ridden for the Duke himself, once or twice.'

'Splendid. I'll go back and find him right away. It's high time I put the money I was left to some useful purpose.'

'There's someone else at Polrudden you might like to talk to. Tom mentioned him this morning. His name is Henry, but Tom couldn't remember his surname. He's a groom for Nathan. Tom says his father worked for Columb Hawkins's father many years ago. He might be able to tell us something.'

'I'll go and find him after I've spoken to Will Hodge's brother.'

Dewi found Henry Mabb feeding and brushing the horses in the stables. She could hear him talking to them as she passed in through the door. He was speaking as though they were children and Dewi smiled as she walked to the stall where he was working.

He was a good-looking, well-built man of about twenty-eight. When he realised Dewi must have heard his one-sided conversation with the horse, a blush spread across his face and turned it scarlet. Dewi thought the groom was probably more at home with horses than with people.

280

'Hello, Miss Morgan. You must have heard me talking to the horses?' Henry Mabb felt the need to explain himself. 'I always talk to 'em when I'm working in here. The sound of a voice seems to calm them down. I never have any trouble with any of 'em.'

'I'm quite sure you don't, Henry – and they're a credit to you. Have you always worked with horses?'

'Since I was a small boy, Miss Morgan.' Henry Mabb was a simple young man and seemed pleased that Dewi wanted to chat to him. 'And my father before me. His father too. We've all worked with horses. It's all I ever wanted to do.'

'Will Hodge must be very pleased to have you working here for him. Tell me, Henry, didn't your father once work for Sir Christopher Hawkins's brother? The father of Mr Columb Hawkins?'

'That's right, miss. He worked there until I was almost sixteen.' Henry Mabb's manner had changed subtly. He had been happier talking about his family's association with horses.

'Did you ever meet Columb's sister? I think her name might be Felicia.'

'That's right, miss. Her name's Felicia, right enough. Yes, I met her.'

From being cheerily talkative, the groom had become tight-lipped and ill-at-ease.

'What can you tell me about her, Henry? Did she ever marry? Would you know if her married name is Brandon? Lady Felicia Brandon?'

'I can't tell you anything about her, miss. Like I said, I left there before I was sixteen.' Turning away from her, Henry Mabb resumed his grooming of the horse, but now he was not talking to the animal.

'Henry, I think you *do* know something about Felicia Hawkins. Probably quite a lot – and it's important that you tell me everything.'

Dewi paused. She was convinced that Henry Mabb was a little simple and did not want to tell him too much. On the other hand, if he knew something about Felicia Brandon that he was reluctant to tell, she needed to know.

'Listen to me, Henry. This Felicia Brandon, or Hawkins, is out to make trouble for Mr Jago. Serious trouble. It's important I learn all I can about her if I'm to put a stop to it.'

Henry Mabb paused in his work once more. 'Oh, she's very good at making trouble for folk, Miss Morgan. Very good, she is – and I should know.'

'Tell me about it.'

Henry Mabb looked about him nervously. 'I don't know whether I should, Miss Morgan. I promised my father I'd never, ever say anything about what happened. He's got a good position over by

281

Padstow now. Head Groom, same as Mr Hodge. He'd likely lose it if ever they found out.'

'Found out *what*, Henry? This is very, *very* important to Mr Jago and I promise I'll do nothing at all that will threaten your father – but you *must* tell me.'

Henry Mabb looked around him and licked his lips nervously. 'It's not an easy thing to tell, Miss Morgan . . . you being a woman.'

'Try, Henry. Please try. Turn away from me, if you like. Pretend you're telling it to the horse.'

The unhappy groom's face had turned scarlet once more and he said, 'It's not a story I'd even want to tell to a horse, Miss Morgan.'

As she was about to emphasise the importance of his information once more, Henry Mabb made up his mind. Taking a deep breath, he said quickly, 'There was trouble about what went on between me and Miss Felicia. But it were her fault, I swear it were. I wouldn't have laid a finger on her if she hadn't told me to. She made me, Miss Morgan. Took me up in the hayloft over the stables, made me take my trousers off and then stood looking at me, for all the world as though I was a horse she was going to buy. Then she laid down in the hay and . . . and made me . . .'

'You said she caused trouble? Did her father find out?'

'Not for a long while. She used to come to the stables about once a week, when my father was out doing something else. Then one day her father came in and caught us. I think he'd probably suspected something and been watching.'

'What happened then?'

'She said I'd made her do it. Said it was all my fault.'

'Did her father believe her?'

'I thought so at the time. He gave me a choice. Take a whipping from him, or go before the magistrate.'

'What did you do?'

'I took the beating.' Now Henry Mabb had revealed his story he seemed eager to tell all. 'Here, Miss Morgan, you look at this.'

Pulling his shirt clear of his trousers, the groom lifted it and turned his back towards her. It was criss-crossed with ugly scars from shoulder to waist that made her wince. It must have been not so much a flogging as a flaying.

'You can't have hidden that for all these years. What have you told others who've seen that?'

'After I'd got over the flogging, Mr Hawkins had me put into the army before dismissing my father without a reference. Two years a soldier, I was. Then I got shot in the stomach and they didn't think I'd live. I did, but I wasn't fit to fight again for a while so they sent me home. The others at Polrudden think I got this from a flogging in the army. You won't tell them the truth?'

'No, Henry, I won't say anything to any of them. Thank you for sharing your secret with me. Now I need to be certain this Felicia Brandon is the same Felicia Hawkins.'

'Felicia Hawkins was married, but it was to a Colonel Barnes and they went off to live somewhere in Kent. He died after they'd been married for less than three years. Then she married again. This husband was quite old too, but very important. He's a "Sir", but I don't know what his name is.'

Dewi was almost at the stable door when Henry Mabb called to her.

'Miss Morgan?'

When she turned, his face had turned scarlet once more.

'I . . . I don't know if it's important, but I wasn't the only one dismissed from the Hawkins's house for . . . the same thing.'

Dewi came back to stand before him again. 'You don't know who the others are, or where they might be now?'

'I can tell you *who* they are. There was Peter Barrow and Daniel Carthew. They're both working up at Carloggas, in the clay pits. Sam Dainty is on a farm, up on Bodmin Moor. Jim Wills is a gardener up at Lanhydrock. There was William and Jem Coutts, too, but I don't know where they are now. I heard that William was taken by a press-gang at Falmouth, but I couldn't be sure.'

'Six of them – and you, *seven*! Were they all flogged by her father?'

'I don't think so, Miss Morgan. You see, although I wasn't the first, I was the first to be caught.'

'Henry Mabb, you've told me more than I dared hope for. If this Felicia Brandon of Golden *is* Felicia Hawkins, she'll not make trouble for anyone.'

Chapter 57

The messenger returning with a reply to Dewi's letter to the Duke of Clarence beat Lady Felicia Brandon to Polrudden by a mere two hours.

It was three o'clock in the afternoon and Dewi still had the Duke's letter on the desk in front of her when one of the servants knocked at the door.

'Come in.'

Dewi turned to see an agitated young maid standing in the doorway.

'Excuse me, Miss Morgan, but there's a lady downstairs wanting to speak to Mr Jago. She's been shown to the library by Ruby.'

Ruby was one of the senior servants, but the maid had not yet imparted all her information. 'Her horse was taken by Henry, the groom. He said I should come and tell you right away that Lady Felicia was here. He said to tell you, "It's her, all right." I don't know what he meant by that, Miss Morgan. That's all he'd say.'

'Is Mr Jago still out of the house?'

'Yes, Miss Morgan. Cook said he hasn't come in for lunch yet.'

'Thank you, Hetty. I'll go and see the lady.'

Glancing out of the window, Dewi could see the schooner *Heron* at anchor off Portgiskey Cove. A small boat was pulling from the ship towards the fish-cellar, hidden by an outcrop of the cliff. Nathan had gone out in the schooner saying he would be back at lunchtime. He was probably in the small boat on his way to shore right now. There was little time to lose. He knew nothing of the contents of the letter she had received. It would probably be better if it remained that way. Dewi would deal with his visitor in her own way.

Lady Felicia Brandon was standing at the window of the room when Dewi entered. Her back was to the door and the riding whip she held in her hand was being tapped impatiently against the back of the elegant riding habit she wore.

When the door closed behind Dewi, Lady Felicia swung around. When she saw Dewi and not Nathan, she frowned in annoyance.

'Where is Mr Jago?'

'He's not here at the moment. Perhaps I can be of help to you?'

'When do you expect him to return?'

'Some time this afternoon, but he'll no doubt be leaving again almost immediately to speak to some of the voters at Tregony.'

'Oh, will he? I suggest you speak to Mr Jago when he returns and pass on a message from me. Tell him that before he wastes any more time on electioneering he should pay me a visit, at Golden.'

Making it patently obvious she had nothing more to say to Dewi, Lady Felicia headed for the door.

Before the visitor reached it, Dewi said, 'I have no intention of passing on your message, Lady Felicia. Nathan Jago will continue to fight this election – and he'll win.'

Lady Felicia swung round to face her. 'You will not . . . How *dare* you!' She eyed Dewi's dark dress and crisp white pinafore. 'Who are you? Are you related to Mr Jago?'

'I'm governess to Sir Beville, Mr Jago's son.'

'An employee!' Lady Felicia's disdain was plain. 'I suggest you remember your station or I will demand your dismissal as well as Nathan Jago's withdrawal from the Tregony by-election.'

'I don't think so, Lady Felicia. I think you'll return to Golden and keep very quiet until the by-election is over. In fact, I *know* you will. You see, you have far more to lose than Nathan Jago.'

Lady Felicia stood with nostrils flared, glaring at Dewi, controlling her anger with great difficulty. 'This is *unforgivable* impertinence. If you were a man I'd have you horse-whipped.'

'As your father horse-whipped Henry Mabb, no doubt?'

'Henry . . . Mabb? I know no one of that name.'

'He was the son of your father's head groom, when you were a young girl.'

Lady Felicia's start of surprise told Dewi that the other woman had remembered – but Dewi had not yet finished reminding her of her past.

'There were others too who perhaps *should* have been thrashed. They did no more and no less than the unfortunate Henry. Peter Barrow; Daniel Carthew; Sam Dainty; Jim Wills; William and Jem Coutts . . . need I continue?'

Dewi had memorised the names given to her by Henry Mabb and she saw that Lady Felicia remembered them too.

'I don't know what you're talking about, young lady. Oh, yes, I vaguely recall some of the names you've mentioned, but they are so far distant from today they can be of no possible relevance to any scheme you may have in mind. You can tell Nathan . . .'

'I haven't finished yet.' Dewi interrupted with such vehemence that she successfully silenced Felicia. 'In the past they may be, but I know where to find them and have no doubt your present husband will be interested in what they have to say. I doubt it would drive him to suicide – as your morals did your first husband. Colonel Barnes, wasn't it?'

285

'I will not remain here and listen to this.'

Lady Felicia made for the door, but Dewi beat her to it and stood with her back firmly against it.

'You *will* listen, Lady Felicia, because if you don't I'll pay a call on your husband – he's in London, I believe. Or should I go direct to Lord Castlereagh, the Foreign Secretary? I'd probably find them together. I believe your husband is there begging Lord Castlereagh for another ambassadorial post. Doing his best to convince his lordship that the stories circulating about you and Princess Caroline during your time together in Naples were a pack of lies. Shall I tell him they were *not* lies after all? That, if he doubts my word, he should question a certain Prussian "secretary" employed by you. I am told he might be persuaded to disclose the truth were he to be questioned with sufficient firmness about his own relationship with you?'

'You insolent bitch!'

'I haven't finished yet, Lady Felicia. There's the scandal of the French military attaché in London. Or did you think that was a secret? Everyone who knows, and there are many of them, is behaving with the utmost discretion – out of compassion for your husband. However, should you try to sully Nathan's name, I can assure you that all your "indiscretions" – many more than I have mentioned – will become public knowledge. Not only will your husband never receive another ambassadorial post, he will be forced to forsake public life and retire to his estate in Ireland. It's a somewhat remote area, I'm told – but no doubt you will find something to amuse you there. If your husband hasn't divorced you by then.'

Lady Felicia Brandon could hardly contain the anger she felt. As she fought to gain control of her feelings she glared at Dewi. Finally she said, 'Did Nathan put you up to this? Is he so much of a coward that he dare not face me himself? *Is* that what this is all about?'

'Mr Jago knows nothing about this . . . yet. I shall no doubt inform him in due course.'

'You are his mistress, of course? Serving him faithfully, even while he was *my* lover. But pride cannot be your strong point. It would be conveniently forgotten should you be in danger of losing Nathan Jago. Polrudden may not be much, but it must be vastly superior to anything *you* will have known before.'

Lady Felicia's words about her own relationship with Nathan hurt more than her vindictive remarks aimed at Dewi. But Dewi had no intention of allowing her to see *how* much.

'I know you must find it difficult to understand, Lady Felicia, but I am not Nathan Jago's mistress and never have been. I am his son's governess and am happy to remain so. I've involved myself in this matter because I don't want to see a good man's name dragged in the mud by a woman who would be trash whether she were a lady, servant, or – more appropriately – harlot. He is worth more. Far more.'

'His worth can no doubt be measured by those who defend him,' retorted Lady Felicia, cuttingly. 'Well, you can have him. You deserve each other. Now, I would be obliged if you would stand aside? I wish to leave.'

'Shall I tell Mr Jago you called? Or shall I say nothing and allow him to get on with his electioneering?'

'You can say as much, or as little, as you damn' well like! From what I've seen of the voters of Tregony since I've been here, they and Nathan Jago deserve each other. I shall return to London, to be with my husband.'

Dewi was filled with a great sense of relief. Her gamble – and it *had* been a gamble – had paid off. She had called Lady Felicia Brandon's bluff, and won.

Moving away from the door, Dewi turned the handle and opened it. 'I'm sure you're being wise, Lady Felicia. Very wise indeed. You will be far more at home in London than here. However, you can be quite sure your visit to Cornwall will be remembered.'

Lady Felicia was actually in the doorway when her anger suddenly erupted. Turning, she raised her riding crop and brought it down with all her force across Dewi's face.

Staggering back, Dewi raised her hand to her cheek. Her fingers came away streaked with blood.

'There's something else for you to remember, Miss whatever-your-name-is. Every time you look in the mirror, I hope. Perhaps it will serve as a reminder to hold your tongue when you're talking to your betters.'

Chapter 58

'I'd give her Lady Felicia Brandon if I could get my hands on her for this!' Nell made the tight-lipped comment as she pressed a cold-water compress against Dewi's cheek in a bid to stem the bleeding. 'The Hawkins family are far too ready with their whips and riding crops. It's high time someone taught them a lesson.'

'It really doesn't matter, Nell. It was an outburst of anger because we'd wrecked all her carefully laid plans. She's lost. That's all that matters.'

Dewi had hurried to Venn Farm as soon as Lady Felicia left Polrudden. By having Nell dress the gash on her face she hoped to avoid having to give explanations to the servants.

'It's you who've ruined her plans, Dewi – and saved our Nathan from a highly embarrassing confrontation with her. He ought to give you a medal at the very least.'

'I'd rather he knew nothing about it . . .'

Nell's noisy exhalation of breath cut her short.

'There's no way you're going to keep this a secret, Dewi. At least, not at Polrudden. You might think you sneaked out of the house without anyone noticing, but I doubt it very much. The servants let Lady Felicia into the house, complete with riding crop. After a few minutes talking to you she stalks off, as angry as an overturned hive of bees, leaving you hurrying from the house with a weal across your face and bleeding all over your dress. Word of what's happened will go round quicker than a bad odour and they'll tell our Nathan the moment he sets a foot inside the house.'

Nell's forecast proved entirely accurate. She had hardly stemmed the bleeding from Dewi's wound when the two women heard Nathan's voice in the yard outside. He was talking to Tom and both men were walking towards the house.

Dewi's face lost much of its colour. She felt far more nervous about facing Nathan than she had when confronting Lady Felicia at Polrudden. She had interfered in something that should have concerned only Nathan and Lady Felicia. It had been done with the best of intentions and the outcome had been entirely successful. However, she *had* interfered . . .

Entering the kitchen with Tom behind him, Nathan saw the two

288

women beside the table, Nell standing, Dewi seated, with her still bleeding cheek turned away.

'What's this I hear about Lady Felicia coming to Polrudden and striking you, Dewi? Is it true?'

'It's true. Look at this,' Nell answered him, at the same time reaching out and turning Dewi's injured cheek towards him.

'She did that!' Appalled, Nathan pulled a handkerchief from his pocket. 'Here, use this. It's still bleeding.'

As Nell bent over to wipe the blood away, Dewi said, 'It looks far worse than it is. There's always a lot of blood when the skin of the face is broken.'

'What on earth made her do such a thing? I'll go straight from here to Golden and demand an explanation . . .'

'No, Nathan.' Dewi brushed away Nell's attentions. 'This is why she did it.'

Reaching out, she took the Duke of Clarence's letter from the table and handed it to him. 'She came to Polrudden with a message for you. I was to tell you that if you wished to avoid a serious scandal you would withdraw from the by-election at Tregony. Instead, I challenged her with the contents of this letter.'

'And a few more things that the Duke of Clarence never knew about,' declared Nell. 'That woman has the morals of a farmyard cat. She and that brother of hers make a good pair, if you ask me. Why you got mixed up with the likes of her, I'll never know.'

'When did you receive this letter – and why did the Duke of Clarence write to you? It's obviously in reply to one you sent to him. What did you tell him?'

'You don't need to concern yourself about your precious reputation, dear brother,' said Nell. 'It's still intact – outside of Venn and Polrudden, anyway. I saw Dewi's letter. It merely said that Columb Hawkins's sister was in Cornwall and seemed intent upon stirring up trouble for you in the election. Dewi said she was writing to the Duke because Lady Felicia had been in Naples with Princess Caroline. She also said you were too much of a gentleman to wish to defend yourself by attacking a lady.'

Nell gave a most unladylike snort. 'Gentleman, indeed! You're as much of a gentleman as this Hawkins woman is a lady! It's lucky for you that Dewi had the gumption to see the threat she posed and did something about it right away. If she hadn't, you'd be slinking away from Golden now with your tail between your legs and Columb Hawkins would have an unopposed ticket to Parliament.'

'I'm grateful to Dewi. Very grateful. But it isn't necessary for anyone to go behind my back to fight my battles for me. I've been fighting them quite successfully myself for many years now.'

'Well! There's gratitude for you. If you ask me . . .'

'No one *is* asking you, Nell.' With an apologetic smile at Nathan

Tom Quicke took his wife's arm. 'Come on, it's time the cows came in for milking. I'll give you a hand. We'll see you later Nathan . . . Dewi.'

'I must get back to Polrudden,' said Dewi. 'I left in such a hurry I never told Pippa where I was going. She'll be worried about me.'

'She'll know you're here,' said Nathan. 'One of the maids said you were hurrying in this direction when you were last seen. Everyone will know by now where you are – probably why, too.'

'I'm sorry . . .'

Nathan placed a hand on Dewi's arm. 'You have no need to apologise to anyone. Least of all to me.' Looking up, he saw that Tom and Nell had stopped in the kitchen doorway. Both seemed to take a great interest in the conversation Nathan was having with Dewi. 'Come along, I'll walk back to Polrudden with you.'

As they were walking across the fields towards Polrudden Nathan said, 'I was extremely churlish back there, Dewi. I'm sorry. Nell was right. Had it not been for you I would have had to withdraw from the Tregony by-election. I could see no way of countering any accusations Felicia made against me.'

Without looking at him, she said, 'Felicia Hawkins or Brandon, whatever you wish to call her, has been destroying the careers of men and boys since she was fifteen years old. She's had considerable experience.'

Nathan winced. 'I don't doubt it.'

They walked on in an awkward silence for some minutes before he said, 'I didn't know she was still married, Dewi. In fact, when we first met – and I suspect that was no accident, either – she told me she was a widow.'

'You don't have to give me explanations of what you do with your life, Nathan. I'm only your son's governess. An employee.' Dewi gave a short, mirthless laugh. 'Your Lady Felicia was very keen to point that out to me.'

'She's not *my* Lady Felicia – and she was wrong. So are you. You're not just another employee. You never have been. Not since that first day at Polrudden when you sat opposite me in my study, taking it for granted you had already been accepted as Beville's governess. You made me feel guilty because I was going to have to tell you there was no post.'

Suddenly warming to his subject, Nathan said, 'Ever since that time, whenever I've done something that perhaps I shouldn't, I find myself wondering how *you* would feel if you knew. Why, Dewi? How is it that you've become my conscience?'

She was more confused than she could ever remember. Nathan was admitting she was in his thoughts a great deal more than she should have been. More than she could ever have dared to hope.

290

But she was uncertain whether the knowledge displeased him.

'I . . . I expect it's because it's because I am . . . what I am. Beville's governess. If you're doing something wrong you feel guilty – for his sake. Because he's too young to understand, you think of me . . .'

Dewi ended her convoluted explanation lamely. She could see that Nathan was no closer to understanding than she was.

They had reached a stile now and Dewi was grateful for the brief respite it gave her. Nathan crossed first, then turned to help her. With Nathan holding her beneath the arms she put her hands lightly upon his shoulders and stepped from the high wooden step.

When he did not immediately release her, she looked up at him questioningly. What she saw made her catch her breath suddenly. He was looking at her injured cheek and on his face was an expression she had only seen before when he watched Beville.

'Your poor cheek is bleeding again, Dewi. Here.'

He released her and, pulling his handkerchief from his pocket, dabbed at the bloody weal which extended from the bottom of her ear, across her cheek, almost reaching her nose.

He was extremely gentle and when she looked up at him, she found he was looking not at her cheek, but at her eyes.

'You know, Dewi, I really am a dull-witted fool. It has taken me all this time to realise why it is you've become my conscience.'

'Why?'

Her voice sounded as though it belonged to someone else.

'Because what you think of me *matters*. I care that you might not approve of whatever it is I'm doing.'

He had finished dabbing at her cheek but did not remove his hands from her face. Instead, they moved to cup her face, his fingers carefully avoiding the wound.

'I think you care too, Dewi. If you didn't you wouldn't have offered me all your money when you thought I needed it. Neither would you have written to the Duke of Clarence when I most certainly had need of help. Thank you, Dewi. Thank you for caring.'

When he kissed her it was as gentle as his hands had been on her cheek. She responded to him, reaching up to his shoulders – but then he pulled her to him and his embrace became more demanding, his body straining against hers.

Suddenly, Nathan's face rubbed against the cut on her cheek and she pulled her head back with a brief cry of pain. Then she was pushing him away.

'No, Nathan. No more . . . please.'

'But . . . I thought you cared too? You *do* care. I know it.'

'Yes, I care.'

Her confession was a signal for him to reach for her again, but she pushed him away and stepped back out of his reach.

'I need to think, Nathan. I need to think about a great many things now.'

He looked hurt and she almost weakened, but his hands dropped to his sides in a gesture of acceptance and he said, 'Of course you do, but don't think for *too* long, Dewi. I want you. It's time Polrudden had a mistress once more.'

Walking beside Nathan as they neared Polrudden, she thought of his words and actions on the walk from Venn. He had said that Polrudden needed a mistress, and the reason she had pushed him away had nothing to do with virtue. It was the thought of another mistress. The one who had bloodied her cheek only hours before. Nathan might have relegated Lady Felicia Brandon to his past. It was too soon for Dewi to do the same.

Chapter 59

The next few weeks were very happy ones for Dewi. Nathan had the sensitivity to realise what was behind her reluctance to commit herself immediately. Lady Felicia Brandon's revelations about her relationship with Nathan had gone much deeper than the wound on Dewi's cheek.

He would take his time. He *wanted* to take his time. Two marriages had ended in tragedy at Polrudden. There was a considerable psychological barrier to be crossed before he contemplated a third.

Instead, he threw himself wholeheartedly into the business of winning the by-election at Tregony. Thanks to Sir Christopher Hawkins, the outcome had become a little less uncertain.

Two of Sir Christopher's tenants had been a little too vociferous in their support of Nathan and had been promptly evicted. The evictions had been intended to serve as a warning for any fellow tenants who might have felt similarly inclined. However, Sir Kenwyn Penhaligon was able to turn it to Nathan's advantage. The two tenants were re-housed in property owned by Sir Kenwyn and were seen to be better off than before.

Worried about the increasing popularity of Nathan, Sir Christopher tried another ploy. Halving the size of a number of his tenancies, the wily baronet brought in more tenants – all of whom would vote for his nephew.

The newcomers were intended to be temporary residents only, but their presence caused great annoyance to the existing tenants and considerable disruption in their everyday lives. When Sir Kenwyn promised them tenancies of at least a comparable size to their original holdings, he won a promise of forty additional votes for Nathan.

'They're like a crowd of small children playing at tit-for-tat,' commented Nell to Dewi as they discussed the election campaign. 'It's hard to believe the winner will go to Parliament and help guide the future of England for the next few years.'

The two women were in the kitchen of Venn Farm once more. It was late evening. Dewi had walked to the farm with one of the servants who had collected a basket of eggs and returned to

Polrudden. Nell was pregnant again and she was very happy.

'This kitchen is a wonderful place to sit and put the world to rights,' commented Dewi. 'It's one of my favourite places – warm, cosy and safe.'

Nell was repairing the torn dress of her four-year-old daughter, Kate. Smoothing the material out on her knee, she looked up at Dewi understandingly. 'You'd feel warm, cosy and safe wherever you were, right now. Has our Nathan said anything more to you lately?'

Dewi had told Nell what had happened on the way home to Polrudden from Venn on the day she had been slashed across the cheek by Lady Felicia Brandon.

'He's hardly ever at Polrudden. I don't suppose he will be until the election has been decided. I don't think either of us wants to hurry things. I'd like the memory of Lady Felicia to fade a little first – for both of us.'

'Don't leave it *too* long, Dewi, and don't allow that titled harlot to come between you. All right, so Nathan didn't exactly fight her off – but she *had* told him she was a widow, and he's a widower.'

'I realise that. I'm also aware that if he wins this election he's going to become a very important man. I don't want him to do or say anything right now that he might regret later. He's very special to me, Nell. I don't ever want to be anything less to him.'

'You won't be, Dewi. You'll see. Are you taking Beville to the hustings at Tregony?'

'Nathan says we should both be there. It will be a very exciting day. Are you and Tom going?'

'Yes. We're taking the whole family. That in itself makes it quite an occasion. I can't remember when we've all gone out somewhere together – and I don't think Tom and I have ever been so far from Venn.'

Dewi smiled, but not unkindly. Tregony was no more than eight miles from Venn. The young farming couple led a very simple life.

The rising sun of a spring morning shone on a great many people making their way to Tregony on election day. In the village the inn-keepers were abroad equally early. There would be a great many thirsts to be quenched this day and voting would be followed by hours of celebration, or commiseration, depending upon which party the inn-keepers supported.

Nathan had gone ahead on horse-back. Dewi followed with Pippa and Beville, riding on a light farm cart with Tom, Nell and their four children.

For the older children it was a great adventure. When they occasionally became bored there was always the opportunity to ride, postillion-style, on the back of the patient cart-horse.

294

As they neared the village, they passed a half-dozen men who called after the two women on the cart. Tom frowned. 'I doubt if they're heading for Tregony to cast their votes.'

'Most likely they're Hawkins's men. Nathan said he's gathered a rough crowd around him during the campaigning and has kept them well occupied. Columb Hawkins will no doubt make full use of them today.'

'I hope the magistrate has brought enough constables in to cope with them. Things might turn nasty if it appears that Nathan is winning.'

'If they do and I'm not with you, take the children to The King's Arms. The inn-keeper there is for Nathan. He'll not allow Hawkins's bully-boys inside. You'll be safe there.'

The campaign had been building to a climax during the last three weeks. During this time the inn-keeper supporting the Hawkins camp had served free drinks to all Hawkins voters – paid for by Sir Christopher, of course.

Similarly, Nathan and Sir Kenwyn had let it be known that during the time either was in the area, their voters would be entertained, free of expense, in The King's Arms.

The wives of voters, wherever their loyalty lay, complained that their husbands had rarely arrived home sober since campaigning had begun in earnest.

At the commencement of polling, both candidates were introduced to the assembled villagers by their respective sponsors. Sir Christopher Hawkins's imported thugs soon showed the part they intended playing in the day's proceedings. The proposal of Columb Hawkins was the signal for an outburst of cheering from some thirty men who pushed their way to the front of the crowd.

The polling booth, with a small platform in front of it, had been set up in the wide main street of Tregony and it was here that the crowd had gathered.

After he had been proposed, Columb made a speech, which was also cheered loudly, often in inappropriate places, by the paid supporters.

When the speech came to an end, the supporters clapped wildly, some of them elbowing less enthusiastic onlookers into following their example.

The proposal of Nathan's candidacy by Sir Kenwyn was greeted with boos from the paid members of the crowd and when Nathan moved to the front of the platform to make his brief speech he was greeted with eggs and bags of flour, thrown by Columb Hawkins's paid followers.

His reception deeply angered Dewi. Nell had physically to restrain her from confronting some of the men who were barracking and jeering Nathan.

When he completed his brief address, it was noticeable that, although he was jeered by the hired mob, far more residents of Tregony were applauding him than had expressed approval of his opponent.

For much of the day the voters trickled slowly through the polling booth, publicly expressing their support for one or other of the two candidates. By early evening there was still no clear winner and word went out to Columb Hawkins's paid supporters that the time had come to deter the remainder of Nathan's supporters from voting.

When a man came nervously to the booth to vote for Nathan he was jostled and manhandled. Leaving the booth, he had his legs kicked from beneath him and whilst on the ground suffered a severe bruising from booted feet.

The next of Nathan's supporters ran into even more trouble. Yet, even though spat at, kicked and punched, he still valiantly announced his support for Nathan.

This time, he was hardly two paces from the booth when he was knocked to the ground and kicked and beaten. Had Nathan not leaped from the platform and personally rescued the man, he would undoubtedly have been severely injured.

There were still at least thirty of Nathan's supporters to vote. After seeing what had happened to the previous two they hung back, jeered by the thugs employed by Columb Hawkins and his uncle.

When there were only thirty minutes of voting time left, Columb Hawkins and his party began to relax. A preliminary count had them in the lead. It was a very slender lead, but it would be enough.

Farther along the road Nathan's would-be voters were still hesitant to advance and be counted. Suddenly, someone came to speak to them and minutes later they had all gone. So too were all the interested bystanders who had just begun to gather to hear the final count. The only people left in the wide main road of Tregony village were the paid supporters of Columb Hawkins.

For some minutes they were jubilant. They had won the day. Their euphoria lasted perhaps ten minutes. Then they began to feel nervous. Things were *too* quiet. There was not another soul on the street.

The hush was broken by the sound of a dog barking. Then another. Moments later there was the clatter of hooves on the road, just around the corner.

Suddenly a very large herd of cows spilled into the broad street – and leading them was a very large bull. The bull advanced along the road with tail up and horned head swinging to and fro, as though scenting trouble. When the animal saw the men grouped in front of the polling booth it stopped momentarily, as though taking in what it saw. Then, without warning, the bull lowered its head and charged.

296

The thirty or so men who a few minutes before had been congratulating each other on winning the day for Columb Hawkins, scattered rapidly. Some sought refuge in The King's Head, which supported Nathan. They found the doors closed and locked against them.

Others tried to climb on to the election platform, only to have their fingers stamped upon by Nathan and forced back to the street.

The cows were careering along the street too now, pursued by excited, barking dogs – and still the bull sought anyone who was moving and charged indiscriminately.

There was only one way for Columb Hawkins's thugs to go. They retreated in a confused, frightened mass along the main street of Tregony, pursued by the bull and its accompanying herd of cows.

The cows might have swept the fragile polling booth away, but guiding whistles from behind the herd sent two cattle-dogs crouching in front of the booth, snapping at the legs of any cow which ventured too close.

It was a complete rout. For twenty minutes the bull-led herd ruled the street.

In the wake of the herd thirty Tregony voters hurried forward to record their votes. By the time order had been restored, the by-election had been decided. Nathan was the winner by twenty-seven votes.

Chapter 60

Nathan had hoped to be able to relax a little once the by-election was over. Instead, the next few weeks were among the most hectic of his life.

Sir Christopher Hawkins wasted no time in evicting the remainder of the tenants who had voted against his nephew. They, their families and their possessions were, in some cases, quite literally thrown out on the street outside their former home.

Fortunately, Sir Kenwyn had anticipated such an immediate and ruthless reaction to the election result. He had planned well. All those dispossessed were swiftly re-housed and, in most cases, to their advantage.

Sir Kenwyn and Nathan both worked hard to ensure the families of these supporters suffered minimum hardship. In addition, there were many other matters requiring Nathan's attention.

Work had resumed on the harbour, but the new manager proved unsatisfactory. The result was that Nathan was faced with far more decisions than would otherwise have been the case.

The *Heron* and the *Charlotte* would soon be setting off for the fishing grounds of Newfoundland and the exciting new venture meant there were many last-minute matters to be settled. Not least was the question of an agent in Italy, the proposed market for the cured fish. It was necessary that Nathan find a reliable one if the *Heron* was to sell the fish caught off Newfoundland and return to Cornwall with a profitable cargo.

The weather was much improved now. Nathan's fishing-boats were putting out each night and returning with a rich harvest, keeping the fish-cellar at Portgiskey busy.

As if all this were not enough, letters were received at Polrudden asking Nathan to go to London and take his seat in the House of Commons at the earliest opportunity.

He decided the latter was the most pressing of his duties and made preparations to travel to London.

However, there was to be one more surprise for him.

Nathan was sitting down to dinner with Beville and Dewi earlier than usual because he was catching an early morning coach from St Austell to London. It was the first time they had enjoyed a meal together since the by-election.

Dinner had hardly begun when a maid came to the room to tell Nathan there was a messenger at the door for him.

Frowning in annoyance at the interruption, he said, 'Tell him to wait until I've eaten.'

'He looks very important. He's wearing some kind of uniform and says he's come from London – on the King's business.'

'Very well.' Resigned to the fact that he would have to interrupt his dinner, Nathan put down his knife and fork and rose from the table. 'I'll come and see him.'

A few minutes later he returned with an official-looking document and tossed it on the table beside his plate as he resumed his seat.

'What is it, Father?'

Beville had only recently forsaken 'Dad' in favour of the more adult 'Father'.

'I don't know. Something to do with my election to Parliament, by the look of it. It carries some sort of royal seal.'

'Aren't you going to open it?' Dewi, at least, was curious.

'Can *I* open it?' asked Beville, eagerly.

'If you like. Here you are.' Nathan was being particularly indulgent towards his son this evening. He felt guilty because he had hardly seen him during recent weeks.

'Do you think he should? It looks very important.'

'Of course he can. Use your knife to open the envelope, Beville. Then you can read me what the letter has to say.'

Pleased to be charged with such an important task, he opened the envelope with exaggerated caution while Dewi looked on with some trepidation and Nathan tucked into his meal.

When Beville opened out the letter it was possible for the others to see another seal attached to the bottom of the page, but for some moments the boy pored over the contents, his brow furrowed in concentration.

'Well, what does it say, Beville?' Dewi put the question to the small boy.

'There are lots of long words,' he protested, 'but I think it's from the King. It says he's pleased to appoint you a knight commander of the . . . something order. I can't read the word . . .'

Nathan paused, a laden fork halfway to his mouth. 'A knight! Show me, Beville.'

'I can read most of the rest,' he protested. 'It's only one or two words.'

'You've done well,' agreed Dewi. 'You've also given your father the shock of his life. Let him read the rest of the letter to us.'

Beville handed over the letter and Nathan read it in increasing disbelief. Lowering it finally he said in a stunned voice, 'It's perfectly true. I've been made a knight.'

'Congratulations, Nathan!' Dewi clapped her hands in delight.

'Is this because of your by-election win?'

'No, it has nothing to do with that. It says here it's for my services on behalf of the Crown and the Honourable East India Company. It must be because of Prince Rao and Abigail!'

'What do you have to do now you're a knight?' Beville put the question.

'Your father doesn't have to do anything, Beville – but it means that he too is now a "Sir". Sir Nathan Jago. Isn't that wonderful?'

Beaming at him, she said, 'It really is *wonderful*, Nathan. I am so proud for you.'

From the back of the room two maids echoed Dewi's congratulations and she knew the news would be all around Pentuan within the hour.

Nathan shook his head in disbelief. 'I just can't believe it.' Suddenly pensive, he said, 'If only my father was still alive to enjoy this.' Grinning sheepishly, he added, 'Mind you, he'd probably say I was getting too far above my station in life. That no good would come of it.'

'You know that isn't true,' declared Dewi. 'He'd be as proud of you as we all are. Why don't you send to Venn Farm and tell Nell and Tom the news? Invite them down here and you can have a small family celebration . . .'

The 'small' family celebration grew rapidly in size as the evening progressed.

Long before Nell and Tom reached Polrudden from Venn Farm, villagers were arriving from Pentuan to congratulate the new knight. Men and women Nathan had known since childhood; his fishermen; even some of the senior men working on the new harbour.

All were invited in for a drink. Before long it became apparent that Nathan's plans for a quiet evening before setting off for London would have to be shelved.

The staff at Polrudden also offered their own congratulations, but young Charlie Philpotts managed to inject a brief note of seriousness into the evening when he succeeded in taking Nathan aside and asking a favour of him.

'You still going to London in the morning?'

'I have to Charlie. I've made arrangements to meet Earl Plucknett and I need to be sworn in as a Member of Parliament.'

'Would you 'ave time to do something for me? I don't like to ask you, what with you being a "Sir" an' all, but there's no one else I can ask.'

'What is it? Do you want me to tell someone where you are?'

'No, not that, Mr Jago . . . I mean, Sir Nathan. The last thing I want is anyone in London knowing where I am. No, I'd just like you to send someone to tell my sister that I'm all right. Just

300

in case she's worrying 'erself about me. I don't think you ought to go there yourself. It's not the sort of area for a nob to go visiting.'

'Oh! And where is this place where I shouldn't go? Where is your sister living?'

'In Hackney. Columbia Road.'

'Do you know the number?'

'No. I've never 'ad to worry about remembering the number. I've always known where it is. Just ask for Ma Scuttle's lodging house. Anyone around there will tell you where it is. I've told you about Liz, that's my sister. She was sent to work for Ma Scuttle from the workhouse when she was about seven. She's ten now. Just tell 'er I'm all right and that I'll come and fetch 'er one day.'

'Is that what you intend doing one day, Charlie? Going to London and taking her away from Ma Scuttle's lodging house?'

'I'd like to. Perhaps I will. Anyway, it'll give 'er something to look forward to. Something to 'ope for. Wiv'out 'ope life ain't worth living in that part of London.'

Further conversation became impossible with the arrival of one of the shopkeepers from Pentuan who had brought his whole family to congratulate the new knight.

It was two o'clock in the morning before the last well-wisher left Polrudden and it would take the servants another two hours to clear up the mess they had left behind.

Nathan went to bed, but Dewi remained behind to help out the servants. Surveying the scene, she thought that Nathan must be one of the most popular men in the county, certainly among his tenants and neighbours. No doubt the landowners would add their own congratulations once the news of Nathan's knighthood became common knowledge.

It would be good for Beville – 'Sir Beville' – to take his rightful place in the county's society, especially now the Prince Regent had made Nathan a knight.

Nevertheless, Dewi's thoughts were not happy ones as she made her way up the stairway to her own room, in the early hours of the morning. She wondered where she, Dewi Morgan, governess to Sir Nathan Jago's child, fitted into the new scheme of things.

Chapter 61

When Nathan set off from Polrudden the next morning, he found Dewi and a very sleepy Beville waiting for him in the gig that would take him to St Austell.

'This is a great surprise,' he said as Beville gave him a hug.

'It's a very special occasion,' explained Dewi. 'I wanted Beville to be able to say he saw his father off when he went to take his seat in the House of Commons for the first time.'

'It's a very nice thought,' agreed Nathan. 'I'm feeling guilty because I haven't seen much of either of you these past few weeks. Now, Will, I think we'd better get these trunks in the gig and set off. They tell me the driver on the mail coach doesn't wait an extra second for lord, lady – or new Member of Parliament.'

Will Hodge was driving the gig to St Austell. A usually cheerful man, he had been celebrating Nathan's knighthood with the other servants the previous evening and any talk was an excruciating chore to him this morning.

It was a cold morning, but everyone was well wrapped-up and huddled together in the small gig. Along the way Nathan was able to tell Dewi of his provisional plans. He did not expect to be in London for much more than a fortnight. There was far too much to be done in Cornwall for him to spend any more time there. He would be travelling to London with Sir Kenwyn, who would board the coach at Lostwithiel, the next stop on the route to Plymouth.

For most of the journey to St Austell, Nathan patiently replied to Beville's many and varied questions about the duties of a Member of Parliament and the people he would meet in London.

It was still dark when the gig reached The Crown Inn at St Austell but the mail coach was already there, the breath of its horses and the heat from their bodies sending vaporous clouds rising above the dimly lit forecourt.

As Will Hodge loaded Nathan's trunks on the mail coach with the aid of the coachman, Nathan said his farewells to his son and to Dewi.

After kissing Beville and telling him to 'be a good boy' while he was away, Nathan turned to Dewi. After only a moment's

302

hesitation he put his hands to her face and kissed her too.

'We must have a talk when I return,' he said quietly, before releasing her.

Dewi nodded, thrilled that Nathan had kissed her publicly, but her reply showed far more coolness than she felt. 'You're a famous man now, *Sir* Nathan. I'll take good care of Beville and we'll both look forward to your return to Polrudden.'

Beville and Dewi waited until the coachman cracked his long whip over the backs of his horses and called on them to 'Gee-up!' Not until the coach and horses had clattered over the cobbled forecourt and disappeared into the darkness of the St Austell street did Dewi and Beville climb on the gig with Will Hodge and head back towards Polrudden.

The Polrudden head groom maintained his silence until they had almost reached Polrudden and Beville was asleep in Dewi's arms. It was growing light now and the groom turned to look at her. His expression revealed that he had seen Nathan kiss her before he left on the mail coach.

'Are you and Nathan likely to make a go of things, Miss Dewi?'

She thought wryly that the question could hardly have been more direct and to the point. She replied in the same fashion.

'It might have been possible once upon a time, Will. But he's *Sir* Nathan now, a Member of Parliament and well on the way to becoming one of the richest men in Cornwall. I'd be foolish to entertain any ideas in that direction.'

'Don't sell yourself short. You remind me – and a lot of other folk – of Amy, Nathan's second wife. She was the daughter of a well-known smuggler. No better and no worse than she ought to have been. Nathan was happier with her than he ever was with Elinor, his first wife – for all that she was Polrudden born and bred.'

Will tautened his left hand on the rein and steered the horse and gig from the lane into the driveway of Polrudden. Without looking at her, he said seriously, 'I can't think of one of us at Polrudden who wouldn't be pleased if you was to become mistress. I say that because we're all fond of Nathan and want what's best for him.'

Looking at her with a slightly embarrassed air as he drew the horse to a halt in front of the house door, he added, 'I thought you'd like to know that.'

'Thank you, Will. I appreciate your telling me. I also want what's best for Nathan – and Beville too.'

On the London-bound mail coach, Sir Kenwyn was talking to Nathan on the same subject, but his views did not coincide with those of Polrudden's head groom.

The only other occupant of the coach was a very old man who

had boarded the coach at Penzance and was fast asleep in the corner.

Nathan had mentioned that Dewi had brought Beville to St Austell to witness his departure and the baronet gave him a quizzical look.

'If you'll pardon a most impertinent question, is there anything between you and this girl?'

'Not yet, but the more I get to know her, the fonder I become of her. Why do you ask?'

'Because I don't want to see you make a mistake, dear boy. You are a man of substance and growing standing within Cornwall. I doubt if it will stop here. I once told you that young Beville would find no difficulty being accepted within the community. The same is now true of yourself. You are the friend of the Duke of Clarence and since the sad death of the Prince Regent's daughter, Clarence is second in line for the throne, after the Prince. Should he become King you would undoubtedly be raised to the peerage. That is bait enough for every family in the country! With such friends, money, and election to Parliament you are in a position to take the pick of any daughter in the land. Choose an alliance that will help you politically, Nathan. Carry you to the highest office in the land. It's yours for the taking!'

He smiled at the other man's enthusiasm. 'It was your idea that I should stand for Parliament, Sir Kenwyn. Your assistance more than anything else that won the election for me. Be content for now that I am a Member of Parliament. Let me be sworn in before ambition runs away with us.'

Chapter 62

Nathan took the oath of allegiance and signed the roll before the assembled House of Commons in St Stephen's Chapel two days after his arrival in London. His inauguration was watched with pride from the public gallery by Sir Kenwyn Penhaligan.

Westminster's newest Member of Parliament had fondly imagined the ceremony would take place in an air of solemnity and with great pomp. Instead, the sitting Members chattered and joked among themselves for all the world as though the Commons was a huge class of schoolboys.

Even the Speaker of the House seemed more intent on searching his pockets for something he had lost than ensuring that Nathan was a proper person to take his place among the lawmakers of the nation.

He took his seat in the packed chapel, which served as the House of Commons, and was congratulated by those Members within hand-shaking distance. For the remainder of that day's sitting, Nathan listened to the arguments for and against a bill to prevent seditious meetings.

When the House rose that evening, Sir Kenwyn was waiting for Nathan. He shook him vigorously by the hand, and congratulated him enthusiastically, adding, 'And now we're both invited to celebrate your success at Brook's Club as guests of Earl Plucknett, whom I understand you met at Bushy Park? It is to be a fairly large party, I believe.'

Putting an arm about his shoulders, Sir Kenwyn said, 'Few new Members will have enjoyed such a welcome, Nathan. You can be quite certain it will be noticed. Quite certain.'

The party was every bit as impressive as Sir Kenwyn had promised it would be. Many of the Whig peers and representatives in the House of Commons were there, as were a number of prominent Whig supporters. Among these was the anti-slavery campaigner William Wilberforce. When he learned that Nathan was in full agreement with his views, he monopolised him for a full half-hour.

Nathan was rescued by another guest, a man he recognised as Frederick Temple. He had been one of the original shareholders in the Pentuan harbour project.

When he led Nathan away from the emancipist politician, he asked after the harbour's progress.

'Slow but steady is probably the best way of describing it,' declared Nathan ruefully. 'Since I took over the majority of the shares, we've had some appalling weather. It has eased now and the men are back at work, but there are still problems.'

'Have you ever thought of selling your shares to an independent company?'

'Not really.' Nathan studied the other man. 'But I wouldn't dismiss the idea. Do you have any particular company in mind?'

'Yes. I have a substantial holding in a company that has just built a harbour in Suffolk. We are now running it profitably. It has been so successful that the shareholders are looking for another, similar project.'

The suggestion appealed to Nathan. The harbour, more than any other of his interests, was taking far too much of his time, energy and money. He would be happy to rid himself of the many headaches it posed. But there would need to be safeguards.

'That can be arranged,' said Temple, when Nathan aired his doubts. 'I will give you a personal guarantee that, should we decide to sell, for any reason whatsoever, you will be offered your shares back at the market price.'

'Then we might well be able to arrange a deal,' said Nathan. 'I will be at the House of Commons for the next couple of weeks. Speak to the other shareholders in your company and come to me with a firm proposal. We'll talk more of it then.'

Nathan told Sir Kenwyn of the offer as they drove back to the baronet's London house where Nathan was staying until he found a suitable house for himself.

'It sounds fair enough,' said Sir Kenwyn. 'But be certain to take advice before agreeing to anything. These London businessmen are among the sharpest you'll find anywhere in the world.'

Dismissing the matter from his mind as being of little account, he said, 'Did I tell you what Earl Plucknett said to me about your prospects in the Whig Party . . . ?

Sir Kenwyn only remained in London for a few days. He had come to see his protégé safely ensconced in the House of Commons. This had been achieved with greater success than he had dared imagine. Nathan's arrival on the political scene had been well received by the grandees in the Whig Party and their powerful friends.

The present ruling Tory administration under the leadership of the Earl of Liverpool was universally detested and was expected to fall before too long. Nathan was well placed to play a part in the revival of Whig fortunes. When it happened, those who had helped the party members would surely not be forgotten.

He had made a good beginning. He also had a number of influential friends. His prospects in Parliament were very good indeed. If he kept clear of scandals and made a good marriage he could go to the very top of the political tree.

Happily day-dreaming, Sir Kenwyn wondered, when the time came, whether it should be Lord Penhaligan of Golant? Or perhaps Lord Penhaligan of Fowey?

The thought of a marriage for Nathan was Sir Kenwyn's only cause for concern. However, Nathan was moving in the right circles now and the baronet had not exaggerated when he told Nathan there was not a man in the land who would deny his daughter to the newly elected Member of Parliament.

Yet Sir Kenwyn had the impression that Nathan had not taken the matter seriously enough. Perhaps he should have explained in greater detail. Marriages at the level of influence Nathan was likely to achieve were intended to cement alliances. A step on the political ladder. No more and no less.

Sir Kenwyn was not at all certain that Nathan realised this basic fact of political life. Sir Kenwyn carried a letter for Dewi, the governess to Nathan's son. Sir Kenwyn wished he could believe it contained nothing more than instructions concerning young Sir Beville. Unfortunately, the baronet feared that Nathan was fond of the girl. He could not marry her, of course. Such a marriage would prove disastrous to his future. Nevertheless, Nathan had proved in the past that his heart was capable of ruling his head.

Nathan Jago was older now than when he had made his earlier marriages, but Sir Kenwyn was not convinced he might not choose a disastrous course if he were not properly advised and 'guided'.

He would have to speak to this girl. He had no doubt she was a sensible young woman. She must realise that such a marriage would ruin Nathan's career. He trusted she was fond enough of Nathan not to wish to wreck his political future.

Of course, once Nathan was satisfactorily married and his course had been set there was nothing to prevent him setting Dewi up as his mistress. Providing a small house for her in London, perhaps, while his wife remained happily in Cornwall. Why, Sir Kenwyn himself had done the same thing himself quite satisfactorily during the early years of his marriage. What was the girl's name. Judy? No, Julie! Yes, that was it. Young, dark-haired Julie. She had been on the stage when he met her. He wondered what she was doing now. No doubt she was married and blowsy . . .

Musing on the love he had once enjoyed, the hours passed more quickly as he travelled home to Golant and the wife who had never seen the inside of Sir Kenwyn's London home.

Chapter 63

Two days after Sir Kenwyn had left London for Golant, Nathan went to look at a small house in Orchard Place, close to Westminster. The house was owned by a Member of Parliament who had suffered a stroke. As a result, he was now confined to his home in Sussex. The family were unable to sell the house off while the unfortunate parliamentarian was still alive, but were anxious to rent it out.

Nathan was let into the house by Miss Henshaw, an elderly, unsmiling housekeeper dressed entirely in black, who declared the stairs were too much for her. She delegated the task of showing him the house to Tilly, a tall, pert young housemaid, who was as cheerily cheeky as the old lady was sombre.

'It's a nice little house, sir,' she declared, tripping up the stairs ahead of him. 'No damp, no noisy neighbours, and within easy reach of the House of Commons.'

Reaching the first floor, she said, 'There's two bedrooms on this floor, Sir Nathan, and two more upstairs. If you take my advice you'll settle for the large back one on this floor. Nice and airy, no draughts and away from the noise of the street.'

Opening the door in question, she eyed him as he glanced about the room. It had a large bed fitted with curtains all round and there was a small washroom off one side.

'Will your wife be spending much time in London with you, Sir Nathan? I'm sure she'd like this room too.'

'I'm a widower.'

'Oh dear, I *am* sorry, Sir Nathan.' The maid did not sound sorry at all as she touched his arm in a brief gesture of bold-eyed sympathy. 'Never you mind. We'll look after you here, I can promise you that. When poor Mr Shaw was in London I'd always bring him a nice hot drink last thing at night. Breakfast in bed too, if he wanted.'

Something in the tone of her voice told Nathan she meant every word of her open-ended promise. He would need to watch himself with her.

The inspection confirmed to him that the house was exactly what he was looking for. Four bedrooms on two floors, with servants' quarters in the attic above. There was ample space for entertaining on the ground floor, should he so wish it. The accommodation also included a kitchen, scullery and pantries on the basement floor, with a separate door to an area below pavement level in the front of the house.

'Yes, I like the house,' Nathan told the unsmiling housekeeper. 'I would like to move in immediately.'

'I don't know about that,' said the black-clad woman. 'I'd need to have a letter from Mr Shaw.'

'Unfortunately, Mr Shaw is unable to write. However, I have a letter of authorisation here from his sister – and another from his solicitor. Everything is quite in order, I can assure you.'

'And so it may be for you, sir, but there's things to be sorted out here. There's no cook, for a start. The one employed by Mr Shaw left two weeks ago. She was offered a better post.'

'I'll do the cooking for you, Sir Nathan. I'm a good cook, you ask Nancy, the other maid. Nothing fancy, but as good as any of the cooks employed by Mr Shaw during the years I've been here.'

In spite of her over-familiar manner, Nathan had taken a liking to this cheery London girl. 'All right, Tilly. I'll move my things in this evening and you can cook dinner for me.' Reaching into a pocket he pulled out two gold coins. 'Here are two guineas. Buy whatever you think necessary and we'll have a chat tomorrow about what you're going to require for the future.'

The delighted maid dropped him a pert curtsy. 'Right you are, Sir Nathan. I'll make certain you have receipts for all I spend.' Casting a mischievous glance in the direction of the disapproving housekeeper, she said, 'Everything in the kitchen, at least, will be run proper, I promise you that.'

Nathan found nothing to complain about in the meal produced for him that evening by Tilly and he told her so.

'Thank you, Sir Nathan. I told you I could cook.'

'You've certainly proved that, Tilly. In fact, I feel so full I wish I wasn't going out tonight.'

'You're out, Sir Nathan?' She sounded disappointed. 'Would you like me to wait up for you? Have something ready for you to eat before you go to bed?'

'No, thank you, Tilly. You've excelled yourself tonight. I look forward to seeing what you can produce for breakfast.'

Leaving her beaming at his lavish compliments, Nathan went to his bedroom to change for the evening. He was going to pay a call on John Gully, landlord of The Plough in Carey Street. It was a Saturday night and Nathan intended keeping his promise to Charlie Philpotts by informing Liz, his young sister, that her brother was well.

Charlie had suggested it might be better if Nathan sent a messenger instead of going himself, but he had other ideas.

The Plough was packed with customers but John Gully greeted Nathan with great enthusiasm, as did the prizefighters frequenting the inn. Most had known Nathan in his own prizefighting days.

'We heard the news that you'd been elected to Parliament,' said John Gully. 'And someone said only yesterday that you'd been knighted. Is it true?'

'It's true,' Nathan confirmed. 'I haven't got used to it myself yet.'

'You hear that, everyone?' John Gully's deep voice carried above the hubbub of the crowded inn. 'Nathan Jago, one of the best fighters ever to step inside the prize-ring, has not only been elected to Parliament, but has been made a knight as well. Gentlemen, a toast. To Sir Nathan Jago!'

'Sir Nathan Jago!' The roar went up from the inn's customers, always eager to have something new to celebrate.

When the sound died away and prizefighting acquaintances had ceased congratulating Nathan, John Gully said, 'It's good to see you again. How's that young governess of yours, Dewi? And the other girl, the troublesome one . . . was it Sally?'

Nathan told John Gully of Sally's murder and gained the sympathy of his listeners when he told how her death had led to the tragedy that had killed his father. Many of the regular visitors to The Plough had met Preacher Jago in the past. They were genuinely upset at the manner of his death.

Talk of Pentuan, and of Dewi and Beville reminded Nathan of how much he missed them both. It was pleasurable to be here, among friends, but he would have preferred to be spending the evening at home, in Polrudden.

'Is this a social visit to old friends, Nathan, or is there something I can do for you?'

'As a matter of fact there is, John. Do you remember a young ragamuffin named Charlie Philpotts? I caught him trying to steal Dewi's bag and suggested you might be able to find some honest work for him.'

'I remember him well,' said John Gully. 'I took a liking to the lad. Thought there was a lot of good in him. It seemed I was right too, for a while. He was settling in quite nicely here. I was convinced he'd given up his thieving ways. Then he had a night off to go to the East End somewhere, to visit his sister – or so he said. He came back late at night and by morning had gone without a word. I never did know why, not for sure. Although I heard a rumour that he'd got into some scrape in Hackney. Knifed a man, it was said, although that doesn't sound like Charlie. Why do you ask, have you seen him again?'

'Yes, he's staying at Polrudden. Working with my carpenter there and doing well. He's asked me to let his young sister know about him, but doesn't want anyone else to know where he is.

310

Now I think I know why. But I promised to give his sister his message. I thought I might go there tonight. She lives in Columbia Road, just off Hackney Road. He doesn't know the number but says the workhouse gave her to a Ma Scuttle who runs a lodging house. Charlie says anyone around there will tell me where it is.'

'You'd go to Columbia Road on a Saturday night? I've no doubt most of them around there would know where this Ma Scuttle has her lodging house, but they'd stick a knife in you as soon as tell you. That's a rough area, Nathan. I should know, I did some of my prizefighting around there.'

'I guessed it would be, but I've promised Charlie I'd find his sister. Tonight seemed as good a time as any to go.'

'Well, you certainly can't go dressed like that. Come upstairs and I'll find you something from my store room. That's where I keep clothes that have been left behind in the rooms. You'd be surprised what people forget when they leave. I could probably dress everyone in here right now. What we want for you is something cheap and nasty, but clean. You'll find that people who live around Columbia Road can't afford to spend much on their clothes, but when they go out on a Saturday night they put on the best they've got.'

Fifteen minutes later Nathan was told by John Gully's wife that he looked for all the world like a costermonger on a night out. Dressed in shirt, muffler, pearl-buttoned waistcoat, fustian trousers and corduroy jacket, it was exactly the impression Nathan wanted to give to those he would meet in the Columbia Road area.

But still John Gully was not satisfied.

'You look the part, certainly, but you don't know the East End well enough to pass yourself off as a costermonger. The best thing I can do is to send Alf with you. He comes from that area and they know him. You won't find anyone starting an argument with you if Alf's keeping you company.'

311

Chapter 64

Nathan and the silent Alf travelled only part of the way to Hackney in a coach. When they were still some distance from Columbia Road, Alf brought the carriage to a halt by the simple expedient of leaning out of the window and tugging the coat tails of the coach driver.

Nevertheless, the sight of two men alighting from a coach was still enough to draw a small crowd of youngsters, many of whom reminded Nathan of Charlie Philpotts. He felt they were in danger of having their pockets picked until a passer-by hailed Alf like an old friend.

'Hello there, Alfie boy. You up here for a prizefight or just visiting old friends?'

Grinning amiably, Alf signalled that he was not in the East End for a fight. Slapping the mute prizefighter on the back, the man went on his way and the small boys drifted away. Alf and Nathan obviously belonged to the area and East End pickpockets did not rob their own kind.

Columbia Road was wider than many of the streets in this part of London, but it was no more salubrious. Even at this late hour the street was cluttered with a variety of stalls and rubbish was strewn everywhere. Much of it lay in evil-smelling pools of water in the gutters. From dark alleyways that separated dingy houses the foul smell of un-emptied communal privies added their odours to the street smells.

There were numerous ale-houses and gin-shops here too, the smell of their wares adding to the general aroma. The voices of the occupants, raised in song or argument, added to the general commotion in the street.

There were many people abroad. Most, as John Gully had predicted, dressed in poor quality clothing. Nathan realised he would have been hopelessly out of place had he been wearing his own clothes.

'Shall we ask if anyone here knows Ma Kettle's?' Nathan put the question to his companion.

Alf shook his head, placing a finger vertically across his lips as a signal for Nathan to remain silent. The two men walked half the length of Columbia Road before Alf suddenly pushed his way through a passing crowd. He took the arm of a girl who was having an increasingly heated argument with another streetwalker.

She at first tried to pull her arm away, but then peered closer at the man who had taken her arm and promptly forgot her quarrel.

'Alf! Wot you doing 'ere? You come looking for me?'

Beckoning for the girl to come with him, and not releasing his grip on her arm, Alf propelled her through the crowd. The watching men and women quickly drifted away, disappointed they were not to witness a fight between two of the girls who patrolled the street, ready to sell their bodies to anyone with the price of a half-bottle of Geneva.

Thrust in front of Nathan, the girl put on a practised smile. ''Ello, luv. You lookin' for a girl to give yer a good time? You're in luck. Alf's brought you to the right place.'

Beside the girl, Alf pointed to his lips and then to the girl and Nathan said, 'I'm not looking for a girl. At least, not for what you have to offer. I'm looking for a young child named Liz. Liz Philpotts. I expect to find her at Ma Kettle's.'

The girl looked at Alf accusingly. 'Wot's the idea of bringing this geezer to me, Alfie? Who is he, a thief-taker?'

Alf shook his head and, pointing to Nathan, raised his arms in a prizefighter's opening stance.

'A fighter? Wot's yer name, mister?'

'Nathan Jago.'

The woman's face showed astonishment.

'Nathan Jago – the champion?'

'Shh! I'd rather not attract a crowd.'

'Cor!' The girl looked at him in open admiration. 'You sure you're not looking for a good time?'

'I just want to find Ma Kettle's and have a word with young Liz Philpotts.'

'Wot you want 'er for?'

'I've a message for her, from her brother.'

'Young Charlie? You know where 'e is? I 'ope 'e's all right?'

'He's fine.' Too many people for Nathan's liking were able to overhear their conversation. 'Can you tell us where to find Ma Kettle's lodging house?'

'Course I can. There's not one of us "working girls" who 'asn't used Ma Kettle's, some time or another. Don't know whether young Liz is still there, though. Ma Kettle always seems to 'ave three or four poor little work'ouse brats working for 'er. None of 'em seems to last very long. I doubt if there's anyone ever asks any questions about 'em, neither.'

Nathan and Alf exchanged concerned glances and Nathan said to the girl, 'Can you show us to this Ma Kettle's?'

'I'm not coming with you. I can't afford to get mixed up in any

313

trouble. The pair of you look as though you might start something, especially if you don't like what you find when you get there. When it's all over you'll just walk away and forget about it. I 'ave to live 'ere. But I'll tell you 'ow to get there . . .'

Following the girl's instructions, Nathan and Alf came to an alleyway. Beside the entrance was a flower seller. Sitting on a stool, the woman cried her wares in a voice rusted from years of gin-swilling.

Turning into the alleyway, Alf touched Nathan's arm and moved ahead of him. Some ten paces along they discovered a doorway. Through the open door was a dimly lit corridor.

Entering the house, Nathan wrinkled his nose. The house stank of stale cooking and equally stale alcohol. The two men followed the corridor until they came to a staircase rising to an equally dimly lit landing.

The corridor divided here and from the shadows a large man rose from a chair to challenge them. 'You looking for something?'

'Yes, Ma Kettle. Is she in?'

'Who wants her?'

'Nathan Jago. Not that she'll be any wiser if you tell her.' While Nathan was talking to the large man a woman came down the stairs with a man who was grumbling that he'd: 'Hardly been upstairs for ten minutes!'

'What's your business with Ma?'

'I'll discuss that with her.'

'Not if she don't want to see you, you won't,' the heavy argued.

'Well, we won't know if you don't go and tell her we're here.'

'All right, but you wait right here. Move so much as an inch and I'll heave you back out through that door.'

The man slouched along the ill-lit corridor, glancing back over his shoulder twice, as though daring Nathan and Alf to defy his words.

'He sounds like a hard man, Alf. I think we might have to put him in his place before the evening's over.'

Alf's grin split the darkness in a silent reply.

Light spilled into the corridor as Ma Kettle's sentry opened the door at the far end. Nathan caught a glimpse of perhaps half-a-dozen or so men and women seated around a table in a smoke-filled room before the door was closed once more.

No more than two minutes later it was opened again and this time laughter spilled into the corridor along with the light.

Standing squarely in front of Nathan and Alf, effectively blocking the narrow corridor, the man said belligerently, 'Ma Kettle says she don't know no Nathan Jago and she's not in anyway.'

'That's all right,' said Nathan cheerfully. 'I only wanted to ask her about Liz Philpotts. As she's not in she can't object to my talking to Liz direct – and unless I'm mistaken that's her I saw in the room along the corridor.'

314

Nathan had made out a pinched young face in the smoke-filled room. The brief glimpse had been sufficient to increase his determination to speak to her.

The big man stood straddle-legged, blocking the corridor. Nathan was confident of dealing with him swiftly and efficiently, but before he could make a move Alf had pushed past him.

A feint by Alf's left hand brought the big man's hands up to guard his face. In an instant, Alf sank his right fist almost wrist-deep in the other man's stomach. The big man folded, chin forward, hands transferred to clutch his belly.

Alf's right struck again, this time to the chin of Ma Kettle's sentry, and he caught his unconscious opponent before he collapsed to the ground.

When he was slung over Alf's shoulder the unconscious man was as limp as a rolled carpet. He never felt a thing when he was pitched into the dark alleyway and the door closed behind him.

'That was a joy to watch,' said Nathan gleefully. 'I don't think I could have done it better myself. Now let's go and find young Charlie's sister. I think she might be pleased to see us.'

When Nathan threw open the door to the room at the end of the corridor, eight faces were turned towards him, their expressions varying from surprise to annoyance.

Six people were seated at a table. Cards, tankards, money and bottles were strewn about in front of them. Two women stood behind their men.

'Good evening.' Nathan skirted the players, heading for a door at the far side of the room. 'Don't let me disturb your game.' He found he was quite enjoying himself.

''Ere! Where do you think you're going! Why didn't Mick stop you?' The oldest of the women at the table posed the questions.

'Mick's gone out for a while. I came here looking for Ma Kettle, but since she's not in I'll have a word with the girl who must be in the next room. I believe her name is Liz Philpotts.'

As Nathan crossed the room to a closed door, the woman protested, '*I'm* Ma Kettle. You get out of my 'ouse before I call in the constable and 'ave you taken before the beak.'

One of the men at the table began to rise from his seat but Alf's hand placed firmly on his head pushed him down again.

Nathan opened the door and found himself in a filthy kitchen that smelled almost as bad as the alleyway outside.

At a sink that was filled with greasy, brown-coloured water was a small, thin girl of about ten years of age, wearing a ragged dress. The sound of the door opening caused her to turn around swiftly and there was an expression of fear upon her face.

'Who are you? Wot you want? If Ma's sent you in 'ere . . .' As she spoke, Liz's hand rested on the wooden handle of a carving knife, the blade of which had been rendered sickle-shape by excessive sharpening.

315

'No one's sent me from in there. I'm here because I promised Charlie I'd come to see how you were.'

'You've seen Charlie? You know where he is?'

For a few moments Liz's face relaxed into an expression of excited delight, only to change to one of suspicion. 'It's a trick. You're just trying to get round me.'

'Charlie's been working for me for some months now. When he heard I was coming to London he asked if I'd find you and tell you he was all right. Here I am.'

Liz's experiences, first in the poor-house, and latterly in Ma Kettle's establishment, had left her with very little trust in anyone. There had been only one flicker of brightness in her young life provided by her affection for Charlie. Concern for him overcame her distrust of Nathan.

'Where is he? Did 'e really ask you to find me?'

At that moment there was a sudden commotion from the room where Nathan had left Alf with the card players.

Opening the door quickly, Nathan saw one of the men stretched on the floor, motionless, with a woman kneeling beside him, vainly attempting to shake him into consciousness. Nearby, Alf was rubbing his knuckles. Around the table the other men sat as though fearing to move a muscle.

Taking in the situation, Nathan spoke to the woman who had identified herself as Ma Kettle. 'I think you and I ought to have a chat. The others can go.'

Chairs scraped back from the table as the card players seized the opportunity to escape from the fight-hardened fists of Alf.

'And take him with you.'

Nathan pointed to the prostrate man on the floor. Unceremoniously, two of the unconscious man's companions gripped his arms. Hurriedly they dragged him from the room in the wake of the others who had wasted no time in obeying Nathan's order.

'If you're after money you're out of luck. This is all there is in the house.'

Ma Kettle flapped a hand towards the pennies, halfpennies and farthings scattered about the table among the cards.

'I'm not interested in your money. I want to talk to you about Liz.'

The girl in question stood in the doorway, bewildered by what was going on. A frightened expression was on her face once more.

'She's not ready to go on the game yet. If you want a girl I can find one for you upstairs. There's a new one, Ivy . . .'

Nathan looked at the old lady in disgust. 'If I frequented bawdy-houses this would be bottom of my list. Let's talk about Liz. I want to take her away from here – to be with her brother.'

'You know Charlie's whereabouts? Where is he?'

Ma Kettle's sudden surge of interest aroused Nathan's suspicions immediately. 'He's in the country.'

'A good boy is Charlie. I've always been very fond of 'im. Think of 'im as a son, I do.'

'I'm here to talk about Liz.'

Ma Kettle gave an exaggerated sigh that caused a violent reaction among the flabby muscles of her considerable body. 'Ah! She's more than a daughter to me, is that one. Don't know what I'd do wiv'out 'er. Does everyfing for me, she does. I suppose it's 'er way of showing 'er gratitude. Wot wiv me taking 'er out of the poor-'ouse and treating 'er as me own flesh and blood.'

'How much do you want to let her go?' Nathan cut through the woman's hypocritical cant.

'Let 'er go? You mean . . . part wiv 'er for good? I couldn't. No. Wrench me bleedin' 'eart out, it would, an' no mistake.'

'I'll give you twenty pounds to release her to me.'

'Twenty!' The amount was more than Ma Kettle had been expecting, but she was both crafty and greedy. 'I've already been offered a considerable sum by a gentleman friend for 'er. A considerable sum 'er being a virgin, an' all.'

'Twenty-five – and I'll make it guineas. That's my final offer.'

'Now if you'd 'a said thirty, sir – guineas, o' course – I'd 'ave 'ad to accept. Even though it'd break me 'eart. I'm a poor woman, you see.'

'Thirty guineas it is.' Anxious to get away from this place, Nathan pulled a pouch from his pocket. He had come prepared for such an eventuality and began to count the money out in front of Ma Kettle's greedy eyes.

'. . . twenty-nine, thirty. There you are.' Looking up at the wide-eyed young girl in the doorway, he said, 'Are you happy to come with me to be with Charlie, Liz?'

'You mean it, mister? I really *will* be with Charlie?'

'I swear it on my life, Liz. If Alf could speak he'd confirm it. Isn't that right, Alf?'

He nodded his head vigorously.

After only a moment's hesitation, Liz said, 'Yeah, I'll come wiv you. Even if Charlie wasn't going to be there, I'd come. Anything to get away from 'er.'

Jabbing a venomous finger in Ma Kettle's direction, she said, 'What she said, about being offered "a considerable sum from a gentleman" is a lie. She was offered a guinea and a bottle of 'ollands – and she was so drunk she nearly accepted it.'

'You lying' little cow!' Ma Kettle tried to struggle to her feet.

The effort proved too much and Nathan said, 'It doesn't matter. Come on, Liz. Do you want to go and pick up any belongings?'

'Belongings? I don't 'ave any. No, mister. You want me, you take me. Let's get out of this place.'

317

Chapter 65

Walking along Columbia Road, with Liz between the two of them, Nathan felt very aware of the girl's dirty and ragged appearance. When they passed a stall where a man was folding and stowing away ready-made clothing, prior to going home, he put out a hand and brought Liz to a halt.

'Here, choose half-a-dozen dresses for yourself. You'd better get some shoes too – soft shoes – and anything else you need.' Nathan was embarrassed by Liz's bare and exceedingly dirty feet.

'Honest! You'll let me 'ave some clothes? *Six* dresses?'

'We'll get you more later, but this should cover your immediate needs.'

Aware that fortune had suddenly brought a good customer his way, the stall-holder was replacing clothes on the stall at a rapid rate.

'Can I have a pair of drawers an' all?' Liz turned wide young eyes up to Nathan. 'I ain't never 'ad no drawers.'

'Yes,' said an embarrassed Nathan, aware of Alf's wide grin. 'You'd better have half-a-dozen pairs of them, too.'

'Cor!' Liz looked up at him in awe. 'You're all right, mister.' Already picking over the dresses being produced at great speed by the stall-holder, she added, 'Just wait 'til Charlie sees me in these.'

When Nathan hailed a Hackney coach in the road of the same name, all three were laden with Liz's purchases. The clothes were piled inside the coach and Nathan and Liz climbed in after them. Alf indicated that he would walk back to The Plough.

Seated beside Nathan, Liz was bubbling with unaccustomed happiness.

'You sure all these clothes are for me? You're not going to take 'em back again?'

'They are all for you, Liz, and when we get to Cornwall I've no doubt Dewi will want to have some more made for you.'

'Is Cornwall where Charlie is?'

'That's right. It's a long way from London and we'll need to travel there by coach. But that won't be for a week or so. In the meantime you'll live in the London house I've just taken on. I'm sure one of the maids there will be happy to look after you.'

'A maid . . . to look after me?' A carriage passed them, travelling in the opposite direction, and the light from the link-boy's torch revealed the incredulity on Liz's face. Suddenly she said, 'Who are you, mister? I don't even know your name.'

Nathan smiled. 'I'm Nathan Jago – Sir Nathan Jago. Once a prizefighter, I own a fishing-cellar in Cornwall, live there and have recently been elected to Parliament.'

'You're a *Sir*? Cor! And I've been calling you "mister"! What should I call you, Sir Nathan?'

'That sounds as good as anything to me.'

He still found the use of his new title slightly embarrassing. In a bid to change the subject, he said, 'Why was Ma Kettle so interested in Charlie? I didn't realise she knew him that well. Charlie certainly didn't say.'

'She didn't. She was only interested in the reward.'

'What reward?'

'Didn't Charlie tell you?' Nathan could sense the same suspicion in her that had been there in the house in Columbia Road.

'I knew Charlie was in trouble when he arrived at my house in Cornwall, but I didn't ask him what it was for fear he might take off again. I'd like you to tell me.'

'For all I know you might be after the reward as well.'

'Is this reward so great that I'd give money to Ma Kettle for you, and buy six dresses, when I could have got away with buying one?'

'No,' admitted Liz. 'But there's twenty pounds on 'is 'ead.'

'What for?'

'Murder!'

There was a long silence while Nathan marshalled his thoughts. Then he said, 'I think you'd better tell me all about it, Liz.'

'It was all my fault, really.' She sounded thoroughly unhappy. 'Charlie came to see me one day and told me 'e was leaving Bethnal Green. Said 'e'd got a good job at an inn up in the city. I told 'im 'e was to come and see me whenever 'e got the chance. 'E came a couple 'o times, even though Ma Kettle told 'im she didn't want 'im in the 'ouse. Said it stopped me working. Charlie came to see me quite late one Friday night, when Ma was in on 'er own. I was 'ungry because I'd busted one of Ma's plates and she'd stopped me supper to 'elp pay for it. Charlie came in, all proud of 'imself because 'e 'ad money in 'is pocket. Honest money. 'E'd just been paid. Well, 'e said 'e'd go off and find a pie man and buy us each a pie. Ma grumbled, but when Charlie said 'e'd buy one for 'er too, she changed 'er tune.'

The Hackney coach had reached Pall Mall now where gas lights had been installed for the length of one side of the street. Nathan could see the young girl's tortured face.

'While Charlie was out, one of Ma's regulars came in. A coal-

319

'eaver from over the docks. It was 'is pay-day too – and 'e'd been drinking 'eavy. Mick 'ad taken a night off, because things were quiet, and the coal-'eaver rolled in and told Ma 'e wanted a whore. She told 'im all 'er girls were out. Then 'e saw me and said I'd do as well any she could offer 'im. Ma told 'im to clear off and for me to shut meself in the kitchen. I tried to do as she said, but this bloke gave 'er a back-'ander that knocked 'er clear back over the table and 'e 'ad 'is foot in the door of the scullery before I could shut it. 'E 'it me then and when I was on the floor, got on top of me. I could 'ardly breathe, 'e was so 'eavy. I was screaming too, I think. That's when Charlie came back with the pies. 'E told this bloke to stop. When 'e didn't, Charlie started kicking 'im, but the coal-'eaver upped with 'is fist and knocked Charlie backwards before starting on me again. When Charlie picked 'imself up 'e saw the carving-knife by the sink. 'E didn't stop to think what 'e was doing. 'E shoved the knife into the coal-'eaver's back and it went right between 'is ribs and into 'is 'eart. Ma Kettle told Charlie to get the 'ell out of it – and 'e did.'

Liz shuddered and Nathan patted her arm sympathetically. 'I think Ma would 'ave 'ad someone carry the coal-'eaver down to the river, dumped 'im in and forgotten all about it, but too many people 'ad 'eard me screaming. They all crowded into the room and saw 'im lying there, dead. Someone told the magistrate and next minute the 'ouse was full of constables. The next thing we 'eard was there was a warrant out for Charlie's arrest and a twenty guinea reward for whoever turned 'im in.'

'But Charlie was defending you. They'd never convict him in any court.'

'Don't you believe it! If Ma Kettle found out where Charlie was she'd turn 'im in and claim the reward. It wouldn't be paid over if it was proved Charlie 'ad killed the coal-'eaver defending either me or 'imself. For twenty guineas Ma Kettle would commit murder 'erself. She'd make up a story that would convince a beak – and produce four or five witnesses to swear that wot she was saying was the truth.'

Thinking about it, Nathan realised Liz was right. Ma Kettle was an evil and mercenary woman. She would think nothing of perjuring herself for twenty pounds.

'You didn't tell 'er where Charlie was?' Liz felt Nathan's concern and reacted to it anxiously.

'No, but I *did* give her my name. She could trace me from that – or get one of the runners from Bow Street to do it for her. We'll need to take some precautions to protect Charlie when we get back to Cornwall.'

The door to the house in Orchard Place was opened by Tilly. Her warm greeting turned quickly to disbelief when she saw Nathan

320

and his young companion, almost hidden beneath piles of clothing.

Inside the house the maid's surprise became dismay when she relieved Liz of the newly bought clothing and saw her ragged state.

'It's far too late for lengthy explanations now, Tilly, but I've just rescued Liz from an abominable house in Columbia Road, in Bethnal Green. She was sent there from a poor-house. Her brother works for me in Cornwall and I'll be taking her to him when I return there. In the meantime she'll be staying here. I've bought some new clothes for her, but I've no doubt she'll need more. Other things too. She doesn't have a single possession in the world. Is the housekeeper about? I suppose I ought to tell her what's happening.'

'Not if you want to get any sleep tonight, Sir Nathan. Upset Miss Henshaw and she keeps on and on about it. I think it'll be better if we leave it until morning. I'll take care of this young lady. Liz did you say her name was? You come with me, miss. I'll take you somewhere where you can get that dirt off you while I cook some food for Sir Nathan. Then I'll come back and feed *you* before tucking you up in bed. Come morning we'll dress you up so that anyone from Bethnal Green would think they was looking at a lady if they was ever to cop eyes on you again.'

'Thank you, Tilly. I knew I'd be able to rely on you. Good night, young Liz. It's been an exciting day for you. Have a good sleep tonight and tomorrow we'll talk about getting you to Cornwall and meeting up with Charlie again.'

Liz was accompanying Tilly when she suddenly turned and ran back to Nathan. Taking him completely by surprise, she flung her arms about him and hugged him in a genuine and spontaneous gesture of affection.

While Nathan was still recovering from this, Tilly spoke to him in a voice that was far removed from the cheekiness she had shown earlier in the day.

'Sir Nathan . . . *I* was a poor-house girl who was put in to "service" when I was a year or two younger than Liz. I worked in one or two places I'd rather not think about before I came here. You don't have to do no more than look at Liz to know what sort of place you've rescued her from. I could hug you for it myself, sir, I really could.'

Helping himself to a drink from the stock left in the house by the previous occupant, Nathan told himself he'd made himself two good friends that day, albeit not two of whom the ambitious Sir Kenwyn would approve.

Thinking of Sir Kenwyn caused Nathan to remember the last conversation the men had held concerning Dewi and her place in Nathan's life. He would need to put the Golant baronet right about Dewi.

He also thought about the evil woman he had met in Columbia Road today. He did not doubt that Liz was right about the lengths to which she would go to in order to gain for herself the twenty pounds' reward put up for Charlie Philpotts. He would write to Dewi and warn her of the possibility of a visit from a runner from the Bow Street Magistrate's court. Charlie must be found work at Venn Farm until Nathan's return. He would sort out a more permanent solution then.

Thinking about writing to Dewi, Nathan poured himself a second drink and sat down to enjoy it in front of the fire in this, his London home.

Chapter 66

Dewi was walking home to Polrudden from Venn Farm accompanied by Pippa and Beville when they met up with Sir Kenwyn Penhaligan. The baronet had already been to Polrudden and been told that Dewi and Beville were at the farm.

Dismounting and greeting the trio with his usual bonhomie, Sir Kenwyn said, 'And how is Cornwall's youngest baronet today, Sir Beville? Are you studying hard so you may one day be a credit to your father?'

'Yes, Sir Kenwyn.'

'Good lad! I left your father in London only a couple of days ago. Saw him take the oath at the House of Commons. An historic moment for the Jago family. Wish you could have been there. Your father sends his love and will no doubt bring you back some small remembrance of the occasion.'

'I hope so. I wish I could have been there too.'

'Never mind, Sir Beville. Your father will one day bring great honours to Polrudden – and yourself of course. No doubt about it.'

Beaming at the small boy, Sir Kenwyn shifted his glance to Dewi. 'Sir Nathan sends his regards to you too, Dewi – and I have a letter for you. He is relieved to know his son is in such capable hands while he is away.'

'Thank you, Sir Kenwyn. You are most kind to say so.'

She felt there was more to Sir Kenwyn's visit than the passing on of Nathan's letter and good wishes to her and to Beville. The baronet's next words confirmed her suspicion.

'May you and I have a little chat together, Dewi? Nothing of great moment, but I do think it might be best were we to talk in private.'

'Beville, you go on to the house with Pippa. You've done well with your lessons this afternoon, you can play in the garden until I come home.'

Shouting back his thanks, Beville began to run, dragging Pippa after him.

Leading his horse, Sir Kenwyn fell in beside Dewi and they followed after Beville and the assistant governess at a more leisurely pace.

'How delightful it is to see the young in good health and with such boundless energy.'

'Yes.'

Dewi was waiting for Sir Kenwyn to explain why he had wanted Pippa and Beville sent away. His apparent reluctance to come to the point made her feel uneasy.

'Sir Beville is a fortunate boy. His future looks very bright indeed. His father is setting out on a parliamentary career with the backing and support of a great many influential men.'

'So I believe.' Now Dewi had an inkling of what Sir Kenwyn had come to Polrudden to say.

'Sir Nathan has a very good relationship with his son. They are very fond of each other.'

'That's so, Sir Kenwyn. It's nice to see.'

'Yes, indeed.'

When Sir Kenwyn hesitated, Dewi thought he was probably at last coming to the reason for his visit to Polrudden.

'They are very fond of you too. Both young Sir Beville and his father.'

'And I of them. Sir Nathan is a good man and Beville is probably the nicest boy I have known.'

'Sir Nathan is more than a good man, Dewi. He is a rather exceptional man whose talent has been recognised in the right places.'

'I'm very pleased to hear it, Sir Kenwyn.'

Dewi was certain now that she knew what the baronet had come to say to her. She was equally determined not to make it easy for him.

'I hope you are fond enough of Sir Nathan to ensure he does nothing in haste that might possibly jeopardise his future, Dewi.'

'He doesn't consult me about his intentions, Sir Kenwyn.'

'Not all of them, perhaps, but you must be aware that Sir Nathan has been a very lonely man since the loss of his second wife . . . Amy, I believe her name was.'

'He has many good friends, Sir Kenwyn. Not least yourself.'

'A good friend may help to ease the pain of losing a wife, Dewi. He or she, can offer advice. But a friend can never take the place of a wife.'

'What is it you're trying to say, Sir Kenwyn? I think you have come from Golant to say something to me. If so, I would prefer you to say it to me directly and not to talk in riddles.'

'Very well. I think that in his loneliness, Sir Nathan might well mistake his affection for you for a much stronger emotion.'

'You're afraid he might ask me to marry him?' asked Dewi bluntly.

'I am glad you have faced the facts, Dewi. Yes, that's exactly what I fear might happen. Such a marriage would be disastrous for his future.'

'You're saying I'm not good enough for him?'

'No, no, my dear. Being *good* enough has nothing to do with it at all. I am saying that Nathan is on the threshold of a great future. A baronetcy is a certainty, a peerage highly probable. With the friends Nathan already has, and is likely to make in the coming years, he could hold high government office. Even bring an earldom to Polrudden. A good marriage would move the prospect much closer, of course. A lady of the royal court, perhaps.'

'What are you suggesting I should do, Sir Kenwyn?'

'Well, my dear, you have done wonders for young Sir Beville's education. He is so well in advance of his years he must be almost ready to go away to school.'

'And then, of course, there would be no reason for me to remain at Polrudden.'

Sir Kenwyn made no reply and they walked on without saying anything more for a few minutes. It was Dewi who eventually broke the silence.

'You may be Sir Nathan's friend, Sir Kenwyn, but you have no knowledge of children. Beville is *not* ready to go away to school. He's just a little boy who happens to be particularly bright. There is still a great deal *I* can teach him – and I *will* teach him, for as long as Sir Nathan wishes me to remain in his employment.'

'I was not suggesting you should leave Polrudden, immediately, Dewi. Dear me, no.'

Sir Kenwyn was alarmed, fearing he had gone too far in his bid to ensure Dewi was no barrier to the future he envisaged for Nathan.

'I merely wanted to have this little talk with you. To impress upon you the great opportunities awaiting Sir Nathan.'

'I realise you are thinking only of him.'

Dewi tried to keep sarcasm out of her voice. She was fully aware that Sir Kenwyn intended to use Nathan to bring a peerage into his own family. Nell had told her the baronet had dabbled in politics himself, for the same reason. He had not stood for Parliament because he had neither the friends nor the exceptional ability to satisfy such an ambition himself.

'It would be a great honour for Cornwall were he to achieve high office.'

'I appreciate that, Sir Kenwyn.' Dewi took a deep breath in a bid to control the very deep hurt his words had caused her. 'I can assure you I will never do anything to stand in the way of Sir Nathan's future. I am far too fond of both Sir Beville and him ever to do anything to harm either of them.'

'That's exactly what I thought you would say.' Sir Kenwyn could hardly hide his relief. 'You're a sensible girl, Dewi. I knew I could speak to you honestly and openly. I trust you may always speak to me in the same manner. Remember, we both have the interests of Sir Nathan and Sir Beville at heart.'

When he left her, Dewi walked on towards Polrudden without seeing anything about her. There was a bottomless emptiness inside her. For weeks she had been content in the knowledge that Nathan was fond of her. It had coloured her whole life. Everything she did. Sir Kenwyn had destroyed that feeling. Yet he had told her no more than she had told herself during her early months at Polrudden.

It was not Sir Kenwyn Penhaligan who was at fault. It was Dewi herself. She had allowed Nell, and perhaps Nathan himself, to persuade her that a romantic attachment to her employer, no matter tenuous the attachment, was possible.

Dewi had not only allowed herself to forget the rules she had set herself, she had gone far beyond foolishness. She had fallen in love with Nathan.

She was a fool – and now she was a very unhappy fool.

Instead of turning in at the gates of Polrudden, Dewi climbed the stile on the other side of the lane. There was a path here that led to a wood. She felt that in her current state of mind she would be more at home in its darkness than in the bright sunshine of a warm Cornish afternoon.

Chapter 67

Nathan's rescue of Liz Philpotts from the Columbia Road bawdy house owned by Ma Kettle did not receive universal approval. When the ageing housekeeper awoke the next morning to find a young girl had spent the night in the house without her knowledge, she was furious.

After a three-cornered argument involving Nathan and Tilly, the housekeeper announced she would not stay in a house where she was not consulted about matters affecting the running of the household. She would, she declared haughtily, leave that day.

From her attitude it was evident she expect Nathan to argue for her to remain. He did not.

'I'm sorry, Sir Nathan. I should have thought to tell her last night. She's always been particular about having visitors in the house. It's my fault,' Tilly apologised to him after the housekeeper had swept out of the room. The maid was fearful she might have upset Nathan.

'The fault lies entirely with her, Tilly. Besides, if I'm perfectly honest, I'm not sorry to see her go.'

It was true. The presence of the sour elderly housekeeper was the only aspect of the house about which Nathan had had reservations when he took up the tenancy. With her gone the whole atmosphere of the house would undergo a change, he felt. Become more relaxed and cheerful.

'It means I'll need to find another housekeeper, but that shouldn't prove too difficult. I'll make some enquiries when I go to the Commons tomorrow.'

Tilly hesitated before saying, 'Begging your pardon, Sir Nathan, but if you was happy with the arrangement, I'd like to put myself forward for the post. I can do it, sir, I know I can – and if it would save you money I could carry on as an upstairs maid at the same time.'

Nathan smiled at the girl's eagerness. It was in marked contrast to the departing housekeeper's surliness. 'Would that be as well as your occasional duties as cook and nursemaid, Tilly?'

She answered his smile. 'Well, I would appreciate a little help, but not a lot. Unless I'm mistaken, young Liz is used to hard work. She'll help me out, I'm sure.'

Nathan thought about the maid's proposition. She was a willing girl, there was no doubt about that. She was also capable.

'How old are you, Tilly?'

'Twenty-seven, sir – as far as I know. The poor-house master said no one bothered to give him a birthdate when I was taken there. He may have added a year to my age so I could be put out to work earlier.'

Nathan remembered what Tilly had said the previous evening, about knowing of the way Liz had been treated by the world.

'All right, I'll give you a trial period. Say three months? If you're satisfactory then the post is yours. Liz can give you a hand with things until I take her to Polrudden, but I'll leave it to you to find another maid to help you out.'

'Thank you, Sir Nathan.' The delighted Tilly dropped him a curtsy. 'You won't regret it, I promise you.'

'No, Tilly, I don't think I will. Now, do you think my new housekeeper can produce some breakfast for me? In all the argument that's gone on this morning, it seems to have been overlooked . . .'

Nathan had intended remaining in London for only another week. Private business coupled with his duties at the House of Commons kept him in the capital for almost three.

During this time he made his maiden speech. Appropriately enough it was in favour of an increased allowance for the Duke of Clarence who was to be married later in the year.

All the royal brothers were now in a race to marry. Each hoped they might produce a son or daughter who would one day inherit the throne of the United Kingdom.

Because the Prince Regent would have nothing more to do with his blowsy Queen, the death of their only daughter had thrown the succession wide open.

The Duke of Clarence had finally found a woman with the breeding and the background to produce a future King or Queen. She was Adelaide, eldest daughter of the Duke of Saxe-Meiningen. Twenty-seven years younger than the Duke, she was considered young and strong enough to bear sufficient children to satisfy the needs of royal succession.

The marriage of the fifty-three-year-old Duke and the bride who was half his age would take place in July. A proposed increase to the Duke's twelve thousand pound annual allowance was facing stiff opposition in Parliament.

Nathan's speech did not win the day for his friend, but it was well received and his position on the issue did not pass unnoticed. He received a note of thanks from the Duke of Clarence and was congratulated on an excellent speech on the Duke's behalf.

Nathan's private business was showing some signs of success

too. Frederick Temple, whose company had expressed a wish to purchase the shares of the Pentuan Harbour Company, called on Nathan at the House of Commons.

Surprisingly, the company had also been able to purchase Sir Christopher Hawkins's block of shares. In view of this, Nathan was quite content to sell his shares too, at a modest profit. He owned so much of the surrounding land that it would be impossible for the company to disrupt life in Pentuan any more than had been allowed for in the original plan.

Nathan was pleased to have the headache of the harbour handed over to someone else. On the same day he found an agent who would act on his behalf in Italy when the *Heron* reached there from Newfoundland with her first cargo of dried cod.

Things were beginning to fall into place, allowing him time for a little modest relaxation. On the last Sunday before setting off for Polrudden, he took Liz and Tilly to the morning service at St Paul's Cathedral.

Liz found the service boring, but she was impressed by a fiery sermon, delivered on 'the evils of the flesh'.

The service took on increased interest for her when she suddenly leaned towards Nathan in the middle of a prayer and said in a stage whisper that made him wince, 'You see that man sitting over there? The one with the big, bulbous nose? 'E's one of Ma Kettle's regulars. Goes there on the first Monday of every month. Says 'is wife goes off to the country then, to see 'er mother.'

Half the congregation in their immediate vicinity looked at Liz, the other half looked at the bulbuous-nosed worshipper.

'Shh!' Nathan tried to cut off her chatter.

'Well, 'e does! I'm not telling any lies,' Liz persisted indignantly.

Now the bulbous-nosed man's wife was looking at her husband too and Nathan writhed in embarrassment. A giggle from Tilly, unsuccessfully stifled, did nothing to help. Fortunately, at that moment the preacher called upon the congregation to stand and the service did not last very much longer.

On the way home Nathan gave Liz a fatherly lecture on the subject of discretion, but he did not feel confident he had succeeded in convincing her.

When the trio arrived at the small house in Orchard Place, a rotund red-faced man was waiting outside the door for Nathan. He introduced himself as Porteous Kenyon, adding, 'I'm a constable employed by the Bow Street Magistrates' Court.'

'You're a bleedin' runner!' Liz made the explosive accusation.

'That's enough from you, Liz. Tilly, take her inside, please.' Turning back to the Bow Street runner, he asked, 'I'm Nathan Jago. Are you waiting for me?'

'I am, Sir Nathan. May we go inside and talk?'

Once inside the house, Nathan took the other man to the small study and sat him down. The policeman refused a drink but Nathan poured one for himself before saying, 'Now, what is your business with me, Mr Kenyon?'

'A warrant has been issued for the arrest of a certain Charles Philpotts to answer to a charge of murder, Sir Nathan. It's a very serious business as I'm sure you'll agree. I have reason to believe you might know where I can find the lad?'

'At this precise moment I have no idea where Charlie is.'

Nathan told himself it was only stretching the truth a little. Charlie might be at Polrudden or at Venn. More likely he was on board the *Heron*, and she would be somewhere at sea, carrying out trials with the new sails and rigging ordered by Nathan.

He had anticipated this visit by a constable and had recently written to Dewi suggesting it would be advisable to send Charlie to sea for a while, on his ship.

'I presume you were given my name by the Kettle woman of Columbia Road? She was also no doubt eager to ensure that any reward for Charlie's arrest came her way?'

'Right on both counts, Sir Nathan. Can you give us any help in the matter?'

'I can, although it may not be what you wish to find. I would like you to listen to the story of the young lady you met outside the house. She is the sister of young Charlie Philpotts. When I spoke to him, many weeks ago, I promised to visit his sister who was living in Columbia Road. I went to this woman Kettle's house and as a result of what I saw brought young Liz away from there. She can tell you rather more of the incident involving her brother than you know at the moment. I suggest that you listen to what she has to say, then return to Ma Kettle and tell her the reward for Charlie's arrest has been withdrawn. She might be more inclined to tell the truth if there is no money to be earned with a lie.'

'Thank you, Sir Nathan. I would like to speak to this young lady if she witnessed something of importance. I'm certain she's better off here, sir. As you say, Ma Kettle's house is no place for a young girl.'

Liz's attitude towards the Bow Street runner was aggressive, but she told him exactly the same story as she had told Nathan and the constable listened to her in silence.

When she finished he remained thoughtful for some minutes before asking her a number of questions. She answered them equally aggressively, but did not stray from her original story.

When Liz had been dismissed from the room, Nathan said, 'I think you have just heard the truthful version of what happened, Mr Kenyon. What happens now is in your hands.'

'Quite so, Sir Nathan. I don't doubt everything happened exactly as the young lady said. Nevertheless, there is still a warrant outstanding for the arrest of Charles Philpotts. My duty is to find

330

him and bring him to answer to the charges against him. In view of this I must warn you against harbouring a wanted felon, sir. But I don't doubt you know that already, you being a Member of Parliament.'

When the Bow Street runner had gone, Nathan was left with the distinct impression that Porteous Kenyon was a man inclined to follow the letter rather than the spirit of the law. He doubted whether he had seen the last of him.

Chapter 68

Nathan's journey from London to Polrudden, accompanied by Liz, was one he would never forget. He had written to Dewi, saying he was bringing Charlie's sister and explaining something of her character. However, he doubted whether she would be ready for the young cockney girl.

Liz's young life had been a hard one, and she had grown up without any of the inhibitions acquired by children from more normal backgrounds.

During the brief time the East End orphan had been at the house in Orchard Place, Tilly had been able to teach Liz only the rudiments of acceptable behaviour. She was unable to curb the young girl's colourful language, or her wonderment at all the things that were new to her.

As the coach left London behind, Liz, who could not stop bouncing up and down on the hide seats, turned to Nathan and asked, 'Why are there so many trees? They don't have as many in London. Look, you can't see any 'ouses for the trees.'

Nathan smiled, 'There aren't very many houses, Liz, and this is what London was like before they built all the houses.'

Liz looked thoughtful for a few moments, then she shook her head. 'Garn! You're 'aving me on. London was never like this. Where would all the people live if there were no 'ouses, only trees?'

Nathan decided he would not argue with Liz's logic.

A few minutes later, she cried excitedly, 'Look! Look! What are they?'

Nathan could not immediately grasp what Liz was so excited about until she said impatiently, 'Them bleedin' animals. I ain't never seen any like them before.'

The animals Liz was so excited about were cows. Nathan could not believe she had never seen them before.

'They're cows. Surely you've seen them before? They're the animals that give us milk.'

'I've never ever seen anything like 'em in all me life.'

Liz watched the cows in silence until they were almost out of sight, then she asked, ''Ow do they give milk?'

Nathan glanced at his travelling companions. There were two

curates who were too busy gossiping about fellow clergymen to bother about a child's excitement. In the far corner was a man who was probably a merchant or a shopkeeper. He reeked of cheap whisky and was snoring intermittently.

Opposite Nathan was a tall, pinch-faced lady, resting both hands on the ivory handle of a closed silk umbrella. She was staring fixedly out of the coach window, determinedly ignoring Liz's chatter.

'All female animals produce milk for their babies. Cows keep on producing milk long after their babies – their calves – have been taken away from them. Farmers milk them and sell the milk. It's very good for you.'

'Women 'ave milk too, for their babies.'

'That's right.'

Nathan had heard the sharp, disapproving intake of breath from the woman seated opposite him. When he glanced at her he saw her lips were drawn into an even tighter line than before. He tried to steer Liz's conversation away from the subject of mammalian feeding.

'Look, there are some sheep over there. They provide lamb and mutton for eating. Their fleeces also provide us with wool, to make clothes.'

Liz glanced at the sheep but, much to Nathan's dismay, immediately returned to the subject of milk.

'Rosie, at Ma Kettle's, 'ad a baby. She 'ad milk too, and was right fed up about it. She couldn't take any customers until it dried up. Ma Kettle said a bloke wasn't going to pay good money just to get an eyeful of milk when 'e . . .'

'I think we'll talk of something else if you don't mind, Liz,' Nathan said hurriedly as the woman passenger tensed on her seat.

He breathed a sigh of relief when he succeeded in silencing Liz before she went into lurid detail about the activities of Rosie, but the uninhibited young girl had not quite completed her observations.

'All right,' she said cheerfully. 'But I bet Rosie didn't know about cows, and about being able to *sell* milk!'

Nathan broke the journey to Cornwall at Salisbury, staying at The Lamb Inn. Much to his relief and, he had no doubt, that of the woman in the coach, the other passengers continued on their way.

Had Nathan been travelling on his own he would have remained on the mail coach for the whole of the journey. But it took forty hours to reach Polrudden from London and he felt it would be too much for Liz. At Salisbury they had ten hours of the journey behind them. They would spend a night and a day at the inn before resuming the long coach ride that evening.

Much to Nathan's relief, Liz behaved well during the meal they

333

enjoyed together that evening. Tilly had taught the young cockney girl the rudiments of table manners and Liz tried very hard to please him.

She was occupying the room next to Nathan's. When he took her up after their meal he realised that, beneath all her worldliness, she was still only a ten-year-old child. Despite the degradation she'd suffered there, Ma Kettle's establishment had been familiar to her. Now she was miles from London in an environment that was totally alien.

At the doorway to her room she kept Nathan talking for many minutes discussing trivial matters. When he eventually said he was going to his room, Liz suddenly blurted out, 'You will still be 'ere in the mornin?' You won't go orf an' leave me . . .'cos I embarrass you?'

'No, Liz. I won't go off and leave you . . . and you don't embarrass me. It's charming to be able to look at things through new eyes. You've reminded me of the pleasures of so many things I've always taken for granted. I'll take you to see Salisbury Cathedral before we catch the evening mail coach. Go and get some sleep now and we'll have breakfast together in the morning.'

Liz hesitated for a few moments then, for the second occasion in the brief time he had known her, she ran to him and gave him an affectionate hug.

Moved by her spontaneous warmth, Nathan ruffled her hair. 'Thank you, young lady. Now off you go and have a good night's sleep. We've got a lot of travelling to do tomorrow – and a brother to look good for at the end of it.'

'What will I do when I get to this house of yours?'

The low-voiced question came to Nathan from the darkness inside the coach as they bumped and swayed through the night at what seemed to him to be an alarming speed.

'I haven't fully made up my mind yet, Liz.' It was a problem he had been trying to resolve when she spoke to him. 'I rather thought you might like to go and help out my sister, Nell. She and her husband have a farm only a short distance from Polrudden. That's where Charlie was working before I sent him to sea in the *Heron*. You'd like it there. She has four children – and is expecting a fifth. They have lots of animals on the farm too. I'm sure she would be glad of your help.'

Liz said nothing for some minutes and Nathan listened to the other sounds about him. The drumming of horses' hooves on the road, the rumbling of the wheels, the creaking of the coach and its leather seat. There was also the measured snoring of the mail coach's only other occupant, a jovial gentleman farmer who had dined exceedingly well before boarding the coach.

'I think I'd rather stay at Polrudden with you.'

'Well, we'll see what Dewi has to say about it. I'm sure we can find you something there. It's just that I thought you'd enjoy yourself more at Venn Farm. Have a bit more freedom, perhaps.'

'Is Dewi your 'ousekeeper? What's she like?'

'Well, Dewi started off as governess to my son, but I rely on her a lot. She's rather taken on the running of Polrudden.'

'Is she old, like the one who left your London 'ouse because of me?'

'No. Dewi's a few years younger than Tilly.'

'Is she pretty?'

'Yes, she is. Dewi's a very attractive girl indeed.'

'You're sweet on 'er, ain't yer? I can tell, the way you speak about 'er.'

'Yes, Liz, I'm definitely "sweet on her", as you so colourfully put it.'

'You going to marry 'er?'

'I'd like to think so, but I haven't even spoken to her about it yet. She might not want me.'

'Course she will,' said Liz scornfully. 'Anyone who turned you down couldn't be right in the 'ead.'

After a few more minutes of silence, Nathan felt Liz's head come to rest against his upper arm. Her hand found his and in a small voice she said wistfully, 'I 'ope she likes me too.'

Chapter 69

Dewi took Liz to her heart immediately. Nathan was the first to alight from the mail coach and Beville ran to him with a cry of 'Father!'

Behind Nathan the young cockney girl stepped to the ground from the coach, clothes crumpled from travelling. She looked tired and very small and alone as father and son enjoyed their reunion.

'Hello! You must be Liz. I'm Dewi.'

'I knew it must be you. He said you were pretty.'

'Did he now?' Dewi glanced over to where Nathan had swung his son high in the air in exuberant greeting. He caught her glance and smiled at her. 'Sometime you must tell me what else Sir Nathan has said to you about me – but for now we'll get your things off the coach and take you home. You must be worn out after all your travelling.'

'Where's Charlie? Will I see him when we get to Polrudden?'

'We'll talk about that when we're all in the carriage, on the way there. There are too many people here to overhear what we say.'

The inn yard where the mail coach had pulled in was the scene of hectic activity. The steaming horses that had brought the coach clattering into the courtyard were being led away and fresh horses brought from the stables. A new driver was taking over too. The two men exchanged instructions surrounded by a dozen men and boys delivering and collecting packages.

From the inn the landlord and his servants were busily supplying refreshments to those passengers who had declined to leave the coach. Other hotel employees were swarming all over the vehicle, disturbing a number of grumbling outside passengers. They were searching for baggage belonging to those leaving the coach at St Austell and doing their best to avoid the articles being thrown on board by others.

Mingling with those who were busily engaged in the business of making the coach ready for its onward journey were many who had nothing better to do than watch the bustling scene.

A private conversation in such surroundings would have been impossible, but Liz had to ask one final question.

'Is Charlie all right?'

'He's fine, Liz. Don't you worry about him.'

Nathan joined them, carrying Beville, and smiled at the governess. 'Hello, Dewi. I see you and Liz have introduced yourselves. It's good to see you again. I've missed you.'

The way he looked at her made Dewi feel weak at the knees, but all she said was, 'It's nice to have you home again, Sir Nathan. Beville has missed you a lot too.'

Nathan's eyebrows went up. 'What's all this *Sir* Nathan stuff? And haven't *you* missed me?'

Dewi wanted to tell him that she had missed him more than he would ever know. That Polrudden without him was not a happy place for her. Instead she said, 'We agreed on formality when we're in public. You're a very important man now.'

'As long as you think so, Dewi.' His hand rested on her shoulder for a moment before she moved away.

'I brought a light carriage from Polrudden, driven by one of the grooms. It's waiting just outside the yard.'

Nathan waved directions to one of the inn servants who was guarding his baggage and the Polrudden-bound party moved through the crowds from the inn yard.

In the carriage as they rode away from St Austell, Dewi explained to Liz why she would say nothing about Charlie until she was certain she would not be overheard.

'He's at Venn Farm, with Nell and Tom Quicke – that's Sir Nathan's sister and her husband. We had him brought ashore by fishing boat from the *Heron* last night. A Bow Street runner arrived here from London a few days ago. He's been nosing around Pentuan with a St Austell constable, carrying a warrant for Charlie's arrest. We heard they intended going on board and searching the *Heron* when it came in, so I decided he should come ashore and go to Venn. One of the fishing boats went out to pick him up. The London magistrates must want him very badly. What do they say he's done?'

When Nathan explained what had happened in Ma Kettle's bawdy house in Columbia Road, Dewi's indignation matched his own.

'That's not *justice*! He should be given a reward for saving his sister from such an attack.'

'I agree with you. Unfortunately, Charlie has run foul of the law before. Most magistrates would believe the worst and say it was a natural progression of his criminal way of life. He wouldn't stand a chance.'

Dewi gave Nathan a concerned look. 'I didn't realise Charlie was facing such a serious charge. It might have repercussions for you if he were caught here.'

'He won't be caught,' replied Nathan confidently. 'No one who works for me will give Charlie up to a London constable – and I have a plan that will get him out of the way until all the excitement dies down.'

'Do we pass the farm where Charlie's hiding before we reach Polrudden? Can we call in and see him first?' Liz had been an apprehensive listener to their conversation.

Calling out of the window of the carriage to the driver, Nathan instructed him to go to Venn Farm.

Tom was out in his fields but Nell met the carriage in the farmyard. She was carrying her youngest child and had the others crowding around her. She greeted Nathan affectionately and then turned to Liz, giving her a big smile. 'So you're Charlie's sister? Yes, I can see the likeness now. We had Charlie in the house for a couple of hours last night and he talked a lot about you. He'll be very pleased to see you, I'm sure. He seemed to think this Ma Kettle wouldn't let you go.'

'She didn't want to,' declared Liz, looking at Nathan proudly. 'But Sir Nathan and Alf laid out Mick and another bloke, then 'e gave 'er thirty guineas for me.' She quoted the sum proudly.

'Did he now?' Nell eyed her brother before saying, 'I thought he'd given up hitting people.'

'I have,' grinned Nathan. 'Not only that, I've slowed down a lot. Alf beat me to the punch every time.'

'Can I see Charlie now?'

'I don't see why not,' agreed Nell. 'As long as you don't mind pigs. Tom boarded off the back part of the pig house for him. It doesn't smell too good in there, but it would be a brave man who'd try to go past our old boar to look for Charlie – or for anything else. You'll need to wait a few minutes while I get him out of the way, then we'll go in.'

Handing the baby to Dewi and telling the other children to take Beville to see the two new calves, Nell disappeared into a low-doored pig house.

For some minutes there was the sound of excited squeals and grunting. Nell could be heard talking too, but whether she was talking to Charlie or to the pigs was impossible to tell.

Looking hot and a little mired when she came outside again, Nell said, 'The old boar was being a bit awkward today. But he's safely tied up now. Come inside. I've called Charlie out.'

Ducking through the doorway, they waited as Charlie lifted a wooden flap at the back of the pig's sty and made his way towards them.

Dewi had expected the young cockney brother and sister to fall upon each other in an emotional reunion. Instead, they greeted each other almost diffidently.

'Hello, Charlie.'

'Hello, Liz. I didn't expect to see you down 'ere in the country, miles away from Bethnal Green.'

'I didn't expect to see *you* ever again. Not when the runners came looking for you.'

'I'm glad Sir Nathan got you out of Ma Kettle's 'ouse. You'll like it 'ere. I do.'

'Yeah, I fink I might.'

That was the reunion. After their brief conversation both children stood silent in apparent indifference.

'Well, if you two have finished talking, we'll put you back in your little room, Charlie, and get Liz sorted out. She'll be tired after her journey.'

'Yeah.' As he turned to return to his make-shift hide-out, he added, 'I wish pigs didn't pong so much.'

'You think these smell?' asked Nell. 'Be grateful I didn't put you in with the hens, young man. Then you'd really know about a smell.'

When Charlie was safely shut inside his hiding place once more and Liz had gone off to find the younger children, Nell asked Nathan, 'What are you going to do with the girl now?'

'I'm not sure . . . No, that's not strictly true. I was rather hoping you might be able to find her something useful to do, here at Venn.'

'All right.'

It was such an unhesitating, categorical acceptance of his suggestion that it took Nathan by surprise.

'You mean . . . you *will* take her?'

'Isn't that what you asked me to do? Actually, I rather like young Charlie. From what you've already said, and the little I've seen of Liz, I think I could become very fond of her too. She can help me about the house – and with the children. There's enough here to keep her occupied.'

'You don't know what a relief that is to me, Nell. I didn't think what I would do with her when I first found her. I was so intent on getting her out of that house. She's a strong-minded little thing and I thought she might prove disruptive at Polrudden. She's had a hard life, a *really* hard life, but I'm convinced she'll be happy here with you.'

'I think she will too, but perhaps we ought to ask her what she thinks of the idea?'

Liz was not too keen on it at first. She kept looking across the room at Nathan, as though hoping he might change his mind.

Nell realised the young girl had grown fond of Nathan and had come to trust and rely upon him.

'Nathan will be around here most days to see how you are, I don't doubt,' she said. 'And there will be lots of errands to take you to Polrudden. In the meantime, I know Charlie will like having you around. You'll be able to spend more time talking to him in his hide-out than I can, that's certain.'

It was this argument that eventually gained Liz's grudging agreement to remain at Venn Farm.

Nathan had sent the carriage on to Polrudden when they had arrived at Venn from St Austell. He had sat in the mail coach for so long he declared a walk home to Polrudden would be a welcome luxury. He would send someone from the house to Venn with Liz's clothes.

Nell came as far as the gate to see Nathan, Dewi and Beville on their way home. 'Don't worry about Liz,' she said. 'She'll soon settle in and will find more love at Venn than she's ever known before in her young life.'

Chapter 70

'Nell's right, you know. There's love enough to spare at Venn. Liz is a lucky little girl. First you rescue her from that horrible place in London, and now she's found a good home with Tom and Nell and their family.'

Nathan and Dewi were walking along the lane to Polrudden in the darkness. Nathan was carrying Beville who had fallen asleep with his head resting against his father's shoulder, exhausted by the excitement of the day.

'There's certainly love enough at Venn, Dewi, but how about at Polrudden? Is there enough love there for you and me to talk about our future?'

After a lengthy silence, she replied, 'There has never been a lack of love at Polrudden, Nathan. It's a very happy household. As for our future . . . I don't think I'm ready to talk about it yet.'

'Why? You're not still holding my foolishness with Columb Hawkins's sister against me?'

Once again there was a lengthy pause as Dewi tried to gather her thoughts in order to give Nathan an honest reply.

'No, that is where it belongs – in the past. But I still believe we should wait a while before making any decision.'

'Why, Dewi? You know how I feel about you. In spite of your reluctance, I think you feel the same way about me. Why wait?'

'Because things are not quite as simple as you make them sound. You have just embarked on one of the biggest adventures of your life and everyone is very proud of you. They say you're destined for greatness. High office, honours . . . no doubt wealth and power too.'

'You know, Dewi, you sound exactly like Sir Kenwyn Penhaligan.'

She was momentarily startled. When she recovered, she said, 'Then you'll know that what I'm saying is perfectly true. There's such a huge gap between the woman I am and the man you will become, I want you to be absolutely certain. Not just for now, for a few weeks, a few months – or even a year or two. If we marry, I want you never to regret it.'

Nathan began to protest that he never would, but Dewi placed a hand on his arm and brought his words to a halt, 'It would be wonderful to say yes and become *Lady* Dewi Jago, wife of the Member of Parliament for Tregony – but that's not what I want most of all, Nathan. I want you to be content with what you have. I don't ever want you to resent not being asked places, or not being given a government post, or high honours, because your wife doesn't come from the right family, or know all the right people.'

'Aren't you forgetting that I am the son of a Methodist preacher? My father probably never had more than a few guineas to call his own during the whole of his lifetime.'

'No, I'm not forgetting that at all. But you've risen above your early years as very few men have. You proved from the very beginning you were someone special. Admiral Lord Nelson recognised it when he had you transferred to his ship to be his helmsman. The Duke of Clarence saw it when he watched you win the Championship of All England in the prize-ring. Your first wife must have seen it when she married you, and your second when she sold you a half-share in the fish-cellar at Portgiskey. Now everyone realises that as a politician you can surpass all your past successes. It's important to many of them that you do so. I think it's important to you too.'

Once again Nathan tried to interrupt her.

'No, hear me out, please. It's very important to both of us to have things clear. You are an ambitious man – and there's nothing wrong with that. Nothing at all. But I'm not ambitious, Nathan. The most important thing for me in marriage would be to love my husband and my family, and the life we would lead together. That, and to have my husband love me in the same way, enjoying the same things. A life of growing together as a family. A man like Sir Kenwyn Penhaligan would say such things are all right for a woman, but not enough for a man who must think of future generations of his family. Of the honours he can bring to them.'

Dewi made a deprecating gesture. 'I expect he's right, really. My idea of marriage is far too simple. I'm thinking only of today. Of the here-and-now. Not concerned enough for those who will come after, and who I'll never know. But there we are! That's the way I am.'

'There's nothing wrong in that, Dewi. Perhaps that's the way I am too . . .'

'No!' It was far too positive an assertion, and she repeated the word, more quietly this time.

'No, Nathan. It might be the way you *were*, but you *can't* be that way any more. You are too important to a great many people. Not only here, in Cornwall, but in London too. To men who seek power in Parliament and outside it. The Whig leaders – and Sir Kenwyn.'

She realised that Sir Kenwyn Penhaligan had come into the

conversation for the third time that evening. She wondered whether he would approve of the line she was taking with Nathan.

'I'm deeply moved by your reasons for not marrying me right away, Dewi. You're a very special girl. Nell can see it, so too could Abigail – and my father. All right, I'll wait for a while longer but *not* because I'm not certain of myself, I'll wait because I want to prove to you that all these things you put up as a barrier between us don't really matter. Much of what goes on in Parliament is a game that's played by the men in London. A great many of them are like Sir Kenwyn, trying to achieve their own ends through others. It's no more than a game of cards to them. They choose a card on which to gamble. If it's not the right one they throw it away and choose another. In no time at all they can't even remember what the first card was, and it no longer matters anyway.'

Suddenly Nathan put out his hand and brought Dewi to a halt. They were not far from Polrudden now and there was still much that needed to be said.

'I'm not talking of playing their games, Dewi. I'm talking of lives. Your life, my life – yes, and Beville's too. It's important for all of us. I want you. I want to marry you and I want things to be right for all of us. I've found happiness twice and had it taken away from me. Don't you take it from me a third time, Dewi, I beg you.'

Reaching out, Nathan pulled her to him and kissed her. When he released her she hoped the hands he kept on her arms could not feel her shaking.

'I love you, Dewi, and I want to marry you. I'll wait so that *you* can be certain – but don't keep me waiting for too long. I need you . . .'

Chapter 71

Bow Street Constable Porteous Kenyon, accompanied by a magistrate and a constable from St Austell, reached Venn Farm late in the afternoon, only two days after Liz's arrival there.

Tom had just brought the cows in from the fields for milking and he and Nell came into the farm yard to greet the three representatives of the law.

'Good afternoon, gentlemen, what can I do for you?' Tom spoke pleasantly enough although he recognised the constable and had a shrewd idea of the purpose of their unexpected visit.

'You are Mr Quicke, I presume? I am Magistrate Willis. My two companions are Constable Lamb from St Austell and Constable Kenyon, from the Bow Street Magistrate's court in London. Acting upon information given to me by Constable Kenyon, I have reason to believe you are harbouring Charles Philpotts, a fugitive.'

'Well, I don't know about all that,' said Tom Quicke, scratching his head and giving the magistrate the impression he was slow-witted. 'But if you want to look around you're quite free to do so. You won't mind if I get on with feeding the cows while you're doing it, will you? They don't understand about such things as fugitives and they've come in to be milked.'

At that moment Liz came out of the house accompanied by one of the younger children and Porteous Kenyon said triumphantly, 'There! That's Charlie Philpotts's sister. I told you we'd find him here.'

Advancing to meet her, he said. 'We've come here to find your brother, girl – and find him we will. If you know where he is you'd better tell us and make it easier on everyone.'

'I don't know where Charlie is,' declared Liz defiantly. 'And if I did I wouldn't tell you.'

'Come now, girl.' The magistrate frowned at her. 'Such an attitude will get you nowhere. If you know anything it will be better for you to tell us immediately.'

'Liz is a waif who was brought here by my brother only two days ago, Mr Willis. She's hardly recovered from the journey yet, I won't have her bullied. I think the best thing you can do is to speak to my brother. Liz, will you go to Polrudden and ask

Sir Nathan to come to Venn, please?'

The magistrate was startled at the mention of Nathan's name. 'Sir Nathan? You are the sister of Sir Nathan Jago of Polrudden? The recently elected Member of Parliament for Tregony?'

'That's right. Off you go, Liz. I'll take Bessie.'

The magistrate rounded on his own constable angrily. 'Were you aware that Mrs Quicke is Sir Nathan Jago's sister?'

'Yes, but if a wanted felon is hiding here . . .'

Without allowing the constable to complete what he was saying, the magistrate said angrily, 'I should have been told of this.'

'What difference does it make?' Porteous Kenyon replied on behalf of his discomfited rural colleague. 'I have a warrent for the arrest of Charlie Philpotts – and Sir Nathan Jago is acquainted with the lad. The identity of whoever's harbouring him doesn't matter.'

'It might not matter in London, Constable Kenyon, but such things matter here. I very much doubt whether Sir Nathan would be acquainted with such a fugitive.'

'I think I can explain that,' said Nell. 'Nathan found this boy living in poverty, in London and helped him. He found work for him and the boy did well until he got into trouble when he found a man attacking his sister. She's the young girl you were speaking to a few minutes ago. He fled from London and came to probably the only man who'd ever helped him – my brother. This was at the end of last year. While he was at Polrudden he told Sir Nathan of his sister and begged him to help her. That's the reason she is with me now. My brother found her living in a wretched state in a very poor part of London and brought her here. Her brother left Polrudden a month or two ago.'

Nell had bent the truth, but felt it had not been distorted too much.

'May I say I think Sir Nathan has acted in a public-spirited manner over this matter? Of course, it is no more than one has come to expect from a man who has always been such a great credit to his home county. We are all proud of him, Mrs Quicke.'

Turning a frosty glance upon the Bow Street runner, he said, 'I don't think we need waste any more of Mr or Mrs Quicke's time, Constable Kenyon. You may return to London happy in the knowledge that you have carried out your duties with all due dilligence.'

'*You* may return to St Austell, sir. I came here because I believe a fugitive from justice is in hiding. I intend to find him.'

The magistrate bridled with anger but Nell said, 'It's all right, Mr Willis. We have nothing to hide. If he wishes to look around, he is at liberty to do so.'

'Then with your permission, ma'am, I too will remain – in order that Constable Kenyon does not try your patience too far.'

As the Bow Street runner began a systematic search of the farm premises, Magistrate Willis worked hard to ingratiate himself with Nell. It seemed he too had a small farm and his speciality was pigs. He was with Nell in the pig-sty when Porteous Kenyon ducked in through the low doorway.

'I presume you have had no success in your search, Constable Kenyon. May I take it you are almost ready to admit you are wrong and return to St Austell to catch the coach for London?'

'Not quite, Magistrate. There are still one or two out-buildings to search . . . Agh!'

While he was talking, the Bow Street runner's hand had dropped over the low wall of the sty to pat the bristly pink back of one of the pigs.

The sight of the hand fondling one of his paramours was anathema to the old boar. With a speed that belied his bulk and years, the bad-tempered animal charged across the sty and snapped at the Bow Street runner's hand.

Porteous Kenyon's cry was not merely one of surprise. The boar's teeth sank into the fleshy part of his hand and inflicted a very nasty wound.

As the London constable freed his hand from the boar's mouth, blood spurted everywhere.

'Oh, you poor man! Here . . .' Nell pulled off her apron and hurriedly wrapped it about the constable's hand. 'I didn't think to warn you. I forgot that coming from London you would know nothing about boars. He's a bad-tempered old creature. Come into the house. I'll put something on that for you and try to stop the bleeding.'

As they walked towards the house, with Porteous Kenyon holding Nell's apron tight about his hand, Magistrate Willis said, with more than a touch of malice in his voice, 'Well, Constable Kenyon, one thing is certain. This young man you're looking for certainly won't be hiding in the pig-sty!'

Porteous Kenyon was a constable in the best tradition of the Bow Street runners. He did not give up easily. The incident with the pig put an end to his search of Venn Farm, but he was waiting for the *Heron* when the ship put in to Pentuan from its sea trials. Before one man was allowed to go ashore, the constable had the ship searched from stem to stern. He found nothing, but not until then did he admit defeat.

The ship had been granted permission by the Pentuan Harbour Company to dock alongside the unfinished wooden breakwater and Nathan was there to meet his captain and crew. It was to him the Bow Street runner acknowledged that time had combined with the close-mouthed Cornish community to beat him.

'I'm still convinced I was right, Sir Nathan, but there's nothing

346

more I can do about it for the time being. If Charlie Philpotts is here, you've got him hidden too well for me to find – but you can warn him from me: if he's anywhere in the King's realm I'll get him, and it has nothing to do with the reward. I'm a conscientious man and do my duty as I see it. I'll be looking for him for as long as I'm employed by the Bow Street Magistrates.'

'If I meet up with him again I'll tell him that, Constable. But, I promise, you'll not arrest Charlie Philpotts on Polrudden land.'

It was a promise that Nathan intended making good. Constable Porteous Kenyon would be on the London-bound mail coach that very night. The *Heron* would be sailing for Newfoundland within forty-eight hours – and Charlie would be on board.

Chapter 72

The departure of the *Heron* and the *Charlotte*, bound for Newfoundland, was an event that brought every man, woman and child to the near-completed wooden jetty owned by the Pentuan Harbour Company.

The company had given Nathan permission for both ships to berth at the jetty. Here they would complete their victualling and load the stores needed to maintain both boats and crews in the cold Newfoundland waters.

The *Heron* would carry spare nets made in Mevagissey for the *Charlotte* and stores to last them a couple of months, should it become necessary to provide for themselves.

During the days before the two ships sailed, Nathan held many meetings with his two captains. Sir Kenwyn was also a regular visitor, catching the excitement of the forthcoming venture. He was standing beside Nathan as the *Charlotte* and the *Heron* cast off their mooring ropes.

The women who had husbands sailing on the two vessels were tearful. To them Newfoundland was no more than a name, but they knew it lay many weeks to westward, across an unpredictable sea that had widowed very many Cornish women.

Pippa Hanna was one of the women whose view of the two departing vessels was clouded by tears, despite her young husband's assertion that the *Charlotte* was unsinkable.

The men and women watched until the two vessels disappeared from sight. Determined to keep the two Newfoundland-bound craft in view until the very last moment, the more energetic children ran along the cliff path that climbed high beyond the fish-cellar at Portgiskey, rounding the headland until they were overlooking Mevagissey and could see the two boats heading westward to the open ocean.

'At least Charlie is beyond the reach of Constable Kenyon,' observed Dewi quietly as she and Pippa walked up the hill to Polrudden behind Nathan, Sir Kenwyn and Beville.

'They're all in God's hands now,' declared Pippa. 'I hope he keeps my Francis safe for me.'

'Francis is the finest sailor I know,' said Nathan reassuringly, as he dropped back with Sir Kenwyn and Beville to walk beside the two women. 'He'll return to you at the end of the season a much richer man.'

'I'll be happy just to have him safely back again,' said Pippa, trying unsuccessfully to hold back her tears.

As Dewi comforted the younger woman, Nathan and Sir Kenwyn drew ahead once more. 'They say a good woman can help a man achieve his ambitions,' commented Sir Kenwyn. 'But a bad one can as easily make him forget them.'

'Pippa and Francis are a very happy young couple,' said Nathan. 'She misses him when he's away from home, but she wouldn't stop him doing anything he really wanted to do. I'm pleased to have them both working for me.'

Sir Kenwyn looked far from convinced, but although he had spoken of Pippa, his mind was on Dewi. When they reached Polrudden he managed to speak to her alone for a few minutes when Beville and Pippa went off to show Nathan a nest they had found in a garden bush.

'Have you thought any more of what we discussed while Nathan was away?'

'I've thought about it a great deal – but perhaps you should speak with him about it and not me?'

'Does that mean you'll do nothing to prevent Sir Nathan throwing away his future? You'd deprive Sir Beville of a peerage?' Sir Kenwyn spoke with tight-lipped disapproval.

'I'm saying that I'll do whatever I believe to be best for both Nathan *and* Sir Beville.'

'I've already told you what is best, girl. Unless you want it on your conscience for the rest of your life, you'll do something about it – and do it quickly.'

Sir Kenwyn spoke sharply, but the reappearance of Nathan and the others prevented him from pursuing the matter any further.

With the *Heron* and the *Charlotte* gone from Pentuan, Nathan had more time on his hands and spent much of it with Sir Kenwyn. Occasionally he would ride to Golant to the baronet's house. More often Sir Kenwyn would call at Polrudden and take Nathan off to meet someone he felt would help further his parliamentary career.

Sir Kenwyn arrived at Polrudden unusually early one morning, as excited as Nathan had ever seen him.

'I had a message last night from John Kendall of Pelyn. The Earl of Wavendon is in Cornwall and staying with him for a while.'

When Nathan failed to react, Sir Kenwyn said, 'You must have heard of him, surely? He has been a major force in politics for almost fifty years. I've heard it said that if the Earl of Warwick was "The Kingmaker", then Wavendon is certainly "The Premiermaker". We have an invitation for lunch at Pelyn today.'

On the ride to Pelyn, a manor house about six or seven miles

349

from Polrudden, Sir Kenwyn told Nathan more of the Earl of Wavendon. A friend of King George III since boyhood, he had always been a trusted and influential member of the royal household. His was said to have been one of the few voices raised in opposition to the disastrous marriage of the present Prince Regent with Princess Caroline. This was sufficient reason in itself to endear Wavendon to the Prince Regent. As a consequence, he was able to maintain his great influence at court and among parliamentarians.

'He did not marry until very late in life,' confided Sir Kenwyn. 'Married a woman much younger than himself and had a daughter when he was almost sixty. His wife died a few years later. He's over eighty now and dotes on the daughter. I understand she's at Pelyn with him. Be nice to her, Nathan – and humour the Earl. He has great influence in London.'

It was not difficult to be pleasant to the ageing Earl of Wavendon. A gentle old man, his manner betrayed nothing of the power he wielded within the royal court. By way of contrast, his daughter, although attractive enough, was a positive, authoritarian woman in her mid-twenties.

Lady Sarah Milton and Nathan seemed to get off on the wrong foot immediately. It began when they disagreed on the emotive issue of the slave trade, Lady Sarah maintaining that the slaves enjoyed a much happier life in America and the West Indies than in their primitive African villages.

Such an argument led to the question of the importance of men being free to secure their own futures. Nathan felt the British artisan needed a trade association. Lady Sarah was of the opinion that such associations would lead to an uprising, similar to that experienced in France at the end of the previous century.

The argument became quite heated at times, and proved discomfiting to the host, to Sir Kenwyn and to the Earl of Wavendon.

When they left Pelyn, Sir Kenwyn upbraided Nathan for disagreeing so violently with Lady Sarah. 'I had hoped you and she would find you had something in common – or at least find nothing about which to argue. A word from Lady Sarah to her father can make a man's career, Nathan. It can just as easily break him.'

'I'm sorry if I've disappointed you, Sir Kenwyn, but anyone with such positive ideas as Lady Sarah must expect to provoke equally strong reactions.'

Behind them, at Pelyn, the Earl of Wavendon was expressing similar disappointment to his daughter.

'It's a great pity you and young Jago don't see eye to eye. He's a promising young man who has a great deal of potential.'

'Oh? What makes you think we didn't get along?'

'I'd say that was perfectly obvious to everyone. You and he

were arguing for the entire evening.'

'So? All that means is that Nathan is the first man I've met for a very long time who had the gumption to disagree with me. All the others are so busy trying to impress me because I am your daughter that they wouldn't dispute it if I said a mouse was a cow. Nathan is a real man. I like him, Father. I like him very much.'

For the next week, Nathan spent much of his time in the company of Sir Kenwyn and they were frequently accompanied by the Earl of Wavendon and Lady Sarah.

Most of their time was spent either at Pelyn or Golant, but Nathan did bring them to Polrudden one afternoon.

He introduced Dewi to Lady Sarah with the words, 'This is the most important lady at Polrudden. She takes care of me, of Beville, and of just about everything else that needs attending to. Dewi is my hostess, my confidante – and, quite frequently, my conscience.'

Nathan smiled affectionately at Dewi, but this warmth was not shared by Lady Sarah. With no more than a cold nod in Dewi's direction, she turned her back.

Telling Nell of the introduction, later that day, Dewi said, 'Why is that Nathan always seems to fall in with arrogant, titled women? If you or I behaved as she did, we would be told we were being rude. I think a different set of rules is handed out for use when a woman is given a title.'

Nell smiled sympathetically. 'I'd have been inclined to punch her on her aristocratic nose. Perhaps she didn't like the way our Nathan talked about you. Jealous maybe. Mind you, Nathan always has fallen for women of her type, although he's never found any true happiness with any of them. I would have thought he'd have learned his lesson after his latest experience with Lady Felicia. But I understand the father of this one is a very important man in parliamentary circles in London. Perhaps Nathan needs him for something.'

'Perhaps. But I can remember our preacher back in Wales quoting from the bible when someone in the congregation was suspected of stealing. He said, "What shall it profit a man, if he shall gain the whole world, and lose his own soul?" I would be surprised if your father didn't quote it to Nathan at some time. I wish he would remember it.'

351

Chapter 73

Nathan returned to London a couple of days earlier than he had intended because he was invited to travel there in the Earl of Wavendon's private coach.

It was a last-minute invitation and Nathan left Polrudden in a great hurry, having time for only the briefest of farewells to Dewi and Beville, and leaving the governess to make his excuses to Nell and Tom.

She did not know whether she was more relieved or upset at Nathan's abrupt departure. She had hoped he might speak more of what was in his mind about their future together – if there *was* to be one at all. At the same time, she was relieved at not being made to come to any firm decision about what she should do.

Sir Kenwyn's words weighed heavily upon her. She desperately wanted a future with Nathan, but knew that so much of what the Golant baronet had said was the truth. In spite of his own humble background, Nathan could carve out a career in politics for himself, because of his own achievements. Indeed, there were many who would admire him for all he had done.

However, they would not forgive a man who married his governess, a woman who had lived beneath his roof for almost a year in his employ. Such a man would be regarded by his fellows as beneath contempt – and a man held in contempt would never hold high office. It was an impossible situation. One for which Dewi could find no solution.

Nathan had been in London for almost a month when Dewi's uncle, Captain Morgan, came to call upon her at Polrudden. He always visited her when his ship came to Pentuan, but on this occasion he had more news and gossip than usual to pass on to her.

They met at Venn farmhouse because the ship's captain felt more at home here than at Polrudden and he had formed a close friendship with Tom and Nell Quicke.

'Your Aunt Phoebe sends her love to you, Dewi. She especially asked me to say that. I was to give her *love* to you, she said.'

'There was precious little of that around when I lived with her at Newport.'

'You mustn't be hard on her, Dewi girl. She just has a different way of showing how she feels, that's all. Never has been very good at showing her emotions hasn't your Aunt Phoebe. She has a kind enough heart, for all that.'

'You're probably right,' acknowledged Dewi. 'She took me in when I had need of a roof over my head. How is she keeping?'

'Not very well. Not well at all. It's the arthritis, you know. Affecting her knees and fingers something awful it is at times. Last time I went to see her it was as much as she could do to stand up out of a chair. As for making tea – I finished up making it for her. Afraid the hot kettle would fall out of her hand, I was. Mind, she's getting on in years. Can't expect her to be doing everything as though she was some spring chicken, can we?'

'You ought to go back and see her some time,' said Nell. 'Our Nathan wouldn't mind, and young Pippa is quite capable of taking care of Beville on her own.'

'That would be nice,' agreed Captain Morgan. 'Your aunt would like that.'

They chatted some more before he said, 'It's likely I'll only be making one more trip here on my old ship.'

'Oh, why's that?' asked Tom. 'They giving you a new ship after all these years?'

'No, it's a bit better than that, Tom. The owner has finally decided to retire. He's putting me in charge of the whole shipping company.'

'But that's *wonderful*!' Dewi jumped up from her chair and kissed her uncle on the cheek. 'But fancy you not telling us all about it when you first arrived! You must have been bursting to tell someone.'

'Me? No, modest I am, girl. As well you know.'

His assertion raised a laugh among the others. Captain Morgan was one of the biggest braggarts sailing the seas.

'Anyway,' said the captain, 'there's so much more news to be telling you. I'm surprised to see them all working down at the new harbour. Rumours are strong among the captains that the Harbour Company's gone bust. No more money, they say.'

'Do they now?' Nell was alarmed. 'You'd best be going down there in the morning, our Tom. They owe us a lot of money for the eggs, fowls and sheep we've sold to them these last few weeks. They've seemed reluctant to pay but I never bothered, thinking they weren't likely to be going anywhere. We can't afford to lose the money they owe us. Thank you for telling us, Captain Morgan.'

'Nathan has said nothing about it to anyone in Pentuan, as far as I know,' said Dewi. 'But then, he hasn't been here for a month and we haven't heard a word from him.'

'He'll be too busy gadding about with that earl's daughter who was staying across at Pelyn,' said Tom. His wink to Nell became a quick blink when she rewarded him with a frosty glare.

'What's this, Dewi?' asked Captain Morgan. 'Don't tell me Sir Nathan is only associating with the aristocracy now he's got a knighthood?'

'*I* wasn't telling you. Tom was,' retorted Dewi. 'Anyway, I doubt if Nathan has much time for gadding about in London. If I know anything of Sir Kenwyn he'll have given him a list of people to cultivate while he's in London. That man won't be satisfied until Nathan is made Prime Minister and in a position to make Sir Kenwyn a marquis, a baron, or whatever it is he wants for the Penhaligan family. I sometimes wish he'd chosen someone else to get it for him. Perhaps we'd be living a normal life up at Polrudden now – and I wouldn't have to listen to Beville asking every night when his father was going to come home to him again.'

Dewi had put far too much feeling into her words. There was a long silence in the kitchen of Venn Farm as everyone there wondered what they could say to change the subject quickly.

Nathan returned to Pentuan the following week – but it was a fleeting visit. He arrived at Polrudden accompanied by two fellow Members of Parliament and Sir Kenwyn. For five days they busied themselves sounding out 'borough mongers' and the powerful landowners who dictated policy to the Members of Parliament they supported.

The present government was becoming increasingly unpopular. It was time for a change. Without the support of the country's landowners the government could not function. All over the country Whig parliamentarians were rallying support for their party.

Dewi hoped Nathan might remain at Polrudden after the other Members of Parliament had returned to London. He looked tired and harassed and she told him so. Nathan's response was to give her a kiss that displayed much of his former warmth and tell her that he felt better for knowing she cared.

But he was not able to remain longer. These were exciting times, he told her. He was needed in London where the Whigs were keeping up constant pressure on the government and voting against every bill it tried to pass through the House of Commons. Sooner or later an election would be forced upon them. This would be the great opportunity to oust the unpopular Prime Minister Liverpool and his Tory government.

Nevertheless, Nathan promised Dewi he would be home for her birthday in a few weeks' time. He hinted that they might have something special to celebrate this year.

It was a frustrating visit for Dewi. She desperately needed to talk to Nathan. Seeing him now, on an equal footing with Sir Kenwyn and the two Members of Parliament, brought home to her that what Sir Kenwyn said was probably right. She could not hope to marry Nathan now.

She knew she was being especially sensitive, but her place in the household was apparent in the way she was treated by Nathan's companions. Following his lead, they behaved respectfully towards her – while he was there. In his absence they treated her as though she was little more than a servant.

Sir Kenwyn was the worst of all. Not even bothering to be condescending in his attitude, he was downright rude for much of the time.

Dewi wanted a chance to sit down and talk to Nathan. She would have liked to go away for a couple of weeks. To have time to think things through without any outside pressures. Her aunt's illness would provide her with a good excuse to return to Wales for a while.

But the opportunity for a private talk never occurred. Nathan and his companions never returned to the house until late at night and then the men would talk until the early hours of the morning. So late were they that Sir Kenwyn spent three nights sleeping at Polrudden.

When morning came the four men would rise and leave the house early to see someone else. Even Beville complained plaintively about his father being too busy to spend any time with him.

'He can't help it, Beville,' explained Dewi. 'Your daddy is a very important man now. He has a great deal to do.'

Beville pouted his disappointment. 'I liked it better when he wasn't so important. We had a lot more fun together then.'

'Yes, Beville,' agreed Dewi sadly, 'I think I enjoyed life more then, too.'

Chapter 74

Nathan and his two fellow Members of Parliament returned to London without Dewi being able to speak to him in private. Things had not been helped by the fact that Pippa had been ill during the visit. It meant that Dewi needed to take care of Beville on her own for the whole of the time.

She consoled herself with the thought that her birthday was only a few weeks away. Nathan had promised he would be home by then.

Then, without any prior warning, work stopped on the Pentuan harbour. It seemed the management in Pentuan had no money to pay wages or to honour their debts. At a mass meeting the manager told the men he had no cash in hand at all. He had repeatedly asked for more from the London office of the company, but none had been forthcoming. Now the local bank had announced it would advance no more. Until money was forthcoming from London, all work would cease.

The news was greeted with dismay in the small village. The workmen had been allowed to run up colossal bills at the village inns and a great deal of money was owed to every village shopkeeper and tradesman. There had been rumours that all was not well, of course, but such rumours had circulated since work was first commenced on the project.

Dewi immediately wrote a letter to Nathan, informing him of the consternation of the villagers and asking him to throw some light on the matter.

The villagers were still reeling under the impact of the collapse of the Harbour Company, when a further calamity befell them.

One morning a ship was seen heading towards the unfinished harbour breakwater. There was great excitement in the village when word went around that it was the *Heron*, returning from Newfoundland.

Villagers flocked to the breakwater as the ship was brought skilfully closer to the shore. There were waves of recognition from those on board when they sighted wives, mothers, fathers or children. However, the mood of those on shore changed from joy to uncertainty when a remark was made that something was surely wrong. The excitement of the villagers was not mirrored in the

356

expressions of the crewmen onboard *Heron*.

So grim were the faces of those on the ship that within minutes the joy of the Pentuan villagers became apprehension. As the ship entered the narrow channel alongside the breakwater, someone called, 'We didn't expect you back so soon. Is something wrong?'

'It's the *Charlotte*. She's been lost off Newfoundland . . . with all hands.'

A woman, wife of one of the crewmen of the *Charlotte*, screamed. Another put her hands to her face and her fingernails drew blood from her cheeks as the realisation that she had lost both husband and son sank home.

Captain Dunne toiled up the hill to Polrudden later that morning. The burden of the news he carried weighed heavily with him.

Eleven men had been lost with the *Charlotte*. The vessel had been carrying more men than usual because it was intended that Francis Hanna would establish a camp in a sheltered cove on Newfoundland's south-eastern coast.

The place for the camp had been chosen before the ships left England, Captain Dunne having acquired maps of the area from a fellow captain who had sailed in Newfoundland waters for many years.

The cove had been suggested as being ideal for their enterprise. Here they would have ample wood for the curing and storage sheds. There was also a deepwater bay in which the *Heron* could safely anchor.

A copy of the map was made so that both vessels held one, in the event that they became separated on the voyage to Newfoundland.

'Everything had been organised so well,' said the captain. 'We had a good, fast crossing and had even met up with some of the Newfoundland fishing fleet.'

Captain Dunne and Dewi were seated in the morning-room at Polrudden. He had come looking for Nathan but, in his absence, was quite ready to tell his story to Dewi.

'We were no more than a hundred miles from our destination when a northerly storm came down upon us. It was as bad as any I've seen in all my forty years at sea.'

The captain shook his head disbelievingly as he remembered. 'I lost sight of the *Charlotte* almost immediately, and I don't suppose poor Francis Hanna had any thought for me. It was every man for himself. I tried to ride it out for a while, but I was forced to give in and run before it. For two days and nights we fought with sea and wind, until it seemed that men and ship could take no more. Just about then it began to ease off.'

The captain was shaking now and Dewi crossed to a brandy decanter and poured him a large drink. The distraught man took a deep draught before resuming his story.

'As soon as I could, I turned the *Heron* around. When I was able to take a bearing, I made for the rendezvous. I found it all right, but there was no sign of Francis or the *Charlotte*. Using our ship's boats I searched every cove and inlet for nigh on a week but never found so much as a timber from the *Charlotte*. Then I landed some of the men to begin building the huts that Francis and his men would have built. While they were doing that I took the *Heron* along the coast to enquire among the fishing villages. The storm had wreaked havoc with them. I found one place where they'd lost their merchantmen, smashed to smithereens on the rocks. I bought all the cured fish they had and took it down to the West Indies. I sold it at a good price to a plantation owner and bought up a full cargo of sugar and rum. It's on board the *Heron* now.'

Captain Dunne took another deep swig of his drink. 'I didn't come straight back here. First of all I sailed back up north, to Newfoundland. I foolishly hoped I would get there and find the *Charlotte* riding at anchor, waiting for me, I suppose. But there was nothing. So I sailed home, leaving a couple of men to finish building the huts. I think we must presume the *Charlotte*'s been lost, although it grieves me to say so. I don't know if I've done what Sir Nathan would have wanted me to do, but I did my best as I saw it. Looking back, I don't think I could have done any more. Despite this tragedy there's money to be made in Newfoundland – if Sir Nathan still has a mind to fish and trade there.'

'I think you've done very well, Captain Dunne. Do you have a list of the men who were on board Francis Hanna's boat when it was lost?'

'I thought one would be wanted. I have it here.'

Captain Dunne handed a sheet of paper to Dewi with eleven names printed on it in a bold, clear hand. Looking down the list Dewi winced as she saw the names of Francis Hanna and young Charlie there.

She would have to break the news of the tragedy to Pippa and to Liz. Pippa was at Venn Farm with Beville for the day. She would find Liz there too.

'What are your plans now, Captain Dunne?'

'I shall take my cargo to Bristol. It will fetch a good price there. When I've unloaded I'll return to Pentuan and remain here for a few days. Shall we say until Friday of next week? Then I'll return to Newfoundland and repeat the journey to the West Indies. I can't afford to wait any longer. The Newfoundland season is short and if I'm to make a good profit for Sir Nathan I need to turn my ship around quickly. Will he be home by then?'

'I'm afraid not. I had hoped he would return to Polrudden this weekend. Those were his plans. Unfortunately, I had a note from him only yesterday to say he had been forced to change them. He's remaining in London. I think it might have something to do with the harbour.'

'You'll write and tell him what's happened?'

'No, Captain Dunne, I think he will want to know about this as quickly as possible. I'll go to London myself. We'll be able to talk about things in detail there. If he can't return to Polrudden right away, I'll come back and tell you what he would like you to do.'

Chapter 75

Dewi took the London-bound mail coach the morning after her discussion with Captain Nicholas Dunne.

There were a number of things she felt she had to discuss with Nathan.

The *Heron*'s master saw it as his duty to turn his ship around as quickly as possible in order to make a profit for his employer. Dewi thought she had been employed by Nathan for long enough to know that profit would not be his first consideration in a tragic matter like this.

It was her belief that Nathan would want Captain Dunne to take his ship back to Newfoundland and make determined efforts to find Francis Hanna and the *Charlotte*. It was highly unlikely any of the missing men were still alive, but he would want to confirm their deaths and discover if any bodies or wreckage had been washed ashore.

In order to give Nathan as much time as possible to think about the matter, Dewi did not break her journey to London. She remained on the mail coach through numerous changes of driver, attendant and horses, enduring forty excruciating hours of bone-jarring motion on different roads.

Leaving St Austell at seven in the morning, Dewi reached the heart of London at eleven the following night.

Catching a Hackney coach from the coaching inn, she drove with her luggage to Nathan's London address in Orchard Place.

She was desperately tired, but along the way she tidied herself as best she could in the confines of the small hire-coach.

She was buoyed up with the exciting prospect of meeting up with Nathan again. She thought that during her stay in London they might find time to talk to each other about the problems of their relationship and reach a decision about the future.

Her hopes took a sharp dive when the coach pulled up at the small house in Orchard Place. She could see no lights on inside. Dewi asked the coach driver to wait for her, but he told her he was already working beyond the hours for which he was paid. He added that if she wanted a coach to take her somewhere else she would need to make other arrangements.

Unloading her single piece of baggage, the coachman accepted the money he demanded, grumbling that she had not added a gratuity. When he drove away, Dewi was left pulling the bell-pull beside the door in the unlit London Street.

She had to pull three times, the bell jingling loudly somewhere inside the small house, before someone came to the door.

It was opened by a tall girl wearing a nightdress with a coat thrown over her shoulders. She had the cross look of someone who had just been wakened from sleep.

Opening the door only slightly, she held a lighted candle in a holder high in the opening. In a shrill, uncertain voice she demanded, 'Who are you? What do you want at this time of night?'

'I'm Dewi Morgan, from Polrudden, in Cornwall. Governess to Sir Nathan's son.'

The candle was thrust to within inches of Dewi's face and from behind it Tilly said suspiciously, 'Sir Nathan's said nothing to me about you coming.'

'He didn't know. Something has happened that needs his urgent attention. I must see him.'

'Well, you're out of luck. He's not here. I don't know about Cornwall, but it's a holiday week-end here in London. He went off straight from the House of Commons this evening. He might be back on Tuesday – or he might stay away for the whole week. He wasn't sure himself.'

It was now Friday – unless time had passed even more quickly than she realised, in which case it would already be Saturday. Captain Dunne of the *Heron* would sail from Pentuan in less than one week from now. Probably on next Friday's morning tide. Even if she saw Nathan on Tuesday it might prove to be too late to return before then.

Suddenly, the strain of the mission Dewi had undertaken, coupled with the sheer physical exhaustion of the long journey she had just completed, caught up with her. She felt deadly tired and totally defeated.

She had expected to be pouring out her story to Nathan by now. Instead, she was standing on the doorstep of a house in the heart of London, facing failure and an inexplicably hostile servant girl – and she had nowhere to stay.

'Look, it's really urgent that I find Sir Nathan. I've just got off the coach from Cornwall . . .' Dewi faltered, suddenly overcome with the knowledge of her failure.

'You'd better come in.'

Tilly realised just how tired her unexpected visitor must be and suddenly felt very sorry for her. She realised she was being hostile to Dewi but was not quite sure why. It was probably because she was happy with things the way they were in the Orchard Place house. She felt this girl from Sir Nathan's Cornwall home, his *real* home, posed a threat to her new found security.

'Thank you,' said Dewi gratefully. 'It's been a long journey. My every bone and muscle are screaming at me.'

'Would you like a cup of tea? It won't take long, the kettle won't have gone far off the boil.'

'I'd love one. I'll leave my bag here in the hall for a while and come to the kitchen with you.'

As they walked down the stairs to the basement, Tilly said unexpectedly, 'I'm sorry I was a bit short with you back there. I wasn't expecting anyone so I'd sent both the other maids off until Monday and had just got off to sleep. What's gone wrong in Cornwall? I hope it's nothing to do with Sir Nathan's son – young Sir Beville, isn't it?'

Opening the kitchen door, she passed in before Dewi and lit a lamp before speaking again. 'Sir Nathan talks a lot about his son. At least, he does when he's here, which isn't very often these days. If he comes in at all it's for a quick breakfast and then he's out again. He's working far too hard and I've told him so.'

'I'm glad he has someone in London who's concerned for him,' said Dewi. 'I told him he looked overtired when he was last in Cornwall. Thankfully my being here has nothing to do with Sir Beville. It concerns the two boats Sir Nathan sent out to Newfoundland to begin a new fishing venture. One of them has been lost in a storm, probably sunk. Sir Nathan knows all the men in the crew. Some of them have been his friends for all his life. The other boat brought the news to Pentuan. Now the captain wants to take his ship back there next week and carry on trading. I think Sir Nathan would want the ship to try to learn the fate of the men instead.'

'I think he would too,' agreed Tilly. 'He cares for people. I saw that when he brought young Liz here.'

She was stirring the red ashes beneath the kettle. Looking up, she asked, 'How is Liz liking Cornwall? Is she settling down?'

'She's very happy on the farm with Sir Nathan's sister,' replied Dewi. 'At least, she has been until now. Her young brother Charlie is one of those lost off Newfoundland with the boat.'

'Oh, the poor girl!' Tears sprang to Tilly's eyes. 'As if she hasn't suffered enough in life. Is there no hope for her brother and the others?'

'Very little,' admitted Dewi. 'But the captain of Sir Nathan's other boat says the Newfoundland coast is a very difficult one to search, and largely unexplored. I'm convinced Sir Nathan would want him to carry on searching until something is found to prove they're dead. That's why I need to find him quickly and get a decision from him before the *Heron* sails again. Where is he, do you know?'

'Yes. He's staying at the home of the Earl of Wavendon in

Middlesex. I don't know what's going on there, but I heard him telling one of the gentleman who came home with him one night that everyone of importance will be there.'

'Oh!' In the excitement of her mission, Dewi had temporarily forgotten the Earl of Wavendon – and his daughter. 'I suppose Lady Sarah Milton will be there too?'

Tilly had been about to take the kettle from the fire. Now she paused and looked sharply at Dewi. 'There's no doubt about it. Lady Sarah wouldn't miss any opportunity to be where Sir Nathan is likely to be. Do I take it that you don't think any more of her than I do?'

'I don't think she's the right woman for Nathan . . . for *Sir* Nathan,' replied Dewi guardedly. 'But then, I look at all of his friends with a governess's eye. I have yet to meet one who would make a good mother for Sir Beville.'

'I don't know young Sir Beville, and I haven't met any of Sir Nathan's lady friends except for Lady Sarah, but I looked at her when she came here one day and I thought: There's hope for you yet, Tilly. You may not have an earl for a father, but there's nothing Lady Sarah can do for Sir Nathan that you couldn't do better.'

'I'm sure you're right.' Dewi was more amused than shocked by Tilly's honest and basic confession. 'Unfortunately, Sir Nathan is in Lady Sarah's company right now and not with you or me. I have to find him to sort out what Captain Dunne and the *Heron* are to do when they sail. Can you tell me how to get to the Earl of Wavendon's house? If Nathan's not likely to return here this week-end then I'll have to go there and find him.'

'Of course I can,' said Tilly, warming to her visitor from Cornwall. 'But first of all you must have this cup of tea and I'll get you something to eat. I guarantee it'll be a sight better than anything you had to eat at any of the inns along the way from Cornwall. Sir Nathan always arrives here absolutely starving after his journey from Cornwall.

'While you're eating you can tell me something of his home in Cornwall – and I'll tell you all I know about Lady Sarah and what's going on here, in London.'

Chapter 76

Dewi woke late with a feeling that she should be doing something. It was a few minutes before her dulled senses had gathered themselves sufficiently for her to throw back the bedclothes and dress hurriedly.

She had spent the night in one of the guest rooms at Nathan's town house and had slept an exhausted sleep. When she was dressed, she dashed downstairs and found Tilly in the kitchen.

'What's the time?' Dewi asked breathlessly.

'Hello,' Tilly answered cheerfully. 'It must be almost two o'clock. I looked in on you once intending to wake you, but you were so fast asleep I didn't have the heart. What would you like to eat? I've got some nice bacon here, with an egg or two – and I've got a couple of sausages. Sir Nathan doesn't like them, but I do. The butcher makes them 'specially for me.'

'Have I time to eat? I want to find Sir Nathan today and tell him what's happened to the *Charlotte*.'

'Is that the name of the boat that's missing? It's a lovely name. I knew a girl in the poor-house by that name. She was lovely . . .'

'Tilly, it's urgent that I find him today and tell him what's happened.'

'You've time to get something inside of you. You'll be in a poor way if you don't eat. The Earl of Wavendon's house is close to Harrow. When you've eaten and dolled yourself up, I'll come out with you. We'll probably find a Hackney for you along by Westminster Abbey. That'll get you to Harrow in about an hour-and-a-half. Come on, sit yourself down. I've had tea on the brew for an age.'

While Tilly prepared the meal and Dewi ate, the London housekeeper questioned her about life at Polrudden. Dewi thought she had given away no secrets, but by the time she had eaten her fill, Tilly knew a lot more about her guest than Dewi would have been comfortable about, had she realised.

'What do you think Sir Nathan is going to say when he sees you over there at Harrow, at the Earl's house?'

'He'll be surprised. I'm the last person he'll be expecting to pitch up there.'

'Will he be pleased to see you, d'you think?'

'Not with the news I'm bringing. It'll be just one more worry for him. But he'll appreciate that there was nothing else I could do. He needs to get a message to the captain of the *Heron* before she sails. It would have been no use sending him a letter.'

'That's true. A letter would have been sitting on a tray in the hall here until he returned – and none of us knows when that'll be.'

Tilly looked at Dewi critically. 'You'll be among real nobs out there at Harrow, not like those around here who only think they are. What do you have to wear?'

She looked dismayed. 'Only what I've got on – and a change of a couple of things in my bag. I came dressed for travelling, not for going to rich men's houses.'

'Never mind, we'll have to make do with what you have. I'll do your hair and face so you'll match anyone there for beauty. It's something I do well. I wanted to be a ladies' maid, once upon a time. Trouble was, I got too tall. Ladies don't like maids who look down on them. Come on, now you've got some food inside you, we'll get you ready.'

Tilly took Dewi in the direction of Westminster Abbey. Outside the ancient building she hailed a Hackney coach and dickered with the driver over the fare to Harrow. He complained that travelling so far he'd need to come all the way back empty. He wanted a return fare, he said, setting it at two pounds and five shillings.

The tirade from Tilly included a few choice words that Dewi had never heard the Polrudden maids use. When it ended, the Hackney coach driver accused the housekeeper of trying to put him out of business, but reduced his fare to one pound and ten shillings.

As she settled back in the small coach, Dewi decided Nathan had found himself an exceptional housekeeper. She was also much younger than Dewi would have expected – and attractive. However, Dewi found comfort in the knowledge that Nathan spent very little time in his cosy little London house.

By the time the driver reported that they were approaching the Earl of Wavendon's residence, it was almost five o'clock.

'There seems to be something going on in the house, miss,' he called down to her as she put her head out of the open coach window. 'Do you want me to take you around to the servants' entrance? I expect it's at the back of the house.'

Dewi almost said yes. The Earl of Wavendon's home was huge. Probably ten times the size of Polrudden and by far the grandest house she had ever seen. It was so large as to be awesome, but something perverse in her made her raise her chin defiantly.

365

'No, thank you, driver. You can take me to the front door, if you please.'

'Right you are, miss. Just so long as you're certain. It makes no difference to me.'

There were a great many coaches and carriages standing in front of the house. All the carriages had at least one liveried retainer in attendance. Many had a coat-of-arms or a monogram inscribed on the doors.

A liveried servant from the house hurried to open the door for Dewi. As she stepped to the ground and saw the expression of surprise on his face, she faltered.

Then determination gripped her. Nathan had said he was very fond of her. Had hinted he wanted to marry her. This would be his opportunity to see her in a setting where he would be expected to take her if she became his wife. She would also be able to see his reaction to having her turn up unexpectedly here, when he was among his friends.

The liveried servant was young and relatively inexperienced, but he was perfectly polite.

'Pardon me, ma'am, but do you have an invitation? The Earl of Wavendon is having a private week-end party and . . . if you'll pardon me for saying so, you're not quite dressed for the occasion.'

'Thank you, but I haven't come to any party.' Dewi's nervousness accentuated her Welsh accent. 'I'm here because I have a very important message for one of the Earl's guests: Sir Nathan Jago of Polrudden, in Cornwall.'

'I see. If you'll come with me, ma'am, I'll see if someone can find him for you.'

In the great marble hallway of the house, Dewi passed two women who wore dresses that she thought must have cost more than most Pentuan fishermen would earn in a lifetime of good seasons. Both women looked at Dewi with haughty disapproval. She raised her chin and walked past them, following in the wake of the servant.

She was shown to a small elegantly furnished room just off the hall and asked politely if she would sit down while the servant went off and found someone to help her.

After waiting for almost a quarter of an hour, Dewi heard voices outside. Women's voices. A few moments later Lady Sarah Milton entered the room.

When she saw Dewi, Lady Sarah frowned. 'One of the servants said you were here looking for Sir Nathan Jago. You have a message for him?'

'That's right, Lady Sarah. It's most important. One of his boats has been sunk in Newfoundland waters.'

'Oh, dear!' Lady Sarah's reaction fell only just short of outright boredom. 'That's very tiresome – but hardly a matter of life-or-death, I would think. After all, Newfoundland is a very long way from here. All this must have happened quite some time ago.'

'There's a little more to it than that, Lady Sarah. It's important enough to bring me all the way from Polrudden to speak to Sir Nathan.'

'Of course, I remember you now! You're Nathan's governess. I must confess, I'm surprised *you* were sent to break the news of a shipwreck to him.'

'No one *sent* me, Lady Sarah. It's something I believe he would want to know about immediately. May I see him, please?'

'That's quite out of the question. I am afraid your long journey has been wasted. Sir Nathan is not here.'

Dewi could not hide her dismay. 'But . . . his London house-keeper told me I'd find him here.'

'Then I regret that Sir Nathan's London housekeeper misinformed you. Sir Nathan is accompanying my father and a few friends on a river trip. I don't know where they are, or when they are expected to return.'

'Oh! That's dreadful news. May I wait for him, please? It *is* most important.'

'I told you, I have no idea when they will return. They may decide to remain at an inn and return tomorrow. It has happened before. As for remaining here, I am afraid I have a house party. It would be most inconvenient. I suggest you return to Cornwall and await him there.'

Dewi knew she was going to receive no co-operation from this woman. Neither could she rely upon her passing on a message of sufficient urgency to bring Nathan hurrying back to Pentuan.

'Do you have writing paper and a pen? I would like to leave a letter for Sir Nathan, telling him exactly what has happened.'

'Of course. I'll find a servant to take you to their sitting room. I think you'll find paper and an envelope there. When you've written the letter, give it to the butler. He will ensure it is delivered.'

Without another word, Lady Sarah Milton turned and left the small room. A few minutes later a maid appeared to guide Dewi to the servants' quarters at the rear of the house. Lady Sarah had left Dewi in no doubt of the place she thought Sir Nathan's governess should occupy in *her* household.

Smarting at the slight, Dewi sat down and wrote a long letter to Nathan, informing him of the tragedy off the Newfoundland coast. She told him why she thought it was important for him to return to Pentuan, or at least send detailed instructions to Captain Dunne about his forthcoming voyage.

When the letter was written and sealed inside an envelope, Dewi asked to give the letter personally to the butler.

A large, dignified man, he seemed even less impressed with Dewi than Lady Sarah had been. He managed to give her the impression that he considered her presence in the servants' quarters to be no more welcome than it had been elsewhere in the great house.

Trudging over the gravel as she made her way around the house, Dewi was glad she had asked the Hackney coachman to wait until she had found Nathan and delivered her message.

She had failed to find him. In this respect, her journey had been wasted. However, she had written a letter explaining all she had come to London to tell him. That would have to suffice. The butler had told her it would be in Nathan's hands by morning at the latest. That meant he would probably hurry to Orchard Street to see her. She would be able to explain more fully then, if need be. It also meant they could travel together back to Polrudden.

She chose to dwell on this thought and wipe out the memory of the attitude of Lady Sarah and her butler towards her. It was really no more than she had expected. It tended to confirm what Sir Kenwyn had told her, and what she had tried not to face fully before today: Nathan could never marry her. She would never belong to the society in which Lady Sarah Milton moved. She would never be Lady Dewi Jago.

In the house of the Earl of Wavendon, the butler entered the hall where the guests were assembling for a concert that had been arranged for that evening.

Approaching Lady Sarah, he said, 'The young lady from Cornwall has left the house, Lady Sarah. She gave me this letter for Sir Nathan Jago. Shall I take it and give it to him now?'

Lady Sarah looked across the crowded room to where Nathan was taking his seat at the front of the room, next to her father and beside the empty seat he was saving for her.

'No, Giles. Have a maid take it to my room. I will see the letter is given to him, but not tonight. It contains depressing news, I believe. Sir Nathan has had enough to cope with recently as a result of the collapse of this wretched harbour company he seems so concerned about. Let him enjoy himself while he's here. I'll give it to him before he leaves.'

Chapter 77

Dewi remained at Nathan's London home for two days awaiting a response to her letter. For the first twenty-four hours she steeled herself for a reunion every time a carriage rattled on the cobble-stones outside the house.

When Sunday night came, she had accepted that he was not going to come. Perhaps he was embarrassed because he had put off returning to Polrudden for her birthday. His reason had been he was 'too busy', yet he had been able to attend a week-end party with the Earl of Wavendon – and the Earl's daughter.

By Monday morning, Dewi had resigned herself to receiving no more than a letter in acknowledgement of the one she had written to Nathan. She felt certain he would at least do this. Unless she had been wrong all along and the loss of the *Charlotte* was not as important to Nathan as she had believed it to be?

Dewi tried to put such a thought aside, but there was no letter. By late-afternoon she knew there was only one course open to her. She would return to Polrudden by that night's mail coach.

Yet, even as she packed the single bag she had brought with her, Dewi could not bring herself to think the worst of Nathan.

'There's always the chance that he went straight to Polrudden from the Earl's house,' she said to Tilly, as the young housekeeper brought to the room a few items of clothing she had washed and ironed for Dewi. 'He was very fond of Francis – and has always been concerned for the well-being of all his men and their families.'

'Parliament changes a man,' declared Tilly, sweepingly. 'I've worked for three Members of Parliament now. I've watched 'em all become so involved in what they were doing, running the country and all, they forgot all about the ordinary people and how they live.'

'Sir Nathan's not like that. He cares about *everyone*. You should know that as well as anyone. You were here when he brought Liz to the house from that horrible place where she'd been living since they put her out of the poor-house.'

'You're sweet on him, aren't you?' Tilly put the question as she handed Dewi a newly washed dress.

'Aren't you?' Dewi evaded the question with her own.

369

'I like him enough to sleep with him, if he asked me,' replied Tilly, with complete openness. 'But it's more than that with you, isn't it? You're *really* fond of him.'

'I admire him,' was all Dewi would admit to the housekeeper. 'And I love his son, very much. He's a dear little boy.'

Tilly looked at her pityingly. 'You're in for a lot of heartache, you know. Sir Nathan Jago is one of the best catches in town at the moment. There isn't a mother in London who wouldn't throw her daughter in his direction if she felt he was looking for a wife.'

'I'm under no illusions,' declared Dewi. 'Lady Sarah made it quite clear to me that my place is in the servants' quarters and not in the front hall.'

'Oh, her!' Tilly made a rude noise with her tongue. 'She's a bitch of the first order. I don't know a maid who's stayed with her for more than a matter of weeks. She thinks every man in London is chasing her and that no woman has what she's got. If Nathan gets himself mixed up with her then I've sadly misjudged him – and I've never been that wrong about a man yet!'

'I hope you're right, for young Beville's sake,' said Dewi, closing her bag. 'I'm off to Cornwall now, Tilly. I doubt if you and I will meet again. Take care of yourself – and of Sir Nathan. I think he's in desperate need of *someone* to look after him.'

'You make that sound as though *you* don't expect to be around to do it. Are you planning to leave Polrudden?'

'I don't know yet what I intend doing. I'll think about it on my way back to Cornwall and make my decision when I get there.'

'Don't do anything hasty, Dewi. Right now it may seem to you that Sir Nathan has the whole world at his feet, but this is London, not Cornwall. He could wake up one morning and find that everything's collapsed about his ears. I've seen it happen before – to some very nice gentlemen. If it does, he'll need someone's shoulder to cry on. I'd like to think it'd be mine, but it's more likely to be yours.'

'Thank you, Tilly, I'll remember, but I think perhaps my mind is made up already. Nathan has achieved a great deal in his lifetime. He has a way to go and the sort of woman to help him get there is more likely to be Lady Sarah Milton than either you or me.'

On the long journey to St Austell on the mail coach, Dewi had plenty of time to think of the future. Her visit to the Earl of Wavendon's home and her meeting with Lady Sarah had finally convinced her there was no future for her with Nathan.

As she had said to Tilly, he was moving into a social circle where she did not belong and never would. She would be a social drawback to him. To imagine he might marry her and still reach the political heights was unrealistic. Sir Kenwyn's words to her

370

had been cruel, but every one had been the truth.

Once again Dewi was travelling without taking a stop for sleep. For two nights and a whole day she remained on the coach, leaving it only during the time it stopped at an inn for a change of horses.

She enjoyed only brief periods of sleep, snatched when the section of road on which the coach travelled was less pot-holed than was normal. During the journey through Cornwall, where the roads were worse than elsewhere, the periods of sleep were brief. Nevertheless, when the coach pulled into the yard of the St Austell inn, it took the coach driver a few minutes to rouse her from her exhausted sleep.

It was now noon on Wednesday. She had boarded the coach shortly before dusk on Monday. She reached Polrudden an hour later, carried there by a St Austell stable owner in his small, fast, two-wheeled cart.

By now, Dewi was so tired she was unable to think straight. Asking after Beville, she was told he was at Venn Farm with Nell. Assuming he was there with Pippa, Dewi took a bath and climbed into bed. She was asleep the moment her head touched the pillow and slept until morning, not stirring when Nell put her head around the bedroom door to check on her, a couple of hours after her return.

Dewi woke to the sound of one of the cockerels in the hen run beyond the stables. It was a safe, comforting sound and something she had missed in London, where the early morning sounds were of carts and carriages rumbling over the cobblestone street outside the house.

Thoughts of all that had happened during the past few days flooded back to her mind during the few minutes she lay there. The memories brought her out of bed far more quickly than had any noisy cockerel or the iron-clad wheels of a London street-cart.

She had woken early. When she reached the kitchen only the scullery maid was awake. She was desultorily brushing circular patterns into the thin film of soapy water moistening the dark grey slate slabs of the kitchen floor as she dwelt in her own overly romantic thoughts.

She started guiltily when she realised that Dewi was watching her and began scrubbing with a vigour that drew an exclamation of amazement from Cook, who reached the kitchen only moments after Dewi.

'Why, bless my soul! What's got into the girl? That scrubbing brush has lasted her for nigh on two years, but the way she's working this morning I doubt if it'll last another week! You'll have to come downstairs early a bit more often, Miss Dewi. Would you like a nice cup of tea? How did you like London? Did you see Sir Nathan?'

As she asked her questions, Gladys Coppin took the huge iron kettle from the hob and pushed it into the red coals of the fire.

'I'd love a cup of tea, Gladys. As for London – I dislike the place. It's noisy and it smells – and I didn't see Sir Nathan. He was spending the week-end at the Earl of Wavendon's house. I had to leave a letter for him.'

'That's a pity, after your travelling such a long way to see him an' all.'

'Yes, a great pity. There were things I wanted to discuss with him quite apart from the instructions I hoped he might have for Captain Dunne.'

Gladys Coppin had taken a loaf of bread from the larder and was cutting thick slices from it when something in the tone of Dewi's voice made her pause and look up at the governess.

'Important things, Miss Dewi?'

She nodded, not trusting herself to speak until she was quite sure she would be able to control her voice, 'Yes, Gladys. I intend leaving Polrudden. I'm going . . . back . . . to Wales.'

She could not bring herself to say she was going *home* to Wales. Polrudden had become her home more than any other place she had ever known.

The ageing cook ceased carving the bread and looked at Dewi with undisguised dismay. 'You're going? But why? I thought you were happy here. . . . We all did.'

'And so I am, Gladys. Too happy, perhaps.' It sounded foolish, but Dewi felt unable to clarify it, either to herself or to the cook. 'I . . . I can't really explain. My aunt is ill, but that isn't the only reason. I think the best thing I can possibly do is to leave.'

'When?'

'I'll probably go with my uncle, Captain Morgan, on his next voyage here.'

'What do you mean by his next voyage? Not this one?'

'Is he here?'

'That's right. His ship's on the beach, down at Pentuan. Came in a couple of days ago. He was up here yesterday, looking for you. He'll be leaving again in the next day or two, I dare say.'

Dewi remembered her last conversation with Captain Morgan. He had said his next voyage to Pentuan would be his last. She had not intended leaving quite so quickly, but now she had made up her mind, the sooner she left Polrudden, the better it would be for everyone.

Captain Morgan was sailing that evening. He was taken by surprise when Dewi requested a passage to Newport, but asked no questions. Dewi's pale face and tortured manner told him this was not the time for quizzing her. He would learn her reason for leaving Polrudden soon enough – and there *had* to be a reason. She had never made any secret of her pleasure at working for Nathan Jago.

Dewi was busily stuffing her belongings into two bags when Nell came into her room after only a perfunctory knock.

Looking at the scene she said, 'So it's true then? You *are* leaving us.'

Dewi could only nod. Somehow, seeing this woman who had been such a very good friend to her, made her want to break down and weep.

'Why, Dewi? Why leave now when you and Nathan have both said you have hopes for a future together?'

'I was being foolish, Nell. Living in a make-believe world. One where the handsome prince kisses the poor little servant girl and she magically becomes a princess and everything is wonderful. Life isn't like that.'

'Of course it isn't, but when two people love each other they make their own magic. Tom and I have.'

When Dewi did not reply, Nell said, 'Did something happen when you were in London, Dewi?'

'No . . . Yes . . .' After this contradictory reply, Dewi went on to tell Nell of her humiliating visit to the home of the Earl of Wavendon.

When Dewi ended her story, Nell took hold of both her hands. 'You can't let one single incident destroy your life, Dewi. One woman like Lady Sarah Milton. This just isn't like you. Why, I remember how you dealt with Columb Hawkins's sister! You were more than a match for her. You would be for this woman too.'

'There's far more to it than the way she treated me, Nell. Nathan is *Sir* Nathan now. He's an important man. He belongs to the world I saw at Harrow. I don't. I never could. I'm just Dewi Morgan, a Welsh girl from the valleys. Nathan couldn't marry me, I can see that, but he *will* want to marry, one day. I just couldn't bear to be around when that happens. I'd rather go now and get it over with than stay here and torture myself.'

'But what about Beville? He'll be heartbroken.'

'I don't think so, Nell. Not now. Pippa's had far more to do with him than I have just lately and he's still got her. I think I'll miss him far more than he's going to miss me.'

'I doubt that, and Pippa hasn't been much use since she heard the news of poor Francis and his crew. Beville has spent most of the time up at Venn. That's where he is now. You *were* going to say goodbye to him?'

Dewi would have liked to evade the truth, but she could not leave Nell on a lie.

'No, Nell. I wasn't going to say goodbye to him, or to you.'

Suddenly tears sprang into her eyes and angrily she tried to brush them away.

'Damn! Damn! Damn! I wasn't going to say goodbye to either of you because I love you too much, Nell – and that's the reason I'm going away from Nathan. Because I've never loved anyone so much in all my life – and I never will.'

Chapter 78

Nathan remained at the Earl of Wavendon's Harrow home until late-afternoon on Tuesday, the day after Dewi had left London for Polrudden. Much of the time there had been spent with the Earl and his Westminster friends, discussing Whig affairs. George Ponsonby, leader of the Whig Party in the House of Commons, had recently collapsed in the House. He was not expected to live and there was feverish activity within the party to choose a new leader.

The Tory Party was shaky enough to be toppled. It wanted only the right opportunity to remove them from office. All the prominent Whig politicians had gathered at the home of the Earl of Wavendon to discuss their tactics.

Victory was in the air and the week-end had combined lavish parties and entertainments with the more serious business of deciding who would be given office in the event of a Whig government.

Nathan felt very much on the fringe of the activities. He was also somewhat uneasy about the manner in which various issues were settled. It seemed to him that if ever the Whigs took office all parliamentary matters would be decided in the stately homes of the members of the House of Lords before being put before the Commons. It was a prospect that filled him with uneasiness.

In the hall, with a number of other guests, Nathan was preparing to take leave of his host when Lady Sarah put in an appearance.

Approaching Nathan, she reached up and with a proprietorial air turned back a folded lapel of his coat.

'Nathan, you haven't spent *nearly* enough time with me this week-end. Hardly any time at all.'

This was entirely untrue. Lady Sarah had monopolised his company for almost every waking hour when he was not in political discussion with the other men.

'I think perhaps you're exaggerating a little.' He was in a good mood. He was going back to Orchard Place where he would be able to relax. He had not been entirely comfortable in the exalted company gathered at Harrow.

'Perhaps . . . but only a little. By the way, this letter came for you during the week-end.' Walking to a side table, Lady Sarah picked up a long envelope from a silver tray and handed it to him.

Frowning, because it was out of the ordinary for a letter to be delivered here, where he was only a guest, Nathan tore open the envelope.

As he read the contents his face expressed concern, anguish and shock in turn.

'When did this arrive?' He looked up at Lady Sarah.

'Oh, some time on Saturday, I believe.'

'Saturday! Why wasn't I given this before? The contents are important. Very important. I need to give instructions to the captain of a ship before he sails from Cornwall on Friday.'

Lady Sarah was not used to having anyone demand an explanation from her. Especially in front of her friends. She replied without pausing to think, 'What's so important about it? Your boat sank weeks ago. You can't do anything to save the crew now. It's too late.'

'You know the contents? How?' Suddenly his anger flared anew. 'Was this letter delivered in person? Did Dewi come here looking for me?'

'If "Dewi" is the name of your governess, yes, she did – but you were in important discussion with my father and his friends. I most certainly would not disturb you to speak to a *servant*.'

Nathan could hardly contain the outrage he felt. Dewi had travelled from Cornwall to London to deliver a message and been turned away by this woman. It was an outrageous slight to Dewi and it was this that caused him to overstep the bounds of discretion.

'She's more than a servant, Lady Sarah. Much more. Dewi Morgan is the girl I intend to marry!'

Outside the house, still angry, Nathan realised he had effectively put an end to any hope of office within the Whig Party, but he did not care. He did not like the way they went about things – and he was still furious about the manner in which Dewi had quite obviously been treated upon her arrival.

A number of Hackney coaches were lined up in readiness for those guests who had not brought their own carriages and Nathan climbed inside the first of them, having ordered the driver to reach Orchard Place as quickly as he possibly could. He hoped he might find Dewi there, or at least news of where she was staying.

Tilly dashed Nathan's hopes immediately upon his arrival at the small house in Orchard Place.

'Miss Dewi, Sir Nathan? No, she's not here now. She waited for a reply to the letter she left at the Earl of Wavendon's house, but yesterday she said she couldn't wait any longer. She caught last night's mail coach back to Cornwall.'

As Nathan let out a groan, Tilly added, 'She was very upset at not seeing you.'

'I should think she would be. After travelling all the way from Cornwall, only to be frustrated by the whim of a spoiled young woman like Lady Sarah Milton—'

Nathan looked at the grandfather clock in the hall. It was after seven o'clock. He had missed the mail coach to Cornwall. There would not be another until tomorrow evening – and that would be too late. The *Heron* would have sailed before he could reach Pentuan.

'I liked Miss Dewi, Sir Nathan. She's a nice girl and very fond of young Sir Beville. Shall I take your coat, sir?'

'No.' Nathan was remembering a conversation with another of the Cornish Members of Parliament. He had described another, faster route from London. It entailed a coach trip to Portsmouth and transfer to a steam-powered vessel which travelled to Falmouth, calling at one or two ports along the way. His informant had said it was possible to save as much as twelve hours on the journey.

'Tilly, do you know where the Portsmouth coach starts from?'

'I don't think I do, Sir Nathan, but it stops at The Three Feathers Inn, just down the road in Victoria. I've seen it there myself.'

'Bless you, Tilly. I'm going to write a letter now and I want you to deliver it to the House of Commons tomorrow.'

'*Me*?! At the House of Commons?'

'That's right.'

In extreme cases, Members of Parliament were allowed to take up to two months' absence of leave from the House. They were supposed to obtain permission first, but this was an emergency. Nathan doubted they would take disciplinary action against him.

Sitting down at his desk while Tilly prepared him a hasty meal, he penned a lengthy but hurried letter. When it was finished he addressed it to 'The Speaker' and handed it to his housekeeper.

'There you are. Make quite sure it gets there in the morning, Tilly. Now, I'm off to catch this coach. I shall be away for anything up to two months but I'm leaving you enough money to take care of anything that may come up during that time. I trust you to do things exactly as you would if I were here. Is that understood?'

'Of course, Sir Nathan. When you return you'll find everything exactly as you would wish it to be.'

'I know I shall, Tilly. One of the best things I ever did when I came to London was to make you my housekeeper. I couldn't have chosen better.'

Glowing from his praise, she said, 'Thank you, sir. I said you'd never regret it, and you never shall. But where will you be for these two months, Sir Nathan? Where can I find you if there should be some emergency.'

'I don't think you'll be able to get in touch with me where I'm going, Tilly. I'm setting off to see if I can find out exactly what happened to the men on board the *Charlotte*. I'm going to Newfoundland.'

Chapter 79

Had the steamship on which Nathan was travelling not run aground in Southampton Water, he would have reached Polrudden before Dewi left. In the event, the tide was ebbing and the vessel was held fast by the mud for ten hours.

When the steamship churned its way into deep water once more only another couple of hours of daylight remained. After talking to his ship's officers, the master decided he would return to the quayside at Portsmouth and remain there until the morning.

Nathan remonstrated with the master, but he achieved nothing. The captain would not put his ship at risk. Entering some of the small harbours along the coast during the hours of darkness was out of the question.

Once the ship got under way, the captain was as helpful as was possible. Off the coast of Cornwall he took his steamship in close to Mevagissey, enabling Nathan to transfer to a small fishing boat. The boat was manned by two young boys who regarded the great, hissing, threshing steam vessel with awe. They had experienced a lean day's fishing and were quite willing to call it a day and take Nathan to the Portgiskey fish-cellar for a guinea.

At the cellar Ahab Arthur was able to tell Nathan something of what had been going on in his absence and the sad news brought by the *Heron* from Newfoundland.

As Ahab related his story in his slow, unhurried way, Nathan became increasingly aware that he was very tired. He had suffered one night driving through the darkness to Portsmouth. The second night, when he might otherwise have slept, he had endured the discomfort of a room booked for him at a waterfront inn by a clerk of the steamship company. The inn was noisy and he had been obliged to share his mattress with a colony of bed bugs.

Eventually, he interrupted Ahab Arthur's rambling tale.

'Ahab, I'm sorry, but I feel so tired that if I stay here any longer I'm likely to fall asleep on the spot. Find Captain Dunne for me and ask him to come to Polrudden in an hour's time. There are many things I need to discuss with him as quickly as possible. Between now and then I'll clean up and shave, and have something to eat and drink. Even more important, I must apologise to Dewi. She was treated shabbily in London by people who should have known better.'

'Dewi? You mean you don't know?'

'Know what? Has something happened to her? Is she all right?'

'She was fit enough when I saw her not many hours ago, although I wouldn't say she looked to be the happiest person in the world. You won't find her at Polrudden, that's certain. She left for Wales on Captain Morgan's ship about four hours ago.'

At Polrudden, Nathan read Dewi's brief and uninformative note for the third time, but could deduce nothing more from it than the stark information that she was terminating her employment at Polrudden and returning to Wales to take care of her ailing aunt.

He was thoroughly bewildered. He realised that Dewi must have suffered a humiliating experience at Lady Sarah's hands, but it was a single incident and he was in no way to blame. Why then had she chosen to leave Polrudden and return to Wales? Could it be because her feelings towards him had undergone a change? She must have known he wanted to discuss marriage with her. He had tried to broach the subject many months before, only to have it held in abeyance, at Dewi's request. He could think of no other reason why she would have left and the thought left him greatly depressed.

Nathan had washed and shaved and was sitting down to a meal when Nell arrived at Polrudden. She had brought Beville back from the farm with her.

He was overjoyed at seeing his father. Climbing on his lap, he clasped his arms about Nathan's neck so tightly he was almost choked – but Beville's first words hurt even more.

'Dad! Why has Dewi gone away? Why wouldn't she stay? Doesn't she like us any more?'

'Her aunt's very ill, Beville. Dewi left to take care of her. I'm quite sure she'll be back at Polrudden as soon as she's able. Here, help me to eat some of this and then I want you to go up to bed early. I've got plans for us tomorrow. I'll come up and tell you all about them before you go to sleep.'

To Nell, he said, 'Why have you got Beville, Nell? Where's Pippa?'

'She's taken the loss of Francis very hard. They were a very happy young couple. She's improving now, but for a couple of days there was nothing anyone could do with her. I had her up at Venn to take care of her. I really don't know how we'd have coped without young Liz. She was as upset as anyone, because of young Charlie, but she's had more kicks than cuddles in her young life, has that one. What she feels for Charlie has gone inside – and it'll stay there until there's no one around to see it come out.'

'I'd like to see her in the morning, Nell – along with Pippa and

380

the relatives of every man who was on the *Charlotte*. I want to tell them what I intend doing, and ensure that no one wants for money in the meantime. Can you ask the servants to arrange that for me?'

Patting Beville's backside affectionately, he said, 'In the meantime I think it's time this young rascal went to bed. Captain Dunne is due here shortly and I want to talk to you before then, Nell.'

'I put *myself* to bed now,' said Beville, proudly. 'No one has to come with me . . . but I want you *both* to come up and say good night to me.'

'We'll be there soon,' promised Nathan. 'And I'll have some very exciting news for you. Off you go now.'

When the door closed behind Beville, Nell asked, 'What's this exciting news you've got for him? Does it have anything to do with Dewi?'

'I wish it had. No, Nell. I intend sailing with Captain Dunne on the *Heron* tomorrow. I want to go to Newfoundland and satisfy myself that everything possible has been done to find the *Charlotte*, or at least to find out what happened to the men. I don't suppose I'll be able to do any more than Captain Dunne, but I'd never be satisfied unless I did. I've seen far too little of Beville just lately, so I intend taking him with me.'

Nell sucked in her breath sharply. 'Is that wise? Will a voyage such as that be safe for a young boy?'

'As safe as I can make it. Besides, he's been brought up in a fishing community and has already spent time out with the men. Sailing comes naturally to him. He'll be all right. But what I really want to talk to you about is Dewi. I was shocked to learn from Ahab that she's gone back to Wales. Do you have an address for her, Nell? I want to write a letter to her before I set sail for Newfoundland. Explain all I can about what went on in London.'

'She didn't leave an address. I think it was deliberate. My impression is that she thought everything out very carefully on her way back to Cornwall from London. This was no spur-of-the-moment decision to leave.'

'But why did she *want* to go, Nell? I intended marrying her. I still do. She knew that – and so does the rest of the world now. I told Lady Sarah Milton and her friends so when I learned Dewi had called at the house and been turned away without speaking to me.'

'You should have told the whole world long before that. It could be too late now.'

'Why, Nell? Surely one misunderstanding wouldn't cause her to throw everything away in such a manner?'

'She was upset at whatever happened in London. You had made excuses for not returning to Cornwall for her birthday and yet you were enjoying a week-end party at Lady Sarah's house.'

381

'It is not Lady Sarah's house, it belongs to the Earl of Wavendon, one of the most influential men in politics. Practically the whole of the week-end was spent discussing ways the Whig Party could oust the government of Lord Liverpool.'

'Did Dewi know that? No, she only knew what she saw – and what your Lady Sarah chose to tell her. Coupled with everything Sir Kenwyn Penhaligan's been saying to her, it was enough to tip the scales. She felt she had no alternative but to leave Polrudden.'

'What has Sir Kenwyn got to do with this?' Nathan spoke sharply.

'He's been taking every opportunity to tell Dewi that any association with you would hold you back from high office. I think she believed him in the finish.'

'He had no right to say anything to her at all. That's insufferable interference . . .'

'What has *right* got to do with anything? Sir Kenwyn is driven by ambition. He's ambitious for you, for whichever party he supports – and ambitious for the Penhaligan family.'

'I don't care about his own ambitions. I'll have words with him about this.'

'Forget him, Nathan. You have far too much to do right now, even though we can do nothing about Dewi until we know exactly where she is. She promised to write to me. When she does she'll hopefully give me an address so I can reply.'

'All right, we'll wait for that, but in case her uncle puts in to Pentuan I'll leave word for one of the fisherman to speak to him and get Dewi's address.'

'Captain Morgan won't be coming to Pentuan again. This trip was his last. He came to Venn to say goodbye to Tom and me.'

'Damn! Either Dewi thought this out very carefully or everything is against us. I'll leave word in the village to make enquiries from any of his company's boats that come in. Talking of the village . . . warn the shopkeepers and the landlords of the inns to give no more credit to anyone claiming to represent the Harbour Company. They've almost certainly gone into liquidation. I tried to contact the shareholders while I was in London, but they seem to have disappeared. Work will stop here very soon, if it hasn't done so already.'

'Tom and I have already done that. I fear it was too late for most of the traders. What will happen to the harbour? Surely they can't just leave it as it is, half-finished?'

'I've left instructions for my solicitor to try to buy up all the shares. If I get them I'll see that the work goes ahead. I'm still not convinced Pentuan needs a harbour but, as you say, we can't just leave things as they are at the moment.'

There was silence for a few moments before Nell said, 'Everything suddenly seems to have got itself in a horrible mess, our

382

Nathan. It's all happened since you left Polrudden to go into politics in London. The harbour, the *Charlotte* – and Dewi. I'm going to miss her. She's the best friend I've ever had.'

Nell paused to rub a hand over her swollen stomach. 'I wish she was going to be around for the birth of this one. It doesn't feel as right as any of the others have done. I've been getting a lot of pain with it already.'

'Politics can't be blamed for the loss of Francis Hanna and his boat, Nell, although it must take responsibility for a lot of other problems. As for your baby . . . I'm hoping we'll have Dewi back before it's due to be born. Talking of children, let's go up to see Beville and I'll tell him about tomorrow.'

Chapter 80

The *Heron* encountered rough weather in mid-Atlantic yet still succeeded in reaching the Newfoundland fishing grounds in twenty-three days. The first call was at the wide, sandy cove that had been selected for the drying-house.

Nathan had hoped that by some miracle he might find the missing men here, but the miracle eluded him. The two men who ran down to the water to meet the boat coming ashore from the *Heron* were those who had been left to construct a drying-room and living quarters.

There were others here, but they were far removed from the missing Cornish fishermen. Somehow, the two men left at the cove had gained two Indian women 'companions' who were delighted to see young Beville and kept peering closely at his blue eyes, much to the small boy's embarrassment.

Somewhat sheepishly, the two men explained that the women had been with a party of Indians who came visiting. They had been left in exchange for a blanket and an old ankle-length coat that would probably have fallen apart if it had been worn for one more winter season. They also asserted that the women worked harder than any man in carrying out chores about the camp.

The two Cornishmen had neither seen nor heard anything of the *Charlotte* or the missing Pentuan men.

'What do you want to do now?' Captain Dunne had come ashore with the small boat and asked the question of Nathan.

'That storm that hit you was a northerly,' he replied. 'And you were heading for this cove at the time, so I suppose we had better search to the south.'

'The *Heron*'s your ship,' said Captain Dunne. 'I'm happy to take you wherever you want to go, but Newfoundland is two-thirds the size of England and some of the bays are the size of Cornwall. In a storm like the one that hit us, the *Charlotte* was likely to have been blown clear of land altogether. If the boat survived – and it's a mighty large if – they might have made landfall anywhere in Eastern Canada – or even gone as far south as America.'

'I appreciate all that, Captain,' agreed Nathan. 'And I know our chance of finding any trace of them is slim, but I have to make the effort, if only to live with my own conscience. I'd like to feel you, or they, would do the same for me.'

'Fair enough,' said Captain Dunne. 'What do you want to do with the two men we left here? Do we take them with us?'

Nathan smiled. 'I think we should. It might upset their two young Indian friends, but I have to face a wife and a mother when I return to Pentuan. They'll come back with us. We'll build a new curing house when you come out here next year.'

'You'll continue fishing and trading from Newfoundland then?'

'You've already shown it to be profitable, Cap'n Dunne. I'd like to try for at least another season. Does that suit you?'

'It would suit any true sailor. There's nothing to compare with deep sea sailing.'

'Then it's settled. Now, let's get the two men back on board, then we'll set off along the coast. On the way we'll stop and buy up all the cured fish we can. Speaking to the fishermen is the most likely way to pick up news of the *Charlotte*.'

It had been Nathan's intention to spend ten days in Newfoundland waters, but at one of the small coves where they called to buy cured fish, one of the fishermen had heard a rumour of men rescued from a shipwrecked vessel immediately after the great storm.

Nathan spent four extra days following up the rumour, only to learn that the vessel involved had been a small fishing boat containing three men. It had been wrecked on a tiny beach beneath sheer cliffs and only one man had survived.

This story, coupled with their lack of success, cast an air of depression over what had proved to be an unexpectedly successful trading voyage.

The Newfoundland season was over and many of the usual trading vessels had been sunk or damaged in the storm. The fishermen who operated curing houses along the coast were anxious to sell the split and lightly salted cured codfish before the long, hard winter set in.

The return voyage to Cornwall was even faster than the outward journey. The *Heron* averaged a hundred and eighty miles a day to complete the voyage in twenty days.

Back at Pentuan, the villagers gathered to hear Nathan give them details of his lack of success. Hopes had never been high that the latest expedition would find their men, but a few of the villagers had been praying that he might pull off a miracle.

As Nathan spoke to them on the quayside, his words were constantly interrupted by sounds from the harbour. When the villagers began to make their sad way homeward, Nathan asked Ahab Arthur, one of the bystanders, what was happening.

'Work's being going on there for more than a week now,'

explained the fisherman. 'Seems like Sir Christopher Hawkins has taken over again. Leastways, it's him who's been down at the harbour getting things organised.'

The news startled Nathan. He had made a private arrangement with the head of the Harbour Company that *he* would be offered the shares should they decide to sell. No doubt the bankruptcy had made this difficult but, as a safeguard, he had instructed a London solicitor to act for him in purchasing the shares.

The news of Sir Christopher's takeover of the harbour and his own lack of success in Newfoundland filled Nathan with a sense of failure as he climbed the hill to Polrudden. The only bright spot of the past few weeks was the new closeness which he had achieved in his relationship with Beville.

This apart, he felt deeply depressed and dissatisfied with life in general. It was not until Polrudden came into view that he realised why. Dewi was not here. For more than a year now the thought of seeing her again had made every return to Polrudden more pleasurable. No matter where he might have been, or what had happened, there was always a sense that all would right itself once he passed through the door.

With Dewi gone the house would seem strangely empty.

Nathan had expected Pippa to be in the village upon the return of the *Heron* but he had not seen her there, neither was she at Polrudden. When he enquired, he was told she had been helping Nell at Venn since he and Beville had sailed to Newfoundland.

He had hoped to find a letter from Dewi at Polrudden, but the only correspondence was from senior Whig politicians, urging him, as a friend of the Duke of Clarence, to return to London as soon as possible. The Duke had married Adelaide. His allowance should have been increased upon his marriage, but it seemed there was still much resistance to this. Much of the opposition came from Tories in the government and stemmed from the Duke's support of the Whig cause.

At Beville's insistence, Nathan set off with his son for Venn within an hour of his return. Beville wanted to tell his cousin, Christian, about his exciting voyage to Newfoundland – especially about the 'savage' Indians he had met there.

The first person Nathan met at Venn was Tom. He was coming from the milking parlour with Liz. When the young cockney girl saw Nathan her face paled, then she ran to meet him.

'Did you find Charlie, Sir Nathan? 'Ave you brought 'im back with you?'

'I'm sorry, Liz. We found nothing at all. We've got just about every fisherman in Newfoundland searching, but I'm afraid the chance of finding Charlie and the others is remote, especially with a Newfoundland winter just around the corner.'

'Oh!' For a few moment Liz seemed close to tears. Then she

said, 'I'll carry on with the cows, Mr Quicke. You 'ave a chat wiv Sir Nathan.'

Liz made her way to a nearby barn. When she had disappeared inside, Tom said, 'She thinks you're something of a hero, Nathan. She was sure you'd find young Charlie and bring him back with you. Poor kid, there haven't been too many good days in her young life. She's a good little worker, though. I don't know what we'd have done without her these past couple of weeks.'

'Why? Nell usually does all the dairy work.'

'She's not been too well. I'm worried about her. She's having a hard time carrying this baby. Things aren't going as well as they did with the others. Pippa's been up here with her to take care of the children, but we've just learned that she's expecting too, poor girl. I tell you, Nathan, I wish Dewi was still around. She had a knack of sorting things out when it was most needed.'

'You don't wish it any more than I do, Tom. On the way home I was hoping it would all turn out to be a bad dream. That I'd get back to Polrudden and find Dewi waiting there, as usual. Do you know if Nell's heard from her?'

'Yes, she's had a letter . . .'

Nathan's face lit up hopefully and Tom added hurriedly. 'Trouble was, it didn't give no address for her. It was just a letter hoping we were all getting along all right.'

'Oh!' Nathan could feel the depression settling on him again. 'I'll go in and speak to Nell. Perhaps we can cheer each other up – although I doubt it. It doesn't sound as though any of us has too much to be cheerful about.'

Chapter 81

Nathan reached London just in time to take part in the debate which would decide whether the Duke of Clarence was to receive an increased allowance as a result of his marriage.

It was the second time since Nathan was elected that the motion had come before the house and things did not look hopeful. Many Tories would vote against it because of the Duke's support for the Whig cause. Others saw this as an opportunity to express general dissatisfaction with the conduct of the sons of King George III. The Prince Regent, in particular, had enraged a number of members of the House of Commons by his treatment of Princess Caroline.

The debate was fierce and the vote that followed very close. The motion was eventually carried when, at the last minute, a number of government supporters decided that support of the royal family came before their duty to the party.

In the lobby voting with the Whigs was Sir Christopher Hawkins. Whether by accident or design, he was only a step behind Nathan as they walked along the corridor from the lobby.

Moving up beside him, Sir Christopher said, 'That was a damned close thing, Sir Nathan.'

The baronet's civil tone and his use of the title told Nathan that Sir Christopher had something special he wished to say to him.

'I'm very pleased the increased allowance was approved by the House.'

'Yes, of course. The Duke is a friend of yours. Well, he had my vote.'

An expression of regret crossed the baronet's face. 'It has pained me for a very long time that the Duke of Clarence and I should have met in such unfortunate circumstances at Pentuan harbour. It was the fault of that hot-headed young nephew of mine. His actions have cost me dearly over the years. They have soured relations between you and me, too. Fortunately for everyone, perhaps, Columb is no longer in Cornwall. He's accepted a minor post in our embassy in Russia. I doubt if he will be able to do much harm there.'

The two men drew apart to allow a small crowd of hurrying

Members of Parliament to pass by. Nathan thought the Cornish baronet had conveniently forgotten much of his own rudeness and underhand scheming.

'Look, Ja— Sir Nathan. I don't want you coming to any wrong conclusions about my taking over the Harbour Company while you were out of the country. In truth, I was merely intent on rescuing it from extinction. It was not until I bought back the company that I learned you had been promised the shares if ever they came back on the market. I honestly believe there has been so much uncertainty that it would be best for everyone if I were to retain control of the company, but I am not an unreasonable man. We must meet up soon and discuss the matter. I suggest I give special terms to you for your various vessels.

'I'd like to discuss my future plans too – and ask your advice about a longer breakwater. I would also like your views on improving the harbour for the benefit of the villagers, as well as getting the best from it for those who will be shipping from Pentuan. In my opinion, it needs a railway line from St Austell to Pentuan. That's the way really to make the whole venture profitable. We'll have a long chat about it some time, eh?'

When Sir Christopher Hawkins had gone on his way, Nathan allowed himself a brief, knowing smile. The motive behind Sir Christopher's unexpected friendliness had been hidden in his apparently idle chatter. Sir Christopher wanted to build a railway to the harbour. It would never pay its way unless the conveyance of goods to and from the little harbour could be speeded up. A railway, with horses pulling the trucks, was an obvious answer.

However, the scheme had a major drawback as far as Sir Christopher was concerned. Nathan owned most of the land along the only practicable route between the harbour and St Austell. His co-operation was essential to the baronet if the harbour were to succeed.

Sir Christopher Hawkins was a devious man, yet no more so than those whose behind-the-scenes dealings decided most issues in Parliament.

Nathan had become thoroughly disillusioned with the workings of British government and became even more so during the course of the next few days. He found himself ostracised by those Members of Parliament and political peers with whom he had spent the weekend at Harrow.

Only one of the peers broke the silence to say, 'Why don't you make things up with Lady Sarah, Jago? Have the whole incident put down to a mere lover's tiff. Everyone will be quite willing to believe the words that were spoken meant nothing at all. Lady Sarah herself will forgive you, I don't doubt.'

'*She* will forgive *me*!'

As he spoke, Nathan remembered the incident that had been

the cause of his angry outburst, but his companion missed the incredulity in his voice.

'Of course – and I am not offering you my own personal view. The Earl of Wavendon spoke to me about it only yesterday. He was speaking for his daughter, but would not do so if she had not given him the words to say. She is a strong-willed, independent girl. Think about it, Jago. You could regain lost ground and play a very important part in any future Whig government.'

The day after Nathan's talk with the peer, the situation took another, quite unexpected turn. Early in the afternoon a piece of tragic news reached the House of Commons. Its progress could be seen around the chamber like wind stirring the trees in a forest.

The Earl of Wavendon was dead. He had passed away during the night, apparently as the result of a heart attack.

Of a sudden there were new alliances to be formed. New allegiances sought. From being a political pariah, Nathan's support was now eagerly sought.

The sheer hypocrisy of his fellow Members sickened Nathan. If this was London politics, he felt more of an outsider than ever before.

That evening, after writing a brief but sincere letter of condolence to Lady Sarah, Nathan put the scheming corridors of Westminster behind him and took a long and thoughtful walk through the streets of London. He headed for Carey Street and John Gully's inn.

Nathan's return to the haunts of his prizefighting days was not an unqualified success. He was welcomed with great enthusiasm by John Gully but tonight the centre of attention was Seth Clements who had just won the championship of London. He was now being strongly tipped as the future champion of All England, a title once held by Nathan.

Perched on the edge of the table at which Nathan sat alone nursing a very large brandy, John Gully looked over to where Clements sat. Bruised and cut from his last fight, the new champion was surrounded by sycophantic admirers.

'Doesn't it take you back to past glories, Nathan? It does me. Why, I can remember when you sat right where Clements is now and admirers hung on your every word. It isn't so many years ago either. I did it myself too – and loved every moment of the adulation. But I suppose we've moved on to greater things now, you and I. Talking of which, how's that fine young son of yours – and his governess? The girl you took to the theatre. Dewi, isn't that her name?'

'Beville's well. He and I have just come back from a voyage to Newfoundland.'

Nathan told John Gully the circumstances that had prompted

390

the voyage. Almost as an afterthought, he added, 'Dewi isn't at Polrudden any longer. She returned to Wales to look after a sick aunt there.'

'Oh. I must admit to being disappointed. My wife and the children will be too. We were all agreed that you and Dewi made a lovely couple. We expected to be receiving an invitation to your wedding before too long.'

A few minutes later John Gully was called upon to help his overworked staff cope with the increased business brought to the inn by the presence of the new champion.

Sitting on his own, Nathan became increasingly morose. He had come here to be among friends and forget his problems, not to be reminded of what he had lost. For the first time for as long as he could remember, he felt alone and uncertain of himself and his life.

That night Nathan drank far more than he was used to and left The Plough encompassed in an alcoholic haze.

Given some lively company, he would have gone on to another inn, made a night of it, purging all his problems in a single night of soul-scouring debauchery. When the hangover cleared, life would have fallen into perspective once more.

It was a formula that had worked for him during his younger days. His problems had been smaller then, it was true, but youth tends to see life through a magnifying glass.

When Nathan reached the house in Orchard Place it was in darkness. There was nothing unusual in this. His hours were so irregular that he was in the habit of letting himself in. It was not fair on Tilly to expect her to be awake at all hours to open the door to him.

The idea of using his own key had seemed a good one when it was first mooted, but tonight he had great problems finding the keyhole.

Grumbling to himself, Nathan put the key partly in the keyhole at an angle, only to have it suddenly slide from his grasp and slip to the ground.

Cursing, he leaned down to look for it and almost overbalanced. He was down on his knees when the door opened and Tilly, dressed in her night attire, stood before him, holding a candle in her hand.

Looking up at her owlishly, he said, 'I'm sorry, Tilly. I seem to have lost my key.'

'No, you haven't, here it is.'

She leaned over and in the moment before her loosened hair obscured his view, he glimpsed her full breasts, hanging loose inside her nightdress.

Nathan took a hold of the railings at the side of the front door

391

in order to pull himself up, but only half succeeded. He was more successful at his next attempt – but only because Tilly put an arm about him and lifted him to his feet.

In the hallway, where Tilly had placed the candle, she closed the door behind him and helped him towards the stairs. Along the way, Nathan felt a need to give her an explanation for his unsteady state.

'I . . . I've been drinking, Tilly.'

'Really, Sir Nathan? I thought that might be drink I could smell on your breath.'

He pulled them both to a halt. Drawing himself up unsteadily to his full height, he looked down at her and asked, 'Are you laughing at me, Tilly?'

'No, of course not, Sir Nathan. I have far too much respect for you ever to do that. Besides, you've had many problems of late. I wouldn't blame you one little bit if you drank yourself silly every night. When poor Mr Shaw was living here he used to get that way at least once or twice each week. There must be something wrong with that House of Commons, I reckon.'

They had reached the stairs now and she guided him towards them, but suddenly he pulled away.

'No, Tilly, I want a drink before I go to bed.'

'Begging your pardon, Sir Nathan, but don't you think you've had enough for one night.'

'You should never tell a gentleman he's had enough to drink, Tilly. Don't even *suggest* it – not even if it's true. You remember that.'

'Of course I'll remember it, Sir Nathan – but I'll tell you what I'll do. It's very late now and I've no doubt you'll want to be up early to go to the House. We'll get you to your room. Then, while you get ready for bed, I'll fetch a bottle for you. Brandy, isn't it?'

Tilly had managed to help Nathan up two stairs before she asked the question.

'That's right . . . brandy. But I can . . . manage quite well . . .'

Tilly just managed to prevent him from swaying backwards and falling down the stairs. In helping him regain his balance she managed to advance up three more stairs.

'We're nearly there, Sir Nathan. Just one or two more. It's a bit difficult round this corner, but we're doing fine. There! Let's go in and sit you down while I light a lamp for you.'

A few minutes later Nathan was sitting lop-sided on his bed while Tilly removed his shoes. They were quickly followed by his coat.

'There you are. Would you like something to eat?'

'No. Just a drink.'

'Right, Sir Nathan. You get yourself ready for bed while I go downstairs and fetch you some brandy.'

'Bring two glasses, Tilly. One for you. You deserve a drink. You're a good girl, Tilly. You look after me. Look after me well.'

On the way downstairs, she thought for a moment of leaving him alone now. He would probably forget about the drink and fall asleep – but she was not at all certain that was what *she* wanted.

Sir Nathan had told her she was a good girl. Many things she might be, but she was not a *good* girl. She could read the danger signs. Going to Nathan's bedroom with two glasses and a bottle of brandy was asking for trouble. The speed at which her heart had begun to beat added weight to the warning. But it would not stop her.

When Tilly returned to the bedroom Nathan had stripped himself only as far as the waist and was seated on the edge of the bed looking vague. It was some years since he had fought in the prize-ring, but he was well muscled and still had a fine physique.

For a moment Nathan seemed surprised to see her, then he caught sight of the bottle of brandy and the glasses she held in her hand.

'Are you quite sure you want this, Sir Nathan? Haven't you had enough?'

'Pour me a large glass, Tilly – and an equally large one for yourself.'

She poured the drinks and handed a glass to Nathan. He took a large gulp and pulled a wry face.

Tilly also took a drink and felt the fire going down her throat to her stomach. She took another, deeper draught this time.

Suddenly, Nathan put the glass down on the table beside his bed and dropped back on his pillow, saying, 'What am I doing in the House of Commons, Tilly? I don't belong there, any more than I belong in London. I've just returned from a sea voyage to Newfoundland. I enjoyed being at sea. I'm at home there. I'm a sailor. A fisherman.'

'You *were*, Sir Nathan. You're a Member of Parliament now. You're going through a bad patch, that's all. You need to have a drink or two and forget about things for a while.'

'You're a good girl, Tilly. A good girl.'

Nathan's hand reached out and rested on her bare arm.

'You keep telling me I'm a good girl and you shouldn't. I don't *want* to be good.' Tilly hesitated, 'But I could be good for you, Sir Nathan . . . if you wanted me to.'

He had been looking up at the ceiling, apparently seeing nothing, but her words got through to him.

With an effort he focused both his eyes upon her. 'That wouldn't be right, Tilly. Not right. No future in it for you.'

'I'm not looking for a future, Sir Nathan. I'm not thinking

beyond tonight, any more than you are really. If you want me, I'm here.'

'I shouldn't, Tilly. It's not fair to you. Not fair at all.'

Even as he was speaking, Nathan's hand was moving up Tilly's arm until it passed beneath the shoulder strap and inside her nightdress. 'I shouldn't . . .'

As his hand moved to her breast, Tilly trembled.

'Wait a minute.'

Slipping from the bed, she cupped a hand over the glass of the lamp and blew it out. In the darkness her nightdress dropped to the floor.

Moments later she was helping his clumsy fingers to unfasten his trousers. When they had followed her nightdress, she slid beneath the bedclothes and pulled his naked body to her.

Chapter 82

When Nathan awoke it was a moment or two before memory parted the curtain of palpitating pain in his head. He turned over quickly in the bed, but there was no one beside him.

For a fleeting second he thought he might have dreamed the events of the night before. Then he saw the impression caused by a head on the pillow next to his. He groaned. The swift movement had increased the hammering his head. But it was not the immediate pain that caused the sound. It was the increasingly clear memories of all that had happened the previous night.

Nathan rose from his bed gingerly and dressed slowly. When he went downstairs he expected to come face-to-face with Tilly at any moment, but reached the breakfast-room without meeting her.

As the maid served his breakfast he querulously asked the whereabouts of the housekeeper.

'She's gone to Billingsgate,' said the maid cheerfully. 'She said to tell you that if you were home for dinner tonight there'd be some nice fresh fish for you.'

As the girl spoke, Nathan watched her for the faintest sign of a knowing smirk. There was nothing.

He ate little of his breakfast and set off early for the House of Commons. Deep in thought, he rounded a corner and almost collided with Tilly, carrying a large basket covered with a white cloth.

Dropping Nathan a curtsey, she said, 'Good morning, Sir Nathan. I hope you're feeling better this morning?'

'Er, yes . . . Thank you, Tilly.' Thoroughly embarrassed, he said, 'Look . . . about last night. I . . . I'm sorry . . .'

'You have nothing to be sorry about. You had a few drinks, that's all – and nobody deserved them more.'

'I'm not talking about that, Tilly.'

'What else was there? You don't have to feel sorry for anything. I don't. I'm very happy to be in your service, Sir Nathan. I did nothing last night that I wouldn't do again – if you wanted. I hope you'll feel the same when you've thought a bit more about it, sir.'

She dropped him another curtsey, and then she was gone. He watched her as she walked towards the house in Orchard Place. She looked happy and carefree and he was forced to accept that she probably meant every word she had said.

By the time another week had gone by, Nathan realised that Tilly was as good as her word. She was neither more nor less pert than she had been before the night she shared his bed. She carried out her work as happily and efficiently as she had before. It was as though nothing had happened between them, although once or twice when their eyes met he was aware that she would be quite happy to share his bed again – on a casual or a permanent basis, if he so wished.

Things were far less satisfactory at Westminster. Rumours were rife that Lord Liverpool intended dissolving Parliament and calling a general election. Consequently, no one seemed to be taking business seriously in the House of Commons.

Nathan also found the intrigues and brokering going on behind the scenes disquieting. It was becoming increasingly apparent to him that personal aggrandisement and family connections were of more importance to men of both Houses of Parliament than was the state of the country.

It was time he went home to Polrudden.

Nathan was listening to a desultory first reading of a bill aimed at imprisoning radical booksellers, when an usher came along the almost empty row of seats behind him.

Leaning over, the parliamentary official whispered, 'There's a gentleman outside asking to speak to you, Sir Nathan. I asked him if it was important and he said it was. To be quite honest with you, sir, I don't like the looks of him. Seems a bit unsavoury. Like a foreign gentleman, 'though I must admit he don't speak very much like one.'

'He sounds intriguing. What's his name?'

'He didn't give no name, sir. He's waiting outside for you.'

When he entered the lobby he saw the man immediately. Gazing out of a window with his back to Nathan, he wore a Portuguese fisherman's hat and coat and heavy boots.

'You wished to speak to me?'

As he spoke, the man turned around – and Nathan gasped in disbelief. 'Francis! I . . . we thought you were dead!'

Francis Hanna grinned. 'Well, as you can see, I'm very much alive, although I came closer to death than any man should and still be alive to tell of it.'

'What of the others? Did any of them survive?'

'All of them. We only landed in London this morning, brought in by a Portuguese vessel. The only person I know in London is the landlord of The Plough so I took the liberty of taking the men and putting them up there. John Gully told me he'd seen you recently and thought you were probably here.'

Suddenly overcome with emotion, Nathan reached out and

embraced the Pentuan fisherman. 'Francis, if you'd put the men up at the most expensive hostelry in London, I would be delighted to meet the bill. Come, let's get out of this place and take a coach to The Plough. On the way you can tell me everything that happened to you. You don't know, of course, that I came to Newfoundland in the *Heron* to look for you . . .'

Francis Hanna's story was one of courage, tenacity and skill. The storm that struck the two Pentuan boats was worse than any experienced before by the *Charlotte*'s owner. It was rendered more terrifying because it came at them from a totally unexpected direction.

In Cornish waters he would have sought shelter long before the storm struck, but the *Charlotte* and the *Heron* were a hundred miles off southern Newfoundland and there was no place to go.

The wind roared in from the north-east, seemingly springing up from nowhere and without warning. It brought with it torrential rain that reduced visibility to no more than a boat's length. Francis knew nothing of the coast of Newfoundland. His fear was that the *Charlotte* would be driven headlong on to a rocky shore and be dashed to pieces.

Francis steered as far south as wind and waves would allow, but not until the second dawn changed the colour of the sky from black to dark grey was he confident they had succeeded in sailing past the southern tip of Newfoundland.

The problem then was to ascertain where they were. That day the rain eased off, although the wind had not decreased to any noticeable extent.

The men on board the *Charlotte* had not slept for two days and nights. During this time eating was out of the question. All the men were too exhausted to function properly. Francis believed he might actually have dropped asleep at the tiller when Charlie shouted that he could see something ahead.

The weary men crowded the bows of the boat and as the coast of the New World became more visible through the rain, were gripped with renewed terror.

The cliffs first spotted by Charlie were not tall by Cornish standards, but between them and the *Charlotte* the sea foamed over a myriad of rocks.

Had the wind not still been so high, Francis would have attempted to bring his boat around and try to sail to safety, but the combination of wind and sea would have overturned the *Charlotte*. The only thing he could do was try to ride over and through the rocks and reach the comparative safety of the beach beyond.

Despite the tremendous odds against him, he almost made it. Steered by Francis, the wind and the strong hand of God, the

Charlotte was no more than twenty feet off the beach when it crashed headlong on a jagged, black rock. It ripped a hole in the boat's hull that two men could comfortably have dived through.

Fortunately, as water poured in, the sea flung the boat on to a shingle beach. Moments later, the men plunged over the side to safety – but when they would have run higher up the shingle, away from the fury of the sea, Francis screamed at them to come back.

The *Charlotte* had carried them to safety – and his life's savings were invested in the boat. He was not going to give it up to the sea without a fight.

With ten strong men and Charlie heaving, pulling and pushing, the boat was eventually run far enough up the beach to be safe from even a storm tide. Not until then did Francis allow his men to vent their relief in a delirium of wild shouting as they pummelled each other on the back in jubilant celebration of their unexpected salvation from the sea.

But they were not safe yet. The cliffs were not the tallest Francis had seen – but there was no way up them. They were trapped at the foot, until Charlie volunteered to make the attempt to climb the near-vertical rock face.

He climbed with a hammer and a cold-chisel tucked in his belt and a rope tied about his waist. When the nimble-footed young boy could find no more foot or hand holds, he made them. Below him, the now silent crew stood holding a sail between them, hoping that should Charlie fall, they might catch him.

He did fall once, but fortunately it was from a height of no more than twenty feet. Yet it was sufficient for everyone to realise that if he fell from farther up the cliff face, he would probably not survive.

But Charlie did not fall again. He reached the top after more than two hours of fiercely determined climbing and was able to make the rope fast around what was, in reality, no more than a bush.

Francis was the first to trust his life to the rope and paled when he reached the cliff edge and saw the frail bulwark that had stood between him and sudden death.

From the cliff top there was no sign of civilisation and before the last men were brought to the top the boat was cleared of provisions and all tools that might double as weapons.

After a debate between them, the men from Pentuan set off northwards.

It was another two days before they stumbled upon a small settlement of Scots men and women who had founded a tiny colony on a more hospitable stretch of coast. These men too were fishermen and had established fish curing houses, of a type the Pentuan men had intended setting up.

Not until now did the Cornishmen learn they had landed on the coast of Nova Scotia, on the mainland of Canada.

The Scots possessed very little material wealth, but they could not have been more hospitable. Now, at last, the men from the *Charlotte* knew they had reached safety.

The story was ended in the bar room of The Plough and John Gully's customers were enthralled with the adventures of the Cornish fishermen.

'How did you get from Nova Scotia to London?' John Gully asked the question to which Nathan had already been given an answer by Francis.

'Ah!' Francis smiled. 'That's a story on its own. The Scotsmen sold their dried fish direct to a Portuguese merchant who came around the fishing communities with his own ship, determined to get the best prices and not be "robbed" by a greedy captain. He would not take us anywhere along the coast to a larger community, where we might have caught a British ship, but he took us direct to Portugal – for a price. It was fortunate I had money with me, taken in case there was anything we needed to buy for our own curing operation.

'We landed in a very small coastal town in Portugal but were lucky enough to find another Portuguese ship that was bringing a cargo to London. We had hoped the captain might put all of us off at Falmouth, but we crept up the Channel in a mist and he wouldn't deviate from his course.'

'What happened to Charlie?' asked John Gully suddenly. 'He didn't come back with you?'

Francis seemed surprised at the question from the landlord, but Nathan explained, 'John knew Charlie. He worked here for a while before he came down to Cornwall.'

'Young Charlie stayed on in Nova Scotia. He liked it there and the people seemed to like him. He's also well on his way to becoming a useful carpenter. His skill will be very useful to them. He sent a message for his young sister to join him there, if she's a mind. Young Charlie has a good head on his shoulders. His intention is to remain with the Scots until he's more skilful, then he intends going to America. It's my opinion that he'll do well, wherever he finds himself. I hope so. We all owe our lives to his keen observation on the boat, and to his courage in climbing the cliff.'

'I always believed that young lad had never been given a chance in life,' said John Gully. 'He deserves all the luck he'll find in the New World. Now, drink up, lads. After your experiences you deserve a celebration. Tonight, you'll pay for nothing in The Plough. All you can drink is on me. We're happy to have you back in England, safe and sound.'

Chapter 83

Nathan entered the house in Orchard Place quietly that night. He particularly did not want to waken Tilly. The lamps were lit in the house and turned down low and on a tray on the hall table he found a letter. He took it into the study to read it.

From a prominent Whig, the letter was to advise him that Parliament had been dissolved that day. Nathan was asked to contact the Whig leader as soon as possible.

Tearing the letter in two, he dropped it in the wastepaper basket beside the desk. He had made up his mind: the House of Commons had seen the last of Sir Nathan Jago.

There was a soft sound from the passage outside the study. Looking up as the door opened, Nathan saw Tilly standing there.

'Hello, Sir Nathan. I heard you come in. Is there anything I can get for you?

Nathan was about to decline her offer, then he suddenly changed his mind. 'Yes, Tilly, you can get a drink for me. A brandy, please – and I think you should have one yourself.'

He saw the sudden expression of anticipation on her face and shook his head. 'No, Tilly. I want to say something to you and I feel it might help if you have a drink.'

Pausing at the drinks cabinet, she said, 'You're getting married! Not to that Lady Sarah?'

'No, not Sarah. I have no intention of marrying Lady Sarah Milton.'

'That's all right then. Who *are* you marrying? Your governess, Dewi Morgan?'

Nathan looked at her in astonishment. 'What made you think I'd be marrying her?'

Tilly shrugged, then set about pouring two drinks. 'You could do a lot worse. She's sweet on you, and I suspect you feel the same way about her.'

As Tilly handed him one of the two half-filled glasses, he said, 'It's not marriage I want to talk to you about. Parliament was dissolved today and I've decided not to stand for re-election.'

Tilly could not hide her dismay. 'Does that mean you'll not be living here any more?'

'That's exactly what it means, Tilly. I intend to return to

Cornwall and build up my fishing interests. That's what I do best. I'm not cut out for politics.'

She sat looking down into her glass for a long time. Suddenly, she raised the brandy to her lips and downed it without a pause. Lowering the glass, she took a deep breath and said, somewhat hoarsely, 'May I have another?'

He nodded. 'I'll leave you with enough housekeeping to last six months – I've paid the rent until then – and I'll pay you until the end of the year. I also want to give you this.'

Pulling a small but heavy bag from his pocket, he passed it across to her. She opened it and then looked up at him sharply. 'It's filled with guineas!'

'You'll find fifty there.' Nathan had obtained them with a bank draft to John Gully. 'I want you to have them.'

'If this is to pay me for what happened that night here, Sir Nathan, you can keep your money! I'm no prostitute.'

'I know, Tilly, and it's nothing to do with that . . . well, not entirely. The money is a present. You're the only one I'll regret leaving when I go from London. Life here would have been unbearable had it not been for you. Nothing I could give you will ever repay my debt to you for that.'

Her eyes suddenly filled with tears. 'That's the nicest thing anyone's ever said to me, Sir Nathan. Can I . . . can I have that other drink now?'

'Of course. Here, I'll pour it for you.' Nathan had seen the size of the drink Tilly had poured for herself. He had a suspicion it was not the first she had drunk that evening.

'Thank you.' She gave Nathan a tearful smile as he handed the drink to her. 'When will you be leaving?'

'Tomorrow, Tilly. I'm going home with some of my men.' He told her about the events of the day and the return of the crew of the *Charlotte*.

She expressed her delight that the men had all been saved, but her thoughts were on his departure from the London house – and from her life.

'It's all so soon! I won't even have time to buy a keepsake for you.'

'You're far too generous, Tilly. I'll be writing a reference for you before I go. I can assure you that if you ever decide to leave your post here, you'll have no difficulty finding work elsewhere. Now, I have a great deal of packing to do if I'm to return to Cornwall tomorrow.'

Tilly drank the last of her brandy and stood up unsteadily. Thoroughly dejected, she said plaintively, 'Can I sleep with you tonight?'

'I don't think that would be a good idea. It will just make my departure more difficult – for both of us.'

'It won't, I promise. I just want to . . . one more time.'

'I'm sorry, Tilly.' Nathan dared not allow her to see that he found the thought of having her one more time tempting. 'I think you'd better go to bed now.'

'Kiss me first.'

She gave him no time to refuse. Before he could reply she had her arms about him and when she became aware of his desire for her she pressed herself to him.

When he pushed her away, as gently as was possible, she said thickly, 'All right, I know. You don't want me. I'm going.'

When the door closed behind her, Nathan breathed a sigh of relief and poured himself another drink. Another night with Tilly and all his plans might have been thrown away. It would have been an exciting prospect to have her as a mistress, available whenever he came to London.

Downing his drink quickly, Nathan extinguished the lamp and made his way upstairs to his bedroom.

He packed hurriedly and had the task completed within the hour. He went to bed but got up again to put the bolt on his door. Half an hour later he heard the handle squeak as someone tried it twice and knew he had been wise to take the precaution.

Tilly was not abroad when Nathan rose early for breakfast the next morning. She appeared, dark-eyed and pale, when the maid brought a Hackney coach to the door to convey Nathan and his luggage to the inn from where he would catch another coach to Portsmouth.

He bade farewell to everyone in his small household staff. When he came to Tilly he tried to give her a farewell kiss, but she turned her face away at the last moment.

Nevertheless, his last memory of the small house in Orchard Place was of her tear-stained face as she watched the coach turn the corner.

The crew of the *Charlotte* were awaiting Nathan, and his arrival was the signal for a rousing cheer. The coach company had put on a special vehicle for the Pentuan men. Those who did not find a seat inside cheerfully clambered to the outside of the vehicle.

They were travelling to Portsmouth where they would catch the steamer bound for Falmouth. However, with eleven passengers heading for Pentuan, the London agent for the steamship company had already agreed the steamer would drop them alongside the half-completed breakwater of the Pentuan harbour.

The evening at The Plough had set the tone for the crew's celebrations. They spent their money freely at the posthouses along the Portsmouth road and had not been on board the Portsmouth steamer for more than ten minutes before it was general knowledge that the steamship was carrying ten men who had

402

miraculously survived a shipwreck in far-off Newfoundland. For the remainder of the voyage not one of them needed to reach in his pocket to pay for a drink.

The arrival of the crew of the *Charlotte* at Pentuan was going to be a joyful occasion, but it would not be a sober one.

Chapter 84

The arrival of a steamship at Pentuan brought the villagers out in force. Not until the large vessel began to edge cautiously towards the wooden breakwater did a woman on the shore recognise her man among the passengers who lined the rail.

She screamed his name hysterically. As others saw their men too, news carried back to the village to be shouted from house to house. Within minutes every man, woman and child was hurrying to the jetty. So contagious was the joy that the men working on the harbour downed tools and hurried to join in the jubilation.

Once on shore, the welcome for the survivors of the *Charlotte* was ecstatic. They were carried shoulder-high to the village, while wives and relatives wept with joy and clung to the hands of their loved ones.

Pippa was one of the last to reach the scene, having been summoned from Polrudden by a breathlessly excited young boy. When she caught sight of Francis, she immediately fell to the ground in a faint. Her husband had to fight his way to her through a crowd of back-slapping well-wishers who had not seen what had occurred.

The celebrations in Pentuan lasted for much of the night. The landlords of all the Pentuan inns served free ale to the returning seamen and their close relatives, and everyone crowded around them to hear the story of their escape from the Newfoundland storm.

While the festivities were underway, Nathan realised that no one had thought of going to Venn Farm to tell Liz of the deliverance of her brother, and he himself had not yet been to Polrudden to see Beville.

Calling at his home, he collected his son and together they went to Venn.

Liz was in the farmhouse kitchen, helping Nell to bake bread. Her hair was untidy and her face red from the heat of the fire, but she looked as though she was thoroughly enjoying herself.

After greeting his heavily pregnant sister, Nathan said to the young girl, 'Liz, I have some news of Charlie for you. Some very good news.'

'He's alive? He's home?'

404

'He's certainly alive, Liz, as are the rest of the *Charlotte*'s crew, but he didn't come home with them, probably because he wanted to stay well clear of the Bow Street runners. He's in a little village in Nova Scotia and looks set fair to becoming the village carpenter from what I hear.'

Nova Scotia was as remote as the moon to Liz, but the news that her brother was alive split her red face in a wide grin that just would not go away.

'He sent a message to you with the other men. If you want to join him in Nova Scotia, he'll make a home for you there. If not, he'll know you're happy here and promises to return to see you sometime, when the runners are no longer looking for him.'

Glancing shyly at Nell, Liz said, 'I'm *very* happy here. Happier than I've ever been. But I don't know if Nell will want me here all the time. She's got her own family around her.'

Nathan noticed that Liz had already begun to lose her cockney accent.

'*Want* you? I don't know what I'd have done without you these last few weeks. What with Pippa getting heavy with her baby, and me not being so well. If you want to stay at Venn, Tom, me and the children will be overjoyed.'

Turning away from the beaming young girl, Nell said, 'She's been an absolute wonder, Nathan. She helps me cook, takes care of the children, cleans about the house – not to mention helping Tom with the milking and feeding the animals. She's a little marvel. We were saying only last night that if she stays we're going to have to give her a wage. She certainly earns one.'

Liz's scarlet cheeks no longer owed their high colour entirely to the heat from the fire. 'I don't want no money for doing what I enjoy . . . but I *would* like to stay on here.'

'Then that's settled,' declared Nell. 'Now, our Nathan, tell Liz and me all about the crew of the *Charlotte* and how they were rescued.'

Sir Kenwyn Penhaligan came to see Nathan when he had been home at Polrudden for ten days. Shown into the study where Nathan was working on the figures from the *Heron*'s voyages, the baronet greeted Nathan cheerfully.

'Good morning. I did not expect to see you involved in desk work. I thought you'd be out and about at Tregony, ensuring you still had the support that is going to ensure your return to Parliament at the election. Not that you should have any problem!'

Laying his quill carefully on the pen-stand in front of him, Nathan looked directly at the other man. 'I don't intend standing for Parliament again, Sir Kenwyn.'

The baronet sat upright in his chair. 'What nonsense is this? You must stand? You owe it to your friends – and to your son.'

'I think I can do far more for him by being around as he grows up than if I am miles away, in London.'

'That's for now. I'm talking of laying a foundation for future generations. Why, you have everything on your side. The right friends in London. Money. Make the right marriage and one day you could become Prime Minister.'

'I presume that by the "right" marriage, you mean I should marry Lady Sarah Milton?'

'You could do far worse. Her father is dead now, of course, but the new Earl is Lady Sarah's uncle. Until he assumed the title he was a sitting member of the Commons. He too is a leading Whig. All of which will stand you in very good stead.'

'None of that is for me, Sir Kenwyn. I didn't enjoy the Commons, and I don't care for London.'

'Good God, man! No one says you have to *enjoy* any of it – although you'll have far more of a social life when you take up office. You're a young man, it's a wonderful challenge – and you'll do damn' well, I know you will.'

'I'm sorry, Sir Kenwyn, but I've made up my mind. A political career is not for me. I enjoy life here at Polrudden far too much.'

Sir Kenwyn looked aggrieved. 'I feel very strongly that you've let me down, Nathan. I set great store on your continuing at Westminster. Bringing honour to Cornwall and those of us who have supported you.'

'I'm sorry you feel that way, Sir Kenwyn, but my life is here at Polrudden. And I valued your friendship far more before politics were involved.'

Sir Kenwyn was not mollified. 'You know, I really believed that together we had the chance to do something really important. I am devastated by your decision.'

'You can still do something important, Sir Kenwyn. You are a man with very many friends and a grasp of politics such as I would never have. Why don't *you* stand for Tregony at the election?'

'*Me*?' It was evident that the idea had not even crossed the baronet's mind. 'But . . . I couldn't spend my life travelling back and forth to London. I'm not as young as you.'

'Nonsense, Sir Kenwyn. You'll still be a young man in the political world, and you're a very fit one too. You would enjoy London – and Cornwall couldn't be in safer hands!'

'Much of what you say is perfectly true. I *am* fit. I hunt, and can keep up with any man there. But London . . . as a Member of Parliament . . . I don't know. I have so many duties here.'

'But your first duty should be to your country, Sir Kenwyn. You've just been trying to convince me that it's so. My London

406

friends are your friends and one day it could be *you* who leads the country. Think about it seriously, Sir Kenwyn. When you've made up your mind I can offer you the tenancy of a charming London house. I guarantee you'll be made comfortable there.'

Chapter 85

The winter of 1818 was a severe one and the bad weather lasted into the early months of 1819. At Venn Farm, Nell alarmed everyone by becoming very ill. She had severe stomach pains, lost weight alarmingly, and seemed to lose interest in everything about her.

Nathan rode through the snow to Bodmin and persuaded a renowned surgeon to accompany him to the farm, but after examining Nell, the surgeon declared there was little he could do. The unborn baby was dead. For the rest, he declared he was prepared to operate to remove the dead child, but the chances of Nell surviving were very slim. The only answer was to hope that nature would take over and provide the answer.

Nathan was not prepared to await the vagaries of nature. He rode to Bodmin Moor, where the snow was thicker than anywhere else in the county, and spoke to a woman whose reputation as a midwife was almost equal to her notoriety as an abortionist.

For an exorbitant fee she agreed to travel to Venn Farm on her ageing and evil-tempered mule, escorted by Nathan.

It was a difficult journey. The mule was smaller than Nathan's mount and so travelled in the path made by the larger animal. Unfortunately, whenever the old woman absent-mindedly forgot to hold the mule in check, it stretched forward and gave Nathan's horse a painful bite.

However, the journey was well worthwhile. Told of the surgeon's prognosis before she examined Nell, the old woman made a disdainful noise that matched the irascibility of her mule.

'This isn't the first of his patients I've had to deal with,' she declared scornfully. ' "Surgeon," he calls himself. I can't for the life of me think what it is he "surgeons". It's certainly not pregnant women. I don't know of one he's cured. Certainly not one in your sister's condition.'

'Can you do anything to help her?' Tom asked anxiously. 'Get her well and you'll have first place in my prayers every night.'

'If I can't help her, I've had a long ride for nothing, and you've wasted a lot of money.' Pursing her mouth, the old woman said, 'I'll get her back on her feet, but if you look on your wife as nothing more than a brood mare you'll be disappointed. She'll have no more children. You'll need to pray at night *instead* of doing anything else, not as well as.'

'I don't care about that,' said Tom, desperately. 'Just get her well, I beg you.'

'I'll need some help,' said the old woman. 'Do you employ a girl about the place?'

'There's Liz,' replied Tom. 'She was in the kitchen when you came in.'

'She's a bit young for the work that needs to be done,' said the woman. 'But she'll do as long as she does as she's told. Send her in and you men go off somewhere. If there's an inn nearby, go and spend an hour or two there.'

'I'd rather stay here,' said Tom. 'So I can be near if I'm needed.'

'You won't be needed. I want you out of the house – and take the children with you. I don't want your wife's screaming alarming them. There's nothing worse than a houseful of crying brats.'

On the way to Polrudden with the children, Tom said anxiously, 'Do you think we're doing the right thing, Nathan? All that talk of Nell screaming . . . I'm frightened.'

Nathan was walking beside the horse which carried the older children. Tom, with the youngest in his arms, tramped through the snow beside them. Putting an arm about his shoulders, Nathan said comfortingly, 'She'll be all right, Tom. I'm sure of it. Besides, we really had no alternative. She'd have died if we'd left her and done nothing. You know that.'

'Yes.' Tom walked on in silence for a while. Then he said, 'I wish Dewi was still here, Nathan. I'd have felt a lot happier had we left her back in the house to help with Nell.'

Nathan said nothing. He too had been thinking a great deal of Dewi in recent weeks. One thing was certain, Polrudden had lost much of its warmth on the day she walked out.

The old woman from Bodmin Moor succeeded where the surgeon had failed. Liz came to Polrudden to tell Nathan and Tom when they could return. The young London girl had a pallor that almost matched the snow she had walked through on the way from Venn and refused to say anything about what had happened.

But Nell survived and, after a further worrying week, became stronger with every day that passed.

When the weather broke, Nathan set his men to work preparing the boats for the forthcoming season. He would be sending two boats to Newfoundland with the *Heron* this time.

Pippa had given birth to a baby son and Francis was overjoyed, but it did not prevent him from asking Nathan to be allowed to return to Newfoundland. He wanted to take extra crewmen and a boatbuilder from Portmellon. Francis intended repairing the

Charlotte on the rocky beach where the boat had gone aground, and recovering her.

It would be a dangerous undertaking. Nathan agreed only after Francis promised he would endanger neither men nor boats in his determination to recover the boat that had once belonged to his grandfather.

The Newfoundland venture was only a part of Nathan's plan for expanding his fishing interests. He intended sending his boats into the southern Irish Sea, believing there was a rich harvest of fish to be reaped here.

After the harsh winter, spring came early to Cornwall and Nathan decided to sail with his boat, the *Marquise*, to explore the prospects of the hundred-mile-square fishing ground, bounded by the coastlines of Ireland, Wales and Cornwall, with the waters of the Atlantic Ocean on the fourth side.

Nathan had been home at Polrudden all winter and Beville had grown accustomed to his company. When Nathan told his son he was going fishing for perhaps two or three weeks, Beville begged to be allowed to go with him.

Nathan's first reaction was to give his son a categorical no. A working fishing-boat at sea was no place for a seven-year-old boy. But when he thought more about it, he realised there was a great deal to recommend the suggestion. Nathan had been familiar with the sea and fishing by the time he was Beville's age – and his son would one day inherit the fishing business. The sooner he learned about it, the better.

There were also problems about having someone to look after Beville at Polrudden if he were left behind. Pippa had her baby and Nell was not yet well enough to take care of her own children. She could not take Beville on. Liz would have accepted the responsibility eagerly, but she was still no more than a child herself. It would be unfair to add to her burden at Venn Farm.

There was no particular servant at Polrudden who had taken charge of Beville since Pippa left. If Nathan had to go away for the day, he was looked after by whoever happened to be available.

It was not a satisfactory arrangement, but there was no one in the village capable of taking on the task of governess, and the severe weather had prevented Nathan from looking farther afield. Besides, there was always the hope at the back of his mind that Dewi would one day return. The hope receded with every day that passed, but it never disappeared altogether.

'Please, Father. Can't I come with you? I promise I won't get in the way – and I'll be sensible.'

The eagerness on Beville's face clinched the matter.

'All right. You can come. But it means an early night tonight. We will be leaving first thing tomorrow morning.'

The warmth of the hug Nathan received from his son dispersed the last lingering doubts in his mind. It was going to be a good trip. He felt it deep in his bones.

Chapter 86

The nights had not entirely shaken off the bite of winter and as Nathan and Beville set off, hand-in-hand in the early morning, Nathan felt his son shiver.

'Never mind,' he sympathised. 'You'll be warm by the time we've walked to Portgiskey.'

'Will I be able to help when you're fishing?'

'I doubt it. At least, not at first. You and I are mere passengers on this trip. Ahab Arthur is the captain. You and I will have to do as we're told.'

Beville pouted. 'Ahab won't let me help. He's too strict.'

'He's a good fisherman, Beville. You watch him carefully and you'll learn how things *should* be done.'

Ahab Arthur and one other fisherman were the only members of Nathan's regular crews accompanying him on this trip. Most of the others were preparing to sail to Newfoundland. Nathan was coming to see for himself what might be caught in this particular area.

It took the *Marquise* twenty-four hours to reach the fishing grounds, by which time Ahab Arthur swore Beville had asked the name and purpose of every single item on board the fishing-boat.

'That's good,' said Nathan. 'Part of the reason for bringing him along was so he could get to know all about fishing and the boats that do the work.'

'That's all very well,' grumbled the fisherman, good-naturedly. 'Trouble is, any more questions and I'm liable to run out of answers. He's bright, that boy. You can't fob him off with a vague answer because he'll come right back at you with another question.'

'Perhaps I should have taken him to Parliament,' commented Nathan. 'He might have been able to teach *them* something.'

'You're not regretting that you didn't put up for Tregony again this time?'

'No, Ahab. I don't belong up there. I'm happier here. One day perhaps Beville might decide that's where his future lies, but I'd like him to see something of this sort of life first. The country might be run from Westminster, but one thing I learned there was that very few of them know – or care – how the rest of the people

412

in the land earn a living. Without that knowledge, I can't see how they can govern efficiently for very much longer. They've been bumbling on for years, but the country's changing. People expect more from life than a wage that keeps them from starving or dying of cold, and no more.'

'I don't know nothing about that, Nathan. That's politics. I've always been happy left to get on with my job, doing what I know best – talking of which, it's time we began shooting our nets if we hope to make a profit from this trip.'

The *Marquise* fished for only twenty-four hours, during which an impressive catch was brought on board, but the weather had begun to turn against them.

During the night the fishing-boat began to rise and fall more noticeably. In the morning, as the nets were being hauled on board, Ahab Arthur looked at the mackerel-patterned sky, painted ominously red by the early morning sun.

'There's a storm coming in from the west, Nathan. I'm not familiar with these waters, so I don't know how hard it will hit us, but if I was fishing off Mevagissey I'd head home. We certainly won't be able to put the nets out again for a day or two.'

'What do you suggest?'

'We've been drifting towards the Welsh coast during the night. I think we should either head for a Welsh port, or go for the British Channel and put land between us and the storm.'

'We'll head for the Bristol Channel. How long before we reach shelter?'

'With the wind increasing from the direction it is, probably no more than six hours. Perhaps less.'

'Fine. Let's take the nets in as quickly as possible and we'll get under way.'

By the time the Welsh coast was on the port side of the *Marquise*, the wind had strengthened considerably. Behind the boat heavy black cloud now filled a third of the sky, billowing up from the horizon.

'We've beaten it,' commented Ahab Arthur, 'and it's as well, I'd say. This storm's going to be a beauty when it arrives. Do you want me to make for the nearest Welsh port?'

'No,' said Nathan, unexpectedly. 'Stay close to the Welsh coast, but keep going until we reach the Bristol Channel.'

Something in his voice brought a frown to the face of the old fisherman, but Nathan said nothing more and Ahab did not question him.

It was three hours more before a belt of rain could be seen lowering over the Welsh mountains. The *Marquise* was in the Bristol Channel now and passing a large seaport.

'That must be Cardiff,' said Ahab. Looking towards the slowly advancing rain, he added, 'Would you like me to head in there?'

'Keep going, Ahab. About ten miles farther on there's a river entrance with a town just upriver a little way. You can turn in there. We've the tide behind us and a fair wind on the quarter, it shouldn't take too long. We might even beat the rain.'

Enlightenment came suddenly to Ahab and his grin was wide enough to show the gaps in his mouth which had once held teeth. 'I've never been to this place where we're heading, but it sounds to me as though it might be Newport.'

'That's right, Ahab. I'm sure we'll find somewhere safe to tie up there.'

'I don't doubt it.'

Ahab shifted the tiller to give a wide berth to a collier, tacking to make Cardiff. For some moments he pursed his lips as though he was about to whistle. Instead he said suddenly, 'Isn't Newport where Dewi came from?'

'Now you mention it, Ahab, I believe it is.'

'That wouldn't be the reason we're making for there when we've passed up a half-dozen places where we could have sheltered just as well?'

'What would you say if I agreed it was?'

The grin returned, this time wider than ever. 'I'd say that it makes a sight more sense than going up to London and getting involved with the likes of them up there. Dewi was right for Polrudden, I knew it. Everyone who ever met the two of you knew it – and the house knows it too. I've heard some of the women who work for you up there say that a lot of the heart went out of Polrudden the day Dewi left to go back to Wales.'

'I wouldn't argue with you, Ahab.'

'What you going to do if you find her? Bring her back to Polrudden with us?'

'Not if, but *when*, I find her, Ahab. As to what I'm going to do . . . that will depend very much on her. It's been nigh on eight months since she left. A lot could have happened in that time. She might have found someone else.'

Finding out where Dewi lived was not easy. Nathan tried first to find Captain Morgan, her uncle. He had thought the owner of the captain's ship had an office in Newport. He made enquiries, only to learn that when Captain Morgan took over from the owner, he promptly moved the office to Cardiff.

But at least Nathan had a name now. The company being managed by Captain Morgan was the Llewellyn Coastal Company.

Hiring a horse, he rode to Cardiff. It was not a good journey. The horse had not been ridden for some time. Each lightning flash and rumble of thunder set it dancing and throwing its head about.

Cardiff was larger than Nathan had realised. He wasted half a day searching for the shipping company before he was given the information that it no longer existed. The owner had died within a few weeks of handing the reins to Captain Morgan.

Upon the old man's death it was discovered he had been deeply in debt for some time. His estate's only asset was the shipping company. It was sold, piecemeal, to pay what he owed. Captain Morgan had purchased his old ship and was now sailing to and from Europe, picking up cargoes as and when he could.

No one knew where the captain or his ship were at this time – or if he was ever likely to return to this part of the country.

Frustrated, cold and wet, Nathan returned to Newport. But he was not yet defeated. This was Captain Morgan's home town and by the seaman's very nature he would have been a well-known character.

After returning his still-fractious horse to the stable, and before walking back to the *Marquise*, Nathan made his way to the coal wharf. The cargo most often brought to Pentuan by the sea captain had been coal. Someone here might know something about him.

Nathan struck lucky on board the third ship on which he made enquiries. The mate had served with Captain Morgan, sailing with him to Pentuan on more than one occasion. He also knew Dewi.

'It's her I particularly want to speak to,' said Nathan eagerly. 'You don't happen to know where she's living?'

'What do you want her for?' asked the Welsh mate, suspicious of Nathan's eagerness.

'She used to be my young boy's governess,' he replied, concerned that this man might refuse to disclose the information if he believed Dewi did not want to see him. 'I've brought my son with me on a fishing trip and we've had to put into Newport because of the weather. I thought that as we're here it would be wonderful for them to meet again. My son was very fond of Dewi. Indeed, we all were at Polrudden.'

'Yes, she's a fine girl,' agreed the mate. 'And I heard she'd been a governess over at Pentuan. She lives up at Maespool village, about ten or so miles from here.'

'I'm very grateful to you,' said a delighted Nathan. 'I'll hire a horse and gig and we'll go to see her tomorrow.'

'Happy to be able to help you,' said the mate. 'I owe her uncle everything I know today. A fine seaman, that man. Wasted on land, he was. Best thing that ever happened was when he was made to go back to sea again. He might not think so, mind, but it's true.'

The mate saw Nathan as far as the gangway leading from his ship. It was still raining just as hard as it had been on the ride to Cardiff, although it seemed to Nathan the wind might have dropped a little. He pulled the high collar of his waterproof up around his face before stepping to the gangway.

He had reached the quay before the mate called to him again.

'Give my regards to Dewi when you see her. My congratulations and best wishes too. Last I heard, she was to be married. Tell her I wish her every happiness in her married life.'

Chapter 87

Dewi stood at the stern of Captain Morgan's ship, the *Miriella*, as it left Pentuan. She was waiting for the vessel to sail clear of the cliffs so she might get a last look at Polrudden, the house where she had spent the past eighteen months.

It would only add to her torture, but she had to see the house where she had spent the happiest period of her life just once more.

Polrudden came into view sooner than she had expected and tears stung her eyes at the knowledge that she would never see it again. She saw the ancient house with its windows overlooking the sea. *Her* window, where she would watch the fishing boats setting off hopefully from Nathan's fish-cellar at Portgiskey. It was the same view she had seen on her first day at Polrudden, when she was seated facing Nathan across his desk, looking out at the sea through the window behind him.

She had observed the sea in its every mood. Churned to foam in its anger; grey and sullen like the mist that rolled in frequently to the land; silver and blue and alive on the rare summer days that were like no others she had known anywhere.

She would see such days no more. She was leaving them behind, together with the friends she had made and the two people she loved more than anyone else in the world. Nathan and Beville. *Sir* Nathan and *Sir* Beville. She must never forget they both had titles. It was the reason she was leaving Polrudden. Sacrificing her future so she would never be an obstacle to theirs.

Suddenly, as she looked back, a small figure ran from the front door of the house, across the lawn, and paused, as though looking up the driveway towards the lane. It was Beville.

As she watched he changed direction and went towards the back of the house, where the stables were situated. He moved slowly, as though looking for something. For someone. Perhaps he was looking for her!

The thought that he would not find her, would *never* find her, was more than Dewi could take. Blinded by her tears she ran from the deck, past her uncle and past the helmsmen to the hatchway that led down to her cabin.

Both men exchanged glances and Captain Morgan said gruffly,

'Upset she is, see. Been working as a governess at Polrudden for a long time. Grew very attached to the young lad up there, Sir Beville Jago. Now she's going home to Maespool to look after her aunt. A good girl is our Dewi.'

Bringing the conversation to an end, the ship's captain said, 'Bring her round to starboard now, Hugh, and keep her head sou'-sou'-west until we're well clear of Chapel Point. We've a fair wind with us so, with luck, we'll all be eating at home tomorrow night.'

Wandering apparently aimlessly to the hatchway where Dewi had gone below, Captain Morgan looked down. The door to her cabin was closed. He had seen how distressed she was when she fled from the upper deck. He would have a good talk with her before they docked at Newport.

What he had told the helmsman had been the truth – as far as it went. Dewi *was* returning to Maespool to take care of her Aunt Phoebe. What he wanted to know was, what had precipitated the decision?

It was dark when Captain Morgan knocked on Dewi's cabin door. 'Dewi? Dewi, girl? The steward says you don't want anything to eat. Is something wrong with you?'

'I'm just not hungry.'

Her voice sounded faint and muffled against the creaking of the ship's timbers and the slap of water against the hull.

'I'd like to have a few words with you, girl. If you don't want me to come in your cabin then you'll find me up on deck. You'd better put a coat on, there's a cool wind up there.'

Captain Morgan was considerate enough to realise that Dewi had probably been crying. She would not want him to see her with puffy and reddened eyes.

Waiting on the deck for his niece, Captain Morgan wondered what could have gone wrong at Polrudden. Dewi had been happy there, he was certain of that. He was equally sure that Sir Nathan Jago was pleased with her and her work. Perhaps there was some-one else. One of the men in the village. He hoped things had not gone too far . . .

One thing he was quite certain of: she was not returning to Maespool purely out of concern for her Aunt Phoebe. She couldn't wait to leave Wales when he had told her of the offer of work at Polrudden.

Dewi kept her uncle waiting for almost half-an-hour before he saw her slight figure emerge from the hatchway.

'Here I am, girl,' he called as he saw her hesitate. When she drew close, he said, 'We'll go for'ard. We won't be overheard there.'

A small cluster of men were standing about the helmsman,

chatting and laughing, the red glow of their pipes visible in the darkness.

'You warm enough?' There was no moon yet, but in the faint glow of the stars he could see she had not taken notice of his suggestion that she should put a coat on, but she did have a shawl thrown about her shoulders.

'Yes, thank you.'

There seemed no life in her reply. It was more of a mechanical response.

'You know why I've asked you to come up here?'

'I can guess.'

Dewi made it no easier for him, and Captain Morgan was more used to dealing with bluff, cursing seamen than with young girls.

'I was very surprised when you came on board and said you wanted to go back to Maespool. I thought you were very happy at Polrudden.'

'I was.'

Once again she gave only a brief reply to his question. Making him do all the work.

'Come now, Dewi. This doesn't make any sense at all. If you were so happy at Polrudden, then why have you left – and in such a hurry? Don't tell me it's because your Aunt Phoebe isn't too well. That might answer others, but not me. I know you couldn't wait to get away from her.'

Dewi was silent for so long that Captain Morgan thought she was not going to reply, but he could almost feel the unhappiness that emanated from her.

'I thought you looked on me as your favourite uncle, Dewi? You can tell me, surely?'

'I was happy there, yes, and I didn't want to leave. I just thought it was best . . . for everyone.'

'Why, what happened? Sir Nathan didn't try anything on with you, did he?'

'No, and perhaps that's more the pity. Had he done so, I might not have been so ready to leave.'

'That's enough of such talk, Dewi. You've had a good decent Wesleyan upbringing. I won't have you speaking that way. I think you'd better tell me what's been going on up at Sir Nathan's house.'

'Nothing's been "going on". Not in that way. It was just . . . well, Nathan Jago said he wanted to marry me.'

'Good God! *Marry* you, girl? That would have made you a *Lady*. Lady Dewi Jago. Don't tell me you refused him?'

'No, I didn't do that. In fact I wanted to marry Nathan Jago more than anything in the world – and I couldn't care whether he was a "Sir", a "Prince", or just "Mr Jago".'

'Well . . . I'm sorry, Dewi, I don't understand. If you both felt

419

that way, then why didn't you stay there and marry him?'

'One of his friends spoke to me about it. Sir Kenwyn Penhaligan. He told me that if I married Nathan, I'd prevent him from taking high office in government, being given high honours – I'd be robbing young Beville of his birthright.'

'He had no right to say such a thing to you. Nobody has.'

'He had every right, Uncle, and it's quite true. If Nathan married me, his son's governess, he'd be scorned by all the lords and ladies who are clamouring around him now because they see him as a man who could one day become Prime Minister of England – but only if he marries the right woman.'

'I'm sure that can't be true, girl. He's the one that matters, not the girl he marries.'

'It's perfectly true, Uncle. I saw it for myself. I went to London last week to see Nathan . . .'

Hearing Captain Morgan's sudden intake of breath, signifying disapproval, Dewi explained, 'I went there to tell him the *Charlotte* had been lost off Newfoundland. It was urgent because the *Heron* is due to sail on Friday. I thought Nathan might want to send her back to Newfoundland or something. It obviously isn't as important as I thought, because he hasn't even troubled to answer my letter. Anyway, that isn't what I was saying. I was telling you what I saw when I went to London.

'Nathan was at a week-end party at the home of the Earl of Wavendon. It was a huge place with lots of expensively dressed men and women. Most of them with titles, I suspect. It was very soon made clear to me that I just didn't belong among them. I knew it and so did they.'

'What was Nathan doing while all this was going on, I'd like to ask?' Captain Morgan was angry. 'What sort of man would let them pick on you like that?'

'Nathan didn't know it was happening. He was off with the Earl and some of the others. On the river, I think Lady Sarah said. But all that doesn't matter. It was clear to me that *she* was the sort of woman he would need to marry. I don't like her one little bit and I hope he finds someone else instead of her, but it needs to be someone *like* her. It would destroy Nathan's career if he were to marry me. I couldn't do that to him, or take away Beville's chance of inheriting a peerage when he's older.'

'It's all a lot of nonsense if you ask me, girl. Sir Nathan Jago has all the money he's likely to need – and there'll be plenty left over for his son to inherit. I'd say that all he needs to make his life complete is a good, loving wife. You'd be that, I've no doubt.'

'Oh, yes, I'd certainly be that, but it's all in the what might have been now. Aunt Phoebe would be the first to say you need to make sacrifices if you're to secure a place in heaven. So I suppose that by going back to Maespool to look after her, I'm making an investment in the hereafter.'

Chapter 88

Aunt Phoebe Morgan was immediately suspicious of Dewi's motives in returning to Maespool. Far from suggesting that she was investing in the hereafter, she seemed to think it more likely that Dewi was atoning for sins committed in the immediate past.

She arrived after dark at the small cottage in the mining village where Aunt Phoebe lived and found great difficulty in waking her. Not until a neighbour provided a ladder and climbed to her ageing aunt's bedroom window and knocked several times was it possible to rouse her.

'Oh, it's you,' was her greeting to Dewi when she eventually made her way downstairs and opened the door to her niece. 'What do you think you're doing, getting me up out of bed and waking all the neighbours at this time of night, girl? Wanting the whole village to be talking about you, is that it? All round the village it will be, tomorrow. I can hear them now. "Have you heard Dewi Morgan's come back? Arrived in the dead of night, thinking no one would see her. Woke her poor old aunt she did." Aye, and half the village too, I've no doubt. You ought to be ashamed of yourself, girl.'

As the time was not yet nine o'clock and only the immediate neighbours had been disturbed, Dewi did not allow herself to be too ashamed of herself.

However, the reception she received made her heart sink. Her aunt had not changed from the cold, narrow-minded woman Dewi had been hoping she had maligned in memory.

Closing the door behind Dewi, her aunt removed a piece of lighted candle from the small recess in the hall wall where an accumulation of wax served as a candle holder.

Carrying the candle shakily to an ancient and smoky lamp in the kitchen, the old woman lit the wick before turning her gaze upon her niece. Significantly, she stared at Dewi's midriff. 'Well, why are you back here? Are you in trouble?'

'No, Auntie, I'm not in trouble. I heard from my uncle that you haven't been too well. I thought you might like me to come home and take care of you.'

'Why should you think such a thing? Did it stop you from going away and leaving me when it suited you? I'm no worse now than

422

I was then. I had a little chest trouble through the winter, and my arthritis bothers me more than it did, but I have a girl who comes in most days from the village. I get by.'

The old woman glared at Dewi suspiciously. 'What did he tell you? Did he lead you to believe I was dying? Have you come home in the hope that you'll inherit this house? Is that it?'

'I don't want your house, Auntie. I have enough money to find myself a little place somewhere and live quietly if you really don't want me here.'

Dewi found the encounter with her aunt overwhelmingly depressing. There was the same coldness, suspicion and narrow-mindedness as before. Returning to Maespool had been a mistake.

'Seeing that you're here, you'd better stay. We'll talk about it in the morning. You don't need me to show you to your room. The bed's made up in there. Don't stay down here too long burning oil and candles. I haven't got money to burn.'

With this parting shot, Dewi's aunt limped from the room, leaving her feeling depressed and close to tears. This was even worse than she had imagined it would be – not that she had ever dreamed of returning here. Not until a few days ago, anyway.

Her aunt had not mellowed in any way during Dewi's absence. Nevertheless, despite her assurance that she was all right, Dewi could see that she walked with considerable difficulty and had observed her fingers when she was lighting the lamp. They were crippled with arthritis. She would have great difficulty in taking care of herself.

When Dewi went to bed soon afterwards she found the bed damp, but there was nothing she could do about it. The kitchen fire was out downstairs, so she could not even put hot coals in the copper bed-warmer that hung on the wall beside the fireplace. She would have to get into the bed exactly as it was.

After she had undressed and blown out the stub of candle she had brought with her from downstairs, Dewi drew back the curtains at the tiny bedroom window.

It had rained since she reached the village and the yellow lights from the windows of the terraced houses on either side of the narrow street were reflected on the wet cobblestone road. It was the type of weather the miners' wives liked best. It prevented coal dust blowing from the giant waste heaps down the hill and into the small houses. It also dampened down the smell of the dust that hung on the air and invaded the nostrils.

Suddenly, deep depression overcame Dewi. She had been trying very hard not to allow it to take her over, but now she could do nothing to prevent it. Climbing into the damp bed, she turned her face into the pillow and wept, as she had often wept into it in years gone by.

* * *

It did not take Dewi long to slip back into the old, soul-destroying routine of earlier days. She rose in the morning and lit the fire. Cooked breakfast for her aunt and scrubbed the stone doorstep before cleaning the house.

Cleaning the step was the opportunity for gossiping with the neighbours. All along the narrow street women were doing the same thing and calling one to the other in their sing-song voices.

'Have you heard? Mrs Roughley around the corner is having *another*? Her thirteenth this one will be. Her thirteenth, and her with only two bedrooms and a drunken husband!'

'Fancy! Well, at least she's *got* a husband. Have you seen young Lily Williams lately? Puppy fat, her mother says – but it's no puppy she's got there, I'm telling you. Well, what can you expect? Two months married her mother was, when Lily was born. I don't know who she's going to snare for this one, but it's not going to be my David, I can tell you that . . .'

Dewi listened to their gossip as she scrubbed. She was not yet included in their conversations. She had not been born in the village so had never fully been accepted by them when she lived here before. Now they would never forgive her for going away and seeing something of the outside world while they had travelled no more than a mile or two from their daily-scrubbed doorsteps.

They would talk among themselves, ignoring her, while they peeped from behind curtains, trying to ascertain whether or not she was in the condition her aunt had expected her to be. When they discovered for certain she was not then they would gradually – very gradually – include her in their conversation. Probing to learn what she had done while she was away from the village. What she had seen. And, most important of all, what had brought her back.

In the meantime, Dewi accepted the old routine, as before. On Mondays she did the washing, on Tuesdays the ironing. Twice a week she did the shopping and twice a week the gardening. Saturdays was the day for cleaning windows and, perhaps once a year, she might venture into Newport.

On Sunday, morning and evening, she took her aunt to chapel. The slow walk had been a ritual for as long as Dewi could remember.

It took longer now, but it followed the old pattern. Her aunt walked with one arm tucked inside Dewi's, the other hand clutching a walking stick, its handle as gnarled and misshapen as the hand that held it.

Along the way, neighbours would overtake them, saying a hello to Aunt Phoebe and nodding solemnly to Dewi. Inside the chapel it even smelled exactly as she remembered. It was the overpowering smell of cheap soap used daily by the miners, and by their families too, for the Saturday evening scrub-down in the bath in front of the kitchen fire.

The only thing that had changed was the preacher. When Dewi left Maespool, the Methodist minister had been an ancient ex-miner with white hair and a face engrained with coal dust like a pencilled design. He had preached of Hellfire and retribution. Of inherent sin and atonement. Evil, the ever-present enemy, and of the never-ending fight in defence of salvation.

The new preacher was an entirely different sort of minister. Educated and well read, he interpreted the story of the bible in a quiet and gentle manner. Spoke of the life to come with hope and optimism. Told of a God who possessed both understanding and compassion.

There were many in the congregation who were disdainful of the new preacher's teaching. Who longed for the Sundays when they would walk home from chapel quaking in their shoes – those who possessed such footwear – fearing they were already beyond redemption.

Aunt Phoebe was one of these. When the young Methodist preacher had bade them farewell at the doorway, pausing over Dewi's hand to ask her whence she had come and where she was staying, she expressed her thoughts in her own inimitable manner.

'He doesn't preach like Minister David. You knew exactly where you stood with him. Obey the Commandments of the Lord and you'll end up in Heaven. Disobey them and Hell's door stands open for you. This one's too full of ifs and buts and "Never mind, the Lord will forgive you". He'll never teach them the difference between right and wrong, not the way he preaches.'

'Well, you must tell him so,' declared Dewi somewhat maliciously. 'He said he was pleased to see me at the service, and asked where I was from, and what I was doing in Maespool. When I told him, he said he'd come calling on us this week. I'll tell him how you feel about his preaching. Perhaps he'll discuss it with you.'

Chapter 89

The Reverend Mervyn Craddock paid a call on Dewi and Aunt Phoebe the day after they had attended his service together in the Maespool chapel.

Despite her criticisms of his ministry, Aunt Phoebe fussed around the minister as though he were royalty when Dewi opened the door to him.

No one had entered the 'front room' since long before Dewi had left Maespool to go to Polrudden, but today the door was opened. When the young minister had been shown in, the curtains were opened wide to announce to the neighbours that a guest worthy of the honour was present in the house.

Aunt Phoebe sat on one uncomfortable chair and the minister on another, while Dewi shuttled between the kitchen and the front room. Soon tea, freshly baked scones and a variety of preserves retrieved from dark recesses of the larder were exhibited on the starched linen table cloth, brought out from a bedroom drawer for the occasion.

'It's nice to welcome you to my house, Reverend Craddock. Especially as my niece, Dewi, has only just returned to the village after working in Cornwall for Sir Nathan Jago. She was governess to his son, you know. Young Sir Beville. A baronet in his own right, I believe. Is that not so, Dewi?'

She nodded, more occupied with the logistics of the Reverend Mervyn Craddock's visit. She had put out all the scones they had in the larder. If he ate more than two they were in trouble – and he looked the sort of preacher who just might.

'That must have been very interesting, Dewi – you don't mind if I call you that? Your aunt has been such a regular at my chapel that I feel I know you too. What does this Sir Nathan do?'

'He's a Member of Parliament,' she said. She would have added more, but mentioning Nathan's name was enough to open wounds that were still far from healed.

'Really?'

The way he spoke revealed a Welshness that reminded Dewi of Nathan even more. She remembered how he would gently mock her about her accent.

'That must have been a most interesting life. Did you meet many interesting people?'

Dewi thought of the many people she had met at Polrudden: The Duke of Clarence; Prince Rao; the Penhaligan girls; the Earl of Wavendon; various baronets and knights . . .

'A few.'

Aunt Phoebe showed her disapproval with a glance. 'Our Dewi has never been a great one for conversation, Reverend Craddock. She seems to have grown even quieter since she went away.'

'I wouldn't say that was a fault, Miss Morgan. Most young women these days have far too much to say for themselves. It seems to me that Dewi has experienced a great deal in the time she has been away from Maespool. I would like to call on you again and speak with you both. I've seen a few places myself. Cardiff, Bristol . . . London too. Incredible city that. Have you ever been to London, Dewi?'

She thought of her first visit to London, travelling on board the *Charlotte*. Of being caught up in a riot at the gates of the Tower of London. The second occasion, and her visit to the great home of the Earl of Wavendon . . .

She nodded.

'A fascinating city. Sinful, perhaps, but truly the capital of the world. We must compare our experiences there sometime, Dewi. Would you mind if I called on you again during the week, Miss Morgan?'

Aunt Phoebe was only too pleased to have the minister call on her. It would not pass unnoticed with the neighbours. There would be a new respect from them when they passed the time of day with her on the way to chapel next Sunday.

The Reverend Mervyn Craddock soon became a regular visitor to the small terraced house. He was obviously very taken with Dewi. For her part she had to admit he was the only person in Maespool, male or female, who had anything of interest to say.

Aunt Phoebe was delighted with the attention Mervyn Craddock was paying Dewi. To be truthful, she could not understand *why*. But then, she realised, she understood little of the modern generation, be they ministers, or miners. It was enough that he found something of interest in her niece. She could not remember when any Morgan had brought a minister of religion into the family. If only her arthritic fingers had enabled her to write she would have penned a triumphant letter to Captain Morgan. He had written to her, soon after Dewi's arrival, suggesting that Aunt Phoebe should use her influence to persuade the girl to return to her post as governess at Polrudden.

Dewi's uncle paid an unexpected visit to Maespool shortly before Christmas that year, but he was not the flamboyant sea

427

captain Dewi had known over the years. Calamity had befallen Captain Morgan. The world with which he was familiar had collapsed about his ears.

Sitting in the kitchen of Aunt Phoebe's house – close relatives were not accorded the privileges of the 'front room' – he told them of his misfortune.

'I thought I had a berth for life,' he confided. 'When the owner of the shipping line retired, he appointed me to take his place. I haven't been in charge for very long, but I've worked hard and we were making a satisfactory profit. Very satisfactory indeed. Then, only last month, the owner died. Very sad it was. Hardly had time to enjoy his retirement. When the solicitors looked into his affairs they found he was terribly in debt to just about every trader in Newport. Everything was passed into the hands of the Official Receiver and he's selling it all. Offices, warehouses, even the ships.'

'That's dreadful,' declared Dewi, genuinely concerned. 'But where does that leave you?'

'It leaves me out of work and with no prospects of ever getting any again.' Captain Morgan shrugged despairingly. 'Who'll want to employ a captain of my age? I'll tell you, Dewi. No one.'

'Well, it's probably time you retired anyway,' said Aunt Phoebe, unfeelingly. Fighting her way to her feet, she said, 'I'm going outside to the privy. Put the kettle on will you, Dewi? And don't use too much tea. The last lot you made for the Reverend Craddock was so strong you could have stood a spoon up in it.'

Tottering dangerously, she left the room. Behind them, Dewi and Captain Morgan sat in a silence that was broken by the rhythmic beat of the pendulum in the clock standing against the wall beside the doorway.

'What's happening to your old ship, the *Miriella*?' asked Dewi, breaking the melancholy silence.

'She's to be sold,' said Captain Morgan sadly. 'I'm as distressed to see her go as I am to find myself out of work. She's a good ship. The best I've ever sailed in. It's a sad day when you see everything you've known going away from you and can do nothing about it. Very sad indeed.'

'What would you do if the *Miriella* was yours? Would you be able to earn a living with her, or would you suffer the same fate as the last owner?'

'Earn a living with her? Why, I'd say I could! You sailed in her, Dewi, you know what she's like. She'll outsail any other ship in her class and take a cargo of anything, anywhere. It doesn't matter whether she has to be beached or docked, she'll do whatever is asked of her. Whoever buys her has a bargain. A wonderful bargain.'

'What price is being asked for her?'

'Five hundred and fifty pounds. I've no doubt the Receiver would take five hundred – but what difference does it make? Five hundred or five thousand, it's all the same to me. I've been a sea captain for all my life yet I have less than a hundred in the bank to show for it.

'If someone bought the *Miriella* for you and offered to share the profits with you, provided you did all the work in finding the cargoes, would you earn enough to live on?'

'Earn enough? If someone made such an offer, I'd promise to make them and me rich men by the time I had to retire.'

He shrugged. 'But there's no one around who's likely to make me an offer like that.'

'Yes, there is,' contradicted Dewi, quietly. 'I'll buy the *Miriella* for you, Uncle. I'll buy it, you'll be her captain, and we'll share all the profits you can make. Would that make you happy?'

'Happy!' Captain Morgan looked at Dewi in disbelief. 'Do you mean it, Dewi?'

'Every word. When you get back to Newport, go and speak to the Official Receiver. Say you have a buyer for the ship. You work out all the details and I'll give you the money when it's needed.'

'Dewi, you're an angel!' Captain Morgan stood up and gave her a warm hug and a kiss. 'God, girl, but that Sir Nathan Jago didn't know what he was losing when he let you slip through his fingers. If I was a younger man and you weren't my niece, I'd marry you myself – and I've never disguised the fact that I'm a confirmed bachelor!'

The mention of Nathan spoiled the pleasure of the moment for Dewi. Captain Morgan saw her sudden change of expression.

'I'm sorry, Dewi. Are you still fond of him?'

She was saved from replying by the arrival of Aunt Phoebe in the kitchen, and the Reverend Craddock at the front door.

As she let the methodist preacher in, Dewi could not help comparing him with the man whose name had just been mentioned. There was no comparison at all. But Nathan Jago lived in one world, and the Reverend Mervyn Craddock in another. As Aunt Phoebe never tired of telling her, it was time she began living in the world of *real* people, and not in the realms of make-believe.

Chapter 90

The Reverend Mervyn Craddock fitted very easily into the life Dewi led in her aunt's house. He was a visitor there three evenings a week and would join the two women for a midday meal after morning service on Sunday.

Dewi had hoped the preacher might bring some new ideas into the house. Perhaps argue with some of the narrower viewpoints held by her aunt. However, the Maespool Methodist minister was not a man given to the cut and thrust of argument. His views were almost as rigid as those of Aunt Phoebe – but by speaking only about those matters which had been the subject of long study, he did not lay himself open to contradiction.

Nevertheless, Mervyn Craddock was a gentle and kindly man.

'He'll make someone a good husband one of these days,' commented Aunt Phoebe as she sat in her chair beside the fireplace, watching Dewi clear the dishes away.

It was a Sunday afternoon and the preacher had set off on his ministerial rounds after enjoying the meal cooked by Dewi.

'I'm sure he will,' she agreed.

'He's sweet on you. The whole village is talking about it.'

'While they're talking about me, they'll be leaving some other poor soul's character alone,' she retorted.

The doorstep chatter had been particularly virulent the morning before, destroying the character of a young widow who was using every means at her disposal to earn money with which to feed her four young children.

'They don't mean anything by it, girl. It's just village chatter. Anyway, the minister is an important man in the community. What he does affects everyone. It's the villagers who will have to provide a home for his wife and any family they have, remember that.'

'Why should I remember? If the Reverend Craddock is any man at all he'll be the one to decide who he's going to marry, not the village.'

'Don't underestimate them, girl. If they decide he should marry you, then he goes against their wishes at his peril.'

Dewi turned to face her aunt, hands on hips. 'And how about me? Don't I have a say in this?'

'Of course you do – but you'd have to be a fool to turn down an ordained minister who wanted to marry you. Many things you may be, Dewi Morgan, but you're not a fool.'

Struggling to her feet with difficulty, Aunt Phoebe said, 'I'm going to lay down on my bed for an hour. That meal was too heavy for me. Be sure you wake me so I can have some tea before we go to chapel.'

Having Aunt Phoebe out of the way was a relief for Dewi. It gave her time to think. She knew her aunt was right. The village was talking about her and Mervyn Craddock. She saw it in their glances when she went out. The silence whenever she passed a group of women.

Nothing had been said by the preacher, but in a small Welsh village like Maespool, words were unnecessary. Marriage, in particular, was accepted as inevitable between certain couples. Formal announcements or declarations were not needed.

Dewi had no intention of allowing such an important matter to be decided for her by popular agreement. She decided it was time a new basis was found for the relationship between herself and Mervyn Craddock.

When the minister next called at the house, Dewi cut through the conversation on aspects of the New Testament by saying, 'I've been thinking, Minister. Why don't you start a school here in Maespool?'

'Don't be foolish, girl. What do we want a school here for? We've managed without one so far.' Aunt Phoebe was scornful of the idea.

'I can foresee certain difficulties,' said the minister hesitantly.

'Of course you can,' agreed Aunt Phoebe. 'What mother is going to send her child to school when he or she can be bringing money into the home from the pit?'

'Are you saying there's not a mother in Maespool who wants more for her son than work in the mine from the time he's old enough to pull a truck underground until the day he dies? I don't believe it.'

'Perhaps it's not so much a question of *wanting* it as a matter of economics?' suggested the minister, seeking to reconcile both viewpoints. 'Most families are hard put to manage these days, with wages poor and so many men clamouring for work.'

'Why don't you make some inquiries? Speak to the families. Most children are on shift work, the same as their parents. They would have an hour or two, either during the day or in the evening. Have words with the mine owners, too. They could surely provide a room up at the mine to serve as a schoolroom.'

'I could ask,' agreed Mervyn. 'But what about a teacher? I don't have the time . . .'

'I have,' declared Dewi, looking directly at her aunt. 'I taught children when I was at Polrudden. I'd be delighted to take it on here.'

'Oh! And may I ask who's going to look after me while you're at this school, wasting everyone's time?'

'I'll get a girl from the village to come in. As you've both just said, there are many people eager for work.'

'I'll have no stranger working in my house,' declared Aunt Phoebe.

'Oh, yes, you will. You had a girl here while I was away. You'd do the same again.'

Aunt Phoebe opened her mouth to argue further, but closed it again without saying another word. This was a new Dewi, one who had never stood up to her in this way before. She would need to give it some thought . . .

'Will you approach the mine owners and the parents about this?'

'If you're quite certain about your own commitment.'

'I am. Will you speak to them tomorrow?'

'Er . . . yes, if you wish.'

'I do.'

Contrary to the expectations of both the Reverend Mervyn Craddock and Aunt Phoebe, there was considerable enthusiasm for the school from the parents of village children, and a more guarded approval from the mine owners.

Only ten days after Dewi first put the idea to the minister she was taking her first class in a room above the mine manager's office.

She had fifteen pupils. Later in the morning two more arrived. Neither more than ten years old, both were bleary-eyed from too little sleep and one already had coal dust engrained in his skin.

During that first day the class was frequently interrupted, on three occasions by mine managers looking in to see what was happening, twice by parents who needed their children to carry out some family duty.

Gradually the lessons became less of a novelty and Dewi was able to get on with the task of teaching her willing, if not always able, pupils.

As more children were enrolled in the school, Dewi received help from the wife of one of the mine managers. She too had once taught and was happy to help out.

In the week after Christmas, Dewi was teaching during the late evening when there was sudden rumble from deep underground. It lasted for several seconds and shook the building. Moments later there was a considerable commotion outside. One of the children, his hearing keener than his fellows, cried, 'There's been an accident, down the mine.'

A minute later, the classroom had emptied and Dewi stood in the room alone. She understood the reason for the anxiety of her pupils. Every one of them had a father, brother, or even a mother or sister working underground. They wanted to know what had happened.

Packing up her things and placing them in her desk, Dewi went out into the night.

Men seemed to be rushing everywhere, some carrying lamps, others picks and shovels.

'What is it?' One of Dewi's pupils was hurrying away from the mine, heading for his home.

'There's been an explosion underground. A bad one, they say. My dad's working down there. I'm going home to fetch Ma.'

None of the families living nearby needed to be told that an accident had occurred. So severe had been the explosion that houses more than a mile away had felt the tremors.

It was an hour before the first casualties were brought to the surface and taken to the chapel. The mine doctor had been joined by others from surrounding mines and soon they were all busily at work.

Dewi had not intended to become involved with tending the casualties, but as she walked away from the mine, two men came along bearing a small girl on a litter. Aged no more than nine, she was almost naked and between her moans was calling out for her mother.

As they passed by, Dewi was faintly illuminated by a light from the office of one of the mine officials and the girl on the litter held out a hand to her. She took hold of the hand and clutched it, murmuring words of useless comfort to the child.

Inside the chapel, Dewi saw her clearly for the first time and could hardly contain the revulsion she felt. She had been severely burned and must have been in dreadful agony.

Dewi remained with her for an hour before her tearful mother appeared just in time to be with her child during her dying moments. By now many others had been brought to the chapel and the doctors assumed that Dewi was there to help them.

She worked all through the night, together with the other women. The Reverend Mervyn Craddock also offered his services when he was not comforting bereaved families or praying with dying miners.

It was the worst accident the Maespool mine had ever known. Thirty-three men, eight women and seven children died, and scores more were injured.

The community reeled under the tragedy. Nevertheless, as Dewi made her way home in the cool of the early morning, the day shift was on its way to work: men and women, deformed from years of underground work, their faces expressionless because they did not want to think about what had happened. What could happen to them too, without the slightest warning.

'Life must go on, even in the midst of such a tragedy of this,' observed Mervyn.

He was walking Dewi home. He still had much to do before his day was done. Most of the bodies from the mine were lying in the churchyard outside the chapel, covered with sheets and blankets brought from beds where they would never lie again.

'Such accidents should never claim young children as their victims,' declared Dewi angrily. She was still haunted by the agony of the young girl who had been among the first brought to the surface.

'It can't be prevented while their families need extra money,' declared the preacher sympathetically. He was aware of the reason why Dewi spoke so bitterly. He had seen her at the side of the dying child.

'You were magnificent back there in the chapel.' Mervyn paid the unexpected compliment as they turned into the street where Aunt Phoebe had her house.

'I only wish there was more I could have done. I felt so . . . so *useless.*'

'You were far from that,' declared the minister emphatically. 'But there is one more thing you could do, Dewi.'

'What's that? At the moment I feel I hardly have the energy to climb the stairs and go to bed.'

'You could marry me.'

It took a moment for his words to sink in, he had spoken them so matter-of-factly.

When she turned her head to stare in disbelief at him, he added, 'We worked well as a team back there, Dewi. We would do the same in my ministry, I know we could.'

She was drained, both physically and emotionally. She did not want such a conversation right now. All she could think of to say was, 'I'm not in love with you.'

'It would be asking too much to expect you to be in love with me after such a brief acquaintance, Dewi, but I love you. I would work hard to make you happy and I believe I could succeed – if you'll let me?'

They had reached the door of Aunt Phoebe's house by now and Dewi said, 'This morning is not a good time to ask me about something of such importance. I can hardly think at all.'

'Of course not.' Mervyn laid a hand gently on her arm. 'I don't want you to make a decision in haste. But you will think of what I have said to you?'

'Of course.'

Mervyn smiled at her, and she could see that he too was very,

very tired. 'That's all I ask. Thank you, Dewi – and thank you for all you have done for the people of Maespool tonight.'

Chapter 91

Dewi prevaricated over her reply to Mervyn for the remaining months of winter, despite continuous pressure from Aunt Phoebe, and more gentle prompting from the minister himself, asking her to declare herself.

There was pressure of another kind. Her actions during the night of the pit disaster had not passed unnoticed among the community. It opened ranks to allow her in and the women took a closer interest in what she was doing. The regular visits of their minister to the house of Phoebe Morgan and her niece had not passed unnoticed and they agreed it could mean only one thing: he and Dewi were going steady. And when a couple were 'going steady' in Maespool, marriage was only a matter of time.

They began to ask questions about when she and the preacher would name the day. It was suggested that an Easter wedding in Maespool would be ideal.

Aunt Phoebe was less tactful and far more direct. She was constantly reminding Dewi that she was not getting any younger. Telling her that if she turned Mervyn Craddock down, she was likely to end her days like Aunt Phoebe herself: 'Dependent upon uncaring strangers for her every need.'

Gradually, the pressure began to tell. Some days Dewi thought she might say yes, just to put an end to the nagging. Other days, on the rare occasions when she was able to turn her back upon Maespool and enjoy the hills and the skies and the song of the birds, she knew she could never love Mervyn Craddock in the way she wanted to love the man she married.

One day, Aunt Phoebe had been particularly insistent in her nagging and Dewi was feeling rattled. In the kitchen, baking, she banged pots and pans around with unnecessary zeal, issuing dire muttered threats at the poor quality coal. Refusing to burn evenly, it spat fragments of slate at her whenever she leaned over the fire to rake it.

She heard the knock at the door and muttered even more vehemently as she brushed back a lank tress that refused to remain in the band that held back the remainder of her hair.

'All right, don't trouble yourself, girl. Your crippled old aunt will answer the door for you.'

As Aunt Phoebe had just come down the stairs and was standing immediately behind the door, it was no trouble for her and Dewi scowled. The remark was typical of her aunt, determined to make her feel guilty over the most trivial of matters.

She heard low voices at the front door, but was too busy launching another attack on the reluctant fire with the poker to pay very much attention.

Suddenly the kitchen door opened and closed behind Aunt Phoebe. 'There's someone at the door to speak to you.'

'Me? Who is it?' Dewi's hand went automatically to her hair and pushed back the recalcitrant tress, which as promptly fell down again.

'I don't know, I've never seen them before. But get rid of them as quickly as you can, I don't like the look of the man.'

Frowning, Dewi made her way from the kitchen along the short passageway which led to the front door. Aunt Phoebe had pulled it closed, no doubt to prevent the callers from prying into what she had in the house.

Dewi opened the door – and her gasp could be heard in the kitchen.

'Nathan . . . and Beville! What . . . what are you doing here in Maespool?'

'We've come to see you!' With this joyful explanation, Beville leaped at Dewi and gave her a hug that almost overbalanced her. He and his father were dressed as Cornish fishermen in working clothes, albeit clean. She could understand why her aunt had been suspicious of them.

Suddenly releasing her, Beville said accusingly, 'Why did you go off and leave us without saying anything, Dewi? You never even said goodbye.'

'No . . . and I'm very sorry for that, Beville. I . . . I left in rather a hurry, you know.'

Suddenly aware that she and her visitors were the focus of a great deal of curiosity from a knot of women standing across the narrow street, Dewi said, 'Come on in and you can tell me how you found me. Why you're here.'

Dewi had hardly looked at Nathan since she first saw him standing in the doorway. She dared not. Her heart was racing wildly and she was having difficulty controlling her breathing.

As she led them into the front room, her aunt came from the kitchen and demanded angrily to know what she thought she was doing.

'Aunt Phoebe, may I introduce Sir Nathan Jago and his son, Sir Beville.'

Beville gravely held out his hand to her, but Aunt Phoebe was too flabbergasted to notice. 'This . . . is Sir Nathan Jago?'

'And my son, Beville. I'm sorry we've called on you dressed

like this, but my son and I were out with one of my crews, fishing in the Irish Sea. A storm blew up and we decided to shelter on the Welsh coast. We found ourselves at Newport and I knew we were close to Dewi's home, so thought we'd pay a visit.'

It was a gross over-simplification of the facts, as Dewi was fully aware. She had covered her tracks very well. She knew Nathan would have had to make a determined effort to find her. It made her feel no easier.

'How is Nell? And Pippa? Has she got over the loss of Francis now?'

'Of course, you wouldn't know. Pippa is very happy with her new baby – and Francis wasn't lost. He and his crew found their way to a village and were rescued by a Portuguese ship . . .'

Nathan told Dewi the story of the rescue and then answered her first question. 'Nell's been very ill. She lost her baby. Young Liz has been marvellous, but Nell could have done with you at Venn, Dewi. We all could.'

She was upset to hear the news of Nell. She was also aware of the accusation in Nathan's voice. To cover her confusion, she said, 'Poor Nell. I must write to her. Is she going to be all right now?'

'She's been told she'll never have more children but, yes, she's almost her old self once more.'

There was an awkward silence for a few moments during which Dewi willed herself not to look at Nathan. Suddenly she said, 'Where are my manners? You'll have a cup of tea, of course? I'll go and make one.'

'Can I come with you?' asked Beville eagerly.

'Of course. And while we're in the kitchen together you can tell me everything that's been happening at Polrudden. I hope you're keeping up with your lessons. I'm teaching boys and girls in a school here, but I don't think they're as clever as you . . .'

When Dewi and Beville had gone, Nathan was left with Aunt Phoebe, doing his best to make small talk. It was not easy. Aunt Phoebe, renowned for her ability to overawe everyone who came in contact with her, was tongue-tied in the presence of *Sir* Nathan Jago.

When her niece eventually returned to the room, Aunt Phoebe seemed more pleased to see her than at any time in Dewi's life, but she was appalled that Beville was carrying a plate of cakes behind her.

'Dewi! What do you mean by making Sir Beville help you? He's a guest.'

'I didn't make him, he asked if he could. Isn't that so, Beville?'

'Yes. Dewi says I'm a good helper . . .' He almost proved her wrong by tilting the plate, but Nathan grabbed it before the cakes were deposited on the floor.

For many minutes the conversation was mainly of people Dewi

had known at Polrudden and in the village. Then Nathan said, 'Dewi, may I speak with you alone, please?'

For a few moments, Aunt Phoebe was her old self as she snapped, 'Young girls in this village don't go off alone with men, Sir Nathan.'

'Oh, Aunt Phoebe. I lived in Sir Nathan's house for more than a year. If anything was going to happen it would have happened by now.'

'That's as may be!' The irascible old woman was shocked. 'You weren't going steady with the Reverend Craddock then.'

Aunt Phoebe's words shook Nathan and he said to Dewi, 'The rumour I heard in Newport *is* true then? You are to be married?'

'That's what everyone assumes. I've said nothing – one way or the other.'

Nathan was greatly relieved. He knew something of village gossip. Turning to her aunt, he said, 'Has Dewi told you that I wanted her to marry me? I still do.'

Before Aunt Phoebe could recover from the astounding news that a 'Sir' had proposed marriage to her niece, and apparently been turned down, Dewi said quickly, 'I'll take Sir Nathan and Beville for a walk up on the hill at the back of the village.'

'Reverend Craddock will be here shortly. What do I tell him?'

'I'm sure you'll think of something, Aunt Phoebe. We won't be long.'

Dewi felt that everyone in Maespool was looking at her as she walked through the village with Nathan at her side and Beville holding tightly to her hand, but she did not care. She could not decide in her own mind whether it was bravado – or happiness.

When they reached the outskirts of the village, Beville ran off in pursuit of a kitten, many of which lived wild up here on the hill.

When he was out of earshot, Nathan said quietly to Dewi, 'I've been living in the hope that you'd come back to Polrudden one day. Why did you walk out on me so suddenly?'

'Because it was the only sensible thing to do. It was best for everyone.' Suddenly she countered, 'How is Lady Sarah Milton?'

'I haven't seen her since the weekend she failed to give me your letter until I was leaving the Earl's house. I hurried back to Polrudden as quickly as I could, but I arrived a couple of hours too late.'

'Oh! I didn't know that. She promised to give you the letter as soon as you returned from your river trip with her father.'

'What river trip? I was in the house all the time, discussing politics with the Earl and his guests.'

Dewi looked at Nathan sharply and saw he was telling the truth.

'Why should she lie to me?'

'I believe she knew you posed a threat to her plans. When I

left she knew for certain. I told her and her friends that I intended to marry you, Dewi.'

'Oh!' There was nothing else she could say. She was thoroughly confused now.

'You still haven't given me your reason for leaving. I don't know who was more hurt, Beville or I.'

'This is foolish, Nathan. You know very well why I left. Ask Sir . . .'

'I don't care what Sir Kenwyn or anyone else said, Dewi! I asked you to marry me. I still want you to marry me.'

'It wouldn't work. As a Member of Parliament you spend your life with important people like the ones I saw in Harrow. I don't fit in with them and I never would.'

'You wouldn't have to. I didn't stand for Parliament in the recent election. Everything I want is at Polrudden. Everything except you.'

Dewi's confusion was worse than ever, and at that moment the last person in the world she wanted to see came along the pathway towards them.

The Reverend Mervyn Craddock had been visiting a sick farmer and had seen and recognised Dewi long before she noticed him. He frowned because she was with a stranger, a man, and they appeared to be having a very serious conversation.

As she approached and Dewi recognised him, the strain she was under was plain to see.

'Hello, Dewi. Is everything all right?'

'Yes.'

Her appearance belied the word. She seemed very close to tears.

'Sir Nathan Jago, this is the Reverend Mervyn Craddock.'

'Ah!' The minister's expression cleared. 'Dewi's former employer. And this young man must be Sir Beville?'

As he nodded, the preacher added, 'I have heard a great deal of you, young man. Dewi was very fond of you. Very fond indeed.'

'We've come to ask her to come back to Polrudden with us,' declared Beville with childlike honesty and bad timing.

'Is this true?' Mervyn looked from Beville to Nathan, and on to Dewi.

'Not quite,' corrected Nathan. 'I came here to ask Dewi to marry me – and not for the first time. I believe you've done the same, Minister?'

Nathan's bluntness took Mervyn by surprise, but he controlled himself admirably. 'I have – and although Dewi has not said 'yes' in so many words, I do believe we have an understanding. If you have asked her before and she refused you, do you have any reason to think she might have changed her mind?'

'I hope I have cleared up a misunderstanding which might persuade her,' said Nathan. 'Has it, Dewi?'

She looked at Nathan, whose whole life had given him an air of assurance that was lacking in lesser men. Then her glance fell upon Mervyn. His life had been dedicated to serving others. Probably the only thing he had asked for since becoming a minister was her hand in marriage. To turn him down now would destroy him.

'There will always be other Sir Kenwyns in your life, Nathan. Men only too ready to tell you what a mistake you have made by marrying a girl who was once your son's governess. I . . . I'm not sure I could live with that.'

'And I'm not sure I can live without you, Dewi. Beville and I both love you – and I believe you love us. Please, Dewi.'

They had turned around when Mervyn met them and now were walking back to the village.

There was a very long silence until they reached the door of Aunt Phoebe's house. Only then did Dewi turn to look up at Nathan. 'Nothing has changed. How could it have?'

The next moment she had run inside the house, leaving Beville and the two men outside.

His face tortured, Nathan could only say to Mervyn Craddock, 'Take care of her, Minister.'

He turned and led Beville away, not hearing the protest that his father's fingers were hurting his shoulder.

Inside the house, Dewi was in the front room, ignoring her aunt's demands for an explanation. She stood at the window, watching Nathan and Beville walking away, tears streaming down her face.

'What's been going on?' Aunt Phoebe asked yet again. 'Is it that Sir Nathan?'

'Yes, Miss Morgan, but not quite in the way you think. I think perhaps we should leave Dewi alone for a while.'

Mervyn Craddock was leading Aunt Phoebe from the room when there was a knock at the door.

The minister saw Beville standing on the well-scrubbed doorstep. In his hand he carried a small package.

Holding it up, he said, 'It's a present for Dewi from my father. He said I shouldn't give it to her, but he made it 'specially. She *should* have it.'

'I think you'd better come and give it to her, young Sir Beville.'

Beville advanced less confidently when he saw Aunt Phoebe, but the minister guided him past her to the room where Dewi stood.

'This young man has something to give you. It's a present from Sir Nathan.'

She took it, trying to avert her face so that the boy could not see her tears.

441

'I think you should open it while Beville is still here.'

Dewi hesitated then tore off the wrapping. Inside was a wooden spoon, hand-carved. On the handle were engraved two names, linked together by carefully carved flowers. They were 'Dewi' and 'Nathan'.

'My father made it especially for you, Dewi. I watched him do it.'

There was no way now that she could keep her tears from Beville, but the Reverend Mervyn Craddock seemed to acquire a new stature.

Taking Beville's hand he put it in Dewi's.

Startled out of her misery, she looked at the minister questioningly.

'Take Beville to his father, Dewi. That's where you both belong.'

'I can't . . .'

'You have never looked at me as I saw you looking at Sir Nathan. I can't take what will never belong to me. Go, Dewi. Sir Nathan has proved his love by coming here to find you. Show him yours by confounding those who say he will lose by marrying you.'

Leading Dewi and Beville to the front door, past a confused Aunt Phoebe, he said, 'Go, Dewi, and go with my blessing.'